The People Up
the Holler

Roger L. Guffey

Lexington, Kentucky

ISBN: 1543052053
ISBN 13: 9781543052053
Library of Congress Control Number: 2017902354
CreateSpace Independent Publishing Platform
North Charleston, South Carolina

Acknowledgments

UMWELT IS A wonderful word psychologists use to describe the collection of environmental factors that can affect the behavior of animals or individuals. Every living thing has a unique umwelt that differs from that of every other living thing. In particular, the members of families and communities have their own umwelts even though they may share much of the same environment.

In a literary sense, everyone's life story is a manifestation of his or her umwelt. That umwelt is the prism through which we see the world around us. Legal experts have long known that if ten different people view exactly the same scene and then asked to describe exactly what they see, ten different stories are likely to emerge. Does that mean that some witnesses are lying? No, they are simply recounting the events they saw viewed from the filters of their personal experience, their umwelts.

Novelists and short story writers weave their stories by knitting the umwelts of the characters into a literary narrative. These literary works do more than tell a story: they reveal truths about the writer, the reader, and the characters in their stories.

Throughout history, storytellers have used stories to teach others lessons they wish them to know. Jesus taught with parables, Aesop told fables, Chaucer recounted tales and Shakespeare wrote his plays. Countless generations have read these stories and pondered their meanings and those stories are just as meaningful today as they were when they were first told.

This was the impetus that compelled me to write this collection of stories. Some of the stories are based on real life people and events from my home community, stories I fear will be lost as the life and culture of inevitably changes.

Others explore the realm of surreal possibility where human foibles play out against a preternatural backdrop. It is hoped that all of these stories have something meaningful to say to every reader.

I am indebted to several people who helped make this book a reality. Sue Wilson, Margaret Jones, Jim Fields, George Ella Lyon and the late Jane Gentry Vance all suggested that I tell these stories before they are lost. Joseph Hayse tirelessly edited various drafts of stories, as did Jeanine Grant Lister. They encouraged me to share little bits of my umwelt that have shaped who I am and I wish to offer them my heartfelt thanks.

Roger L. Guffey

Trees I Have Known

THE HISTORY OF my family is so intertwined with the timber industry that as a child I had a difficult time separating the literal meaning of "family tree" from the metaphorical construct it represents. The first Bible stories I heard told of Adam and Eve's fall from grace for eating from the Tree of the Knowledge of Good and Evil and of the saving grace of Christ's sacrifice on a tree. All the eternal damnation and the immortal salvation of the human race hung from the branches of trees in my innocent mind, and with the increasing introspection of age, I find that trees have become the mileposts of my memory.

Forests did not comprise any significant portion of my life as a child as they were not real in my world. A forest was an imaginary construct of fairy tales inhabited by talking animals in cottages, lost woodcutters' children and little blond girls in red riding hoods. No one in my family or even in my county ever used the word "forest" except when reading children's tales. I lived in a landscape swathed in woods and mountains whose inhabitants were flesh and blood men. The "woods" for me meant the quarter-mile stretch of scraggly redbud and dogwood cut-over scrub timber lying between the west end of Mom's garden and the eastern edge of Silas Correll's burley tobacco patch. The "mountains" were a mature near-virginal stand of maples, oaks, ashes, walnuts, and hickories lying on the steep slopes above our house. The vertical limit of the woods merged into the lower limit of the mountains just west of our hog-lot. That boundary was delineated into my young mind at an early age. As a seven-year-old child, I was permitted to play in the portion of the woods visible from the back yard, on the condition that I watch out for two dangers: copperheads and poison ivy. Many years would pass before I could go into the mountains unattended, for real and more subtle dangers lay there.

The nine-acre farm my father homesteaded in 1949 was sprinkled with black walnuts and pignut hickories strewn randomly across the portion we used as a hog-lot where Dad sometimes raised Hampshire and Yorkshire hogs. The house, perched atop a steep grassy incline, overlooked Rufus Burton's farm: a sea of fescue, corn, and soybeans dotted with black walnut trees, bordered by red cedar bushes laced into the fence rows, and watched over by a lone persimmon tree standing vigil on a distant slope. Burton's farm ran the length of Hall Valley, covering the half-mile wide strip of land between Highway Ninety and the secondary road to my house. The secondary road separated Burton's farm from Matt Shearer's farm, a particularly narrow section that, in turn, abutted Raeburn Criswell's land, a peninsula jutting out from a wide hollow at the base of Turkey Ridge, which hid the tree that turned boys into men.

In retrospect, I realize that I had to reach a certain age before I could know certain kinds of trees. When Dad had graded off the land for the house and garage, he left a single big red oak standing on a small prominence behind the garage. To my young eyes, that tree seemed massive. It had two large branches sweeping low to the ground and splotchy, age-darkened bark like the skin of a grandparent. Every spring Mom and Dad fixed a foot wide board to a new rough hemp rope with extruding fibers to suspend a tree swing from the upper arm of the oak. My older siblings had enjoyed this annual ritual and passed it along to us younger children when they outgrew the swing.

The swing captured my fancy in spells throughout the summer but it was the network of miniature roadways and tunnels coursing under the ancient oak's exposed roots that endlessly diverted my young imagination. My older brothers had forged the first thoroughfares around and under arching gnarled roots, and each new son had expanded the highway system so extensively that only Providence must have kept the tree upright in the ground. For hours my younger brother and I would race our die-cast metal cars — so old that no trace of paint still flecked their surfaces — along the dusty trails making the requisite "vroom" noises as we played. We stopped only when Mom discovered the red clay staining my brother through his urine-soaked diaper.

My sisters, Sally and Judy, sought a more genteel use of the tree by gathering ink-balls that had fallen from the canopy. The oak tree responded defensively to an attack by a parasitic cochineal wasp by encapsulating the intruder in a mass of cells that produced a rich red dye that could be extracted using a solution of water and a bit of rubbing alcohol. With this bright red mixture, my sisters would write letters and poems they composed while swinging in the rope swing. During a year of good acorn mast, they liked to find perfect acorns with cupules they imagined as tiny cups and saucers or wee hats for their smaller dolls.

Daddy's brother, C.H., owned a lumberyard, but dismissed the idea of buying the oak from Dad when he examined it more closely. Previous owners of the land had accidentally left two large pieces of iron lying in a crotch, and the growing tree had claimed them as trophies. One end of Mom's clothesline was nailed to the trunk of the tree and we boys had practiced nail driving in its trunk. Occasionally, Daddy used to set a trotline for catfish, and he would clean them by nailing their still-flopping bodies to the oak tree and peeling the outer skin off with wire pliers. I watched this horrific spectacle only once, yet the memory of gory crucifixion still haunts me.

None of us children feared our staid "grandfather tree" whose red shirt rippled in the autumn breeze as we clamored over the lower branches or pushed our toys under its arching roots. Once, in spite of our parents' disapproval, we laid a single plank bridge from a branch to the roof of the garage and scampered over to view Burton's farm from the vantage point of the top of the garage.

The red oak tree's days were numbered when Daddy decided to reconfigure the land around the house to remove rock outcroppings. I do not remember the felling of the tree, but I do remember hearing the dynamite blast that tore the roots out of the ground one morning as I was riding the school bus. That afternoon, I ran up the hill only to find roughly disfigured ground where my childhood buddy had once stood. Curiously, as I age I frequently find myself daydreaming of playing under the leafy wooden boughs of that old guardian, bedecked in swings, dull gray metal trucks, ink balls, and crucified catfish.

If the red oak tree occupied my life for only a few years, the red cedar perennially evokes fond memories of Christmas even today. The red cedar tree or juniper was **the** Christmas tree for the vast majority of people where I grew up. Birds feasted on the frosty blue berries, spreading the tiny seeds along every fencerow and pasture. My Dad purposely planted one beside the front porch as some sort of superstitious offering for good health for my older sister, Sally. I can only vaguely recall finding a sparrow's nest in its branches, because Daddy cut it down when it had grown so big that its shadow might cover an area that could determine her future grave. By the time she had married, the cedar was a distant memory.

Sally was the only one who had her own personal cedar tree, but we all celebrated Christmas around a red cedar every year. The aroma of red cedar is unmistakable, and the lightest whiff of its pungent, woodsy smell reminds me of Christmas to this day.

My older brothers would climb the steep slope to search the mountains for the perfect tree, full and roundly balanced, preferably one with an abandoned bird's nest for good luck. Once I got to go along with Leonard and Charlie to get the tree. I remember watching through the softly falling snow as Leonard, hidden by his bushy load, trudged through the foot-deep snow.

Dad or my older brothers would saw the end off flat so a cross-like support could be nailed to the trunk to keep the tree upright. On Christmas morning we would wake up and rush downstairs to find our presents under the tree we had decorated with a hodgepodge of tinsel, lights, and ornaments as old as our parents' marriage. We knew that Mom and Dad hid the presents in the house somewhere, but in all the years my sister Judy and I searched, we never found the presents before Christmas. Presents were simple -- a toy for a young child, a pocketknife for older boys, costume jewelry for older girls and a box of candy and fruit for everyone -- but the quality and quantity of gifts did not matter. The red cedar is the family tree of the family I always wanted to have: the times when we were all together, happy (or naïve enough to believe that we were), innocent, and unscarred by the world for which our parents had tried to prepare us.

Christmas was special in another way for it was the only time of the year my parents would indulge in exotic nuts: pecans, English walnuts, hazelnuts, Brazil nuts, and almonds. A few pecan trees grew in my county, but none of us had any clue as to what kinds of trees produced these other nuts. They were as alien to us as caviar, but everybody had a favorite. Mom liked almonds, which she called peach seeds as the uncracked nut bears a strong resemblance to a peach pit. The older boys liked English walnuts and pecans because they could crush them with their bare hands;

feeding the image they had of themselves as virile, powerful men to be reckoned with. Daddy would start off each Christmas liking Brazil nuts, but would soon grow frustrated as their tough triangular shells resisted even the claw hammer by slipping away from the crushing blow. The girls liked hazelnuts, which they could crack with pliers without losing their gentility. I liked whatever anyone else would feed me.

The woods and fields around my home were replete with various other nut trees, however -- hickory, walnut, and beech -- and one of the most enjoyable tasks a kid could do was to go on nut-gathering forays, climbing the mountain on a sunny morning in October, a light frost underfoot, a brown paper bag in his hand and a heart filled with childhood joy and carefree purpose. Though small, a boy knew that he was helping to feed his family by gathering the abundance nature rained down. And he was doing it like a vagabond, wallowing in leaf clutter whose rustling told him stories of pioneers and Indians still stalking the woods.

Children did not go to the mountains unattended, but the gathering instinct was so ingrained that my brother and I would gather the nuts from the pignut hickories that grew in the fence-rows and in the pile of boulders pushed up by the bulldozer when Daddy re-contoured the land around our home. One enormous pignut tree, about fifty feet from the back door, had the dubious honor of being the tree Daddy tied Charlie to for flattening his new fire truck with a ball-peen hammer. This was also the tree where I tested my archery skills by launching a brand new arrow high over the lofty tiptop branches only to hear it shatter on a large rock when it fell back to earth.

That tree towered over a large flat limestone rock with a bowl-shaped depression that held enough rainwater for the birds to bathe in. The pignuts themselves were covered in a thin husk that separated easily into quarters. They were actually easy to crack, but fat, white, weevil larvae usually infested most of the nuts. As a small child I learned quickly not to gather any nuts with exit holes left by the larvae emerging from the shell. If the larvae were still inside these holes were not present, so many nuts I gathered had to be thrown away after they were cracked open to reveal a curious mixture of kernel and smashed worm innards. Mom and Dad encouraged us to gather these nuts as sort of training for the real thing, but they never used the nuts for anything. The kernels were either sweet and watery or bitter and, when they were dried, they shriveled up into a tough chewy mass.

The black walnuts in our valley produced large crops at roughly regular intervals of three years. Gathering black walnuts is a bit more problematic than gathering hickory nuts. The outer walnut husk produces an ugly yellow liquid that will ruin your clothes and stain your hands for weeks. I once tried to remove the stain by using ammonia, only to find that the chemical interaction left my hands a dull purple. Leaving the nuts in the sun dried the husk so that the stain leached free. The Burton boys went a step further, dumping them into the roads used by their tractors so the traffic would abrade the husk away while leaving the inner nut intact.

I was much older before I learned that the nuts produced by individual walnut trees vary wildly in quality, but there is no way to tell which trees produce good nuts and which produce bad nuts. The nuts from all walnut trees stain as badly, but the kernels of bad trees are watery and tasteless and shrivel up into a mass resembling slime mold on a pasture fence board. Good nuts contain large plump meaty kernels wrapped in a golden membrane that seals in the rich woodsy taste and insures minimal water loss during drying. The flavor is addictive, enticing the unwary connoisseur to eat more and more kernels, unless a kind soul warns that eating too many black walnuts at once gives the diner a world-class case of diarrhea.

Minute larvae occasionally infest the outer husk of walnuts, but finding larvae inside a black walnut was rare. Cracking walnuts occupied many a long fall or winter night, but seldom did anyone crack alone. A black walnut has to be smashed by a hammer on a hard surface. Mom and Dad often used an old flat iron that had lost its handle. They would cradle a walnut in a crevice between the handle attachment points and rap it sharply with a claw hammer or a ball peen hammer. Judy, Jack and I used to sit on the basement steps where we would place the nut in a small depression on the end of each of three steps, indentations formed by countless poundings of walnuts by our older brothers and sisters. Occasionally, someone would smash a finger and yell "Oh shit!" and the rest of us got a good laugh, at least until it happened to us.

Mom and Dad would often talk about cracking walnuts and hickory nuts for Christmas money. A quart Mason jar of hickory nut kernels would fetch a dime, a jar of walnuts, a quarter. This seemed like a shaky investment of time and energy to us younger children, who did not realize that our parents had lived in a time when houses had no electricity and most people no education, so there was little else to do at night except crack nuts while swapping stories.

One story Dad loved to tell was about the big chestnut tree in the backfield of his childhood home. The tree's canopy varied somewhat with each retelling, but our youthful imaginations always sparked enthusiasm when he would tell of mast years when he could scoop up chestnuts with a shovel instead of picking them up one at a time. His huge hands would indicate clearly the circumference of the burrs as well as the nuts themselves, and he often dovetailed the story of the chestnut fruits with the legendary durability and utility of the wood itself, boasting of chestnut rail fences that were still standing more than a hundred years after they were built.

Invariably, his monologue would assume a more somber tone to tell us children that we would never see a chestnut tree since the blight had killed them all off. He could recount with amazing accuracy the dates on which the chestnut trees near his home contracted the disease and the date they were given up as dead. He would finish his soliloquy by heaping scorn on the imported Chinese chestnuts, which were immune to the blight but came in a distant second to its American cousin for both majesty and quality of nuts.

Mom liked to tell of gathering nuts from the chestnut's smaller cousin, the chinquapin, which grew as bushes alongside the creeks. The chinquapin produces smaller nuts that are as black as ebony, a characteristic that gave rise to the saying 'eyes as black as a chinquapin'. In contrast to the broad gesticulations of my father, Mom always measured off a small length of her forefinger to indicate the size of the chinquapin nut. Ironically, while I remember their stories vividly, I would never see the trees or nuts that colored my parents' childhood memories. A foreign invader extinguished the chestnut and the chinquapin was pushed into hiding.

So it was that my generation's story contented itself with walnuts and hickories. Eight walnut trees grew on my home-place when I was a boy, but only one produced edible fruit on a regular basis. We called it "Old Faithful", for it bore a few walnuts every year. Another, standing above the barn beside an enormous wooden barrel full of rainwater and small catfish we had brought from fishing trips, occasionally bore a dozen or so walnuts, but most fell irretrievably into the barrel. The two tall, sparsely-leafed trees that stood near the mountain edge seemed so distant to me as a child that I never tried to go there by myself; I see now the distance is about sixty yards. Dad finally planted a young walnut tree beside the house so he would not have to walk so far to get them in his old age. The farm cats used the young tree as a scratching post so much that Dad wrapped the trunk in burlap sacks to prevent its tender bark from being scratched away. At maturity, the tree produced enough walnuts to keep my Dad's hammer busy for years after his retirement, and it provided shade from the afternoon sun.

We children preferred hickory nuts to avoid the delayed gratification of waiting for the walnut's stain-filled husks to dry. Unlike walnuts, hickory trees producing edible nuts grew all through the woods, distinguishable by their rough bark. Squirrels, chipmunks, and deer mice competed with us for hickory nuts, and we learned to tell what kind of animal had beaten us to a kernel. Squirrels and chipmunks fragment the shell into tiny pieces on a nearby rock or scatter them over a small area on the forest floor, while deer mice just cut a small hole in one end so they can extract the kernel with their slender incisors. Various members of my family kept gray squirrels, chipmunks, flying squirrels, and deer mice as pets and we always shared some of our gathered bounty with them, watching in wonder as their small hand-like forepaws grasped the nuts firmly, rotating them like a woodcrafter turning wood on a lathe.

Hickory wood is tough and makes the best handles for axes and hammers. Hickory splints, soaked in water to increase flexibility, formed the seat and back of many a chair in our part of Kentucky. Only two or three good trees grew in woodlands around my home, but Mom and Dad let us go hickory nut hunting to these trees as soon as we turned eight or so. We knew to watch for snakes and, though hidden from view out the back porch, the trees lay in earshot of a yell to come home. Copperheads posed the only real danger to us, but they had already found a place to hibernate by October, when the nuts were ripe.

Some years the trees did not produce any nuts; in others the ground would be covered with them. This pattern is typical for many kinds of trees because neither the animals nor we could possibly consume all the nuts in a really good year. I always enjoyed watching squirrels bury nuts for the winter. There is a flurry of scratching, clouds of dust and litter, then a quick thrust of the nut into the crevice and another of flurry of dirt to hide it. Finally, the squirrel tamps the soil firmly with the same motion a cat uses to knead a blanket. Dad told us that squirrels forget where they stash their hidden winter stores, thus planting the seeds for the next generation of trees.

Young trees produced enough nuts for a few pies and a batch of fudge. More mature trees grew in the boundary fencerow between Raeburn Criswell's land and George Horton's mountaintop pasture about a mile across the top of Turkey Ridge. Until I was twelve, I was allowed to gather there only if a parent or older sibling went with me. The journey across the mountaintop was a joy in itself. The smell of the dead leaves from dozens of kinds of trees and the soft rustle of the leaf litter beneath our feet filled the air. Sometimes we sang verses of *Barbara Allen* or old gospel songs. Occasionally, we would see deer or a fox fleeing our approach.

A few beech trees grew in one stretch of woods, and it was a rare year that we did not return home with a hornets' nest taken from one of their lower branches. Mom always asked if the nest was high or low in the tree, saying a high nest meant a lot of snow in the coming winter. Though the beeches rarely produced nuts, we did not consider it much of a loss. One year dad took us out to Lonesome where there was a bumper crop of beechnuts. The small, triangular nuts were borne in a spiny husk that could be opened easily with fingernails. They were quite tasty, but you could starve to death if they were all you had to eat. We gathered half a bushel of the nuts but grew so tired of shelling them that we gave most of them to our pet squirrels.

We knew we had to get quiet as we neared the base of a small rise near the end of our destination if we wanted to see the flocks of migrating geese or ducks that rested on the huge pond in the middle of Horton's field. A small thicket of persimmon trees blocked the pond view so we used to sneak through it to see the pond clearly. Cow pies, as well as possum and coon droppings sprouting persimmon seeds, littered the ground beneath the trees, so our eyes were simultaneously trying to watch the pond and our step. We had no intention of shooting the birds, and we felt a sense of regret when they flew away.

Nine big hickory trees lined the fencerow and a row of cedar trees acted as a buffer to discourage the cows (and bull) from browsing under the trees. One year, Sally's dog, a cocker spaniel mix, Lady, got so badly entangled in the fence-row that she could not get loose. When Lady did not show up for supper after repeated callings, Daddy, Charlie, Leonard, and Ottis combed through the mountains in the middle of the night until they found her and took turns carrying her back home. I was still awake when they returned at about one in the morning, and I remember feeling both proud and envious of their rescue mission, wondering if I would ever be called upon to perform so heroic a deed.

We brought burlap bags with us to gather the nuts from these hickory trees. The nuts were bigger in a rainy year; smaller if the year were dry. But in the bounty of a mast year we could almost fill one of the big burlap sacks with the nuts. The older boys would take turns displaying their marksmanship with a twenty-two rifle by shooting hickory nuts out of the treetops. We sometimes found lost relics from the old Marley Brown house that had stood there in the thirties, and rarely missed a chance to fish in the pond unless we saw the big Hereford bull nearby.

The species of these trees did not matter, as long the nuts were good. The only hickory tree we identified by a specific name was a big shellbark hickory that lay another mile around the ridge in the head of Raeburn's hollow. That was the tree that separated the men from the boys. I can still recall my older brothers setting out on a Saturday morning and returning late that afternoon with burlap sacks half-full of enormous nuts over an inch and a half in diameter. Unlike the big shagbark hickory trees that produced large nuts with very thick shells, this shellbark hickory produced large nuts with thinner shells making them easier to crack.

I accompanied my brothers or my Dad when I was younger, but I was not allowed to go to the big shellbark tree alone until I was fourteen. I particularly remember one trip when Dad took Jack and me to the tree because it is the first image I have of the extent of Dad's bowlegged-ness brought on by worn out kneecaps and tendons. In my youthful naiveté, I assumed that his tan khaki pants and shirt were sweat-stained from the physical exertion of walking across the mountain. I would not learn until years later, when he had knee replacement surgery, that the trek caused him a great deal of pain. He sat sprawled-legged under the tree, picking up nuts he could reach while Jack and I emptied capfuls into the sack.

In later years, my younger brother asked why we did not just walk out the road and cut through Raeburn's fields to get to the tree, since Raeburn did not mind us picking up the nuts. As I saw it, the fun lay in the challenge of the journey across the mountain. Are you old enough to follow the right path and to find your way again if you get lost? Do you see that the easiest way is not always the best way? Can you stay focused enough to complete the task you have taken on without turning back and covering your ineptitude with a lie that the tree had no nuts? Can you deal with the disappointment of finding no nuts after walking two miles through the woods?

I can recall my first solo trip to the shellbark hickory. The mid-October afternoon was clear blue. I called up our old dog Pooch, a black and tan mutt borne to Lady years before, and, clutching a paper bag from the IGA, I set out across the mountain. Without the comforting companionship of my father or brothers, I heard sounds I had never heard before: spooky noises that made me start or shiver. The rustle of a single squirrel in fallen leaves sounded like a herd of buffalo, and the roar of the autumn breeze through the trees was like the ghoulish screams from horror movies. The random play of light on colored leaves surely resembled a copperhead though I knew they were in hibernation by now. All the things I did not fear when I was bolstered by the presence of others now terrified me in my solitude.

Presently, something amazing happened. Building on the small steps my parents had permitted me, I found an easy rhythm in my gait so that I whistled while scanning the landscape. I had little training in identifying birdcalls, but I did not have to know the singers to enjoy the music. I took the wrong fork going over the hill on the outer rim of Horton's field, but righted myself after a few yards. I began to envision a sack so full of nuts it would take me hours to drag it home. The thought of such a bountiful, triumphant return hastened my pace across the ravines and outcroppings so that I was surprised to discover I had burst out of the woods into the presence of the tree, which stood at the edge of the field beside a fallen rock fence covered in saw briers.

Though I had seen the tree before, I stood there in awe of its majesty. The tree was sixty feet tall with a span of forty feet and a trunk diameter of over two feet. Leaves, twigs, and nut husks were trapped between its shards of curling bark. A squirrel scampered down the trunk and into the woods where crumpled leaves carpeted the ground. The tree had produced a modest crop of nuts. It was considerably smaller than the bonanza I was expecting, but I soon collected a peck of the nuts and returned home, walking with the long sure strides of a boy who had become a man.

Epilogue

The pilgrimages to the big shellbark hickory tree stopped when I left for college, as weekend trips home were so overscheduled I could not find the time to go. The pleasures of foraging in the woods for nuts or hunting for the perfect cedar tree for Christmas were not the only elements of my childhood that were disappearing. The religious foundations of my upbringing were shaken by my studies in evolutionary ecology and I began to re-evaluate my understanding of the trees I knew as a child. The cedar trees are pyramidal to shed heavy snows more easily; tannin compounds cause the bitterness of acorns and bitternuts to discourage insect attack. The nut weevils evolved new ways of metabolizing the chemical so a kind of evolutionary arms race is always in progress. The walnut husks that stained my hands contain juglone to inhibit seed germination of plants near a walnut tree.

The neat packages and logical explanations that scientists have figured out to explain the natural order of the world fascinated me, yet I was totally unprepared for an obvious observation my advisor made about the fecundity of oak and other nut bearing trees. An oak tree that lives for four hundred years produces billions of acorns yet, on the average, only one will mature to replace the parent — otherwise the world would be inundated with oak trees. All the acorns a tree produces are just compact experiments in genetic adaptation to the rigors of a harsh and changing environment and they are randomly dispersed as widely as possible. There is no way to predict which acorn will be the seed of the next generation, or from which crop it will come, but I often find myself idling away an October afternoon watching acorns fall from the tree, wondering if I am seeing the future tree fall.

The fatalism of that argument used to bother me, for I quickly realized that the same analogy could be applied to the human race. Evidence shows clearly that the human race did not begin under the Tree of the Knowledge of Good and Evil. Two million years ago our apelike ancestors abandoned the safe havens and bountiful larders of their trees to venture out onto the wide savannas of the African veldt. Speculative arm-waving scenarios can only guess at the mysterious impetus that drove these primates to abandon their arboreal homes for the scarcity of the grasslands. Is the story of the "Descent of Man" only a mindless and goalless evolutionary process fueled by survival? These primitive pioneers survived only because living in the three dimensional world framed by trees had endowed them with binocular vision, grasping hands and a large brain that gave them the edge to survive and evolve for generations. Like the snake that swallowed its own tail, the descendants of this unlikely lot ultimately erected a civilization that would betray their heritage, turning to destroy the jungles and the trees from whence they came.

Mellowed now by age and experience, I have learned to see things through the lenses of compromise and wonder-filled ignorance. Playing under the oak tree in my early years taught me to have an active imagination and gave my parents a reference point to mind me. Gathering nuts did not save my family from starvation, but it did teach me a sense of responsibility and a work ethic. All the pies and cookies and candy we made with kernels extracted by long hours of hard work would not make a large pile, but the love and warmth and spirituality I received in gathering and cracking the nuts with my family are my warm security blankets in troubled times.

As I have grown, I have learned that people are like the trees and nuts I knew as a child. A few are obviously bad but easy to avoid; others require a closer scrutiny to find their evil. People can stain you for life in a good way while others mark you with scars. Some people are simple but easily understood; others take more work. Occasionally, the reward is worth the work, but often the payoff is not commensurate with the effort. True friends are always there; others are seasonal. Certain people offer me no benefit nor threaten me with detriment, but because they are here I must get along with them. There are trees of joy, trees of security and trees of punishment: all qualities I see in people I know.

So it is that the memories of my long-ago childhood resonate through the years as I join my siblings to prepare the home place for sale. The big oak tree is long gone, as are many of the hickory trees skirting the property. Most of the walnut trees are still standing, though the one in the back yard has a curious architecture wrought by Dad's continued topping and pruning to keep it away from the power lines and house roof. It still bears a few green spherical fruits. Lightning struck the big shellbark hickory years ago; Don Burton cut it down when he bought Raeburn's farm and extended his monoculture of corn further into the rich loamy earth of the hollow. A few small cedar trees peek over the top of the grasses and dewberry briers in the hog-lot that is now home only to sparrows and voles.

My siblings have already gone, having shown their grandchildren or even great-grandchildren one last look at the home of their childhood. I am still single, weighing the freedom of the single life with the responsibility of marriage and parenthood. My siblings have either adopted children, had daughters, or chosen to have no children, so this branch of our family name will die out with our passing. The rooms are bare upstairs and down, but I want to check the basement windows one last time. The stale musty odor of dirty moist cement fills my nose as I take the steps down, past the knotholes on the end of the middle steps. I pull the string to turn on the bulb that casts dim light and weird shadows in all directions. Satisfied that the windows are locked securely and the water taps are off, I meander around the basement one last time.

Something is nearly hidden in the darkness on the wall plate above the can shelf where Mom used to store her summer fruits and vegetables. Placing my right foot on the lower shelf, I mount up the shelf quickly to grab the object. As I pull it out, I can see it is the old flatiron Mom and Dad used to crack nuts on. The iron sweeps a handful of small hickory nuts hollowed out by mice off the wall plate onto the floor, and I see another nut on the iron. I trap it with my forefinger so that it does not fall as I dismount the shelf and go to the steps to sit down.

From the size and shape of the nut I know it came from Raeburn's tree, but I have no idea how long it has lain on the shelf. Though my examination of the nut reveals no evidence of worms, I know the shell could be filled with dead worms and frass, a shriveled rotten kernel, or a plump kernel, a last vestige to my lost youth or a new shellbark tree for future generations to enjoy.

With the iron in my left hand and the nut in my right, I pull the string to turn off the light, climb the steps to exit the house and lock up. I place the iron on the floorboard of my car and stand between the door and car, rolling the nut over between my fingers. I wonder if this is the one.

Ghostly Figures Coming Out of the Ground

MARVIN RIDDLE HAD lived his entire life in the Hall Valley community with its scattered houses and baby farms strung along Kentucky 858 like beads on a fine necklace. At seventy-five, he was its most senior citizen, having been born in the big wooden house and having spent his entire life there; his parents willed him the family farm for "love and affection" during their dotage. He had seen the march of time dissipate family farms to seed and ruin as no one attempted to tend them. Fires had destroyed houses and the vast Burton farm had absorbed smaller acreages, yet he kept an indelible mental and written record of every house and family who ever lived or died in the valley during his lifetime.

Occasionally, he would reminiscence with his wife Evalee about the people who had passed through the valley, but this bright May morning his sole recollection was her directive to have the potatoes hilled up by the time she got back from town. Together they raised a small vegetable garden more out of tradition and boredom than actual need as their retirement checks and money from their children up north amply supplied any financial need. He used his hoe to scratch a few morning glory seedlings out of the last hill of potatoes before he scraped up a mound of dusty soil around the emerging potato shoots and left the garden. After returning the hoe to the shed, he took up his favorite position underneath a walnut tree where he spent hours practicing the age old art of whittling a red cedar stake into a soft pile of curly cedar shavings.

Very little traffic ventured onto this road at ten o'clock in the morning so when he saw the same Cadillac make two passes in front of his house, he figured that the driver was lost and would eventually stop to ask for directions. He continued to whittle nonchalantly even as the car eased up the hill to his backyard, waiting to hear a car door open before acknowledging the woman's hailing.

"Excuse me, sir. I seem to be lost. Could you please help me?" she asked politely.

Marvin stood up from his cane-bottomed chair, laying his knife and cedar stick on the seat as he rose. He stretched a leg muscle before walking toward the woman.

"Sure, I'd be glad to help. What are you looking... Wait a minute! You are one of Arlie Sweet's kids!" he cried.

"Why yes, I am. My maiden name was Lora Sweet, but it's Eastridge now. How did you know that?" she stammered, obviously taken aback.

"Well, honey, I didn't know which one you was but I knew you had to be one of Arlie's. He used to live out the road a piece and so help me God all of his children looked exactly alike. All ten of them. Warn't like Arlie nor Thelma but all of you favored each other something fierce. 'Course I don't know about the last four. I think he did wind up with fourteen kids, didn't he?"

"Yes, there were fourteen of us," Lora replied. "Maybe you can help me find what I am looking for here. I was born somewhere in this valley in this house." She handed Marvin a photograph of a small gray house. "I guess it has been torn down over the years. Could you tell me where it was and tell me as much about it as you can?"

Marvin returned the photograph, nodding agreement. "Tell you what I know, but why do you want to know now? That house has been gone for nigh unto fifty years."

"I have recently been named editor of Country Homes Digest. I thought it would be an inspirational human-interest story to tell how I was born into such poverty but worked my way up to my present position. Could you take me to the site of my birthplace and tell me a little about the community then? I believe Mom said we moved to it when I was around four so I don't know much about it."

Marvin nodded again as he raised his age-speckled hand to point across the fields. "That was Russell Criswell's rent house your family lived in. It stood close to the road just this side of that big white house yonder. Let me get my hat and some ice water to take with us and we can go out there to see what's left of it."

Lora started the car while he retrieved his hat and she gingerly guided the car over the hill to the road. "I guess this place has changed a lot since we lived here."

"Oh, you don't know. When I was a kid, there was fifteen houses along this road. There was the Brown place, the Hicks place, the Correll place and so on but the house you grew up in never had a name. It was always Russell Criswell's rent house. Here, pull into that gravelly place there."

The car glided to a halt and they got out.

"Now as I recall, the house was right near the road in that curve yonder. It's been gone a while but we might find a few foundation stones. Used to be a big walnut tree right there but they cut it down when they tore the house down. Wait, that's my wife coming out the road. Let me go wave her down and tell her where I am so she won't worry."

He began to shout, flailing his arms wildly as he walked to the roadway. The car eased to the side of the road.

"Honey, this woman is one of Arlie Sweet's girls that was born in the old Russell Criswell's rent house. She's here doing some research about her home place. This may take a while so I will just eat a sandwich when I get home. And don't worry, you're the only woman for me," he said, eyes a-twinkle.

"That's cause I'm the only one who'd have you," Evalee replied. "Did you get all the taters hilled up?" she asked teasingly.

Marvin nodded his head.

"Then take all the time you need. Chicken okay for supper?"

"Yeah, that's fine."

Marvin returned to the yard of the old house place. "You married, Lora?"

"Yes, my husband's name is Michael Eastridge. He's an architect in Chicago where we live. I flew into Lexington last night and drove down this morning. I was planning to go back to Lexington tonight but this may take longer than I thought. Is there a hotel around here?"

"Oh, you can stay with us if you need to. But let's see if we can find out what you want to know. You can't tell it from the picture but this was a board and batten house… boards nailed up vertically and then another board nailed over the cracks. I was never inside the house but my sister was. I believe she said there was three rooms down and two rooms up. Let's see if we can find the outlines of the house foundation."

Marvin began to shuffle his feet through the fescue and eventually he uncovered two faint rectangles joined in a T formation. The larger rectangle measured about twenty-five feet by thirty-five feet and the smaller one about fifteen by thirty.

"It's amazing how long some of these old house-places can still mark the ground. This warn't a big house for two adults and fourteen kids. 'Course one of your brothers got killed in a wreck while you was living here."

Lora was stepping off the house measurements, but she relied, "Yes, that was Johnny. Jimmy got killed when we were living at Parnell. I don't remember Johnny very well except through pictures. I remember Jimmy since he was only two years older. I guess with fourteen kids…"

"If you don't mind, help me lay a stone on top of the other one so I can sit down."

With some effort, they made a makeshift stone seat near the stump of the walnut tree. Each wiped small beads of sweat from their foreheads and caught their breath.

Lora said, "I was about to say that with that many kids, it wasn't too unusual to lose a couple of them in those days."

"No, but losing two boys in separate car wrecks was a tragedy. I was about five when Johnny died. People brought so much food that some of the men had to cobble up tables outside to hold it. Folks around here thought a lot of your family. Your dad was a good worker for Russell. Good neighbors."

"So why did they move from here? I never heard Mom say. My sister Judy told me one time that Mom thought the house was haunted."

"Well, if it was, they had to be awfully little ghosts. The house was too small for such a big family and your mom and dad showed no signs of letting up. Arlie got on full time at the sawmill and they moved so he could walk to work. I'm getting thirsty. Mind if I get that water bottle out of your car?"

"No, I think I'll join you."

They stood up and fetched the quart of ice water from the car. Marvin offered Lora the first drink before draining a healthy swig himself.

"I don't mind drinking after a pretty woman," he smiled, "but I doubt you would want to drink after me. Let's take it back to the seat."

After they resumed their seats, Lora asked, "So what about it? Was this place haunted? Would you mind if I tape this?"

Marvin sighed as he gazed distantly toward his home on the hillside. "Go right ahead. I guess every place is haunted for someone. My kids is all still alive but I still see the ghosts of them as children playing in the yard sometimes. Now I'll tell you what I know about the house here and a little of what I heard from the old people who lived in the valley before it was built."

He plucked a long yellow straw from a patch of fescue as he settled in to his seat before he continued, "From what I gathered, a lot of people around here thought the house was cursed from the git-go. You see that big house in that curve over there? Matthew Bertram built that one around 1910. The Russell house was built by his wife's granddaddy, Ike Sharp, a couple of years later. The story goes that Ike Sharp and Matthew Shearer was in cahoots to buy the timber rights to a big tract of virgin timber up around Slickford. That's about twenty miles from here in wild country, especially then. Trouble was, a young farmer by the name of Newt Piercy had bought a passel of land smack dab in the middle of the land they wanted. Now, you know all this is just hearsay from the old people?"

"Yes," Lora replied as she realized that the tale Marvin was spinning would make great copy. "Please continue."

"Well, the story goes that Piercy and his wife Nellie was living in a tent until they could build their own house. They had the framework up and would start with the siding as soon as the spring crops were laid by. He had a big stack of yellow poplar boards piled up near the house site. One day Shearer and Sharp showed up to buy the land but he wasn't selling. Some sort of argument broke out and they shot Newt and ran off. Nellie heard the commotion and ran over to find her husband dying. She helped him onto the pile of poplar where he laid until he bled to death. They say some of his blood soaked into the lumber."

"Did she press charges?"

"She tried, but some things don't change. People with money can afford a different brand of justice. The county assessor seized the property, which it quickly sold to Sharp and Shearer for a song. Nellie left the country and was never heard from again."

"So let me guess. That poplar was used to build this house."

Marvin flicked the wet straw out of his hand, plucked a new dry one and continued, "Not exactly. There was a pretty good pile of lumber lying there and yellow poplar is ideal for building. Termites won't eat it."

"You're kidding, right?"

"Nope, my daddy told me that. I can take you to the old Dry Hollow School nearly a hundred years old with yellow poplar joist touching the ground and nary any sign of termites. No, they split the lumber up fifty-fifty. Matthew built a dogtrot house and Ike stored his in that big tobacco barn yonder. At that time his farm was not big enough to need a hired hand so he saw no need to waste the lumber."

"Now, Matthew had two girls, Analee and Cassie. Analee wound up being an old spinster who lived with her father her whole life. Cassie was a mite addled. Took wild spells from time to time. Still, she was pretty, and soon she had a lot of gentlemen callers. Most saw that she was crazier than hell but eventually she married a man not much smarter than she was. I think his name was Willard something. Anyway, Matthew knew that they had no chance of living on their own so he built this dogtrot house for them so he could keep an eye on them. They'd have fighting matches like you wouldn't believe. One day they showed up at Matthew's door with a big hank of each other's hair to give Matt as a birthday present."

Lora shuddered, "Why didn't he commit them to an asylum? Guess there weren't many around then, were there?"

"No, and besides she was still his daughter. 'Course it all ended badly. Got real cold in early December one year and Cassie set the house on fire. By the time Matt got out to the house, he was too late. All he could do was listen to Cassie singing as the house burned down around her. I never saw the house myself, never even seen a picture of it, but my older sister remembered all this very well. Burned about 1949."

He rose slowly from the rock seat. "Got to stretch my legs a bit. Us old folks have to stay a little limber or we stiffen up."

"I think I need a stretch too," Lora replied. "Are you getting hungry?"

"Not really. I can finish telling you about this place at the house unless you just want to hear it here."

"Actually, this place has a nice atmosphere to it. How come the man who farms these fields never plowed this place up?"

"Don Burton told me that the little increase in his crops he might get wouldn't be worth the aggravation of old metal pieces and junk that had collected around the house over the years. Said it gave him a convenient place to rest when he was working these fields."

"So I guess the rest of the lumber was used to build this house. Do you know when it was built?"

"Late forties I think. It was here when the other one burned. By the time Ike had finished clearing this farm off, it was nearly three hundred acres of good farmland. He needed help to tend it so he built this house. And I will say this, his son-in-law Russell had a knack for renting this house to the scum of the earth, present company excepted of course."

"For example..."

"Now, again, this is just what I heard. The first tenant, a man named Everett Coffey, was a drunkard and a bootlegger. Used to haul liquor in from Bald Rock. That's the closest place to get booze here. Used to quarrel something awful. Showed up drunk to work one day and Ike fired him. I think the next renter was a man named Willy Hubbard. Another bootlegger."

Marvin paused to scan the mountainside before he pointed to a low place in the outline of the mountain's edge. "You see that swag in them mountains there? There's a little cave about halfway up the mountain just big enough for a man and a moonshine still. Willy wasn't married so nobody paid any attention when he wasn't home. Ran a still out of that cave for nigh unto twenty years. Then the feds really cracked down again on moonshine in the early sixties. Caught old Willy in the act in that cave. He tried to hide behind the still but a stray bullet ruptured it when it was at full bore. Blew Willy to smithereens. They buried what they could find of him next to his folks in Bethesda graveyard. I think your daddy was the next tenant."

"So why does everybody call it Russell Criswell's rent house if it belonged to Ike?"

"Ike gave the whole farm to Russell when Russell married his only daughter, Frances. Willy was still living here then. Somewhere along the way, the name just took. No disrespect was intended, but it was the only house people lived in that they didn't own. That's all I ever heard it called...Russell's rent house."

"So Daddy was just a farmhand here?"

"He was a damned fine neighbor the whole time he lived here. Hardworking man. I don't recall how many of you children were born in that house. You were and your brother, Jimmy. No, wait, they had another baby just before they moved, but I forget her name."

"That would be Maggie. She's almost two years younger than me."

Marvin stood up again and flexed his legs. "I never could figure out how two adults and fourteen children squeezed into that little house. And I sure could never see how they made more kids with all them other kids around. Back then times were a lot different."

"Judy said that Mom and Dad and the babies slept together in the downstairs bedroom. The rest of us split the upstairs bedrooms between four girls and six boys. I remember in the winter it was really cold up there."

"I know Arlie died fairly young from lung cancer. Heavy smoker his whole life. What about your Mom?"

"She died of a stroke a few years later. So who moved in after we left?"

Marvin stroked his chin. "I don't think anybody lived there for a while after Russell and Frances moved to Bowling Green and closed the farm down. Probably put his father-in-law in an early grave."

"Why did he care? He gave it to Russell years before."

Marvin spat the chewed-up straw out, flicking his tongue in and out like a snake to get the last slivery pieces from under his tongue before continuing. He plucked another long honey-colored straw from a foxtail and resumed. "Ike Sharp was the last of a dying breed and if we're lucky, they'll stay dead. Once bragged in the pool hall that he owned land he had never set foot on, couldn't even find it if his life depended it. He'd fight a circular saw for disagreeing with him. Owned a big farm of rich bottom land up in Beech Valley. Used to get drunker than a skunk and try to shoot pop bottles off the fence posts while he was playing Lone Ranger on an old mule. Killed one of his milk cows and shot the window out of his house before Clony — that was his wife — jerked a knot in him. Him and the Koger boys and Matt Shearer had this philosophy that it didn't matter if the land was used for anything as long as they had it and nobody else did. Stories were told that Ike was involved in more than one murder over it.

"But see, this farm was different. He and Clony had worked and slaved and grubbed roots out to make a good dowry and home for their daughter. Now, don't get me wrong here. Russell Criswell was as fine a man as God ever breathed life into, but he was sort like a reverse King Midas. Everything he touched turned to shit. Ike could read the writing on the wall. If Russell began a new enterprise in Bowling Green it was just a matter of time until he would be in hock up to his ass and the farm would have to be sold. He begged Frances to divorce Russell so the farm would revert back to her alone."

Lora stood up and adjusted her clothes before sitting down, amazed that Marvin could remember all these details and wondering how he would get back to her natal home. "So did she divorce him?"

"I know you think I'm making this all up. But so help me God it's true. Turns out that Frances was pregnant and was on the verge of a mental break-down. That was really the reason they were moving to Bowling Green. In them days pregnant teachers had to take leave anyway. I heard that she tried to file the divorce papers but the court decided she was not mentally competent to make such a big decision.

"So now Ike tries to buy the land back, but he faced the same problem. Both of their names were on the deed and Russell was not selling it come hell or high water. Ike tried to get Russell to rent the big house and farm to someone to keep the farm going. All Russell agreed to was to rent the rent house to needy families who would be expected to keep an eye on things and let them know if anything was wrong. So with Frances four months pregnant, they closed the big house down and moved to Bowling Green — for eleven years I think. The farm went fallow, the fencerows grew up and the big house began to show its age.

"The rent house set empty for a little less than a year before Russell rented it to Annabelle Slagle and her son Nick. A logging accident had killed her husband

and I believe Nick had epilepsy so he had to live with his mom. He was a hard worker in putting up hay and tobacco. Good turned feller, always in a good mood. He loved to hunt, but Annabelle always went with him. She was afraid he would have a spell and die."

Marvin leaned forward with a grin and said, "Here's the funny part. Of course, Nick could never get a license. They lived about a mile from Sexton's store and they used to walk there to get groceries. Well, Nick got an idea. He bought a riding lawn mower to ride to the store. His mom walked behind him to carry the groceries back. I guess some people thought that was not fair, so he built a little four wheeled cart with a big couch cushion in it so Annabelle could ride in style."

Lora chuckled. "I bet that was a sight."

"Yeah, it was, but you had to admire his creativity. They lived there for about five years. One day, somebody hit and run over Nick on his mower. Knocked off the wheel and bent the axle. He never could get it to run right again. I think they moved into a little house in town. Lost track of them, till I heard Annabelle had died. Don't know what happened to Nick. Say, are you getting hungry?"

"Believe it or not, I am not the least bit hungry. If you're hungry, we can finish this back at your house."

"Nah, us old people don't eat much. Besides, it is just getting to the good part."

Lora caught her breath. "The good part? You don't think this has been the good part?"

"No, I mean the good part. After the Slagles, Russell rented the house to James Tuttle. Pure trash. Four kids used to ride the bus. I only remember the oldest, Jimmy Tuttle. Always put me in the mind of Screwy Squirrel in the cartoons. Beady eyes and buckteeth. Stayed in trouble from running his mouth. Bus driver reserved the front seat for him. Always wore a checked CPO jacket he got out of Goodwill."

"How can you remember such details of someone you barely knew?"

Marvin got up to stroll around and whistle as if in deep thought. He picked up a likely piece of stray tree branch, returned to his seat while wrestling his pocketknife out of his pants pocket. He flicked the blade open and as he began to whittle small curlicues of weathered wood from the stick, he said, "Well, these were the first occupants of the house I ever had any dealing with. I wanted to plant some March flowers in Mom's garden and I had noticed that there were several bunches growing in the ditch across the road from the house. I figured they didn't belong to anyone so I figured I'd help myself."

Lora adjusted herself on the stump. "How did March flowers get to be there? Did somebody plant them?"

Marvin bit his lower lip. "I guess chipmunks moved them around. They'll eat the bulbs. Or they could have washed there in a rain.

"That was the year that my dad decided to go into the chicken business. He reworked the barn to have roosts and nest boxes. He ordered one hundred roosters to kill for the freezer and a hundred pullets to lay eggs. After the pullets were grown and started laying, Bob Vickery over in Shearer Valley asked Daddy if he would sell him some of the pullets so he would not have to buy eggs. Daddy sold him fifteen pullets at two dollars apiece. I remember helping catch and load them. The Vickery farm is pretty big and Bob had fixed up an old building on the backside to use as a chicken house. So everybody was happy. Now, come here."

They got up and walked a few paces toward the back of the yard. Marvin gently turned Lora's head while he pointed to the low swag in the mountain skyline. "You see that saddle yonder? Well, that's a pass over to the Vickery Farm." He released her head before continuing, "About a week after he got the chickens, Bob went out to feed and water them. Every one of them was gone. Turns out that Tuttle had snuck through that pass at night and stole every chicken. Bob called the sheriff, but it didn't take no rocket scientist to track down the thieves. There was feathers strewn all over the woods from the Vickery place to here. The sheriff broke the door down and sure enough they had two of them pullets on the stove cooking and were picking the feathers off another. They put the parents in jail and the children in foster homes."

Lora interrupted, "So now the house is empty again."

Marvin nodded his head. "Yep, the house set empty for a few months before the Miller family moved in. A young woman and her two sons, Johnny and Mike. Johnny used to ride the school bus, but I think Mike had not started school. Johnny was a very handsome boy, beautiful smile and cheery disposition. Odd thing was, neither he nor Mike made any effort to mix with the rest of us kids in the neighborhood, and there was a lot of kids to mix with. Never saw them playing in their own yard. Stayed in the house."

"I had driven to town to visit my sister in town on Christmas Eve and was coming home about 9:30. The house was all lit up and there set the big green Thunderbird in that little driveway there. I recognized it as belonging to Ina Jean Coffey, Granny Wilma Brown's daughter. Ina Jean and her children moved back home with Wilma. Wilma Brown was as fine a Christian woman as God ever made. Daddy always said that if Wilma Brown ain't in heaven, there ain't nobody there. Wilma was always taking food to the needy or delivering fruit baskets from church so I didn't give it a second thought. What sticks in my mind sixty year later is that scraggly little Charlie Brown Christmas tree bearing a few lights, strands of icicles and a dime store angel visible through the front window."

Marvin paused to retrieve a handkerchief from his back pocket and wipe a few tears away and quietly sniffle his nose. Lora felt how hard this was for him and quietly reassured him, "Take your time. You don't have to finish this if you don't want to."

Marvin took a few deep breaths to compose himself. "No, I need to tell this. I never found out the truth until a month later. I used to go to Wilma's house to work jigsaw puzzles. I remarked to Ina Jean one night how surprised I was to see her car out there. She straightened herself in the chair and said, 'That woman died of cancer that Christmas Eve night and we was setting up with her.' And I said, 'But nobody knew anything about her or her family. How did you know to go out there? Did they call you?'"

"Well, Ina Jean turned as pale as a ghost. She said the phone rang that night and when Wilma answered, someone told her that the Millers in the rent house needed her. We assumed it was one of the kids, but when we got out there, they didn't have a phone. To this day, we do not know who called us."

"So what happened to the boys?" Lora asked.

"Ina Jean said they went to live with relatives in Indiana. They tore the house down the following spring when Russell sold the property to Don Burton. Say, I am really tired. What say we go home?"

They returned home where Lora told Marvin and Evalee about her family and her job and all the wonderful things she had seen in her career. Marvin dug out his collection of photographs so Lora could put faces with some of the names. They carried on a lively conversation until it was too late for her to return to Lexington. She called her business and family while Evalee prepared dinner. After dinner, she helped Evalee clean up the kitchen before joining Marvin sitting in the glider on the west side of the front porch. They sat quietly watching fireflies flickering in the cool spring twilight and the nighthawks coursing in long waves over the rolling fields trying to catch them.

Marvin coughed shallowly. "You know, Lora, when I was a kid, there was only one come-on light in this whole valley and that was over there by Fox Cooper's chicken-house. We could sit out here and really enjoy trying to count the fireflies. Then everybody got to be so mean and crooked that everybody and his uncle put up a come-on light to keep an eye on things. I can sit here and count eight of the damned things. Now your home set in a direct line between here and the sunset until early June. On moonlit nights you could barely make out the shape of the house but you could always see the warm glow of its lights. They were the only lights you could see because the big hemlock trees blocked the Russell house and the maples blocked the old Shearer house. Sometimes I sit out here, close my eyes and I can still see them as little glowing rectangles floating over the pale fields between here and there and the dark of the mountains beyond."

Wearied, yet exhilarated by her long day, Lora peered in the same direction trying desperately to see her childhood home as Marvin saw it. Sighing, she rested her head on her doubled back fist and whispered, "Marvin, do you ever see any ghosts in those little rectangles of light?"

A look of an exuberant hope washed over his face as he whispered back, "No, Lora, I just see angels."

The Field at Anathoth

The Field

PEARL UPROOTED THE last tangled bit of dewberry briars and honeysuckle from within the circle of sheep-skull rocks that enclosed the small plot and leaned wearily on her hoe. The plot lay within an area bounded by chestnut rails, an acre of land she would shortly own free and clear; she nodded approvingly as she wiped the rivulets of sweat from her freckled brow. She straightened up, sighing and pecking disinterestedly at the root-laced ground with the back of her hoe. Laying the hoe across her shoulder she exited the opening between the rails and began the short walk to the house down a dusty road peppered with the last knotty blackberries of the summer.

She stood the hoe in the lop-sided smokehouse and entered the kitchen, letting the white longhaired cat sneak in just ahead of the battered screen door as it clapped shut behind her. The cat meowed expectantly and rubbed against her legs until she poured a bowl of milk for his supper. After she poured a glass of milk for herself, she walked through the house, turned on the bug-fouled light that bathed the porch in a pale glow and took a seat in the slatted swing. As she swung to and fro sipping her milk, she looked into the darkening woods past the dried up-creek. A whip-poor-will called and she echoed his call as she had taught the children to do.

"Whip-poor-will, whip-poor will, whip-poor-will."

She stopped after the third call, knowing instinctively the correct tempo that occasionally had lured curious birds close enough to the house for children to see. The forest across the creek began to fill up with the sounds of katydids and tree frogs. Her mantle clock struck seven o'clock and she peered expectantly in the direction of the road through the forest because she was expecting a visitor. She had asked him to stop at the country store at the head of the hollow and call before coming up because she had a chore that needed finishing that day, the day of his visit, because his services would bring to legal and irrevocable closure the plan she had designed over the last month and a half but had prayed over for forty years.

The cat pushed the front screen door open and joined her now on the porch. Pearl stroked him, saying to herself, "He may have called while I was out so I'd better call to see."

She re-entered the house, dialed the phone and waited for the whirring ring. When Willis Bertram answered, she asked, "Willis, is that lawyer feller there yet? Tell him I'm home and to come on up."

"Oh, hello, Pearl. Yeah, he's here. He got into a checker game with Chester Hancock and cain't win or git out, either. If you got them chores finished, I'll hurry him along. Good night."

Willis hung up the phone and walked to the back of the store where the men were playing checkers before a small audience.

"That was Pearl Kelsay on the phone, Mr. Gabriel. You probably ought to head up there soon. She don't stay up too late."

Gabriel pushed himself away from the checkerboard and said "Well, Mr. Hancock, how about calling this one a draw? We each won a game but I do have business with Mrs. Kelsay."

Chester looked up with disgust. "Jest lak a lawyer tryin' to make a deal. Well, I guess that's okay."

They stood up and shook hands. Gabriel laid down a couple of dollars on the counter to pay for the snacks he had eaten while waiting. He put a piece of gum in his mouth and waved off the change Willis offered him.

"Keep it. Is there a good road to the house?"

"Oh, there is a good road after the county widened and graveled it so you won't have any trouble. What did you say you are seeing Pearl about?"

"I can't tell you that Mr. Bertram. It's confidential."

"Oh, sure, but now let me tell you Pearl is one fine woman. A fine woman. Ain't she, boys?"

The men in the back nodded and Chester said, "She's been up here fer nigh onto forty-five years and has always been a good neighbor to help anyone. Let me tell you about the time she took care of me when I was bit by a copperhead."

"I'd like to hear about it over some more checkers, Mr. Hancock, but I have to go now. It's been nice meeting all you."

Gabriel left the store, got into his Bronco and forded the ankle deep creek to head into the hollow where Pearl lived.

Purchase

The road to Pearl's house clung like a spider web to the cliffs but the driver's side plunged off about a hundred feet to the creek bottomlands. The road had been widened recently, for Gabriel could still see some signs of the erosion caused by the clearing of the land. Still, the graveled stretch exceeded the width of his van only by about three feet on either side and he shuddered to think what the road must have been like before it was widened. Two raccoons shrank from the light of his headlights and scurried up a beech tree near the roadside just before he forded the creek again to emerge in front of a huge two-story clapboard house. He saw Pearl rise from the swing and walk over to the steps, motioning him to come to the house.

He could see that she was a big woman as she stood silhouetted against the glow of the porch light. Waving as he walked over the weedy yard he said, "Mrs. Kelsay? I'm Ben Gabriel, the attorney you called last week. I'm sorry I'm late, but it's hard to leave those fellows in a checker game."

"I'm glad to meet you, Mr. Gabriel. You can call me Pearl like everybody else."

Gabriel stepped up the three steps to the front porch and shook her hand. Her age-freckled hand engulfed his own, surprising him with the firmness of her grip. She had short wavy hair clipped to the same length as most of the hill women he had met. Fire still burned behind her tortoise-shell glasses and her hearty smile exposed a gold-capped lateral incisor. Her gingham dress was still stained with sweat stains suffused with the musty odor of her perspiration and traces of Ivory soap. The scent surprised him with a fleeting recollection of his childhood, of his own lost mother rocking him to sleep.

"I really appreciate you coming here to do this because I don't drive anymore and I don't have a way into town. I wish we could have done this today before it got late but I didn't have everything finished until a while ago. I wanted everything done so I can show you exactly where everything is and there won't be any confusion."

"I understand, Pearl, and don't worry about being a little late. As a new part of the community it never hurts to meet people. Should we go into the house where we can go over the papers?"

"First, I want to show you exactly where the ground is. Let me get a flashlight. Come on through the kitchen to the back door."

They entered the house where Pearl picked up a six-volt flashlight, led him out the back door and up the road to the plot she had carefully bordered by stick and stone. She swept the beam clockwise around the rail fence boundary saying, "This here is the acre I am buying, marked off by them rails. Jimmy convinced the other children to sell me this one acre. The money is at the house, and Jimmy knows what to do with it."

"Please excuse me, but I'm a little confused. You're buying this one-acre from your children? If you don't mind me saying so, that seems a little peculiar. I mean you are living here and, according to your late husband's will, you can stay here as long as you live, even though the land legally belongs to your eight children."

"They're not my children, only stepchildren. You know how families are these days, always fighting and bickering over wills. The will says I can live in the house until I die, but I got to thinking that they could sell the farm from under me and I just wanted to make sure I had a little plot of my own. I doubt that any of them would ever do that, but if one of them got into a bind where they needed money, they might want to sell the farmland. Better safe than sorry, I guess."

Gabriel nodded uncertainly, feeling too uncomfortable to push the issue. "So you and Jimmy agreed on the price of a thousand dollars for this one acre. That seems like a high price for one acre in this part of the county."

"Well, the money is going back to the kids, so it don't really matter much. Let's go back to the house and sign the papers so you can get back home."

They walked back to the house and spread the legal papers on the kitchen table. While Pearl read the papers over, Gabriel scanned the roomy kitchen.

Windows filled the long wall for about half of its length, and an electric stove and an old wood-burning stove framed the door. A refrigerator stood across from the electric stove. An enormous baker's cupboard and walnut hutch occupied most of the rest of the space. A homemade table and a long bench of seats crowded the rest of the room.

Quietly, he asked, "How many children are there in the family?"

Pearl paused to look up from her reading. "There's eight of them: Mary, Bill, Bob, Dan, Alice, Faith, Ginny and Jimmy. Ginny and Jimmy are twins. All of them but Jimmy live in Indiana now; he lives in Louisville."

She dropped the ending of her answer with a finality that made Gabriel flush because he knew he was asking questions with answers he had no reason or business to know. He sat quietly while she finished reading.

"So I need to sign both copies of the deed and purchase agreement?"

"Yes. Then I'll meet with Jimmy to give him the money."

Pearl scratched his Cross pen along the dotted line on each deed. Gabriel countersigned them and handed Pearl back a copy. She rose from her chair to retrieve an envelope from the cupboard, quietly folded the deed, and stuffed it into the envelope. After returning the envelope to the cupboard, she left the kitchen and returned with a fat stack of hundred dollar bills.

"You said that your charge was two hundred dollars? Well, here it is, Mr. Gabriel." She handed him the money and said, "I really appreciate all that you have done. Be sure them papers are filed in the courthouse and that Jimmy gets the money. Call me if I need to do any thing else. Oh, I almost forgot."

She returned to the cupboard and retrieved a sealed envelope with a scrawled message:

For Jimmy to share with the other children.

Gabriel started from his chair. "Pearl, what are..".

Pearl laughed, "Oh, don't get scared. There's just a few things in there for you to be sure gets done when I do die. I've already told Jimmy that you'll help him settle my affairs."

Gabriel hesitantly placed the envelope in his briefcase along with the other papers and snapped the lid shut. "Well, Pearl, I hope that my services have been satisfactory, but I must admit I am still a little confused. Of course, all of this is confidential, but I get the feeling there is something more I should do."

"I cain't think of anything right now, but thanks again for all of your help. If can come back sometime, I'll cook you a big dinner. Do you like rhubarb pie?"

"I've never had rhubarb pie, but don't be surprised if you get a call from me making a date. When does rhubarb get ripe and what does it taste like?"

"In the spring. You just use the stalks. The leaves and roots are poison. It has a sour whang to it but it makes a real good pie with strawberries. I'll call you next spring when mine gets ready to eat."

"It's a deal, if I can bring my wife and son! I'll be looking forward to seeing you again. Good night."

"That'll be fine. Now be careful getting back out the holler. It can be scary at night if you ain't used to it."

Gabriel shook her hand and left the house. She watched him get back into his Bronco and waited for him to start the engine and turn on the headlights. He waved out the window, turned the van around, forded the creek again and watched the porch light blink out in his rear view mirror. When he reached a low spot in the forest outline from which he could still see the lights in the house, he stepped out into the warm night and watched the house until the lights went out. Puzzled, he got back into his vehicle and continued down the road, mulling the same questions over and over in his head:

Why in the hell would you want or even feel the need to buy land from your children? At her age? Up here in the middle of nowhere?

A Little Piece of Heaven

"Come in, Mr. Roberts."

The door to Ben Gabriel's office opened and a thin young man stepped inside. He walked over to the desk, extended his hand, and said "John Roberts,

Mr. Gabriel. Your secretary called and said that you had some questions about my Aunt Pearl. Is there something wrong?"

"Ben Gabriel, Mr. Roberts. Thank you for coming in so promptly. No, there is nothing wrong, but your aunt retained me to handle some legal affairs last month for her. I am very new to the community and I want to try to make some new contacts and find out more about my clients. I am not at liberty to disclose the details of the transactions, but I was very impressed with your Aunt. The men at the store up there told me that you are quite close to her."

"Well, I'll tell you what I can, especially if it'll help my Aunt Pearl. It's the least I could do, considering. She has always been my favorite relative. Aunt Pearl is my father's sister, the oldest child of my Grandpa Ira Roberts by his second wife Sarah. Aunt Pearl's first husband, Charlie Littrell, committed suicide. My sister Sally was the one who found him. She was twelve, I think. I never knew him or either of my paternal grandparents. I know that Aunt Pearl and Charlie Littrell helped my mom and dad get started after they got married. They lived just outside Decatur, Illinois, and helped Daddy get a job on a farm up there in '36. They all moved back here, but after Charlie died, she moved back to Grandpa's for a year before she married Pat Kelsay and moved up to the farm at Sunnybrook."

"Do you know much about her life on the farm?"

Roberts smiled before answering, "Mr. Gabriel, have you ever thought much about what heaven is like or at least the heaven you wanted to go to? Well, my vision of heaven is to be six or seven years old and live on Aunt Pearl's farm with all of her children. She used to come over every summer and get one of us kids and take them back up to the farm for a week or two. I remember the first time she came to get me in that old faded blue Chevrolet truck. They only went to town a few times a year because they grew everything they ate, but she and Pat would come by and pick us up on the way home. Both Aunt Pearl and Pat were big and fat, so I was squeezed in between them in the cab with the groceries in the bed of the truck. It's funny how the trips up there seemed to take so long, but now they seem so short."

He paused reflectively before continuing. "You turned off at Bertram's store at the head of the holler, got the mail..."

"Got the mail?"

"Back then the mail did not come to every house in some of the hills and hollers. There were a whole bunch of post offices, usually at a small country store. One of the joys of going to Aunt Pearl's was getting to go to get the mail every day. Most of the time, she would give us a nickel or a dime for a Coke or a candy bar. I loved the Hollywood candy bars in a blue wrapper, but you can't find them anymore. Now most of the post offices are shut down because everybody gets the mail at home."

He paused again, pursing his lips and knitting his brow. "Maybe that's one reason people are not so friendly anymore. Everybody back then took a few minutes to visit with each other, and everybody knew what was going on and who needed help haying or who was sick."

"Anyway, the only part of the journey that I dreaded was the trip up the holler. The road now is a good road, but back then it was a nightmare. Just dirt road and rocks as big as a couch jutting up in places. Some places there was only a few inches of clearance on the creek side. I always wondered if Aunt Pearl or Pat was heavy enough to tip us over the edge. Only trucks could get up the road, so sometimes in winter people parked at the store and walked up. I remember my first trip up that road because a squirrel ran up the road ahead of us and hid in a knot hole in a big beech tree by the road."

"So what did you do up there?"

"What we didn't do! Aunt Pearl had two big horses they used to work the farm, Doll and Betsy. Doll was black with a blaze and had a wild disposition but Betsy was a soft gray and was real gentle. My brother Charlie was already up there helping with the tobacco, and he gave me my first horseback ride on Betsy. He swung me up in front of him and we rode her to the barn for the night."

Roberts laughed and slapped his knee. "He had set me down in a bad position so that my weight was bearing down on my nuts and it hurt like hell. He asked what was wrong and I said my kidneys were hurting. He must have understood what I meant, because he laughed and shifted my position for me."

Gabriel smiled at the image of all this and stretched back in his chair preparing to relish what he knew was an excursion into a rural lifestyle unfamiliar to him. "This is all sort of foreign to me because I grew up in Chicago. I take it that the kind of life you are describing was pretty common back then."

"Oh, yeah, all the big farms up there were being farmed. People had big families and grew a lot of their food, but Aunt Pearl's farm was special. She had ducks and geese she picked for feathers for her pillows and feather beds. That creek up there used to run year round and was just deep enough to play in without risking drowning, but in a few places it was deep enough to fish. They raised pigs for meat in the winter and kept beehives for honey. She had cows for milk to drink and sell. Aunt Pearl churned her own butter. In late summer, they made molasses for the winter and to sell. They raised turkeys to sell and corn to feed the hogs and grind into meal. Back then flour came in big cloth bags that people could use to make shirts and quilts with. I still have a flour sack shirt she gave me.

"And chickens. Aunt Pearl always had a big flock of chickens for eggs and meat. She had brown leghorns, White Rocks, Rhode Island Reds, Domineckers, and Topknots. One of my jobs as a little kid was to find nests of chickens hidden in the fencerows. One time I found one that had fifty-two eggs in it. Every time I came home Aunt Pearl would give me an old hen and her brood of little chickens.

"I even got to play cowboy, because I would have to go to the upper pastures to get the cows for milking in the morning and at night. There was a small Jersey, a brown Swiss and a Hereford. They never had names like the horses. The horses you sort of built a relationship with and taught them to work with you, but the cows were just there. I never could milk the cows, because my grip was not strong enough, but Aunt Pearl could sure make them squirt milk like crazy."

"I noticed that she had a firm handshake."

"Firm? We used to go up there for Sunday dinner sometimes and that meant chicken dinner. She'd go out and call the chickens close enough to reach down and grab a couple. I've seen her grab a chicken in each hand, wring their heads off and throw the flopping bodies over her shoulder like paper wads. My Aunt Pearl is a powerful woman."

"So there was always a lot for me to do up there. We hunted arrowheads in the tobacco patch. Found some real beauties. I helped chop tobacco or corn, pick blackberries, feed the stock or whatever chore I was able to do and when I got ready to go home, she would give me a little tobacco sack with a handful of change. I felt as rich as a king."

"A tobacco sack?"

"Pat used to roll his own cigarettes from Camel tobacco and papers. I remember he always had short stubby fingers stained yellow from tobacco. The tobacco came in a little cloth bag with a yellow drawstring. I'd give anything if I had kept just one of them, but I lost them over the years."

"So were all of her children still there when you began to go up there for these vacations?"

"No, only Ginny, Jimmy. The rest had all got married and moved to Kokomo or Indianapolis to work in the factories up there. Ginny and I were real close, but I liked all of her kids. Actually they were her stepchildren. Their mother, Nellie, died of cancer a year before Pearl married Pat. You know, one thing always puzzled me: I called my mother 'Mom', but they always called Aunt Pearl 'Mother'. It always sounded sort of formal and strange to me."

"One thing for sure is that she probably saved their lives. Mary was about fourteen and Ginny and Jimmy were only about two years old when Aunt Pearl went up there. They were dirt poor. No furniture. Not enough food and not much of a future, but Aunt Pearl changed all of that. She brought some furniture and livestock from Grandpa's. Then she cleaned them kids up, took them to church, and taught them to do an honest day's work."

"So the kids had not been going to church?"

"No, I think that Pat had only been out of jail for a little while when he and Aunt Pearl got married so he had not taken much interest in church, so in a lot of ways, she was an angel of mercy sent to save that family. But she wasn't like one of them angels playing harps. She was more like the angel in the lions' den with Daniel who locked the jaws of the lions. She never swore or anything, and she always took religious matters very seriously. And she always looked out for her family."

Roberts paused and bit his lower lip. "The one thing I could never figure out. Aunt Pearl was so good with kids. All kids loved her and she loved kids. When she laughed she would just shake all over. You could just see genuine love and compassion oozing out of every pore. But I can't figure why the God she put so much faith in never gave her children of her own. It just don't seem fair, you know?"

"Well, it sounds like God did the next best thing by giving her a ready made family to raise. Isn't that just as good?"

Roberts grimaced and rose slowly to leave, nodding in ambivalent agreement. "In some people's eyes, maybe, but it's not the same as having your own flesh and blood. I need to go. I have to meet my wife for lunch."

Gabriel shook his hand and watched from the window as Roberts crossed the street and got into his car. He knew that life would be different here in a small southern town, but he and his wife had decided that they did not want to bring their children up in Chicago. As he replayed the images of the country life Roberts's reminiscences had evoked, his lawyer's mind quickly recalled the one incongruous phrase that he regretted not interrupting to inquire about:

What did he mean the least I could do for my Aunt Pearl, 'considering'?

Siege

Gabriel and his family went to Pearl's farm for dinner in the spring. He discovered that he had a real taste for rhubarb pie, a specialty of Pearl's culinary skill. Just as Roberts had told him, his five-year-old son, Benjamin Junior, had taken an instant liking to Pearl so while she entertained his wife, Jill, and their son, Gabriel decided to walk around the farm.

The fields lay fallow, overgrown with briars and weeds that years ago would have fallen to the hoe or tiller. Some of the woven wire fences sagged, but the barn and other outbuildings looked solid enough with only little signs of disrepair. The creek that Roberts described was a sluggish trickle now, even shallower than it was on his visit the previous year. He sauntered up the dusty road to the land Pearl had bought. In the bright sun of the May afternoon, he could now clearly see the small ten by ten plot surrounded by stones that Pearl had cleared the previous year.

There has to be something I am missing here.

He walked back to the house, thinking about all that Roberts had told him, trying to envision the farm buzzing with the sounds of laughter intermingled with the gee and haw of horses plowing and roosters crowing and a loud, stern voice yelling "DINNER'S READY."

There has to be something I am missing here. Has to be.

As they left, Gabriel promised Pearl they would return. Driving back down the road to the highway he convinced himself that the key to the mystery might lie in a time before Roberts had been born. None of Pearl's children lived close by, but he remembered that Roberts had four older siblings and two of them still lived in town. He had mentioned an older sister, Sally; perhaps she could provide a clue.

In a few days he managed to locate Sally, or Sarah Belle, which was her real name, under her married name, Davis. He called her at home to arrange a time to meet.

"Hello, Sarah Belle Davis, please... Oh, hello, Mrs. Davis. My name is Ben Gabriel. I am doing some legal work for your Aunt Pearl and I would like to know some of the details of her early life before she moved to Sunnybrook. Yes, I know that your father was her brother and could probably be a great deal of help, but I understand you were especially close to her first husband, Charlie Littrell. Would you mind meeting with me to clear up a few details? Fine. How about Thursday morning at ten? I'll see you then."

Gabriel was sitting in the outer office on Thursday reviewing a new partnership agreement when Sarah Belle arrived. He stood up quickly, extending his hand. "Good morning, Mrs. Davis, I'm Ben Gabriel. I really appreciate you coming in. Would you like a cup of coffee?"

"Just call me Sally like everybody else. Yes, black, please."

Gabriel poured the coffee and escorted Sally to a leather chair before taking a seat behind his desk.

"So what's this all about?"

"Well, Sally, I'm doing some legal work for your Aunt Pearl Kelsay so I can't go into much detail. I need to clarify some information about her life before she married Pat Kelsay. I've already talked to your brother, John, but of course he could only tell me about her life at Sunnybrook. He did tell me that you were pretty close to her first husband, Charlie Littrell."

"You must be writing a will if you're going to this much trouble."

Gabriel smiled, hoping that he had not given any sign of affirmation at her astute conclusion. "As I said, I'm bound by attorney-client confidentiality, Sally, so I - ..."

"That's fine. I can put two and two together. So what do you want to know?"

"I need to know about her life with Charlie Littrell."

"Did Johnny tell you about Grandpa and Grandma Roberts?"

"He did mention that your Grandpa's first wife died in a fire, but he didn't go into details."

Sally sipped her coffee and set the cup back into the saucer. "It was winter with a big snow on the ground. Uncle Newt had hurt his leg falling from a horse and was staying with Grandpa Ira and his wife, Alta Morgan. They had one son then, my Uncle Charlie Roberts, C.H. as we call him. He was about two. A fire broke out but by the time Ira woke up, flames engulfed the house. He ran to C.H.'s room, grabbed him and threw him out the window into a snowdrift. Uncle Newt had already got out of the house, and he dug C.H. out of the snow and wrapped his coat around him. Grandpa tried to fight his way back into the bedroom to get Alta but he couldn't get in. He just had to watch his wife burn to death. Uncle Newt had to hold Grandpa back from going back into the house to get Alta. His arms and hands were all burned and scarred for the rest of his life from the fire. He seldom talked about Alta, but I think he thought about her a lot. He buried her in the family's graveyard at Walnut Grove. When he raised a new family with my Grandma, he made certain that all of his children knew the importance of looking out for your children. I heard my own dad say that Grandpa once told him that children are the only things that you leave behind to prove you were ever here at all.

"He remarried Sarah Vickery. I'm named for my two grandmas: Sarah Clementine Roberts and Maggie Belle Denney."

Sally leaned back in her chair, chuckling "I'm glad they never called me Maggie Clementine!"

"Sarah Belle is a very pretty name. It has a lyrical, almost musical sound to it."

"Thank you. Daddy just started calling me Sally. So, anyway, Grandpa and Grandma raised a new family. Aunt Pearl was their oldest child that lived, then

Bill, Haywood, my dad Grady, Eula and Helen. Pearl married Charlie Littrell when she was fourteen and he was about thirty."

"Fourteen? Isn't that awfully young?"

Sally finished her coffee and shifted her position in the chair. "Yes and no. Don't get me wrong. All of the kids loved Grandpa and Grandma, but Grandpa was hard on them. He made them work almost as soon as they could walk and he was a very strict disciplinarian. My Daddy has told me many times about how Granny would take him to the tobacco patch when he was just two or three and laid a big rock on his shirttail to keep him from crawling away while she chopped out tobacco. I used to think that maybe Pearl felt that if she was going to have to work so hard it might as well be for a family of her own but, as I have gotten older, I wonder if there was another reason."

Gabriel raised his eyebrows questioningly, hoping that the gesture would coax an answer to an unasked question.

"Uncle Hiram Catron. I'd heard that he and Aunt Pearl had a thing going on, but I didn't believe it."

Gabriel stuck his head forward dumbfounded. "Do you mean an intimate relationship? With a girl that young?"

Sally nodded, hesitantly, a nod filled with disgust and sorrow and anger. "I guess it wouldn't have been the first time something like that happened. Especially back then."

"You say that you didn't believe it at first but now you do. What changed your mind?"

"Hiram Catron was so tight that he raised his family on groundhogs and possums. Daddy says that Lizzie Catron could cook a good possum."

They both made a face of disgust and shuddered at the thought of such a meal.

"Uncle Charlie and I were close, so I used to stay with Aunt Pearl and him when they ran a boarding house called The White Way Inn. Sometimes Uncle Charlie would be out working and Hiram would drop by. He nearly always gave me a nickel or a dime to run to the store to get some candy. I used to think it was because he liked me but, as I have gotten older, I see a different reason. Like I said, I can put two and two together."

"Yes, I can see why you think that now."

"Well, for whatever reason, Pearl married Charlie and they moved to Illinois to raise a family. Johnny probably told you how good Pearl is with kids, so she was looking forward to having a big family. May I trouble you for some more coffee?"

Gabriel picked up the carafe and refilled her cup. "Certainly. Please go on."

"It's funny how things don't work out the way we plan them to. Turns out that they couldn't have children."

"Why?"

"That depends on who you listen to. My Mom told me that Charlie had been kicked by a mule and that had, as she said, 'interrupted' him. But some folks will tell you that Aunt Pearl had caught some kind of disease from Hiram that had left her sterile. I really don't know which one it is, because it was something polite people didn't ask about. It was just God's will."

"And Pearl is a very religious woman."

"So am I. My husband is a Baptist minister and I have learned to see that God works for good in all things. It's just sometimes it's a lot easier to accept God's will than others. Some people never accept it."

"You mean that Pearl was destined to marry Pat and raise his family?"

"Not just that. When Dad and Mom got married, they moved to Illinois where Pearl and Charlie lived, but Mom didn't know the first thing about how to keep house. They laugh that Daddy had to show her how to cut up a chicken the first time she tried to fry chicken. Aunt Pearl took Mom under her wing and taught her how to cook, and everything else. She was all Mom had to rely on up there, five hundred miles from home. Mom was only seventeen when she got married and came from a dirt poor, backward family. I sort of get the feeling that she had a lot in common with Aunt Pearl, if you get my drift."

Gabriel nodded pensively.

"So here Mom and Dad were in the depression trying to start a family. Dad had to work for six weeks for a farmer up there, Clinton Kaiser, without pay just to prove that he could do the job. I don't know how they could have made it without Pearl and Charlie. My brother Ottis was born about a year after they were married, and I followed two years later, then my brother Charlie."

"Lots of Charlies in your family history."

Sally laughed, "When C.H. named his last son Charlie we said that we was so poor that we couldn't afford any new names, but my brother was named in honor of both Charlie Littrell and C.H. Those were hard times in the early forties, what with the war and all. Mom was not always in the best of health so Ottis and me spent a lot of time with Aunt Pearl. Once when I was about three she had cleaned us both up nice and pretty and Ottis threw ashes in my hair. He knew that he would be in trouble if Aunt Pearl found out, so he had me sit under the pump while he pumped water all over me to get the ashes out. When Aunt Pearl found us, I was a real mess!"

Gabriel laughed at the image the story conjured. "Did Ottis get a spanking?"

"No, I don't recall Aunt Pearl ever whipping a kid. She had a tone and a look that hurt worse than any whipping. And you just idolized this woman so you felt bad about misbehaving. I never heard any of Pat's kids say she ever whipped any of them."

"That was probably unusual for that time and this part of the country. Isn't whipping a child who misbehaves sort of the stereotype of poor Southerners?"

"I guess, but Aunt Pearl was pretty much her own person. She and Charlie had some real good fights, but I think he finally understood that he may rule the roost, but she was going to rule the rooster."

Gabriel snickered, "That's a colorful way of putting it."

"Like my Daddy says, plain talk is easy understood. Anyway, Ottis and me spent a lot of time over there. I remember one time my brother Charlie had typhoid fever and just about died. He was about two. Mom and Daddy were both sick with it, but the doctor told Mom that she had to keep Charlie awake until the fever broke or he could die. Aunt Pearl carried him around day and night for almost thirty straight hours until the fever broke. Just set him down to go the toilet. She had that iron will to overcome anything that threatened her family, and we were pretty much just as much her children as Mom and Dad's."

Gabriel muttered under his breath, "Angel in a lion's den."

"Pardon me?"

"Oh, nothing, I was just thinking about what a job that was."

"Oh. About Charlie Littrell and me. He and Daddy were really very close. They worked together on the farm and they drank together in them days. Dad don't drink now, but he used to. Times were so hard that once they had to steal chickens to feed our family. C.H. somehow kept them from going to the pen. Paid a big fine or something."

Sally paused and wiped the tears from her eyes. "You know that has haunted my Dad his whole life. When he came to my house a few years ago to get my husband Daniel to hear his profession of faith in Jesus Christ, that was the first thing out of his mouth. All he and Charlie were trying to do was to feed their family."

Gabriel reached her a Kleenex and paused while she composed herself. "Thank you. You know, it is probably a good thing that I am to go over some of these times. It's easy to forget who you are these days, and where you came from."

"Yes, especially today."

"Both Daddy and Charlie spoiled me rotten in some ways. I was made to feel that I was the most precious thing in the world to them. I wonder why our ties with some people are so strong and so weak with others. It was real hard for me when Uncle Charlie died."

"Please tell me about that."

"Charlie and Pearl ran the boarding house and I was staying with them. I was about twelve outside playing when I heard a gunshot in the barn. I ran in to see Uncle Charlie laying across his shotgun and his brains splattered across the wall."

She halted and wept quietly for a while. "I thought that I was over all of this."

"Take your time. It must have been a dreadful shock for a young girl, or anyone for that matter. Do you know why he killed himself?"

Sally drew in a few deep breaths and stared at the ceiling.

"No. I know that him and Aunt Pearl had just had a big argument about something. Looking back, I can see where he would have real bad spells of depression. Some people told me that he had gotten into a drunken brawl with a man two days before and had cut the other man with a knife. One person told me that the doctor had told Charlie that he had cancer and was dying. Then there are those who thought that one of Aunt Pearl's boy friends killed Charlie."

"Did she have such boyfriends?"

"I don't know for sure. But I do know that some of the men boarders used to give her some very expensive gifts. I got two of them, a manicure set and a set of hair combs. I don't know who gave them to her, but I do know that's where they came from."

"How did Pearl take all of this?"

"Pearl has always been, I guess the word is 'stoic'. At first she was real grief-stricken. She moved back in with Grandpa and Grandma for a year. For about two years she took regular trips to Walnut Grove Cemetery to visit Charlie's grave and put flowers on it. She would just stand there and stare at the tomb-stone. I always went on Decoration Day and put a yellow rose on Uncle Charlie's grave. That was his favorite flower."

Sally began to cry again and dropped her head, heaving quietly with the weight of memories long thought extinguished. Gabriel sat silently, aware of his own heart quivering as he heard the story. He handed Sally another Kleenex. She dried her eyes, blew her nose and gave him a weak smile.

"You know how some things always get to you no matter how much you hear them? Well, this is one of them things for me. I loved Uncle Charlie so much and I think that Aunt Pearl did too for all of their arguing. I know Daddy thought the world of him. Sometimes we can't figure out why things happen the way they do. Maybe I'm one of them people who still has trouble accepting God's will."

"I'm not much of a churchgoer, but I expect everybody's faith wavers from time to time."

"Probably. Aunt Pearl lived at home for about a year before she married Pat and moved up to Sunnybrook. It was not long after that she quit visiting Charlie's grave."

"I guess she felt the need to move on with this new family."

"Maybe, but she always used to say that people should not put flowers on her grave. She wanted her flowers while she was alive. Grandpa and Grandma both died not long after she married Pat and were buried not far from Charlie Littrell's grave at Walnut Grove."

"So it sounds like she is a kind of person who brings closure to the episodes in her life and then moves on."

"Aunt Pearl always believed that God would give her the strength to overcome any tribulation. Oh, she gossiped some about other people, and at times could be judgmental, but she never cussed anybody. When she was able to get around better, she would go out of her way to help anybody who needed it. She quickly became one of the matrons of Sunnybrook."

She looked at her watch. "Well, I need to be going to a beauty shop appointment. I hope I have been helpful. Don't misunderstand. I have a lot of affection for my Aunt Pearl."

"Sally, you can't imagine how helpful you have been. I really have a much better feel for the kind of person Pearl is. But I still feel there is something missing here. A woman who desperately wants children but doesn't have any is handed a ready-made family of eight. I wonder how Pat's children accepted her?"

Sally stood up and gave Gabriel a little smile as if she knew more than she was willing to say. "I suppose you would have to ask them. I really have to be going now, but I want you to understand that we all make mistakes because we are all only human. Maybe that's why Pearl moved back into that holler two years ago."

"Moved back into the holler? You mean she left...? Sally! Wait, Sally!"

But she had already given him that same knowing smile, closed the door behind her and hurried down the stairs.

Captivity

Gabriel felt in his gut that John's cryptic remark and Sally's implication that Pearl had once left the holler she seemed to love so much were related in some way, but since neither elaborated in response to his inquiries, he deduced that whatever they were concealing might cause embarrassment or even shame to both them and Pearl. He recognized that both of their stories relied at times on rumors or malicious speculation, and he hesitated roiling up gossip about matters long since past and forgotten. Pearl was probably the only person who would tell him the truth, and obviously she had gone to considerable lengths to hide it.

In his frustration, Gabriel questioned why this legal transfer of a small plot of land for a simple hill woman he barely knew had so ensnared his interest. What had triggered his desire to know the story of this woman who had paid him a pittance of legal fees? Why did the purchase of an acre of land from her own children, land that she could live on until she died, nettle him so that he felt driven to know the reasons for her action, even to the point of wasting time to seek hearsay evidence and rose-colored recollections of childhood from her kinfolk?

He drained the last sip of coffee from his cup and took the cup over to the small sink in the bathroom to rinse it out. After relieving himself, he turned on the water to wash his hands and began to scrub with the Ivory soap. A sudden memory made him jerk himself upright when the odor-laced vapors from the sink smacked him in the face, reminding him of the same aromas he smelled when he first met Pearl and of a more deeply buried memory, a memory of his own mother's sweet fragrance as she rocked him to sleep. Inexplicably, he began to weep as images of drunken fights, spilled diaper pails full of dirty diapers and Ivory detergent, punctuated by cursing and the sounds of heavy blows that drowned out his mother's cries for mercy dying unheeded in the hot July night, leaving him in a room with one body slowly oozing life away and another succumbing to alcoholic poisoning.

Now sobbing uncontrollably, he kicked the door of the bathroom shut, sat down on the commode, wanting to banish the demons of forgotten trauma and fear of abandonment. Fleeting glimpses of his own loving Aunt Judy and Uncle Harold rearing him as their own son, of their granting his every wish but one: to know the truth about the death of his parents. As he grew older, he had detected slight inconsistencies in the stories they had told him. Perhaps it was this early ability to discern fact from fiction that drew him into the legal profession. By his teenage years he had recognized that for all intents and purposes, his aunt and uncle were his parents for they were the ones who fed him, cleaned him, nurtured and taught him how to live his life. They had given him the best life they could, but at the same time, they had shielded him from a truth they felt he did not need to know, a truth that could only bring him pain.

He bit his lip as he considered the irony: that their efforts to protect him had failed because of his obsession with the life of a woman who had eked out a living for herself and those she loved, sublimating her own desperate need to know the joy of childbirth. She had been denied the one thing that defined her as a woman, the God-given ability to conceive and bear a child, a bridge to a time and a place she could dream of but not visit, to a future where the sins of the parents are not visited upon their children.

He had only an hour to focus his attention on his work with his next client and compose himself by washing his face with cold water; he wondered if he should share his revelation with Jill or if he should continue to pursue Pearl's past. Somehow, an inner voice assured him that he must be patient for an answer to those questions.

Indenture

Gabriel had called Jimmy to come complete the paperwork that Pearl had commissioned. Jimmy promised to come back home the next weekend to finish the process.

On Friday, Jimmy arrived at his office to discuss the disposition of Pearl's property.

"Good morning, Mr. Kelsay. Come in and have a seat. Would you like a cup of coffee?"

"Good morning, Mr. Gabriel. Yes, with cream, please. Before we get started I just want to say how much I appreciate you taking an interest in Mother. She really thinks a lot of you."

"Believe me, Jimmy, — may I call you Jimmy? — the feeling is very mutual. I'm very fond of Pearl. She is a very special person."

He handed Jimmy the coffee and a stir stick. "Thank you. You can call me Jimmy if I can call you Ben."

"You've got a deal. The will is very straightforward. All of you children are to share equally in everything, as far as household goods and financial holdings. Do you think there will be a problem with that?"

"No, we all agreed to that, whether Mother had a will or not."

"Of course, the farm and all of its buildings will be left to you children. Selling the farm requires the written consent of all parties. There is one other matter to address."

He handed Jimmy the deed to Pearl's plot and the letter in the envelope Pearl had given him. He sat quietly while Jimmy read the short handwritten letter aloud.

"Jimmy, I am trusting you to see that this gets done. I marked off an acre of land in the pasture like I told you I was going to do. The lawyer has the money for you to share with the others. All I want is to be buried there on that plot when I die. This here farm is my home and this is where I belong."

Jimmy looked up, wiping tears from his eyes, but he sat speechlessly twiddling the paper in his hands. Finally, he spoke haltingly. "I'd no idea this is what she wanted the land for."

Gabriel spoke softly, "It is a rather unusual request. To be honest, Jimmy, when I first met Pearl she so intrigued me that I did a little snooping into her past, but I found nothing to indicate why she felt it necessary to own this plot of land."

"Who did you ask?"

"I'd rather not say. But there were some hints that maybe Pearl felt that some of your brothers and sisters may have not accepted her when she married your dad. Is there any truth to that?"

A wave of disbelief, then anger, crossed Jimmy's face. "I can't believe people would think that. Ginny and I were only two years old when Dad married Pearl. We don't even remember our real mother, Nellie. But without Pearl we probably would not have survived. I was too young to remember how poor we were, but the older kids told me. Dad had a bed but the rest of us slept on pallets on the floor. There was almost no furniture. The older kids told me that they often went hungry and dirty because Dad wouldn't take care of us. My dad was a good man but he was pretty damned lazy. And it didn't help any that he had just gotten out of prison for killing his brother-in-law. I'm not sure how he met Pearl, but when they got married she brought furniture and livestock from her father's place.

"Maybe the older kids resented how she made us mind and made us work when we had just been growing up wild. But she put everybody to work, even Dad. Before long the farm was producing enough food for us to live almost entirely on what we grew. We sold milk, eggs, honey, molasses, corn, tobacco and a lot of other things. But if we wanted spending money we had to earn it. I remember getting up at three in the morning to go milk the cows before I hitched a ride to go pick beans in Tennessee for money for my first car. Mother made sure we all went at least to the eighth grade at the Sunnybrook School. We all got good jobs and made good lives for our families because Mother taught us to work."

Gabriel watched Jimmy struggle to contain his rage before continuing. "Maybe some of the older kids didn't like going to church or having to go help other people put up hay or strip tobacco. Maybe they didn't like going to every revival at Pleasant Hill or Chestnut Grove. Maybe it's only natural for anybody to resent a woman who came into our lives trying to be our mother, but if she's a good mother to you and you have any sense, you get over it."

"From what I've been told, Pearl was a very good mother."

Jimmy laughed at his remark. "You don't know the half of it. Somebody left the gear room open and the cow got in there and ate a bunch of fertilizer and died. We never did know who it was but Pearl just went out and worked out enough money to buy another one so we could have milk. One time my brother Dan was working on the tractor and it caught fire. He was about fourteen. Burned his leg so bad the doctors thought he would lose it. Mother carried him everywhere he went for six months so that the leg could heal. He would get mad and cuss at her and try to hit her but he was no match for her. I think he just wanted to die and get it over with. But Mother would not let him. She said she had had enough dying in her life.

"Mother never told us to do anything she wouldn't do herself. She showed us how to milk, chop tobacco, work the garden, carry water from the spring, drive the tractor, or whatever else needed to be done. One time the tractor turned over on her on the road to the store. She laid underneath that tractor for four hours until we found her. Broke some ribs, but after she healed that didn't stop her."

"I get the feeling that not much stopped Pearl."

Jimmy stood up to stretch before sitting down again.

"The only time that I saw her almost give up was when she had to have gall-bladder surgery. That was in early sixty-nine. Back then gall bladder surgery was pretty serious and it laid you up for a long time. People down here have always had a fear of surgery of any kind and I know that Mother did."

"Why?"

"Her brother Haywood and her mother both died from complications of surgery. Haywood had served in the Pacific during the war and returned home to raise a family. He and his wife Mason had a little girl they named Ruby Carol. She was about a month old when Haywood broke his leg in a car wreck. They had to do surgery to reset the leg but he never woke up from the anesthesia. That was in '47, before Mother married Dad. Pearl's mother died on the operating table in '56. Her whole family is terrified of surgery. That operation was difficult to recover from and I think it broke her spirit. And then there was that whole thing with C.H. didn't help things any."

"Her brother? What happened?"

"C.H. was killed in a logging accident in March of '69. Mother was still very sick from the surgery and didn't feel that she could make it to the funeral. It caused a lot of hard feelings from her brothers and sisters and a lot of gossip that must have hurt a lot."

"Gossip?"

"Down here, when somebody dies especially your kinfolks, you are supposed to show respect by visiting the funeral home and going to the funeral. Before long people were talking about Pearl Kelsay not even going to her own brother's funeral. It didn't seem to matter that she was still quite sick herself and probably severely depressed, wondering if each day would be her last. They seemed to forget all she the good she had done for us and for anyone else she could. That whole thing caused a real rift between her and her brothers and sisters. They were all convinced Mother could have gone to the funeral if she had really wanted to."

"Can you think of any reason why she would not have wanted to?"

"No, Mother always loved her brothers and sisters. C.H.'s wife Roxie and his son Charlie Herbert used to come up to the house to hunt rabbits and squirrels all the time. She practically raised Grady's three oldest kids, and she hired Eula's sons to work in the summer. When anybody died in the community, Mother was always there first with food to help out the family. Maybe she was just too afraid of dying herself or maybe she was just too sick to go, but there was nothing else I know of that caused hard feelings between her and C.H.'s family. But she and Roxie did not speak for many years over that. You know that Mother will be the only one of Grandpa Roberts's children who is not buried there at Walnut Grove."

"Had you ever discussed funeral arrangements? I mean she must have known about the tombstone you had bought when your father died. Was there any disagreement over the arrangements for his funeral?"

"None. Dad had a prostrate cancer operation two years before he died. After her surgery, Mother let her license expire, so she bad no way to get him to the hospital. But my brother Bill, who had not been home in years, volunteered to come home for a couple of months to help out while Dad recovered."

"Why had he not been home to visit? That seems a little odd."

"I don't know. Maybe that's one reason some people think that some of the kids resented Mother. Most of us came home every holiday, and that was a houseful with eight kids and their spouses and grandchildren. But you know how you get tied up in your own life and you just can't seem to find the time to get home as often. I probably got home more often than anybody else because Louisville is closer than Kokomo or Indianapolis. I believe Bill had just retired from his job when he came home to help. The night before Dad's surgery a big storm flooded the creek so bad that Bill and Mother had to lay planks across it to drive the truck over the creek without drowning out. Dad's surgery was in '78 and he seemed just fine afterwards. Bill went back home, leaving him and Mother up here to live. Of course, they didn't do any farming by then."

"So Pat recovered from his surgery and died two years later?"

Jimmy pursed his lips, pausing as if considering his answer. "I remember Mother calling and telling me that he had died. They had eaten supper and had gone to bed like always. A little after midnight, she heard a loud groan and the bed shook enough to wake her up. It was my Dad's death rattle."

He paused again, tears welling up in his eyes as his body shuddered violently. Gabriel reached him a tissue and waited for him to regain his composure.

"That has always given me the willies. To be sleeping beside someone and feel them die beside you."

Gabriel watched as Jimmy knotted the tissue up in his hands before continuing. "We all decided then to go ahead and put up a triple rock at Gap Creek. Mother never objected. That's why this is all a surprise to me."

"One of the people I talked to hinted that Pearl moved out of the holler for a while. Is that true?"

Jimmy leaned back in his chair and shook his head as a look of revelation swept across his face. "Maybe that's what this is all about. Sam Riddle."

"Who is Sam Riddle?"

"After Dad died, Mother insisted on staying up here in the holler even though all of us asked her to leave and come live with us. She refused, saying that these hills were home and she would not leave them. None of us were too keen on having her up there alone, but I had a renter living in the old Ben Lowe house farther up the holler and she had a phone to call for help. By then everybody had got over their sore spot about C.H.'s funeral, and I think they were all concerned about her being up here alone, what with her age and high blood pressure. I guess some of us even discussed having somebody come stay with her, but she refused. Then the rumors started that she had a boyfriend. People had seen a strange car turn off the main road to come up the holler. Finally, somebody figured out it was Sam Riddle.

"Now, Sam Riddle was just about as poor an excuse for a human being there was. He was a bootlegger and a home wrecker, though God only knows how or why any woman would want him. Still, it was all just gossip. Then one Sunday Grady came up to check on Mother and, just as he was fixing to leave, Sam's car pulls out of the holler."

"What did Grady do?"

"He just said hello and talked a few minutes before he left. He may not have approved of it, but Grady had enough sense to mind his own business. A couple of days later, Mother called over to Grady's and he asked how Sam was doing. From what Grady told me, Mother slammed the phone down in his ear."

"Do you know how Pearl got involved with this man?"

"Nobody is real sure. But the cat was out of the bag now, so there was no point in trying to hide it. Mother moved out of the holler to live with Sam. She told people they were married but I don't think anybody ever found a marriage license."

Jimmy stopped to lean forward as if to whisper a secret to Gabriel.

"Guess where Sam lived."

Gabriel shrugged his ignorance.

"Directly across the road from Roxie, C.H.'s widow. Ain't that a kick in the ass? It wasn't long until we all knew what was going on."

"And how did all this go over with you kids?"

"Some of us were disgusted and madder than hell about it. None of us would have minded if Mother had wanted to get married again, but why take up with such scum as Sam Riddle? I'm ashamed to say that we abandoned Mother for almost two years when she first moved over there. After all she had done for us, we sure picked a hell of a way to show our gratitude, uh? But I guess time heals all wounds, and eventually most of us got over our mad spell and started to visit Mother over at Sam's. Looking back, I guess it was really none of our business. After all, she had lived her whole life for us, so why should we have cared if she wanted to live her life for herself? But, for Christ's sake, Sam Riddle!"

He shook his head before looking up reflectively. "Still, who can say what kind of relationship they had. Maybe they were just two lonely old people who didn't want to spend their last days alone. When Mother became very sick, Sam was there to get her to the hospital. By now, Mother had patched up her differences with Grady and he took Sam to Lexington to visit Mother when she had to be transferred to the hospital up there.

"She and Roxie kept a check on each other, because they, too, had mended fences. Roxie was the one who called Grady and told him that she had seen an ambulance over there late one night. Sam's intestines had gone into spasms and set up gangrene. If Mother hadn't been there he would have died. He recovered, but died a few months later and Mother moved back up to the holler. Maybe Mother felt that we all still harbored a grudge about that, and maybe a few of us did. But when most of us could sit back in our comfortable homes and think it over, we realized that all that Mother gave us far outweighed this little episode - that really was none of our business anyway. I bet that is what this letter is all about."

Jimmy sat quietly, contemplative and remorseful for the pain that he felt he and his siblings had caused Pearl. Abruptly he broke down, crying tears of regret helplessness that ran in tiny streams down his ruddy cheeks. "I guess she felt that old farm in the holler was her one true home, but she never could be sure of who was her family."

By now Gabriel had lost his self-control and they sat in the room's uncomfortable silence punctuated spasmodically by heavy sighs as they desperately hoped that someone they both had loved would some day find peace.

Still choking back his grief, Jimmy took Gabriel by the hand. "Ben, I hope you'll keep all of this to yourself."

Gabriel nodded as he gently blew his nose, "Of course. This conversation will be our secret."

Jimmy braced himself on the arms of the chair and heaved himself into an upright position. "It really doesn't matter, Ben. We certainly are not going to go against her will and dig her up and move her. Besides, I guess that holler may have been her home.

"I'll call you when Mother passes and arrange for her funeral and burial. It'll take some time to probate the will, but it should not be too hard as it is very clear we kids inherit it. Not sure what Mother wanted to do with anything she has, but I guess she just wants it thrown into the settlement. I really would like for you to keep in touch with me even after all this is settled. You have my number."

"You can count on it, Jimmy."

Jeremiad

Gabriel and his family managed to visit Pearl one more time before she died of a heart attack. With Jimmy's permission, he hired some people to dig a grave in the acre of ground Pearl had bought. Jimmy had already told the children about her request and everyone agreed to abide by it.

The will cleared probate in two months and the children met at their home place to clear out the house and Gabriel met them there to complete the tasks.

After each took what they wanted, they donated some to charity and threw the rest away. Jimmy took the long bench from the dining room, Ginny took the old stainless milk buckets and cans, but Faith only cut a big square out of the bright scarlet red rose and paisley wall paper from the bedroom. The holler rang out once again with their laughter as they recalled past days and their life together here. Each had some little embarrassing story to tell on another, and their laughter echoed up the deserted holler and down the near-dry creek bed.

As Gabriel watched them work he would occasionally catch one of them wiping away an errant tear. He found Dan alone in the barn leaning against the old International Harvester tractor, sobbing and cursing himself, but he managed to slip away without Dan noticing him.

The rest of the farm had passed to them through their mother and they all shared in it equally. They agreed to make Jimmy the overseer of the property but none of them seemed anxious to discuss selling it, even though it was unlikely that any of them would return there to live, or even to visit. Mary said it best, "You visit people, not houses."

They finished their work and stood on the banks of the creek bed in front of the house. When they realized what had happened they began to hug and console each other amid loud weeping. This was the closing of the first chapter written into the books of their lives. Then, one by one, each bid the others farewell before driving off to resume their lives.

Finally, only Jimmy and Gabriel remained, staring wistfully at the old white house with its green shutters and black vacant windows. Each knew what the other felt, so they did not break the silence that settled in, not just on this family, but on the way of life that had flourished here. They breathed deeply and, still without speaking, got into our cars and drove away.

Ransom

Ten years have passed since Gabriel moved here and began a strange voyage of self-discovery on a ship captained by haunted pasts and navigated by destiny. He found himself lapsing a bit into the Southern accent and dialect clients, spoke and made a good living for myself with a good reputation in the legal community in the state.

Bertram's store closed and was demolished, so few people ventured into the holler. Gabriel kept Jimmy apprised of the condition of the farm and the house, but it became increasingly difficult. He feared someone would burn the house for a prank and soon kids had thrown rocks from the creek bed through most of the windows that now looked like jagged blank eyes. Someone stole the glass doorknobs from the two front doors and scattered beer bottles and cans across the yard and porch. After he found used condoms and drug syringes in the house, Gabriel decided to buy the property.

Because they all shared equally in ownership of the property, they also shared equally in the tax assessment. Ten years of paying taxes on property that did not benefit them had become more burdensome, especially since they had all neared or reached retirement age. Gabriel took pictures to show them how the inevitable march of time had taken its toll on the house, so that it was now unlivable. He assured them that he would build a new house to which they would always be welcome if they ever wanted to visit. With Jimmy on his side, they needed little persuasion to agree to the sale.

Gabriel decided to keep the house in town for business purposes, but he soon had a new two-story country home built on the farm. He built a smaller house at the Ben Lowe place and hired a young man and his family to stay there as caretakers of the farm.

After his son left for college, Gabriel and Jill spent more time on the farm. They started a nursery cultivating irises, day lilies, and dahlias for mail order sales and put in a small commercial apple orchard with raspberry and blueberry bushes and some rhubarb. The bottomlands were sown in wild birdseed and the rest of the land was left natural habitat for wildlife. Beavers built a small dam upstream from the house so there was water in the creek year 'round and wood ducks settled in near the pools.

He often sat in the porch swing near dusk, intermittently fanning away the insects and listening to the sounds of the night. Occasionally, he heard whip-poor-will's mournful call from deep in the woods and sometime the wind would change bringing a familiar musty odor that made him rock the swing back and forth.

Gabriel and Jill began going to church at Pleasant Hill and came to appreciate the beautiful lyricism of many passages of the Bible and felt a new spirituality. One day as he was flipping through the Bible, he found himself in the book of Jeremiah. God commanded Jeremiah to purchase a field at Anathoth from his cousin, even though the field is in imminent danger of capture by the Babylonians. God ordered Jeremiah to buy the land because the right of redemption is his, and he must show his faith in God's promises of redemption.

When he bought the farm from the children, Gabriel had left the deed to Pearl's plot in her name, although eventually managed to transfer it to himself. He rewrote his will to establish a home for abused women under the title Pearl Kelsay Foundation.

One April morning, Gabriel finally told Jill of the horrors of the loss of his parents and how, in some mysterious way, Pearl had helped him remember and recover from that awful night. He instinctively knew that he had to run away as far and as fast as he could to hide his shame and guilt for the sin of losing his family. He spent his life searching for the grail that would absolve him of blame and redeem his soul and had found it in the most unlikely of places.

After telling Jill of the secrets he had kept hidden, he hugged her close as he felt a lifetime of anguish rise and leave him to dissipate over the dewy fields. They walked down the dusty path to the newly designated Anathoth Cemetery where they had already planted their tombstone. As they stood there, thinking of how the threads of their lives had intertwined with those of a woman seeking salvation from demons they could scarcely imagine, the morning breeze rippled the spring beauties in pink and white splendor in front of a simple gray granite tombstone inscribed with this epitaph:

PEARL KELSAY
HERE SHE FOUND A SHELTERED REST,
WHILE OTHERS GO AND COME.
NO MORE A STRANGER OR A GUEST,
BUT LIKE A CHILD AT HOME.

A Servant of Two Masters

FLONNIE STOOD, ARMS akimbo, watching and hearing the bees sporadically blurt out low humming choruses as they wove an invisible network over her flowerbed. She had suffered from a sting just last week, but she gave little sign of apprehension as she ambled over to the end of the flower bed, plopped herself down onto the sere, sparse patches of crabgrass and weeds, and began to pull weeds from the flowerbed. The lawn was man's work and if he was content with the sorry excuse for a yard, so be it. Her joy in life lay in knowing that the flowerbeds flanking the gray tar-shingled house were the envy of everyone in the small rural valley.

She hummed along with the droning refrain of the bees as she slid her leathery, liver-spotted hands among the flowers to find and uproot stubborn clumps of dandelions and plantain that invaded her beds. Occasionally, she would find a small pokeweed among the tall multicolored zinnias and touch-me-nots or even the petite rusty marigolds and sprawling petunias. She had tended these same beds for thirty-seven years. Each year she had felt secure that she had rid the beds of the last of these tenacious vagrants only to have them reappear the following year from seeds that lay dormant in the soil. Even now in July after repeated weedings, she found one six inches tall that she used to shoo a bee away from her sweat-beaded face.

She paused to sweep the wisps of thin gray hair from her blue eyes before plunging in again to clear weeds and random scraps of tarry shingles littering the ground. The sun lay in the west so she benefited from the shade cast by the squat house whose sides and roof were punctuated at irregular intervals by missing or slightly askew shingles. Spencer cared little that the house had fallen into such disarray: he and their son, Jerry, saw no financial merit in maintaining a building which they used only as a diner and a flophouse. Flonnie answered the questions of neighbors by saying they were too busy in the crop fields to do much about it. Still, in her heart she wished they took more pride in keeping the place up, so that maybe someday her flower beds would be on the cover of the local newspaper, of maybe even in color in RECC magazine.

She sighed. "They don't seem to unnerstan' that you has to work to have anythin' purty. Ever' year I pull weeds until I'm blue in the face and they keep comin' back, but I don't quit. I guess maybe I miss some and the seeds come back next year. No matter what you try to have nice, they's always something trying to tear it down. Dog digs in my flowers or Jerry walks through them, they's always something. This old house could be so purty with these all flowers here, but it is so ugly. I think that's the reason nobody comes to visit. They think the house might fall in on them. Only people that comes here anymore are trying to get Spencer to haul coal or wood or mow a field. Spencer says nobody visits because they are scared of me after they had to take me to Danville. No reason to be scared of me. I ain't goin' to hurt nobody."

She struggled to her feet, but the effort of raising herself made her head spin and she fainted. She collapsed into a heap beside the flowerbeds.

Of course you wouldn't hurt a fly, but everybody thinks you would because they think **she** *is you. You do look alike they say.* **She** *uses your clothes and your house and threatens the neighbors and Spencer with your voice. And nobody has ever seen you both together at the same time. What are they supposed to think? Every time* **she** *appears you disappear and come back saying the same old excuse of a bad headache. Even Spencer can't tell you apart and neither he nor Jerry believes your story that* **she** *isn't you. Is it any wonder that Spencer is letting the house go to ruin? Maybe he hopes it will fall in on you. Why shouldn't Jerry curse you to your face? Maybe he thinks* **she** *is you and he is simply trying to banish* **her** *to get his natural mother back. Wouldn't you? Would you want people to think that your mother had to be carried off in a straitjacket to the nut house in Danville? You remember Danville, don't you, Flonnie? Laying there watching the ceiling fan go round and round and round like a whirligig in the wind. Remember how thirsty you got? They told you it was the drugs, but it was Spencer and Jerry and this whole community trying to poison you. Trust me, Flonnie, they are out to get you.*

She reawakened with a start so violent that butterflies feeding on flowers fluttered away abruptly. She heaved herself vertical, staggering to the corner of the house to steady herself lest she black out again. Equilibrium regained, she noticed the grayish clouds rolling in over the top of Poplar Mountain.

"Gosh, it looks like rain is headin' this way. If I'm goin' to do any visitin' this afternoon, I'd better get to it."

She slipped her dusty, grass-stained hand into the pocket of her flowery broadcloth dress to retrieve a tube of Chapstick, removed the cap and slid the waxy stick over her dry lips. A gnarled apple tree stood over a rickety washstand leaning against the lichen-encrusted trunk for support. She splashed a small dollop of water into the white porcelain pan and reached for the Lava soap resting in the upturned carapace of a terrapin stuck in a crotch of the tree. She smiled at the bony shell bleached by exposure after she had recovered it from the roadside a few years before.

"I don't see why them kids around here are so afraid of that thing. They say it looks like a skull. Looks like a turtle shell upside down to me. Makes a good soap dish. And it didn't cost nothin'."

From the galvanized bucket, she ladled a dipperful of clean water from the galvanized bucket over her hands and dried them on her dress. A gray tabby cat carrying a field mouse emerged from the pasture field next to the yard.

"Well, kitty, ain't you the smart one? I'll give you some milk in a minute to go with your mouse."

The rusty screen door, warped by uneven tension over the years, clapped against the doorjamb behind her as she entered the kitchen. A worn linoleum rug patterned in huge swirls of floral swirls covered the uneven floor that creaked softly as she walked toward the bedroom to comb her hair. She raked a wide tortoise-shell comb through the thinning strands of hair and leaned closer to the mirror to check her chapped lips. She picked up the bright cylinder that she bought herself once a year and contemplated using the bright red lipstick to conceal her cracked lips

"It's just Wilma. She knows how bad my lips get in the summer. I'll save that lipstick for a special occasion. Chapstick is good enough for everyday visitin'."

A fine mist of cologne from a small atomizer obscured the musty odor of perspiration staining her dress in splotches. She folded a floral handkerchief and shoved it into her right pocket and ambled back into the kitchen to remove her pearly dentures from a teacup over the sink. A quick flick removed the water from the dentures and she gingerly placed them in her mouth. A half glass of milk and two drop biscuits still sat on the table from her lunch: she gathered them up to feed the cat and dog waiting outside the back door.

"Here, kitty," she cooed as she poured the milk into a cracked saucer. A scraggly yellow dog ran up to her wagging his tail expectantly.

"Here you go, fella." The dog took the biscuits from her hand and slunk over to the shade of the apple tree to dine in peace. Flonnie seldom petted the gaunt dog, which spent the biggest part of the day dodging cars on the road where he scrounged the fat brown grasshoppers killed by passing traffic. He contented himself with keeping Flonnie company for the irregular offerings of table scraps even though many days she would forget to feed him so he relied on the grasshoppers as his sole meals. In exchange, he protected Flonnie, growling at anyone who entered the yard, and chased hobos away when they tried to panhandle a sandwich from Flonnie. The gray tabby cat left the scant serving of milk to rub against Flonnie's calves in an effort to garner some affection. With some effort, Flonnie picked the cat up and cradled her as a mother with a baby.

Closing her eyes, she sighed, remembering. At sixty-two, her fertile years were behind her in a dreamtime with visions of a large family: stout sons with strong arms tanned in the summer sun as they worked alongside their stoic father, and daughters so beautiful they should be in fairy tales. In the early days of her marriage, she had dreamed of standing in Keene's Chapel Methodist Church in her finest dress and cultured pearls beside Spencer in his cheap suit as they watched their children getting married to start their own families.

Yes, Flonnie, that is the natural order of things isn't it? But who says you're natural? You can't be, as long as **she** *is alive because everybody thinks* **she** *and you are the same person. Can you really blame Spencer for not wanting to give you any more children? He still remembers that fit* **she** *threw in Jerry's room and what a tussle it was to wrestle you down to the floor until it passed. You know he told everybody that you had that wild glazed look in your eyes like you were going to hurt his son for crying too loud. You know that's why he always had Wilma*

*Brown come stay with you and Jerry until the baby got big enough to walk. He didn't trust you. He thinks you are **her**, Flonnie, and when **she** is in you, you are too strong to hold. And you know Spencer told Jerry the whole thing as soon as he could understand it.*

Why do you think that Jerry abandoned his mother, the heart that beat out the first sounds he would ever hear? Spencer knew that he could not take a girl on farm machinery.

*Remember the mysterious visit from Doctor Roberts when he and Spencer stayed alone in the tobacco barn for over an hour? Remember how Spencer picked at his food at supper and slept in a separate room that night? Oh, they are all in on it, Flonnie, all of them: Wilma making up stories of your weird behavior when it was really **her**. Dr. Roberts convinced Spencer to forsake the marriage bed lest some other devil seed issue from your union. Oh, that Doctor Roberts took your husband and your dreams of those beautiful children that you would take to Sunday School: the little girls in dresses you had made of broadcloth and the little boys in shirts you wrenched out of Spencer's feed sacks. He was the one who led the two men in white coats here, invading the sanctity of your home, to strap you into that straitjacket so that he could give you a shot to knock you out. He is the devil himself my dear, the devil himself...*

The cat wriggled in Flonnie's thick arms that were contracting violently around her body. Flonnie snapped her eyes open and set the cat on the grassless ground near the weather-curled planks of the back porch. She stepped inside to check the time.

"I've got time for a cup of tea before I go to Wilma's," she said to herself.

She always kept a teakettle warm on the wood stove for little sips of tea during the day, dropping a Lipton teabag into a black and gold porcelain teapot decorated with bright roses and fancy curlicues and adding a cupful of hot water to refill the pot and returned it to the stovetop.

"Maybe I better check that fire before I leave. I just hate having to relight it for supper. Still, it might catch the house on fire if I'm gone too long."

She opened the door to the firebox to see how much longer the fire would burn. The fire she had lit to fix Spencer and Jerry their breakfast that morning had nearly died out, leaving just a few embers glowing in the soft ashes. Licking her finger she gingerly checked the temperature of the stovetop. Satisfied that the stove was safe to be left unattended, she sat down at the table to enjoy her tea. She smiled as she sipped her tea and began to talk to the cat that had let herself in through the battered screen door.

"That teapot shore is purty, don't you think, kitty? I was lucky to win it from Kay's Drugstore. Spencer had took me up to see Doc Roberts and while I was waiting I saw this teapot in a contest. All I had to do was to play a punchboard for a quarter for three punches. Spencer gave me a quarter and I won this teapot on the first punch. Then I didn't win anything else. But I was happy to have this teapot. I like tea, kitty, like you like milk."

The warm tea and the tick-tock of the clock lulled her into closing her eyes, to savor the warm tea, before picking up the cup and moving to the front room to finish it. A velvety duskiness filled the room that smelled faintly of perfume and perspiration seeping from an overstuffed chair and sofa. A few neighborhood children who ignored the rumors about Flonnie would stop by to sell her seeds. Invariably they would find themselves nodding off into a light nap brought on by the aromas of dust bunnies under the heavy walnut furniture and her houseplants.

As she sat in the huge velveteen chair, she set the teacup down on a small end table before she leaned over to inspect her amaryllis plant. Its solitary pedicel bore a lone vermilion bud, pleated with deep flutes of scarlet. Each day for the past week, the elliptical bud had grown more fiery, more impatient to burst open into a glorious display. Flonnie sat there at least once each day, cooing softly as she gently caressed its plump form. Nobody else could get them to bloom in the summer, as they were often given as Christmas presents that bloomed only by forcing them during the winter months. Its red trumpet would grace the room for a week or ten days before shriveling into a moist clump. A sheaf of shiny green blades would emerge from the bulb and begin to store the food for the next season. When they yellowed, signaling a dormancy, Flonnie would put the pot to a dark corner of a seldom-used closet.

"You'll be blooming any day now. You're awfully red this year. You are about the reddest thing I'd ever seen. Everybody ought to like red. I bet the forbidden fruit was red; that's why Eve couldn't resist it."

As she drained the last drop of tea from the floral china teacup she relaxed, gradually slumping over the arm of the chair.

But Flonnie, you know everyone wondered how you knew the right hole to punch. A lot of people wanted that teapot and you got it on the first try. You must be a witch. You do look the part, don't you? Your hair is thin and stringy, your nose is an eagle's beak. Then here you are coming out of the office of the devil himself eating his magic pills and drinking his potions to bolster your powers of divination. That teapot had set there for three weeks and you won it on the first punch. It was **her** *evil eye, wasn't it? The right one that jitters just a little bit as it searches out the depths of people's souls. It's not even your eye, it's* **hers**; *but everybody thinks it's yours. Remember how they told you how that eye went to jittering just before you chased that Charlie Roberts out of the house with a poker? It wasn't even hot. How could you have hurt him? You wanted to scare him away before he could steal a start off your lilac bush. The next thing you know is his parents and Doctor Roberts are here and that van arrives with the men carrying the white jackets, trussing you up again for another stay in the crazy house. You put up a good fight for a while, didn't you? Screaming and kicking, tearing the rug in the front room. The neighbors all say that you keep those pretty little rugs down in there to hide the tracks of your fingernails on the hard wood floor. Could a normal human do that, Flonnie?*

But then you just gave up and let them throw you into that ambulance like a slab of hog. You kept telling yourself that it was just a dream, that you would wake up from the last thirty years to find a whole houseful of beautiful children standing over you, mopping your forehead with a cool cloth to relieve the fever that had driven you to madness. They would call you 'Mother', the mother that nurtures and protects her family at all costs, not the Mother' emblazoned on a shiny red ribbon around a bouquet of long stem red roses and white carnations enshrouding a granite-colored box burnished so fine to reflect the dimmest light streaming through the church window. But every time you woke up, all you could think of was the only son who cursed you to your face and a husband who tolerated your presence only because you kept house for him. And you had to think about them as you lay there staring at the ceiling, discolored with age and the fumes of urine, among people crying aloud. Most of them wore straitjackets, some bashed their heads against tables or walls, and others slobbered and chewed their tongues to the quick.

But you could escape: all you had to do was to talk to the doctors there and admit that you and **she** *were the same person. They wanted to blame you for all the evil* **she** *had done: winning the teapot, chasing after the boy with a poker, throwing fits. Do you remember how they tried to make you admit that you threw a whole litter of new puppies into a ditch to starve because you didn't want to be bothered feeding them? They didn't know their mother had been run over or you had tried to nurse them yourself. Which is better: to have Spencer sling their brains out on a rock or to let them die of starvation? You knew it was* **her** *that made the decision to throw the pups in the ditch; you could not admit to something that you had not done. So you* *lay there, strapped to a bed as comforting and loving as your bed at home, denying and crying and retching and praying that God heal you, waiting for an answer that would never come. You prayed the wrong prayer, Flonnie. God knew it was* **she** *that was sick, not you. How could he cure you when you were not sick? Finally, even you confused* **her** *with you and you began to take the blame for things* **she** *had done. They said that you could go home if you would admit to every wrong* **she** *had done. You had no choice; this was your cross to bear, a cross that you bore upon your shoulders more out of exhaustion and resignation than repentance, for you could never decide which was the greater sin: refusing to admit to sins you had committed or confessing to sins that you had not committed. Does that sound familiar, Flonnie? Yes, Flonnie, they convinced even you that you are a witch. No wonder your neighbors hide from you when you go visiting. You knock and knock and no one answers, but you know they are in there, hiding behind their doors with their fears and superstitions, waiting for you to give up and leave in search of an unfortunate victim working outside who did not have time to hide before you stopped by. So go, Flonnie. Walk the hot narrow road that bubbles with tar in the afternoon sun when any sane person would sit in the shade resting or breaking beans. Walk up to Wilma's or out to Evalee's or Ora's or even all the way around to Mally's. Go, and I'll tell you what you'll find: empty houses full of people scared of the old witch who everyone, even her husband and son, hates and fears. But go, Flon....*

Flonnie jerked herself upright in the chair so suddenly the startled cat scrambled out the back door. She stood up, smoothed her dress and exited the back door into the hot July afternoon. The clouds she had seen earlier had grown larger, looming a little higher above the horizon. She hesitated, calculating whether she had time for even a short trip up to Wilma Brown's house. A storm seemed inevitable, but her past experience had taught her that she still had plenty of time to make the half-mile trek up the country road to Wilma's.

The swallowtails and fritillary butterflies fluttered briefly when she walked by the house toward the hot, sticky, asphalt road where heat mirages of snakes slithered across the shimmering surface to disappear in the tangle of weeds and fescue alongside the road. The thrushes and sparrows that had sung so gleefully in the cool morning now sat hushed and hidden in the stands of sassafras saplings. The humidity was stifling, forcing her to mop her brow with the handkerchief, a ritual part and parcel to the neighbors of Flonnie Correll: the crazy old woman with false teeth making clacking noises because they no longer fit properly. Sometimes her dentures would be so troublesome that she would have to interrupt her conversation to take them out to reposition them or even stand holding them in her hand while she continued talking without them, her sunken cheeks so altering her speech that she sounded like a different person. Both Wilma and Doctor Roberts had cautioned her about wearing them as she might swallow them during a seizure. She agreed and wore them only when she was away from home.

Two cars passed her, but neither driver slowed to offer her a lift. She would have demurred anyway unless she knew the driver. Sweat ran in little rivulets down her body, staining her dress by the time she had reached the shaded incline to Wilma's house. Her breathing became labored as she mounted the hill to Wilma's house, a small house surrounded by cleome, touch-me-not and zinnias.

She climbed the three steps to the front door and knocked loudly. No answer. She knocked again and cried, "Wilma? Is anybody home? It's just Flonnie. I thought I'd come up to visit, maybe help you break beans. Anybody home?"

Hearing no answer, she walked around the side of the house to try her luck at the kitchen door.

"Wilma, is anybody home?"

She tried the door, but it was locked. Maybe Wilma's sugar got high again and she had to go to the doctor, she thought. Or maybe she's gone to get groceries. I might as well go on back. Maybe stop off by Ora's.

"I'll just wait a few minutes in the shade in case they come back. I need the rest anyway."

As she leaned against the white oak tree at the edge of the yard, she eyed the house that the Bethesda Methodist Church had built to replace the one burned by burglars six years ago. Wilma's husband, Marvin, was a second cousin to Flonnie. She and Wilma had grown up with Marvin and his brother, Joe Willie, playing and attending church together as children, going to weddings and funerals as adults. Wilma was highly regarded by everyone in the community, for she was always quick to help and offer a kind word to anybody. Many people said that if Wilma Brown wasn't going to be in heaven, they didn't want to be there, because there wasn't anybody more fit for it if Wilma wasn't. She and Flonnie had traded flower starts and seeds and used to spend the long winter days piecing quilts, most of which had burned up in the fire. Once she had told Flonnie that Marvin's family, especially Joe Willie, had not wanted Marvin to marry her, a secret that Flonnie pondered occasionally but kept to herself.

She shrugged off the daydream and, satisfied that no one was home, she began the journey home. She did not see the lacy curtain in the bedroom move to one side to expose Wilma's bespectacled face, relieved that Flonnie had abandoned her search for company.

Wilma watched Flonnie disappear down the road before she turned to talk to Ora. She shook her head, sighing, "Poor old thing. I feel so ashamed to hide from her. But with just us two women here, I'm afraid to be alone with her. If she had one of them spells, there ain't no way we could hold her down. She could hurt one of us or herself."

"I know, Wilma. That's the way I am. Flonnie and Spencer have always been good neighbors to us. We used to carry water from their house until our well got drilled. But since she started having them spells, I'm afraid to be alone with her. If it's just me and the kids there and we see her coming, we lock the door and hide. I am really ashamed of it. And she is such good company when she is acting okay. Once she stopped to check on Roger when he was sick. She just kept on admiring the quilt I had over him. Poor thing forgot that she helped me quilt it in the basement a few years ago. How many times have they had to take her off to Danville?"

Wilma dropped her head. "Two, I think. I tell you, Ora, the way Spencer and Jerry treat her, it's a wonder she is still alive. They won't let her go anywhere or buy anything nice for herself. They spend all their money on tractors and machinery."

Ora nodded her agreement. "They are awfully mean to her. One day Johnny was collecting butterflies for his science class down there in the woods above their house and he said that Jerry cussed Flonnie up one side and down the other. We can hear him sometimes all the way up to the house, yelling at her."

Wilma picked up her crocheting and sat back down. "It's a shame."

"Have they ever figured out why she has them attacks?"

Wilma's eyes teared up again. "She's had them off and on her whole life. They just got worse lately. Flonnie and I grew up together, you know. I know that when she had that attack after she married Spencer, just after Jerry was born, Doc Roberts stopped by here one day to talk to me. He told me that they thought Flonnie had a tumor in her head. There's a big knot at the base of her skull, right here. He thought the tumor was putting pressure on her brain from time to time, causing her to go off. He asked Spencer if it would be okay for me to go help Flonnie out until Jerry got old enough to go with him. He was afraid that she would have one of them spells and hurt Jerry. Spencer said that it was fine with him if I'd do it. Doc told Spencer that Flonnie could die from that tumor and leave him with a houseful of kids to raise by himself. Spencer and Flonnie had wanted a big family, but Doc told Spencer there was no way to guarantee how long she would live or if she could handle another pregnancy. Now, Ora, I'll tell you, Spencer really loved Flonnie when they got married, but over the years all that changed. 'Course, now Flonnie has lived a long life, Jerry is grown and they don't even have each other."

She paused to scoot her chair closer to Ora. "Now Ora, I'm going to tell you something that I have never told anybody else. Marvin knows it 'cause he was there. You got to promise not to tell anybody."

Ora saw the serious look in Wilma's eyes. "I promise," she whispered.

"I know where that tumor came from. Once me, Flonnie and Marvin and Joe Willie was riding to town in the back of a wagon. Joe Willie started teasing Flonnie about being a tomboy 'cause she is so big and raw boned. Flonnie kept telling him to leave her alone. That just encouraged him. Finally, she got up in the wagon and punched him in the arm. He hauled off and pushed her out of the wagon. She hit her head on a big rock. That's where that big knot came from. We thought she had died. Mom and Dad rushed her to the nearest house and sent for Doc Powers. He finally managed to revive her. Now don't you tell a soul. My own children don't know that. I'm telling you, Ora, it breaks my heart to hide from Flonnie, but I ain't as strong as I used to be and she scares me. I'd give anything if she could be well again and, God knows, I pray for her every night. I don't think she even remembers what happened. If it would have made any difference, I'd have told on Joe…"

Flonnie had stopped by Ora's house, not knowing she was at Wilma's. She paused to look at the zinnias, larkspurs and gladioli growing along the top of the retaining wall formed by the rocks children had carried off the land. No one answered when she knocked and she decided to go back home before the storm.

She had walked only a few paces when the rain clouds began to drizzle. First one, two, and then a slow sprinkling of cool raindrops pitter-patted on her sweaty body. The soft rustle of the summer shower on the thirsty thistles and milkweeds enticed her to slow her pace before a sudden cloudburst made her run, cow-like, home.

She burst into the kitchen through the backdoor, scaring the cat that had already came in out of the rain. Shivering, she snatched up a dishtowel to dry her face and hair. The kettle contained enough water for a pot of tea; she decided to use the same teabag she had used before and sat breathing heavily as the tea steeped in the lukewarm water. As her breathing eased, she felt her face flush as she crumpled, exhausted from the exertion of her short run, onto the oilcloth-covered table. Without warning, she jerked herself upright, screamed unintelligibly, and flung the teapot across the room, where it shattered. The table vibrated so violently from the thundering tremors of her feet on the floor that the salt and pepper shakers and saucer plummeted to the floor. The cat hissed and arched her back as she dodged the flying debris. She escaped through the hole in the screen door to seek the safety of the haystacks in the barn.

Flonnie's eyes bulged and rolled erratically in their sockets and she staggered into the front room where she collapsed into a trembling heap in the easy chair. The room faded to black as she sank into a heaving mass of mindless flesh. Her quivering was punctuated irregularly by spasms, striking herself, her chair, and finally, the fragile amaryllis bud that recoiled and broke free to tumble onto the musty floor. The spasms ceased; she slept fitfully.

Sleep, my dear. Maybe even dream of starting over far away from here, in an Eden so remote even **she** *can't find you. Just you and your dreams of beautiful little girls in long tresses curled on your fingers and freshly pressed and starched dresses, sipping tea and eating dainty cookies. Dream of you and Wilma teaching the girls to piece and quilt, and how deep to plant the seed of every flower you can imagine, or of chatting with Ora and her children as they fill their water buckets at the pump behind the house. Dream of Spencer and your sons coming home, the sons greeting you with sweaty, musky kisses and Spencer stealing a peck on your rouged and powdered cheek before you all sit down to a huge meal you and the girls have fixed. Dream* *of the carefree days of childhood, riding up Harmon Hollow on a buckboard, laughing with Wilma and Marvin and Joe Willie. Dream of lying in a crib, blowing little bubbles of drool as your Mom tickles your face with posies of violets. Dream that* **she** *never existed: there is only you and your family and friends, and the flowers. Dream that all of your life is but a dream.*

The mantle clock struck four, rousing her from sleep. She stood up, rubbing her eyes as she headed toward the kitchen to prepare supper. She heard the crunch of a shard of pottery before she saw the broken teapot in the kitchen. Leaning heavily on the doorjamb, she sobbed uncontrollably, asking loudly "Why, why, oh Lord, why did this happen?"

Hoarse from crying and the yelling of the attack, she found herself speechless, other than the soft murmurings of choked back tears as she swept the broken pottery into a dustpan, then into the trashcan. She washed her face and started a fire in the stove to fix supper for Spencer. The rain had stopped for now, so that the only sounds in the room were the soft creaking of the floor sagging under her weight, the tick-tock of the clock, and the occasional sizzling pop of the burning wood. Mechanically, she peeled the potatoes into a porcelain pan, rinsing them off before placing them in an iron skillet with a spoonful of lard. She placed a few strips of jowl bacon in another skillet and sliced some cucumbers and tomatoes.

By the time she finished, Spencer had pulled his red International truck into the back yard. He stopped at the rickety washstand to wash up before entering the house. He trudged across the grassless patch, stepped into the kitchen and grunted a rough greeting. Muddy clumps and bits of sawdust littered the rug.

"Rain here much?" he grunted.

"Quite a bit I guess. I dozed off just as it started so I don't know. We needed it. Some of my flowers was getting awfully dry. I'm frying taters and bacon for supper. There's cold biscuits from dinner I didn't want to waste."

"Jesus Christ, woman, ain't I good enough for hot bread? You got time to sleep and work in them goddamned flowers but you ain't got time to cook hot bread! We get any mail?"

"No, you didn't."

"Anybody come looking to get something hauled or mowed? You been here all day or did you go gallivanting around again?"

"I went up to Wilma's, but she wasn't home. I wonder if her sugar is acting up again."

"I ain't heard nobody say. Is supper about ready? I got some things to do in the barn. Jerry broke a tine on the hay rake that needs to be replaced."

Flonnie took the simple meal up into china bowls networked with cracks and chips. She set plates on the table and they ate in silence. She decided not to mention the teapot since Spencer did not drink tea anyway, but she bolstered her courage to ask, "Spencer, I've been thinking if we could take some of that tobacco money and buy a television to keep me company. It gits real lonesome around here. There's lots of westerns and Lassie on Sunday night."

"Everybody says that we can't get a good picture here. Too far from Nashville. Besides, we need that money to buy a new disk. You got your flowers and radio and animals."

Flonnie dropped her head disconsolately while Spencer gobbled down the last bits of food off his plate. He sat picking his teeth, watching her stack the dishes on the counter top by the sink.

"I'd better get that rake fixed for tomorrow. Supposed to cut hay for Willie McCutcheon."

As he started out to the barn, he noticed that the hole in the screen door was larger than it was when he left that morning.

"Did you kick the door?"

"No, it must have been the cat. She came in to keep me company."

"Umph. Damned cat got no business in here. House ain't the place for animals."

"I'm going to rest a few minutes before I do the dishes. It's about time for the local news," she said as he left the kitchen for the barn.

"It's starting to rain again. If it starts to thunder and lightning, turn the radio off. I don't want the house struck by lightning."

Flonnie shuffled into the living room, flipped the switch on the radio and took a seat in the chair. As she sat down, her eye caught a glimpse of a patch of red on the rug. Frantically, she turned on the lamp beside the table to reveal the broken amaryllis bud lying beside the pot.

"Oh no. Not this, too. Oh Lord, why do you let these things happen to me? I try to live…"

She gasped audibly.

"If Spencer sees this, he'll start looking around and find the teapot. He'll know what happened and he'll have me put back in Danville. I can't go there again. I've got to hide it! I'd rather wait another year for this to bloom than go back up there!"

She pushed the pot out of view behind the big chair, and thrust the bud into her dress pocket until she could throw it away. The radio cracked with the static of a new storm; each pop of electrical discharge stabbed her brain with a flash of light. Dizzy and confused, Flonnie stumbled into the bedroom and fell stomach-down into the soft feather mattress. She stared blankly, clenching the red bud, the crimson juices flowing out, leaving pale reddish trails on the yellow chenille bedspread. Her mind alternately raced and stalled in random misfires of synaptic connections: *kitty… takers… Wilmaareyouhome… pokeweed … rain … rock … hurt … black…*

That's right, Flonnie, go to sleep. Sleep deep and still where no one, not even **her***, can find you. Here's your chance to be free of* **her** *once and for all. Sleep, sleep, my dear, among the beautiful flowers and soft church music…*

Spencer entered through the kitchen door and heard the radio popping and crackling. The storm had arrived full force and he ran into the front room to turn the radio off.

"Flonnie, didn't I tell you not to have that thing on if the storm got bad? Where are you, anyway?"

He walked into the bedroom where Flonnie lay.

"Goddamn it, woman, answer me when I call you. You trying to burn the house down? The best thing I could do is send you back to Danville. Is that what you want? Flonnie, are you listening to me? Flonnie?"

A Chasing After Wind

THE POOR AND socially awkward folks of the countryside constituted the clientele of Blevins's Grocery, a small white block building trimmed in red stripes. A flat-roofed porch supported by four-inch iron pipes painted white offered temporary storage space and shelter from rainstorms, or just a place to while away hours discussing coon hunting with the rough farmers and hill people who came there to shop. Willard and Fannie Blevins, proprietors, offered the kinds of food and service that many of their customers had grown up with. The store was situated on the outskirts of town, and provided a place to shop for people who felt out of place in the bigger, fancier stores. More importantly, Blevins's accepted people's food stamps and money without passing judgment. Where else could a man like Delmar Tucker and his family find a place to shop?

The people of the rural county knew two things about Delmar Tucker. His life was inextricably intertwined with a stonework chimney that stood a lonely sentinel in a pasture in Shearer Valley, and Delmar's family were notorious as being the dirtiest, nastiest people on the face of the earth. Delmar's dark-skinned face was perpetually covered in a salt and pepper stubble which occasionally betrayed a trickle of tobacco stain that had escaped from his mouth. He was a little over six feet tall and wore a dirty bill cap askew atop his thick head of graying unwashed hair. His pants and shirts always carried stains of sweat and dirt from places few people would even visit. Perhaps the setting of his face imparted a lucidity to the hazel eyes that made it seem as if he never looked at people, but rather through them; like the eyes of the Great Sphinx of Giza, his eyes seemed to be permanently transfixed on nothing but the horizon. Delmar drove an old beat-up '63 Ford pickup truck whose shallow bed was secured to the cab and frame with baling twine and bits of multicolored electrical wire; most people thought that luck, rather than these cables, actually maintained the integrity of the truck.

Delmar's wife, Adeline, was no prize; she shared her husband's disdain for personal hygiene, and she had considerably fewer teeth. She seldom left the shelter of the truck cab, preferring to let Delmar shop for groceries, while she smoked her Camels in the cab, and occasionally wiped the thin strands of dirty hair away from her face. Her eyes were a study in burdensome and tragic circumstances, but no one knew what those were.

Delmar's only son, Danny, had made a new life for himself, and apparently disavowed any kinship to his parents. Their younger daughter, Clytie, was much younger than her siblings. Sometimes she rode to town in the truck with her parents; when she was a little girl, she would ride in the back of the truck, peering wide-eyed as a calf heading to market between the stock racks; upon reaching puberty she assumed the luxury of the cab. Schoolchildren used to tease boys about having a crush on Clytie Tucker.

Even if she had been born into a family of bluebloods, Clytie would have still been called homely. She had mousy-colored curly hair and eyes that bore the vacant look of a Yorkshire hog that had been hit with a ball peen hammer prior to butchering. Her stomach protruded prominently as though she were pregnant, a claim that the poor girl suffered in silence throughout junior high school before she dropped out in the tenth grade. People whispered accusations that Delmar must be the father, for what other loathsome creature would be so bold as to impregnate so ugly a girl? Perhaps an incestuous relationship was easier to stomach than imagining the existence of families which might produce prospective suitors. Eventually, a health care nurse determined that her little pot belly resulted from a poor diet and bad overall health, not pregnancy. The nurse discovered this during a home visit, an excursion not for the faint-hearted, to treat Clytie for such a severe ear infection that the stench of pus and grimy earwax would empty a room.

Delmar and his family lived at Griffin in what ostensibly passed for a house, but more closely resembled a junkyard or a landfill. Worn out tires, oil cans, empty food cans, old bedsprings and other pieces of domestic or commercial refuse were piled higgledy-piggledy in the yard so deep that no grass grew there. The house, covered in asphalt shingles, looked more like camouflage in a war zone than a dwelling. From time to time, the state health department would go down there and serve notice that the place had to be cleaned up; Delmar would dutifully re-arrange stuff to foster the illusion of disposal. On two occasions, trash spilled onto the road so much that the state highway department used a small bulldozer to push it back into the yard.

Nearly every day, Delmar would stop by to pick up a few groceries with food stamps even though he nearly always carried a wad of bills that would choke a mule. No one seemed to know where he got the money: welfare checks were not that generous and his small tobacco base could not provide such bounty. No one could muster the courage to ask where the money came from and Delmar never said much to *anyone*.

So it was that the enigma of the Delmar Tucker family presented itself to the good people of Blevins's Grocery several times a week when they shuffled into the store to pick up a few groceries before resuming their seats in their decrepit automobiles to fade into the far-flung hinterlands of Griffin.

II

"Howdy, Delmar. How you doing?" Fannie asked as Delmar entered the store.

"Tolerable, but it's hot," came the reply.

"Been working in the bakker?"

"Chopped a few weeds and pulled a few suckers before it got too hot. The old lady needed a few groceries. Willard at the meat counter?"

"He's back there talking to a salesman. Go on back."

Delmar wound his way along the oiled hardwood floor between the plain shelves to the meat freezer where Willard stood chatting to a man in a white short-sleeved shirt. The man was scribbling notes for Willard's grocery order for next week's shipment.

"Delmar, how you doing?" Willard asked.

"Tolerable. Got to get a little meat for the old lady."

"What can I get you?"

"A pound of that Dixie loaf and a pound of pork chops. This here the meat salesman?"

The man stuck the pen behind the metal clip on the clipboard and extended his hand without thinking. "Bob Malone, glad to meet you."

Delmar shook the man's hand and said, "Delmar Tucker."

Malone pulled his hand back and let it drop limply by his side as he stood and quickly surveyed Delmar's unkempt frame. He realized Delmar needed a bath for he smelled of an aroma of perspiration-stained cotton mixed with moist earth after a spring shower. Out of the corner of his eye, he noticed that Willard was matter-of-factly preparing the meat Delmar had requested while engaged in some garbled conversation with him as he stared at motion of the slicer. Malone focused on the conversation when he heard his name mentioned.

"Do you know what Mr. Malone here told me, Delmar? He told me that them little lines and numbers are some kind of code and that they contain all the information about the product in the package. What it is, size of the package, manufacturer. Why, he even tells me that someday grocers will have a way to read them lines and place orders for inventory over the phone. Have you ever heard of such a thing, Delmar?"

"Nope," came the tacit reply.

"Hard to believe, ain't it? That'll put him out of a job!" Willard teased.

Malone stammered, "Not exactly, but it will change the job of salesmen. We will still have to make visits on clients like you, Willard."

"Well, that's a relief. Here you go, Delmar. Anything else?" Willard asked as he reached the packages over the counter.

"No, that'll be it. Got to git home and chop a little bakker."

Willard cleaned the slicer and replaced the pork loin in the counter while Malone watched Delmar pay Fannie and leave the store.

"Willard, may I wash my hands?" he asked.

Willard grinned knowingly and nodded. As he washed his hands in the sink on the back wall Malone continued, "That is the dirtiest man I have ever seen in my life! How could anybody let himself go so badly? How can you stand to have him come into your store? What is he— a bootlegger?"

Willard smiled and answered quietly, "Oh no, not Delmar. There is nothing wrong with Delmar. He just don't take much pride in his appearance. Been that way for years. Doubt that he'll ever change. You ought to see where he lives. The Health Department condemned it twice, but he still lives there. We have a lot of people come in our store who are poor and dirty. Most of them have had hard lives and we just try to provide them a place to shop. You're not from here, are you?"

Malone shook his head, "No, I am from Lexington originally. We have poor dirty people there too, but not like that."

"You have just never had to deal with them on a one-to-one basis."

Malone started to say something, but the screaking of the front door and a thunderous voice interrupted him. "Willard, do you have a chain saw I can borrow?" bellowed a barrel-chested man as he walked toward the back of the store.

"Charlie Poore, you good-for-nothing varmint. What do you need a chainsaw for? You don't do no work."

Charlie leaned up against the counter before answering, "I am trying to dig a well down there. They drilled three dry holes a hundred fifty feet deep. Cost me a fortune."

"So what's the chain saw for?"

"I'm going to cut them holes up into three foot lengths and sell them for postholes to get my money back."

They all laughed heartily. "Charlie, you won't do. This here is Bob Malone. He sells groceries from Malone and Hyde."

Malone and Poore shook hands and Willard continued, "We're just talking about one of your neighbors, Charlie."

"Who's that?"

"Delmar Tucker."

"Ah, Delmar Tucker. Was he just in here?"

"Just left. Mr. Malone was asking me if he was a bootlegger and what his story was."

Charlie shook his head, "No, Delmar is not a bootlegger. I doubt that he has enough gumption to even try to make the stuff. But he's a sight, ain't he?"

Malone nodded in agreement. "Has he always been so filthy and poor?"

"Has been for years, but somebody told me that he didn't use to be that way. I heard that he used to be quite respectable. Seems like they told me he once worked as a lineman for the electric company. Delmar is a mystery. Now I'll tell you boys something you'll not believe, but I saw it with my own eyes."

"What's that, Charlie? By the way, you need anything here?"

"Yeah, a pound of that Colby cheese and a mess of them neck bones.

Virgie's got a hankering for neck bones."

"So what were you going to tell us?' Malone asked.

"Well, a few years ago a bunch of us men at Griffin used to go to Shell Chriswell for a haircut. He used to cut hair in the army and bought a pair of clippers to cut his kids' hair. All the men in the neighborhood went there for a haircut. He charged fifty cents if you could afford it, a dozen eggs if you couldn't. We're all gathered down there Saturday and Delmar came up for a haircut. While he's getting his haircut, somebody started talking about the war. Old man Jeb Bridgeman had served in World War One, Marion Hines, had served in World War Two. Directly, somebody asked Delmar if he'd ever been in the war. Delmar never even looked up, but quietly said that he'd earned some medals in the Korean War. Well, I'll tell you that broke everybody up. Some of them laughed so hard they fell down. I felt sort of sorry for Delmar, because he couldn't get up and leave. He just had to sit there and take their ribbing. They teased him about what kind of medals and made up jokes about it. Delmar sat there and never opened his mouth. Shell finished his haircut, and Delmar paid him fifty cents. Then he got into the old truck and left. Them fellers just kept on laughing and joking about Delmar Tucker, the war hero."

"Well, you got to admit, it's pretty funny," interjected Malone. "He's not exactly my idea of a war hero."

"He wasn't theirs, either. They were still sitting there laughing about it and Delmar drove his old truck into the driveway. He got out and walked over to the porch and handed Shell a beat-up old cigar box. Shell opened it and it was full of all kinds of war medals and papers showing that they belonged to Delmar. We didn't know what to say. Talk about embarrassed! Everybody wanted to see and hold the medals. They apologized to Delmar. He let everybody look at them medals. Then he took his cigar box and went home. We all just stood there scratching our heads."

Malone was flabbergasted. "You mean to tell me that man was a decorated war hero?"

"Yep. I saw two purple hearts, a silver star, and I forgot the rest. Harry Truman had signed the papers. Shocked the hell out of us."

Willard grinned to hide his astonishment. "I had never heard that story about Delmar. Seems like I had heard other stories."

Charlie nodded, "One time I ran into Delmar fishing on Beaver Creek. He was just sitting there, so I struck up a little conversation. He don't talk much, you know. Directly, he says that the nice thing about fishing is that nobody is disappointed if you don't catch nothing. Said he got tired trying to live up to everybody's expectations. I asked him what he meant, but he never said anything. I told him that I had heard that he used to work on the lines for the RECC. He said that he did. I asked why he quit, but he never answered. In fact, he just quit talking altogether, so I went on up the creek bank."

"What were his parents like?" Malone asked.

"Don't nobody know much about them. I think Delmar was adopted. Seems like I heard his folks was killed."

Willard listened as he wiped down the counter top and cleaned the slicer. "Didn't they live over in Shearer Valley?"

"Maybe, but I'm not sure. I heard Delmar say that he got tired of hearing people say God must have something special planned for him. I got the impression that he had been hearing that all of his life. You know Delmar. He never has too much to say about anything."

Malone snapped to as if from a trance. "Well, gentlemen, I have to be going. This has been an interesting visit with you, Willard. I still just don't see any excuse for a human being to allow himself get so low. By the way, is it just me or does he have two glass eyes?"

Charlie replied, "No. Ever since I've known him his eyes have had that distant look in them. Sort like he was looking through you. He don't mean nothing by it. That's just Delmar."

Malone shrugged, waved goodbye and left Willard and Charlie to discuss the big coon hunt in two weeks.

III

"Next!" shouted the employment counselor.

Delmar hastily wiped the tops of his shoes with a handkerchief and straightened his tie as he stood up. He walked over to the young man who extended his hand, grasping Delmar's hand and saying, "Gene Edwards. And you are..."

"Delmar Tucker," answered Delmar. "Glad to meet you."

"Likewise. Now, Mr. Tucker, tell me a little about yourself. What job skills do you have?"

"Well, I just got out of the army and..."

"Wait a minute! I thought I recognized your name. Are you that Delmar Tucker from over in Shearer Valley?"

"Yes, that's me," answered Delmar shyly.

"Somebody told me that you rescued several of the men in your platoon in the war. Maybe that's the reason God spared your life, for saving those other men."

Delmar fidgeted uncomfortably before answering, "I don't know."

"You must be proud of yourself, a real war hero."

"Not really, sir. I just want a job to start my family."

"Didn't the army provide you with a pension of some kind?"

"Yes, but I want a job. A man has to work."

"What kind of work do you want, Mr. Tucker?"

"I used to work with an electrician, so I know a lot about that. Are they still hiring for the RECC?"

"Well, yes, they are, and they need linemen to run lines and install electrical lines to houses. I'm sure they would be happy to hire you with your background. Here's the address. Why don't you go over there and see what they say?"

Delmar's eyes lit up expectantly, "Can I go to meet them now?"

"I'll call and tell them to expect you in the next few minutes. Good luck, Mr. Tucker. It's not every day I get to meet someone who is a real celebrity."

"Thank you, Mr. Edwards. I really appreciate your help."

Delmar left the office, got into his Chevrolet sedan and drove to the RECC office. A little bell jingled as he entered the office, and a pretty young woman in a crisply starched skirt and blouse appeared from around the corner. Delmar felt his heart leap as he glanced at the nameplate on her desk: Adeline Hubbard.

"May I help you?" she asked sweetly.

"I am Delmar Tucker. The employment office sent me over about a job."

"Oh, you're him! Well this is certainly a pleasure, Mr. Tucker. Come on around to meet Mr. Lyons."

Delmar followed her around the counter to a small office where a small-framed man sat reading over applications. He looked up over his glasses.

The man extended his hand and said, "Everett Lyons, Mr. Tucker. I just talked to Gene Edwards. He told me a lot about you. This is a real honor. I wondered what had happened to you after you left Shearer Valley. You know that old chimney is still there."

"I wouldn't know. I don't go around there anymore."

"I can understand that. Lots of bad memories, I suppose. Still I don't understand why the paper didn't do a story about your war experiences."

"I asked them not to," Delmar replied quietly.

"I can understand that. I guess it would make some people uncomfortable."

"Yeah, sort of."

"Well, Gene tells me you have experience with electricity. Are you pretty good at it?"

"I did it before the war and helped string wires in Korea. I know what I'm doing pretty well."

"Well, we need people to go back into these hills and hollers and string lines. Sometimes you'll be a part of a crew, sometimes you'll be by yourself. You know how backward and distrustful a lot of the country people are. Your name will help a lot."

Delmar squirmed nervously. "What do you mean?"

"I imagine that a lot of people consider you a hero. A lot of people figure the Lord has big plans for you."

Delmar shifted his position in the chair. "Yeah, I have heard that a lot. Do I get the job?"

"Of course, you get the job. Just report in here every morning to get a list of places to go to from Adeline. We'll have a truck, tools and a map for you every morning. The first month or so you'll be working with some men to learn the ropes. Then you can be on your own. It's a pleasure to have you with us, Mr. Tucker."

Delmar felt a spring in his step as he left the office. He smiled at Adeline who returned the smile. Over the next few months, he learned all of the crewmembers, and how to install power lines for the Rural Electrical Co-Op. Each day he showed up early so that he could chat with Adeline. They began to date and married within a year. Their son Danny was born a year later, followed by Clytie two years later. Delmar bought a nice little house at Griffin where he could farm a little and have a garden. They attended Reagan's Flat Baptist Church nearly every Sunday, for Delmar was very thankful for all of his good fortune.

Mr. Lyons was right about one thing: a lot of people knew Delmar's name. Most of them repeated the same mantra: God must have big plans for you. Eventually, Delmar learned to just smile and nod graciously before going about his work.

Delmar had just sat down to breakfast with his family one Fourth of July when Mr. Lyons pulled up.

"Delmar! Are you in there?"

Delmar went to the door, and stepped out of the house and walked over to meet Mr. Lyons.

"Hello, Mr. Lyons. What brings you down here?"

"I hate to ask this, but there was a windstorm over in Shearer Valley last night. Blew some trees across the lines and snapped them. The power is out for two miles in either direction. Can you go over there and repair it? They really need their power back on."

"Let me eat dinner and I'll go. Shouldn't be too hard to fix."

Delmar wolfed down his food, jumped into his truck and headed off to the location Mr. Lyons had shown him on the map. By the time he got there, the sun was out, but the air had the fresh scent of a summer rain. The lines lay broken in a pasture field where a ramshackle stone chimney stood. Delmar glanced at it quickly before he climbed over the woven wire fence and headed to the pole nearest the break. He strapped on his spikes, secured his tool belt and began to scale the pole. When he reached the top of the pole, he realized he would have to splice the wires until they could be replaced so he secured his safety belt round the pole and prepared to splice the wires. He steadied himself by grasping one of the glass insulators on the horizontal beam. The motion pulled the insulator toward him and snapped off its wooden peg, and Delmar fell backwards off the pole. Frantically, he grabbed at anything he could reach, forgetting that he was holding metal pliers and wire. The wire whip-lashed wildly over two other wires and caused a flash that showered Delmar with electric sparks. He lost consciousness, went limp, and twisted slowly in the wind. His spikes and belt held firm and suspended him between heaven and earth. His body jerked to one side and memories of his wartime experiences flooded his mind.

Tucker, get over behind that hill and see what's going on.

Sarge, half the platoon is pinned down by a bunch of snipers. I think that I can sneak around that rise to the left and maybe get a few of them.

Then do it!

Got to keep my head down. Zing. Ping. Kaboom. Zing.

I only see five. Got to load and shoot quick before they find me. RATATATTAT! They are all down but one. Oh, God! I'm hit. You son of a bitch. Where are you? Goddam, that hurts! There he is. Crack! Take that you, little bastard.

Delmar flailed upwards violently, then fell back, and twisted in counter-clockwise circles as he heard a quiet voice talking to him.

Delmar, why did you kill all those men? I protected you as a baby, but I did not save your life so that you could take the lives of others.

But, Lord! We were at war. They were trying to kill my buddies.

Delmar, do you doubt that I would have taken care of them? You of all people should know that I will watch over my children.

But everyone has always told me that you had great plans for me. I thought saving my platoon was part of your plan for my life.

Did you really think that was my plan, Delmar? Or was that your plan? Pride goeth before a fall. Did you really believe that any of those people knew what I had planned for them, let alone you? Have you read Job? He suffered too, but he did not quit trusting me. I spared you, and how have you shown your gratitude? You have used that gift for personal glory. You need to think about what you have done. Watch for me, Delmar, be ever watchful for me, for one day I will demand a settlement of your account. Will you be as proud then?

Delmar regained consciousness slowly. He steadied himself on the pole, but was too groggy to know what he was doing. The acrid smell of burnt hair and singed flesh flooded his nostrils and he stared confusedly at the wires and the poles. He dismounted the pole carefully, but blacked out on the ground where he lay until a backup crew found him.

The doctors at the hospital realized that Delmar suffered from temporary amnesia. They pieced the bits of information they had, and deduced that he had accidentally shocked himself with enough electricity to cause brain damage. Apparently, the shock also damaged his optic nerves for his eyes now stared distantly, as if watching for something on the horizon.

Even though he was riddled by guilt, Mr. Lyons had no choice but to let Delmar go, because he could not remember how to do the job. He managed to finagle some paperwork to insure that Delmar got a sizable severance pay from the RECC. For Delmar Tucker, one life had ended and another begun.

IV

The storm blew in suddenly from the East, a bad sign as most storms came from the west. Ephraim Tucker hurried to get the horses into the barn and carry a bundle of wood into the house. His wife and children huddled in the two-story house as lightning crackled and thunder filled the skies. Ephraim hugged his wife and children close to him as the house shuddered in the wind. Suddenly, the house creaked loudly as the tornado ripped it and all of its contents off the ground. The house disintegrated in the swirling maelstrom, and vomited the family and its contents to the ground.

Abraham, Ephraim's brother, who shared ownership of the farm with him, had watched all of this from one window he had left unshuttered. He cried to God for mercy as he watched the house go airborne, but he realized that he dared not to leave his house until the storm passed. His own family hid themselves under beds and prayed for God Almighty to spare them.

The storm passed and Abraham dashed across the field to survey the damage. Ephraim lay dead of a broken neck. His wife, Beatrice, was partially covered by a large table that had crushed her skull. The two daughters, Linda and Susan, lay in crumpled, lifeless heaps. Pots, pans, feathers from bedclothes, and pieces of furniture littered the countryside. As he stood crying and shaking in fear, Abraham heard a slight whimper. He followed the cries and found a baby who lay crying in a homemade crib in front of a limestone chimney.

"My God! Oh Lord, at least the baby is still alive!"

He grabbed the baby in his arms and ran back home.

"Opal, open the door! I got my hands full."

His wife opened the door and took the baby in her arms. Abraham trembled and sobbed as he recounted what he had seen. He spent a few minutes collecting himself before he decided that someone needed to let the undertaker know. As he put on a coat and headed to the barn to saddle his horse, Opal asked, "What are we going to do with little Delmar? He's only a month old."

Abraham walked over and took the baby in his arms. "I'll tell you what we are going to do. God used that chimney to protect this baby, and we're not about to tear down a sign from God as long as this field is here. He must have great plans for this child. We're going to raise this baby as one of our own."

He tickled the baby under the chin. "Yes, sir, the Lord's got big plans for you, Delmar Tucker. Big plans."

The Poor Shall Not Give Less

DOZENS OF ONE-ROOM schoolhouses sprinkled over the hills and hollows of Wayne County defined the communities of subsistence farmers and unskilled laborers living there. They punctuated the forested expanse at irregular intervals determined by topography and walking distance from the families whose lives were inextricably linked to their small plots of land. Most families made sure their children attended, as much as possible, albeit with prolonged interruptions dictated by the demands of an agrarian way of life. Some only let their children go to school long enough to learn to read some of the Bible and write a cursive signature for the purpose of signing legal documents but others did not send their children to school at all, secure in their knowledge that preachers and a scrawled X in the presence of witness would suit the same purpose.

Those children who attended school were granted a respite from the meager existence their families had endured for generations. They could read the Bible and occasionally the works of secular authors who described faraway places and strange customs of people they would never see. When the weather turned cold, the older boys carried in wood to keep the fires roaring in the potbellied stoves that heated the one-room schools and carried out the ashes. Younger children swept the floors and cleaned the blackboard erasers and carried in pails of drinking water. Everyone had some task to do to keep the school going and give them a sense of belonging. After school, they returned to the life of poor dirt farmers whose survival was at the mercy of the vagaries of weather. Tobacco crop sales might return a small profit just in time for Christmas and to pay for the seed to re-start the cycle over again next year.

This was the world into which Emma Troxell was born to Arvin and Betty Troxell and where she would receive the first three years of her education.

II

Emma was so excited about her first day of school that she woke up before her parents, rousting them out of bed to get her ready for school.

"Mommy! Daddy? Wake up. I get to go to school today! Hurry! I don't want to be late!"

Her Dad growled, "For Christ's sake, Emma! You will wake everybody up. It's only four-thirty in the morning! I can get another hour of sleep. School don't meet till eight. I promise we'll get you there on time. Now go back to bed!"

He turned over, but her mother said quietly, "I know you are excited, and I am too. Let me get up and fix breakfast while you tell me what you are going to do today. Why don't you go wash your face and hands?"

Emma raced into the small kitchen and ladled some water into the wash pan and dipped a wash cloth into the water with a dab of soap to clean her face and hands. She could hear her mother starting a fire in the cook stove and rattling pans.

"You and me can have our breakfast now so just us girls can talk before the men get up," her mom purred.

She winked at Emma and they giggled at their mischief. "Go look under the cabinet there and you will find a surprise."

Emma ran over to the cabinet where she found a Fischer's Lard bucket with EMMA TROXELL scratched into the large blue band around the top.

"That's your lunch pail. The boys can all share the bigger bucket but you need a lady-sized bucket. How does an egg and sausage sandwich sound for dinner? Dad bought some bananas at the store yesterday and there is enough for all of you to have one today."

"That sounds good, Mommy."

"I guess today though I'll pack egg sandwiches for all of you. You better go get your brothers up while I wake up daddy."

Emma raced through the small home yelling "Get up! It's the first day of school! You have to get ready!"

Her brothers, Randy, Tommy and Rusty, rolled out of their shared bed in single file and sleepily pulled on their pants and rubbed their eyes.

Randy mumbled, "All right Emma, we heard you the first three times. Now get out of here so we can get dressed!"

In a few minutes her brothers were standing by the stove warming the morning chill from their bodies. Mom said. "Randy, it's your turn to feed the hogs, Rusty get the wood and Tommy go draw a bucket of water. Now hop to it. I have to go to put Emma in school today and I don't want to be late."

The boys shook off the chill and ran outside barefooted to do their assigned chores. When they returned, their Dad was sitting at the breakfast table sipping a cup of coffee and taking long drags off a cigarette. He blew a smoke ring toward Emma and teased, "So today my little pumpkin is off to school! You're going to be the smartest one there, ain't you?"

Emma beamed, "Yes, sir, Daddy. I'm going to be the best student ever. Better than the boys."

The boy burst back into the kitchen just in time to hear her brag and teased her, "Emma, the smartest girl in town!" as she chased them around the table.

Her father pounded the table "That's enough foolishness. Get your breakfast eat and get on out of here. I got to be at work to start topping that bakker patch. Now you all behave and learn something today and boys — watch after your sister."

Mom said, "I'll wash the dishes after I get you to school. I done packed your lunches so get your stuff and let's go. I got things to do today."

The children grabbed a new pencil, a tablet of paper and their lunch buckets and rushed out the door. The shortest route to Griffin School was to cut across the pasture fields glistening in the dewy morning light. Clay Stinson's Jersey cattle watched disinterestedly as the children ran across their field before they mooed softly and before resuming their grazing.

Randy reminded Emma, "If the bull is in this field you don't come this way. You take the long way round, yonder by Stinson's barn. Them old cows ain't gonna hurt you, but that bull could kill you and we wouldn't want to lose the smartest girl in class, would we?"

Several other children were already waiting at the school by the time they arrived. Her mother brushed Emma's light brown hair out of her eyes and led her into the school, where a dark-haired woman sitting at a desk stopped her work long enough to peer over her glasses at Emma as she came toward the desk.

"Well, good morning, young lady. I'm Mrs. Cooper. Now, can you tell me who you are?"

"Emma Troxell," she replied quietly.

"Well, Emma, we're very glad to have you with us. Is this your Mother with you? Hi, Mrs. Troxell. I see you finally got a girl here for us. The boys ok? Will they be back with us?"

"Oh yes, they're outside with the other children. I think their daddy about worked them to death this summer, so they're glad to be back in school. They always tell me that school is their vacation."

"Well, a little hard work never hurt anybody, and it's good for kids to learn that early. Would you please fill out these forms for Emma or would you like me to?"

"No, I'll be glad to do that. Emma and I have been practicing our writing. Do you want to show Mrs. Cooper how good you can write your name?"

Emma smiled shyly. "Yes'm." as Mrs. Cooper handed her a paper and pencil. She printed "EMMA TROXELL" in all capital letters and handed the paper back to the teacher.

"That's mighty fine penmanship, Emma. Can you write cursive too?"

"Not yet, but I know my ABC's and I can count to a hundred. And I can read. A little."

"Well, an eager mind is an easy one to teach. Now the youngest students sit over there on the left two rows, and the oldest ones on the right with everybody else in the middle. Why don't you sit in the front seat while I get everybody in to start? Mrs. Troxell, do you want to stay around for a spell to see how things go?"

"I might stay a few minutes, but I need to get back. Just sit there beside Emma?"

"That'll be fine," Mrs. Cooper replied as she hefted a large brass bell off her desk and strode over to the door, ringing vigorously and shouting, "All right, it's time to start school. Come on in now!"

The children rushed from all directions toward the door of the wooden school and took their seats according to age.

"Now, class, let's go around the room and introduce ourselves. Tell us your name and who your parents are and how old you are."

When her turn came, Emma stood slowly, averting her eyes to the floor as she said softly, "My name is Emma Troxell. I'm six years old. My mom and dad are Arvin and Betty Troxell. And I'm new to school this year."

III

During the first few days of school Emma noted with some relief that most of the class was girls. A lot of the neighborhood boys never came because they worked beside their fathers in the fields rather than being cooped up in a building all day. Most of them never had any ambition to be anything other than what their fathers were: hardworking hill people who led simple lives and dreamed simple dreams. A few fathers, tired of the years of hard labor that aged them far beyond their years, insisted their sons attend school to have a better life than they had. Many local people felt that girls should be more educated even though they often had to work alongside their brothers in the fields. Though the little community was a patriarchal society, everyone seemed to agree that women are much better at the paperwork need to survive in their world. Everyone knew that Arzella Cooper was just the woman to teach them as she had been doing for twenty years.

Mrs. Cooper was the law within the confines of the Griffin School. As a strict disciplinarian, she was on a first name basis with the hickory switch in the corner near her desk. She mentored all of her charges who ranged from first grade to eighth grade since Griffin School stopped at the eighth grade. Three small high schools scattered around the county afforded some students more education, but only a few earned a high school diploma. Many people resisted anything new that might challenge their simple world view.

Arzella was no stranger to the plight of the hill folk youngsters as she watched each year diminish the enrollment of the upper grades as older boys dropped out to farm or take menial jobs at nearby sawmills or flooring mills. She counted herself lucky if two or three boys reached eighth grade, even luckier if one went on to high school. Frequently, she resorted to bribery with candy treats or small monetary rewards for lessons well done.

Arzella's gentle prodding eventually coaxed Emma and her classmates out of their shells and they became becoming active and eager learners. Emma and her newfound friends sat together and spent recess time playing on the swings that hung from two white oak trees behind the school. The boys preferred to climb trees, chuck rocks at tin cans or root around rotting logs to find squiggly critters to scare the teacher and girls. Arzella kept two goldfish in a large pickled bologna jar as an aquarium in the school and the boys would feed them small bugs.

Emma quickly forged comfortable friendships with Hazel and Thelma Stinson, who were a year older. This friendship blossomed by the sheer coincidence that they all wore dresses made from the same blue patterned feed sack material on one day.

At first sight of the two identical dresses, Emma snickered "We must be triplets! Did your mom make those dresses from a feed sack?"

Hazel laughed and replied, "Of course, that is where mom gets most of her material for our clothes."

Their birdlike twittering attracted Arzella who sauntered over to see what they were up to. "Oh, you girls are just having a good time. From the looks of you, I think I will call you my little bluebirds!"

Emma's brothers teased her on the way home. "Tweet, little bird, wanna eat a bug?" Randy asked.

She chased them home across the fields, but the teasing continued at the supper table before her dad made them stop. After supper she went to bed and dreamed of the coming school year.

IV

The humid dog days of late summer gradually eased into the cooler days of Indian summer. As the weather cooled, Arvin loaded his kids and wife into his old Ford truck to go buy shoes for everyone shoes for the winter with the money he had made helping other farmers cut and store their tobacco. The salesman helped the children select shoes that would be big enough to last and accommodate their growth until the next year's winter, because one pair would have to last until then. The boys were lucky, because they could pass their shoes down to one another, but Betty insisted that Emma get a more ladylike pair.

Though the weather was still warm enough to go barefoot, Betty insisted the children wear the shoes a little every day to break them in so their stiffness would not cause blisters of sores. By the time the weather turned cold, the shoes were pliable enough to be comfortable enough to wear all day. Emma could hardly wait to show her new shoes to the other children because they were the first new store-bought thing she had worn to school. But nearly everyone at school had new shoes as if a fairy godmother had magically bestowed the luxury of new shoes and boots on all of the children.

When she saw her friends, Emma raced over, shouting, "Thelma! Hazel! Look at my new shoes! Ain't they pretty?"

"Not as pretty as ours!" came the reply. The girls compared the shoes, which had not a whit's worth of difference and wiped away dirt and scuff marks to keep them looking new. Hazel suddenly motioned for the girls to bend over so they could whisper, "The weather is turning cold now and that means it won't be long to Christmas. I can't wait!"

Emma was trying to pay attention, but she found herself watching her brothers kicking rocks and a tin can with their new shoes.

"Will you look at that? I am going to tell Mom and Dad how they are not taking care of their shoes and they will get a whipping!"

Hazel put her arm around Emma's neck and whispered in her ear, "Don't do that, Emma. My brother Jimmy did the same thing when he got new shoes. Them boys don't want people to know they only get one pair of shoes a year. Jimmy told me that boys always scuff their shoes up to fool people into thinking they always had shoes to wear. You would really hurt your brothers' feelings if you told on them."

Emma nodded knowing of her brothers' pride and how fiercely they resented any deprecation of their humble lifestyle. She had heard the same resentment in her father's voice when a census taker asked him if the family was on welfare: 'Hell, no we ain't on welfare! We may be poor, but we are too proud to take charity!'

When they neared home, Emma ran ahead to meet her mother who was bringing in a few sticks of kindling to start the fire for supper. "Look Mommy, look! My shoes still look brand new! I'm going to keep them looking new all year long."

Even as she finished her pledge, her brothers walked by, ignoring her comments implying that they did not take care of their shoes. Betty replied, "Well, I hope you can do that Emma, but, boys, it sure looks like you all are getting good use out of yours!"

V

As autumn deepened, so did the layer of leaves in the woods around the school, allowing all sorts of new games and mischief for the children at recess. Often, Arzella would bring sacks for the children to collect hickory nuts to use in holiday pastries. Some of the older boys began to miss school regularly, as they were needed to help strip tobacco or collect firewood for the winter. Randy assumed the task of starting the fire in the stove and keeping a supply of coal and wood nearby; his best pal, Delmar Marcum, carried the ashes out to the ash-heap behind the school. Arzella bought some heavy plastic to cover the windows to conserve heat; it made the outside world seem as wavy and indistinct as a reflection in rippling pond.

The first snow fell in early December, blanketing the school grounds with white, speckled with minute particles of soot from the stove. Open fields nearby lay quietly muted in the snow cover, with tracings of footprints from all directions leading to the school, a Mecca in the wintry scene. The boys had snow ball fights at recess while the girls made snow angels in the shallow powder.

Some of the older kids began to scout out potential Christmas trees with five-foot red cedar trees in great demand. For the country folk Christmas was not Christmas unless there was a red cedar tree bedecked for the holidays. With luck, you might even find one with a bird nest in it, a sign of good fortune.

Arzella had taught long enough to realize that the excitement of Christmas would sabotage her teaching efforts if she did not develop activities that were both instructive and celebratory of the season. Daily readings turned to the Christmas story in the Gospel of Luke, the visit of the Magi in Matthew, or learning about Christmas traditions of other peoples, with caroling at the end of each day. She collected Sears and Roebucks catalogs from anyone who did not want them and let the kids peruse them to make Christmas lists. They wrote essays on what they wanted for Christmas, but for most of these children these were exercises in optimistic futility to keep them going for another year.

The week before Christmas, the older boys ventured up the hollow to cut a Christmas tree. The tree had only two strings of working lights, but homemade ornaments from colored paper, pipe cleaners, and a large tinfoil star provided a festive atmosphere for the week before the Christmas break. A few kids had managed to scrimp enough money to buy a friend a gift or some nice handkerchiefs for the teacher, but most children brought cookies or cakes or homemade gifts from their parents to show their appreciation to the teacher. Arzella, knowing the poverty of her charges, always bought each child a two-pound box of peppermint candy. Occasionally, she bought a pair of gloves for a child who did not have any and put them under the tree as a gift from Santa.

The presents and decorations were simple, but for some of the children these were the only sugar plum fairies that would dance in their world. Arzella knew that for most the "wish book" was exactly that: a compendium of the hopes and dreams of dozens of children whose families were trapped in poverty. Her own wish book was a list she secretly kept of the students whom she thought had the most potential to break out of the cycle of poverty and ignorance. This year she placed Emma and her friends first on the list, but scratched off Randy, Tommy and Delmar for she saw them already succumbing to the tradition of being poor dirt farmers like their fathers.

The festive atmosphere in the school the last day before the break included games and swapping gifts with special friends. Every family presented Arzella a small token of appreciation for educating their children. Emma joined her friends near the stove and said, "Merry Christmas! I have a present for you. Mom and me made it." She handed each girl a small box wrapped in brown paper decorated with Christmas designs.

"Why, thank you, Emma. Here's your present." They handed her a small box wrapped in tinfoil with a red ribbon around it.

Emma replied, "Thank you so much!" she exclaimed as she tore open the foil and box to reveal a pair of hair barrettes made of tortoise shell. She gasped in genuine surprise "Oh, thank you so much! Where did you find them?"

Thelma replied, "Our mom remembered seeing them at the dime store so she got them last week. Now let's see what our present is."

Hazel tore the paper off and opened the box to find several pieces of homemade fruitcake decorated with small candy animals. Each of the girls snatched a piece out and took a big bite. "This is delicious. Your mom always makes the best cake. This must have been expensive to make with all these nuts and candies."

"I don't know what it cost, but I helped Mom mix it up and decorate it. There's enough there to share with your family. Here, help me put these in my hair."

Other children were also exchanging handmade gifts with their best friends, but most were just laughing and discussing what they wanted for Christmas. Toward the end of the day, Arzella passed out the peppermint candy and sent the kids home early so she could attend to her own holiday obligations. She put out the fire, emptied the water bucket and locked the door for the two-week winter break.

VI

The children raced home over the frozen ground, scarred by the hoof prints of the cattle that stood placidly blowing soft puffs of breath into the chill winter air. They had learned that the children presented neither reward or threat and they no longer wasted any energy mooing their annoyance at the children's presence.

Randy lifted Emma over the fence while his brothers climbed and straddled the fence near a post. Emma dashed the rest of the way home shouting, "Mommy! Mommy! Look what I got!"

Her mother opened the door for the children and Emma turned her head to show the barrettes, "Looky, Mommy. Ain't they beautiful? Thelma and Hazel gave them to me. And they liked our cake and said thank you and..."

Betty laughed, "Calm down, Emma, before you have a conniption fit. Now let me see them. Oh, they are pretty!"

"Wait till Daddy sees them."

"I am sure he'll like them. Boys, go tend to the chores before your dad gets here. He brung a tree back today at dinner and we can put it up tonight. It's only a week till Christmas and you ain't even wrote your letters to Santa yet."

Rusty interrupted, "Oh, Mom, we all know that there ain't no...."

Betty shook her head quickly and put her finger to her mouth. "Now Rusty, don't argue with me or Santa won't come to you. Just do as I say," she said with a wink to her sons.

After supper, Arvin nailed a board to the sawed-off end of the cedar tree and stood it in front of the window facing the road. The children hung some weathered garland, ornaments and two strings of lights around the tree. Betty laid the big Sears Roebuck catalog opened to the toy section on the table they so could gather round and make lists. Emma wanted dolls and a music box, but the boys dreamed of knives and BB guns. Emma chattered about sitting up all night to see Santa, and the boys fanned the flames of her expectations but they knew the letters would be thrown into the stove when they went to bed.

On Christmas morning, the children got up very early to see what Santa had left them. The boys each found a new pocketknife, die-cast metal cars and trucks powered by imagination instead of batteries. There was one Daisy BB gun that they had to share. Emma found a doll that went to sleep when you laid it down, and a paper doll book with lots of clothes and accessories. Betty had bought Arvin a new wallet and he had bought her a new gingham dress. At the Christmas dinner of baked chicken, Arvin had each child say a prayer of grace to thank God for their Christmas. After the grace, his eye caught Betty's and they both knew what they were thankful for.

The children did not know they were poor.

VII

The confluence of three great social upheavals in the late fifties hastened the demise of the community one-room school house: the desegregation of the public school after 1954, the continuing cold war and red scare, and the launch of Sputnik in 1957. A fear of Russian domination initiated efforts to improve education in general and science education in particular. The federal government realized the enormous discrepancies in the breadth and rigor of subjects in different schools lent a sense of urgency to consolidate smaller community schools into large centralized schools. State legislatures and school boards thought that larger schools would be more cost effective in the long run, so they restructured a two hundred year old system to fit their new vision of public education.

One by one, old one-room school houses around the county were closed, as busses and antiquated military vehicles coursed through the remote hills and valleys to transport students to the new consolidated schools. Two large elementary schools at Rocky Branch and Big Sinking remained open, and a small modern elementary school was built at Powersburg, but by '65 all the isolated community schools were closed. Two of the old school buildings were moved into town and served as offices; one became a museum to preserve the educational history of the county, and but most were simply torn down.

The dismantling of the local schools disguised a more sinister upheaval. Educators and politicians ignored a painful truth in the naïve assumption that children from the vastly different worlds of the poor rural communities and the children living in or near the city could not be homogenized into classrooms grouped by age. Few of the people in the county could even charitably be called middle class, and there were sufficient make distinctions to make class and income levels tragically evident. Not surprisingly, at recesses or lunch, the children from particular schools flocked together like little backward coveys of quail. They attempted to form a microcosm of their world insulated from those whom they deemed better than themselves, who might pity them or patronize them as charity cases.

Emma and Rusty sat with others from their school, dining on the meals their mothers knew they could safely pack: egg and biscuit sandwiches or peanut butter and jelly. For several weeks, they withdrew from the crowd of students they did not know, but eventually an acceptance overcame even the most reticent children and small groups began to form, obscuring any lingering fears of inferiority with the exuberance of children at play.

One day, a young blond girl asked Emma to join her in a walk around the playground. "Hi, there. My name is Shelia Duncan. I'm in Mrs. York's room with you, but I forgot your name."

Emma answered softly, "Emma Troxell."

"So, do you want to walk around a while? Daddy always says you can't have too many friends."

"That would be nice. Most of the time I play with my brother Rusty over there or kids I know from my school." Quietly, she demurred "I'm too shy to meet strangers."

"Daddy says that a stranger is a friend you haven't met yet, so now we can be friends. Let's go! Tag, you're it!"

Shelia raced off, laughing at her trickery, watching as Emma hesitated before she gathered enough courage to chase her around the playground. Shelia ran to the huge swing set and launched herself into the air.

In exasperation, Emma cried, "That's not fair! I can't tag you back!"

"Sure you can, but you have to do it from a swing!"

Emma rushed to the swing adjacent to Shelia's and eventually the two girls synchronized their swings as they bubbled with the giddiness that only young children possess. The bell rang, and they ran quickly toward the building.

Shelia gasped, "That was fun. Let's do it again this afternoon."

"Okay. Let's meet at the swings before they are all taken."

Over the next few weeks both Emma and Rusty made several new friends and the uneasy divisions between castes slowly ebbed away. The seeds of friendship that Emma and Shelia had planted on that first encounter had fallen on fertile ground and they shared secret desires and fantasies of the approaching Christmas break.

One day Shelia whispered, "I heard Mrs. York and other teachers talking today about drawing names this afternoon for Christmas. Maybe we'll get each others' names."

Without thinking, Emma agreed, oblivious for the moment that her parents were too poor to afford much of a present for anyone other than family. That afternoon, Emma did indeed draw Shelia's name, but Shelia got another child's name, a boy named Charlie Hicks.

After school, the girls talked excitedly about what the search for the perfect gifts. Shelia sighed, "I guess I'll get Charlie a model car to put together. Boys always like them and that is about all you can get for under five dollars. They're so easy to please. So whose name did you get?"

"I am afraid to tell you because you might tell them."

"If I guess it, will you tell me? Did you get my name? Did you?"

Emma giggled, "You will just have to wait and see. Do you think you can wait two weeks?"

"I guess I'll have to, but I bet I find out before then."

VIII

After school Emma sat with Rusty on the bus home. Rusty had realized that his parents could not afford to exchange gifts with the city folks because they could not reciprocate in the value of gifts given. When Emma told him she got Shelia's name, he chided, "You shouldn't have drawn names. Mom says we don't have the money to spend."

Emma said, "Maybe I can give it back. I was so excited about maybe drawing my best friend's name I never thought about it. Do you think Mom and Dad will be mad?"

"Well, you can't give it back. Maybe Mom can think of something so we won't be embarrassed. I bet she can make something that Shelia might like."

Neither Emma nor Rusty said anything about her *faux pas* until supper that night. Rusty whispered barely loud enough to be heard, "Emma drew names for Christmas today at school. She got her best friend's name."

A moment of silence seized the room before her Mother said in a conciliatory tone, "Why that's wonderful, Emma. Does Shelia know you got her name?"

"I wouldn't tell her. Rusty says I shouldn't have drawn names but I forgot."

Her father interjected, "Emma, you need to realize that we're not made of money and can't buy presents for just anyone. She is Gene Duncan's girl, isn't she? You know he is a rich real estate man in town. So I don't think we can afford to buy his daughter anything she ain't already got. Can you give…"

Mom stopped him before he could finish. "Maybe we can make her something that she can't buy anywhere else. Do you know what she likes?"

Emma bit her lip. "I know she likes dolls. She brings a lot of different ones to school all the time. She likes ponies. And jewelry."

Dad harrumphed, "Well, we can't buy no pony or jewelry she ain't got already. Guess between us we can come up with something she can't get anywhere else. I won't let my daughter be embarrassed just because we ain't rich."

Mom sat up straight suddenly, beaming with the smile of discovery. "Emma, if Shelia likes dolls so much, we can make her some dolls that I bet she ain't got none like. We'll get started after supper. Robert, do you still have that cigar box?"

"I still have it. Just put a few nails in it but it I still clean on the inside. What do you want it for? I thought you was making dolls."

"Well, we are, but we're going to surprise everyone. Can you get a couple of strawberry baskets from Burton's barn tomorrow? Try to get ones that ain't dirty. Now, Randy, sometime tomorrow I want you to go to Thelma Coffey's and see if she can give you some quilt scraps of pretty cloth. The color don't matter, but if she has some fancy stuff like velvet or satin, tell her I'll trade her a dozen eggs for them. I have some leftover sweet corn seeds and butter beans, but ask her if she has some different kinds of seeds. Different colors and shapes and sizes like Indian corn and kidney beans. Anything real colorful. Just tell her we need this stuff for a school project and we'll make it up to her or pay her for them later."

She turned to Emma and said, "Now, you bring some glue home from school tomorrow and we can get started. We'll get it finished by the Christmas break."

IX

Thelma was all too happy to help out with the project and sent several scraps of satin and velvet in bright colors as well as various kinds of brightly colored seeds and embroidery thread. She smiled as she sent Rusty off and said, "Just be sure to tell your mom I want to see it when she's finished. It sounds like she has something pretty in mind."

Rusty replied, "Thank you, Ms. Brown. I'll tell mom you want to see it. I'm sorta curious what she has in mind."

After they had cleaned up the supper dishes, Mom gathered up the materials she had assembled and sat Emma down at the table. "Now sort these seeds out by color and size. Then we will make a design for the box and glue these seeds onto it."

Emma quickly sorted the seeds out and tried to think of a design she thought Shelia would like. "I wish I could make a pony, but I can't draw good enough."

Mom smiled and said, "Why don't you just make pretty curlicues and star shapes on it and write her name in these red kidney beans? That would make it personal just for her."

"That would be really neat."

Emma's mother and brothers labored over the next few nights to make her mother's vision a reality. Her mother often hummed Christmas carols while she sewed the bits of cloth into robes intended for the mysterious figures whose identities only she knew. Finally, three days before the Christmas break, Emma came home to find the finished present sitting on the table: a Nativity scene complete with clothespins wrapped in rich velvet and satin for the Magi, broadcloth robes for the holy family and rough wool blanket strips for the shepherds. The cigar box opened to reveal a stable scene in which to pose the scene and it doubled for a storage box as well. The strawberry baskets had been transformed into a small manger for the sawed-off clothespin that was the baby Jesus. There were even three angels with paper wings floating above the stable as they wavered on their straight pin supports.

Emma's eyes teared up, overcome with the emotion of how such everyday objects could be made into something so beautiful. "Oh, Mom, this is so beautiful! I almost want to keep it for myself but I know it will be something very special for Shelia. Can we make one for me sometime?"

Mom nodded and smiled, "Why, of course we can. Maybe not this year, but maybe next year. We can have a whole year to gather stuff together and we can use it every Christmas. Now let's wrap this in a pretty paper and put a bow on it so it will be all ready for Friday."

X

Emma could barely contain herself at school thinking about how everyone would be envious of Shelia's present. She struggled to keep the secret at school but went on and on about it at home. On the Friday before break, she was up early, anxious to have her day of triumph for giving the most beautiful gift. She had not even thought much about who got her name or what they might be giving her for a present, but she knew in her heart that nothing could match the gift she was giving.

The school was abuzz with holiday excitement and cheer as the children placed their gifts under the scraggly cedar tree adorned with a puny string of lights, chains of garland made from links of construction paper, and a tinfoil star. Some packages were large, others small but Mrs. York had made no attempt to disguise the small boxes of candy that she would give to each child. By the end of the day the excitement boiled over into the pandemonium only children can bring to Christmas and, one by one, Mrs. York called out the names on the tags — both who the gifts were for and who had given them. She came to Emma's present early "To Emma Troxell from Sara Vaughn." Emma raced to the tree to get her gift and then to Sara, a quiet little girl to thank her.

"Sara, this is a beautiful wrapping. I think I will save the paper to use at home. Would you mind?"

"Why of course not," Sara replied softly.

Emma began to unwrap the present carefully to avoid unnecessary tears. When the last fold of paper fell away, a gorgeous blue-eyed doll with brunette hair appeared, dressed in a plaid dress with golden threads running through it.

"Oh, she is beautiful! She is the prettiest doll I have ever seen. I have never had one this fancy."

Sara bubbled, "Take her out of the package and pick her up."

When Emma took the doll from the box, the doll cried "Mama" bringing a wide beaming smile to Emma's face.

"She can even talk! This is the best present I've ever had!"

While the girls chatted about the doll, Mrs. York continued to pass out presents. Emma's ears perked up when she heard her say, "To Shelia Duncan from Emma Troxell." Immediately, Emma shifted her focus and walked over to stand next to Shelia while she opened the present."

"I hope you like it, Shelia. Mom helped me make it just for you."

"I am sure it will be very wonderful," Shelia replied as the last scraps of paper fell away. A quizzical look crossed her face when she saw the seed covered box with her name on it.

"Open it! Open it!" Emma cried.

Shelia opened the box to see the little figures inside.

"It is a little nativity scene. Let's set it up to see how it looks."

Shelia replied, "Emma this is beautiful! I have never got a handmade present before. It must have taken a long time to make."

Emma smiled in triumph, "Oh, my whole family worked on it, but it was mostly my mom. Do you like really it?"

"Why, who wouldn't like something this special? Here, let's set it up. Oh, I see! The box becomes the stable! That is so neat!"

They anxiously positioned the little dolls in front of the open box and stood back to admire the scene.

"Emma, this is so nice! Wait till my folks see this!" Shelia hugged Emma and said, "Thank you so much!"

A group of boys sauntered over to see why Shelia was so excited.

Timmy York cried out, "Hey, everybody look at this old box covered in seeds that Emma gave Shelia! Is this corny or what?"

In a twinkling, several of the children gathered around the girls giggling and pointing to the present. Emma began to shrink away blushing at their teasing.

Timmy snorted, "Maybe we should call Emma 'Seed Girl?' Seed girl! Seed girl!"

Some of the kids picked up the chorus until Mrs. York came over to quiet them down. Both Shelia and Emma were red-faced, one from the ridicule of the present she had worked on so long, the other out of how to respond to such mean-spiritedness.

Mrs. York looked at the scene and said quietly, "Why, I think this is a wonderful gift. This is something you can't buy anywhere. Shelia you are so lucky to have a friend who thought enough of you to make this for you."

Timmy continued his merciless taunting, "Seed girl, seed girl worst present in the world!"

Emma began to cry. Mrs. York looked at Timmy and said "Timmy! That will be enough. You have hurt Emma's feelings. The value of a gift is not how much it cost but what you want it to mean to the person you gave it to. Anybody can buy a store-bought present, but nobody else can have a present like this."

The children turned quiet at their teacher's conciliatory comments, but when school dismissed, some of them shouted at Emma, "Seed girl, Seed girl!"

Chagrined beyond measure, Emma sobbed from embarrassment all the way home, despite her brothers' efforts to cheer her up.

"Emma, don't you tell Mom about the kids teasing you. Shelia really liked it, so just tell her that. It would hurt Mom's feelings to hear about the other stuff. Quit crying so Mom won't know anything. Now you see why we should not draw names. We can't give nice presents like them city kids."

Emma struggled to quell her tears, wiping her face with her sleeve. She had indeed learned why she should not draw names when any gift she could afford to give could never match the store-bought gifts that the wealthier kids expected.

More importantly, she had learned her place in the world.

XI

A person's entire life may well turn on a single event. In the succeeding years, Emma did not draw names again but she still had to endure the teasing from the kids who knew what had happened. Little by little, the teasing subsided but little by little Emma began to lose interest in school. She and Shelia remained best friends, but she occasionally felt a guardedness that was not there when they first met. From time to time, Shelia would comment on how she showed the gift to relatives visiting from out of town, but sensing that such comments seemed insincere, she eventually quit saying anything at all.

As she entered eighth grade, Emma's absences had caused her to fall behind so she was not promoted to high school. Realizing that she would not see Shelia every day, she dropped out of school. Hard times had befallen her family, so she helped out by working in the tobacco fields or, later, the tomato and pepper fields that the state had introduced to farmers to reduce their dependence on tobacco. The everyday exposure to the sun's relentless rays gradually turned her skin to a deep leathery tan and the hard work left her rail-thin with a hank of sun-bleached light brown hair.

By the time she was sixteen her hope of improving her station in life lay in marriage to a man with a steady income that reliance on the vagaries of weather and the agrarian way of life did not threaten. Her brothers and indeed most of the men, near Emma's age had moved north to the booming states with heavy industry and the high wages of automobile production. Torn between marrying a man intent on following the exodus north and the sense of obligation to remain near her parents, whose health had deteriorated from the years of endless and fruitless toil and their ignorant exposure to agricultural chemicals, she finally agreed to marry Bob Vaughn, a logger for Grissom and Rakestraw, a local sawmill. The only benefit Vaughn's job offered was the advantage of constant income instead of the episodic ebb and flow of a farm-based lifestyle.

To spare the humiliation of not having even a modestly respectful wedding, the couple eloped to Jamestown, Tennessee for a slapdash ceremony performed by a justice of the peace. They returned to Bob's simple home at Mount Pisgah twenty five miles and worlds away from the only town in the county. Five years later, Eugene and Aliceann, tied Emma to the obligations of motherhood and the struggle to make ends meet on an income that hovered only marginally above poverty level.

Her marriage to Bob was not unhappy, but Bob's taciturn nature kept the communication between man and wife at a minimum: there were no 'I love you's' exchanged, for Bob assumed that his providing them with food and shelter was sufficient evidence of his love. Sexual intimacy amounted to little more than Emma's performing her "wifely duties."

She found her real pleasure and, for that matter, treasure, in her children. Between the daily tedium of housekeeping and the monotony of cooking their rough fare, she managed to steal time each day to enjoy their innocence and inquisitive natures.

"Mommy, why are trees so big?"

"Because they are so old and have been growing for a long time."

"Why are bugs so small?"

"So they can hide from the birds who want to eat them."

"Why do birds want to eat them? I bet they are not very good."

"Maybe not to us, but to birds they are good as our chicken and corn."

Between these curious dialogues, and sometimes during them, she took time each day to push them in the swing Bob had made from a smooth oak board nailed to a rough hemp rope hung from the lowest branch of the walnut tree in the back yard. In these moments of her children's blissful and trusting glee, Emma found herself reminiscing about her days swinging with Shelia in the schoolyard swings. She had long since lost contact with Shelia, now a registered nurse at the local hospital. The isolation of her life so far from town did not allow their worlds to intersect. She missed those school days and rued her decision to drop out of school, wondering if a high school diploma would have guaranteed her a better position in life, with more money and a better home — maybe even an educated husband, whom she could not love any more than she did Bob, but who might possess the advantage of conversation with her.

By the time the children could walk and talk, Emma found herself thinking more and more about their schooling and that awakened the specter of her embarrassment when she assumed a homemade gift would be valued in a society where even children paid homage to the god of rampant consumerism and one-upmanship. She was determined that her children would be spared that shame.

XII

In middle America grandparents often lavished affection and gifts with the express purpose of spoiling children they were not responsible for rearing, but Eugene and Aliceann did not have that luxury. Bob's parents had died in a car crash before he and Emma were married and now Emma's parents struggled to get by on their meager Social Security checks and wages earned in doing odd jobs. Neither Emma nor Rusty had told her mother of the reaction to the gift she gave Shelia, but on the twins' sixth birthday in July, celebrated by a simple one layer cake and candles, she decided to seek her mother's advice.

After the children had made a wish and blown out the candles, Emma found an opportunity to talk with her mother alone after the men had retired to the white oak shade tree in the rear of the house to talk and whittle.

"Mom, do you remember the special gift you helped me make for Shelia Duncan when I was in grade school?"

Betty leaned over with her elbow on the table. "You mean the little nativity scene we made? Land's sake, I had nearly forgotten about that. My mind ain't what it used to be, you know. Seems like we used some seeds to decorate it, but I can't recall much else about it. Why do you want to know?"

Emma stammered, "Oh, no particular reason. You know the kids will be starting school next year and it's times like these makes you remember things from a long time ago."

A brief pall passed over Betty's face and a bittersweet smile curled the corners of her mouth, "You know I was so embarrassed that we couldn't afford to buy your little friend a store-bought gift, but we just didn't have the money."

Emma patted her arm softly, "That's okay Mom, you did the best you could and that was more than enough. Still times are different these days. You know the kids will start school in August and I was wondering if you can help me think of a way to make some extra money so we can buy some gifts for Christmas if they still draw names."

"Oh, I expect they still do, kids being kids and all. Gee, honey, I don't know. I am not much help I am afraid. Bob needs the car to drive to work and you really need to be there for your kids as much as you can be and keep the fires burning on the home front so to speak. Maybe there is something you can do at home to make a little. I used to do a little ironing for people while you were at school. Is there anybody out your way who still irons clothes but don't have the time to do it?"

Emma bit her lip in concentration. "There's some teachers live out near Pisgah. I bet they could afford to pay me something after school starts."

"I bet you they would too. Teachers have to look so neat and all. Now when I was doing it, I charged by the size of the load but some people I know charged so much for each piece. You know you might have to do both depending on the teacher. And make sure they pay you in cash. Easier to do than checks especially when you don't get to town much. And you better keep some kind of record of what you make."

She paused, dropping her head before resuming in a quavering, rueful voice, "Honey, I know what happened with Shelia's present. Some of the kids in the neighborhood had told their moms about the mean things kids said about you and they told me. I am sorry that we could not have provided you with a better present to give your friend, but we just didn't have the money. I guess you was too young to understand that then and I hope you understand now that we did the best we could. I didn't mean to shame you."

Emma felt tears streaming down her face as she stood up abruptly and hugged her mom closer. "Oh, Mom, you don't need to apologize. I was so proud of that present you helped me make. I look back at how some of the other kids made fun of me and I am even more grateful that you and dad raised me to never make fun of anyone else. I look back at all that and I really can't say if Shelia really liked it or not but at least she never let on. I was never ashamed of you and never will be. I was so proud of that present and I thought we were going to make me one as well but never did. But now that I see you knew all along you can understand that I don't want my kids to be put in the same spot."

The two women embraced each other, crying softly, their bodies heaving as they freed themselves of burdens they had carried in pain and regret for so many years. As they wiped away each other's tears, Emma whispered, "You know what, Mom? Maybe I don't give the best presents, but I know I got the best present a girl can have: the best mom in the world. I love you Mom. More than you know."

XIII

Two weeks before school started, Emma placed a radio ad on the Trading Post where people sold goods or offered their services.

'Will do ironing in my home. Will work by the piece or by the load. Call Emma Vaughn at Mt. Pisgah 348-5678.'

The ad would run free of charge for a week, but by the time school had started two teachers and a traveling salesman had already called Emma and negotiated prices. Emma asked them to bring their first loads after school started.

She rode the bus into town on the opening day of school to enroll Eugene and Aliceann into first grade and to see they were with the same teacher. While she was waiting in the line with a child tugging at each hand, she heard some one say, "Emma? Is that you, Emma?"

Turning to see who called her name, it took a few seconds before she recognized the woman. "Shelia? My God, it is you!" The women fell into each other's arms at once laughing and crying at their unlikely reunion.

Shelia gasped, "You know, I always wondered what happened with you, but once you leave school it is hard to keep those connections. I don't know if you knew this, but after college I moved up to Louisville for twelve years working in Community East Hospital. My husband just took a job here managing the cable factory two months ago and I took the job as head nurse in the Hospital here. My God, how many years has it been?"

Emma smiled, shaking her head in ignorance of the passage of time, "Gee, Shelia, I don't know. These two here are my twins. Eugene and Aliceann. I am putting them in first grade and I want them to be in the same room. Is that your little boy?"

"Where are my manners? Yep, that is little Jackson. I named him after his daddy, Jack Coffey. So who did you marry? Where do you live?"

"I married Bob Vaughn. We live way out yonder past Mt. Pisgah. We have about three acres, enough for a garden and room for the kids to run around in. Bob works for Grissom and Rakestraw Lumber Company. Your boy is awfully cute. He has your eyes."

"Yeah, that's what everybody says. Makes it hard for me to see though." Shelia grinned mischievously at her joke. "Your kids remind me of you when you were young. You know in a general way. Maybe it is the eyes. Or the smile."

Seeing that Emma was feeling self conscious, Shelia changed the subject, "I hope we can get our kids in the same room. Maybe then we might have more opportunities to se each other. You know PTA open houses and such."

Emma nodded, knowing that the chances of her making it to open house were slim to none. "That would be good, wouldn't it?"

Shelia's face brightened as she whispered, "Wait here. I see someone I know that might could help us out." She squeezed her way through the crowd, whispered to a tall well-dressed woman standing near the registration line and pulled her aside. Emma could see them talking, occasionally glancing her way before

Shelia thanked the woman, patted her on the shoulder and began to wind her way back.

"Don't worry. I explained the situation to Mrs. Walker. She's the principal here. Dad sold her a house when I was in high school. We are all set."

Emma's face reddened even more before she replied almost inaudibly, " Thank you, Shelia. I am too shy I guess to do something like that, but you were always pretty outspoken."

The principal motioned for them to join her. They made their way over to talk to her.

Mrs. Walker said quietly, "You must be Mrs. Vaughn. I am glad to meet you. Looks like you have a handful there. Are they twins?"

"Yes, they are. That is why I want them to be with the same teacher. This is Eugene and Aliceann. I really appreciate your help."

"That's no problem. We just want the children to be successful and if that helps them, we will be glad to help out. We are putting your children and Jack in Mrs. Cooper's room. That's room 103. Let me show you where it is. Follow me."

After the children settled in, Shelia asked Emma, "So, what are you doing the rest of the day? Going back home?"

"No, I can't drive. I thought I would just stay here and ride the bus back home with the kids, it being their first day and all."

"I am sure they will be fine. I can call the hospital and explain to them that I have to deal with a situation and will be a little late, so I can give you a ride home. That sound okay?"

"No, that's too much trouble. I will just wait. I can probably read some books in the library. Wonder if they still have some of the same books as when we were here."

"Well, I thought I would offer. I am sure they do. I have to go to work. Here's my card. Call me if I can do anything to help."

Feeling awkward, Emma said, "Do you have a pencil? I can give you my number."

"Sure, wait a sec. Okay, go for it."

"348-5678. It's listed under Bob Vaughn in the book."

"Emma, it is so good to see you again. Let's try to keep in touch better. Gotta run. Take care."

"Bye, and thanks again."

XIV

By Wednesday of that week, Wanda Twyford brought the first load of clothes by for Emma to iron. She knocked on the outer screen door and waited for Emma to answer.

"Hi, are you Emma Vaughn?"

"Yes. I guess you're Mrs. Twyford."

"That's me. I met your children yesterday at recess. Fine looking kids. My room is right across from Mrs. Cooper's room. Here, let me get the clothes."

She trotted to her car and returned with a large wicker basket of rumpled clothes that she sat down by the door.

"How do you charge? By the piece or by the load?"

"Whichever you want."

"You know there are a lot of clothes there, I got behind getting ready for school. Let's say twenty dollars for the load. We can always change it later if we need to. Oh, just use enough starch on my husband's shirts to make them look nice and crisp. He claims that too much starch makes him itch."

"I have a can of light starch I can use. When do you want to pick them up?"

"Can you have them done by Friday? I just live about two miles from here. I am so glad to find someone so close by who can do this for me."

"That should be no problem. Did you bring hangers? I don't have any extra ones."

"Oh yeah, I put them in the bottom of the basket. I figured you would probably sort the clothes into shirts and pants and so on. Would you prefer having them on top of the pile?"

"I guess it might make it a little easier."

"Okay, I will see you Friday. I think it best if I pay in cash. Is that okay with you?"

"That would be great. I will see you Friday."

After Twyford left, Emma got out her ironing board, iron, and starch to begin. She laid a broom handle between two chairs to hold the clothes after she had ironed them. She dumped the basket onto the couch, retrieved the hangers and began to iron, humming old hymns as she worked. By the time the children got home, she had finished the job and hung the clothes in a closet by the door.

Eugene and Aliceann were giddy with excitement, full of stories of their first day at school.

Eugene said breathlessly, "Oh, Mom, they have such a wonderful playground. The biggest swing set I have ever seen! I could swing so high it was like I was flying!"

Aliceann added, "And the longest slide. Smooth metal with no splinters. And we colored pictures and played games learning each other's names. A boy named Jack told us that you and his mother went to school once."

Emma smiled, "Yeah, his mother and I were best friends for eight years. She helped me get you into the same room. Maybe you and Jack can be friends like we were."

After they changed their good clothes into play clothes, the kids ran outside to play. Emma watched them through the screen door before she turned away to fix supper.

So Emma's life settled into a new and welcome routine: iron clothes during the day and listen to her children's school stories at night. She had discussed her ironing job with Bob, explaining what had happened to her when she was a child. He agreed that he did not want his children feeling ashamed of their poverty nor be recipients of charity if Emma's ironing job could circumvent those two alternatives. He even noticed that Emma seemed happier now that she had fixed her eyes on a goal that offered her purpose other than the drudgery of being a rural housewife and mother. Little by little, her earnings from her ironing grew into a sizable income, enough to afford other things around the house that they could not have on Bob's salary alone.

As the year wore on toward the Christmas season, Emma felt a sense of anticipation and, perhaps, even pride that she could spare her children the pain she endured a child. But her joy ended when her mother died suddenly in late October. She had come to realize and grudgingly accept the mortality of her father as he labored to breathe under the yoke of emphysema and lung cancer brought on by years of smoking, but she was completely blindsided by her mother's passing from a stroke. She sank into a deep depression, not because she had to use part of the money she had earned to help pay her mother's funeral expenses for she still had enough for the children's Christmas presents, but the loss of the woman who had always been a wellspring of hope sapped her of the newfound joy she had found in life. She found herself taking longer to iron the clothes as she surrendered to an overwhelming urge to cry.

Her grief took a respite when Eugene and Aliceann came home frenzied with joy and announced that they were going to draw names to exchange Christmas presents with their classmates. She and Bob joined their celebration because of Emma's hard work, their children would participate in the seasonal ritual that brought a sense of joy to everyone.

In her heart, Emma prayed that one of the kids would get Jack's name so perhaps she could earn a second chance to demonstrate by proxy the affection she had for Sheila, but Eugene drew Ricky Roberts's name and Aliceann drew Earlene Foster's name. Her hopes of somehow salvaging a lost opportunity were dashed. The only compensation would be to hide her children's poverty.

She and Bob took the kids into town to McWhorter's Variety Store where Eugene bought a set of die-cast metal construction vehicles and Aliceann chose a Barbie doll and accessories. Emma let them pick out the paper they wanted to wrap the gifts in and by the Monday before Christmas break, the gifts were ready to go.

XV

On Tuesday of that week Emma saw her moment of fulfillment yanked away; her children contracted chicken pox. They would not be able to return to school until after the Christmas break. Though she tried to console her children's tears by reminding them that they would just have to delay the gift exchange until after New Year's, she found herself choking with a sense of frustration at the dissolution of the plans she had worked so hard to realize.

Wednesday night the phone rang after the children had gone to sleep.

"Hi, Emma? This is Shelia. I just heard that your kids have the chicken pox and can't come to school the rest of the week. I called Mrs. Cooper and she said it would be okay if I came by your house tomorrow and bring your presents to school and then bring your kids' presents back to you on Friday. Would that be okay with you?"

Emma could barely contain the sense of joy that lifted her spirits as she replied, "Oh, Shelia, this must be a gift from God Himself. I know it is a real bother for you, but it would mean so much to my kids. I would pay you for the gas."

"Oh, nonsense. I am happy to do it for you. You have enough to deal with your Mom's passing right at the holiday season. I'll come by tomorrow after I get off work. Just have a cup of coffee made for me. See ya then."

The children's spirits were buoyed a little but they were still disappointed that they would not see the expressions of the children to whom they would give gifts. True to her word, Shelia drove up about six o'clock as Emma was finishing the supper dishes. She knocked on the door and hugged Emma as she entered the house. "Oh, Emma, I know it has been hard for you and I want to apologize for not coming to your Mom's funeral, but I had to be in California for a week-long training program. Did you get the flowers we sent?"

Emma released her and said, "Yes, they were so beautiful. You had explained in your card that you would not be able to make it in person, but you would be here in spirit. You have always been so kind to me, Shelia. I don't know how I will ever repay your kindness."

"Who said you have to? That's what friends are for. We all need others' help sometimes and I am just sorry I couldn't do more. Now, where are the kids?"

Eugene and Aliceann ran over to meet her gave her the presents to deliver for them. Aliceann said, "Oh, Ms. Shelia, we are so grateful that you can do this for us. Will you be able to tell us how the kids liked them?"

"Well I can certainly try. Now, Emma, where is that cup of coffee?"

The women and the kids sat around the table talking. "Where's Bob?" Shelia asked.

"He went up on the mountain after supper to get a Christmas tree. after supper. He shouldn't be gone long if you want to wait."

"I would like to do that but I have to get back. This is good coffee. I will bring your presents tomorrow, kids. Now hurry and get well."

Eugene asked, " Did Jack get my name or Aliceann's?"

Shelia made a face and shrugged, "Guess we will just have to wait and see won't we?"

With that, she ducked out the door and drove off.

The kids were dancing with excitement by the time Shelia returned on Friday evening. She was carrying a large shopping bag with presents sticking out the top. The kids raced to hold the door for her. "Hi, Ms. Shelia. Thank you for bringing us the presents! Did Bobby and Earlene like theirs?"

"They LOVED them. Ricky pretty much had a whole new school built by the time school let out and Earlene was showing off all the new clothes she could put on Barbie. You did good, kids."

She winked at Emma, "Now it's your turn. Eugene, this is from Jack.

Aliceann, this is from Valerie Piercy. Here you go."

She and Emma watched as the kids tore open the packages. Jack had given Eugene a battery-powered train set and Valerie had bought a doll that talked when you pulled her string.

"Oh, Ms. Shelia, thank you, thank you, thank you! These are the best presents ever!" the kids chorused before running off to play.

Shelia sat he bag on the table as she pulled up a chair. "Got any of that coffee left, Emma?"

"We always have coffee around here. Glad you take it black."

"That's the way God made it. Have a seat. Got your tree up yet?"

"Not yet. We are doing that tomorrow morning. It's Saturday so we can take our time. Thanks again, Shelia."

"My pleasure. Oh, by the way, I brought you a present, so shut your eyes."

Emma feigned surprise and shut her eyes.

Shelia said softly, "Open them."

A beautifully wrapped box lay before her on the table. "Well, go ahead and open it. I know it's not Christmas, but you're allowed."

Emma slit the tape with a knife and unfolded the paper to reveal a plain brown cardboard box. She took the lid off and gasped aloud as she pulled out the contents: It was the seed covered box she had given Shelia so many years ago. She sat slack jawed, crying as memories washed over her.

Shelia said, "I think it's mostly there. I lost one of the shepherds somewhere. The lid to the cigar box tore lose and a few seeds are missing. But I have really enjoyed it over the years and I thought you might like to have it back to remember your Mom by."

Emma sat speechless, catching her breaths in fits and starts. She looked into Shelia's eyes and tearfully whispered, "Thank you", and, laughing joyously, they fell into each other arms, two little girls again, swinging wild and free in their innocence.

To Whom Much Is Given

SNOWFLAKES FLITTED ACROSS the cold windshield of Mike Thompson's car as he turned his ramshackle Ford Granada into the cul-de-sac where his coworkers at the Good As New Car Wash lived with their families. Neither Jose Garcia nor Quentin Marksberry owned a car that actually would run reliably, so his friends depended on Mike for transportation, and gave him gas money in exchange. This arrangement illustrated the glue that held the projects together, in spite of the divisive forces of race and ethnicity that tore many neighborhoods apart. Everybody here needed something: better food, rent money, medical care, money for toys for Christmas or just time to relax and not worry about all the things they needed.

Mike swung his car parallel to the curb and tooted the horn with the "Shave and Haircut-Two Bits" jingle he used to call Jose and Quentin while he sat waiting in the warm car. A few strings of multicolored Christmas lights dangled in the soft morning wind. The big bulbs, long since banished from the ritzier neighborhoods, found safe havens in the projects, where they filled the children's eyes with delightful visions of presents in bright paper and ribbons. As he watched the glowing strings, he wondered if he could afford to buy a set of lights to decorate a tree for his two small sons. He had scavenged an artificial tree from the curb in a wealthier part of town and had a few ornaments from Goodwill, but his twin sons were now four years old and had started to ask why their tree never had lights. Perhaps this year the owner of the car wash would give them a Christmas bonus this year that would allow him to buy Christmas tree lights.

He thought of the big bulb lights on the Christmas trees of his youth in his hometown of Monticello. Life there had been hard; the town was located in the foothills of the Cumberland Mountains where families living a rural lifestyle struggled to survive just above the poverty level. Discouraged by bleak economic prospects, many young people abandoned their hometowns and moved north to earn higher wages in the manufacturing plants of big industrial cities in Indiana, Ohio, and Michigan.

But the collapse and outsourcing of the manufacturing economy forced many into unemployment and they had to scramble to earn any wages at all. Fortunately, Mike and two of his friends from the Chrysler plant had found work in a car wash and had languished there for several months, hoping that a better job would turn up soon.

Mike said to himself "Maybe I should just chuck all this and move back home. At least, there I have family and the cost of living is lower. I want something better for my kids than what I had and if I move back, that ain't going to happen, but I don't know how much longer we can make it here."

He heard voices and watched as the doors to the second floor apartments on either side of the street opened, pouring forth a weak yellowish light that silhouetted Jose's wife, Brenda, and Quentin's wife, Tonya, waving good-bye before they shut the door. The men bolted down the stairs, racing to the car where they jostled good-naturedly for the front seat where the heater was strongest. Finally, Quentin slid in beside Mike and Jose piled into the back seat.

"Mike, my man! Give me some skin!" cried Quentin, exchanging a brief slap of hands.

"Leave the man alone, Quentin. Can't you see the man is trying to sleep?" responded Jose. "How you doing today, Mike? Three more days till Christmas and an extra day off."

Mike nodded thoughtfully. "Yeah, but I could use the overtime if they would pay us. Weatherman says we are getting a big snow heading this way. You know what that means."

Quentin chimed, "Yeah, close early one day; make up for the next when it's colder. There has to be an easier way to make living, guys."

Jose snorted, "Yeah, buy lottery tickets, win a gazillion bucks and retire!"

As the car returned to the street, they all laughed at Jose's pipe dream because they all knew that each one of them harbored the same hope. The sounds of their shivering *brrrr* could be heard as they fell silent, calculating how much a gazillion dollars is.

Mike said quietly, "You know, guys, up until now, I sorta got used to giving the boys presents from the Salvation Army, or one donated to the church, but I really would like to have lights on the tree this year."

Quentin nodded. "The old lady got a string of lights on sale last year, but we ain't got no star for the top of the tree. When we put the tree up last week, my daughter, Shania asked me why our tree don't have a star. I told her that was going to be our present for the tree this year."

Jose said, "My wife found this little ceramic angel at a yard sale last summer that has a light bulb in it. She brought it home and the damned bulb is burnt out. I can't find one to fit it anywhere."

The radio crackled out a weather bulletin about a snowstorm by late afternoon, before it returned to Perry Como and Bing Crosby crooning Christmas carols. The flurries had stopped by the time they reached the car wash, but the leaden clouds that filled the early morning sky hung ominously over the city like a cat waiting to pounce on its prey. After Mike parked the car and they went to office to clock in for the day, pulling on fingerless gloves as they went. The owner, Randy Donnelly, sat behind his desk, furiously punching numbers into a calculator, stopping only briefly to see who had entered before he hurriedly finished his task while the men stood warming themselves by the heat register. He pushed himself out from the desk and joined the men.

"Morning, fellas. You'd better start the fire in that barrel as soon as you go out today. Them gloves you're wearing ain't going to do you much good today and it is going to get colder.

"By the way, I've got good news and bad news for you guys. The bad news is that your other three coworkers got arrested last night for public intoxication and won't be working here anymore. The good news is that all the tips today are split three ways, not six. You know you can come in and warm up when we don't have any customers, but try to spend some time outside so people will know we are open."

Quentin nodded. "No problem, Mr. D. You get used to the cold after a while anyway. I just hope we don't have enough snow to close down for a day because we need the money for Christmas."

"Well, you know these weathermen, always claiming the sky is falling. If we close, I can advance you enough money from next week's check to buy a presents and a good meal on Christmas. Well, I am doing year-end reports and you boys need to get that fire barrel started. Stay warm."

"You betcha, boss," Quentin said as the men left the office. They to started the fire and waited for it to flare up to keep them warm their. Intermittently, they darted out to pick up litter from the paved lanes leading into the carwash. The men took turns driving cars through the automated wash, but all three worked quickly to dry the car before thin sheets of ice glazed the windshields. Irregular fingers of ice began to creep out of the carwash exit and occasionally they would slip and fall. Most customers dropped a couple of dollars into the Plexiglas tip box when they picked up their cars, but a few just forgot as they just drove back into the Christmas traffic.

The line of cars slowed to a mere trickle by noon. The winds died down, but more snowflakes soon obscured the tracks made by the cars and the men's footprints. Heavy snow reduced visibility and traction causing some cars on the street to collide in fender-benders but no real injuries. Twice the police came over to see if any of the men had seen the accident in question.

As the snow deepened and drivers stopped getting a wash, Randy closed the wash for the day and gave each of them an envelope containing a Christmas bonus of fifty dollars. He pulled alongside the barrel and said, "You guys go on home. We'll open at ten tomorrow," he said.

A black Mercedes sedan crept into the service lanes around one thirty. A spry little man with wire rim glasses got out of the car as Mike walked over to greet him.

"Are you open for business?" the man asked.

"For about another thirty minutes, sir," Mike replied. "Are you sure you want to waste your time and money getting your car washed today? I mean a black car and all will really show the salt."

"As best I can tell, they haven't started spreading salt yet and I only live a few blocks away. I get the car washed every day, but I have not been satisfied the last two times at the other place, so I thought I would give you fellas a go," the man replied.

Suddenly, the man sneezed hard enough to lose his glasses onto the concrete. Mike picked the glasses up from the dirty snow and handed them back to their owner who wiped the lenses clean with a handkerchief. The man hooked the glasses over his ears so that the frames sat atop a raised whitish scar below his right eye.

"Thank you kindly, sonny. Sometimes these damned things are a nuisance, but after sixty years I can't get by without them. See that scar? I can tell when it is going to snow when that thing tingles a certain way. Say, what's your name?" the man asked as he removed the glove from his right hand to shake Mike's hand.

"Mike Thompson," Mike replied, shaking the man's hand firmly, noticing the large diamond ring on his hand.

"Ronnie Strickland, Mr. Thompson. Can you wash my car before you close?"

"I'll drive the car through while you wait inside, Mr. Strickland."

"Actually, I think I'll stand out there by your fire barrel and chat with you guys stout enough to brave this weather."

Mike placed a paper mat in the driver's side floorboard, stomped the snow from his feet and slowly guided the sedan through the car wash. In a few minutes he emerged to find Strickland laughing with Quentin and Jose. He joined them and the three of them quickly completed the job.

Strickland walked past the tip box, shoving a bill into it as he came to reclaim the car. "I guess you were right that getting the car washed was pretty foolish," he said with a twinkle in his eye, "but then I have been known to do some foolish things. Besides, I'll have a laugh when I tell my brother. It'll really piss him off! You guys have a Merry Christmas and a Happy New Year. I'll be out of town for a few days, but I'll be back here when I get back."

Still waving good-bye, Strickland inched the Mercedes into the street. Quentin blocked the entrance with a huge CLOSED sign. Mike grabbed the tip box and tromped back into the warm office where he dumped the money onto the table.

"Wow," laughed Quentin, "twelve bills! That's four apiece! Who says there ain't no Santa Claus?"

Mike separated the bills by denomination as the other giggled. The men stopped laughing when Mike unfurled a bill with 1000 in its four corners. They stood there numbed by the presence of so large a bill before Mike gave low whistle.

"Holy shit!" said Quentin, "Where did *that* come from?"

Mike swallowed hard and replied, "Quit the bullshitting! We all know where it came from. The question is, did he do it by mistake. He was pretty old and he did just drop his glasses."

"Wait a minute," Jose interrupted, "Didn't he say that he liked to do things just to piss his brother off? From the looks of that card and that diamond ring he had on, I'd say he could afford to lose a thou or two and never even think about it. Looks like Christmas came early for us, boys."

"Amen, brother!" cried Quentin, " Toys R Us, here I come!"

Mike slapped the table loudly. "Guys, think! That old man was old but he wasn't stupid. Suppose he remembers where he dropped this bill and comes back to get it. Meantime we have spent it and we're up shit creek if he comes back to get it. We could do jail time or lose our jobs. Who is going to believe us peons earned that money honestly? I say we try to return it to him and hope for a reward or at least a clear conscience."

The three fell silent, knitting their brows and wrestling with what to do. Quentin spoke hesitantly, "How we gonna get it back to him? Anybody know his name?"

Mike said in a dry whisper, "All I heard was Strickland. What about you, Jose?"

Jose shook his head, "I can't remember his first name. Let's check the phone book."

Quentin laughed, "Ain't nobody living in that kind of luxury gonna have a listed number."

Mike was already leafing through the telephone, running his finger down the pages until he found the first listing for Strickland. "Looks like there's one, two…eight Stricklands here. How are we gonna do this? Call up and ask "Did you leave a thousand dollar bill at the car wash?"

After a spell of laughter, Mike said, "We call up and casually ask to speak to Mr. Strickland. If he answers we ask "Is this the Mr. Strickland who drives a black late model Mercedes who got his car washed today on Broadway? He left some important papers here and we would like to return them to him. If he ain't listed, at least we tried, so we can split the money. Who wants to call first?"

Quentin sat the phone in the center of the table, pulling the book closer to him. "Try not to sound like one of the brothers," Mike teased.

Quentin flipped him off and grinned as he dialed the phone. The men took turns dialing receiving rejections or disconnection notices until they had called all the Stricklands in the book. After he'd hung up the last call, Mike proclaimed, "Boys, I guess the money is ours barring a disaster of some kind, but we have another problem. Look around the table. Which one of us is going to sashay into a bank and get change for a thousand-dollar bill that they don't even make anymore? Besides, big bills take a few days to turn over and are tracked by banks."

Quentin and Jose quickly looked at each other and grasped Mike's point all too well: their frostbitten hands and ragtag appearance would not instill confidence in a bank teller. A check cashing service or a pawnbroker would charge an exorbitant fee. None of them had a checking account, so depositing the check in the bank would not work and no store would take such a large bill. They slumped into their chairs, trying desperately to think of a solution.

Mike leaned forward onto the table. "Say, if they don't make these anymore, I bet coin collectors would pay to get one. One of us could tell them that his grandfather left us this in a will, but we really need the hard cash now. Maybe even pay more than face value for it."

Jose shook his head, "Let's not push our luck. We sell it for face value, maybe a little more if we can. Mike, I think you have the best chance of pulling this off. No offense, Quent, but a black man or a Hispanic man with a thousand dollar bill is trouble looking to happen. Since we are opening late tomorrow, you can get it changed to smaller bills."

Quentin interjected, "Why don't we call around coin shops now so we can know where we're going and if they will exchange it? No sense running all over town when we can let our fingers do the walking."

Mike retrieved the yellow pages and flipped to the section for Coin Collectors. Six stores were listed, but the first two owners were gone for the day and the third dealer was not interested. When they called Addison's Numismatic Emporium a cheery answered, "Merry Christmas, Addison's Coin Shop, Jeff Addison speaking."

Mike responded, "Mr. Addison, my name is Michael Thompson and I have bit of a problem. My grandfather died last month and left me a thousand dollar bill. I really need the money to do some Christmas shopping but no store will take the money. I was hoping I could sell it to you at face value and get it off my hands. I am just a working Joe who can't afford to have a thousand dollar bill laying around I can't use."

"Well, well, this is interesting. You may or may not know that the government no longer prints those big bills and collectors pay a hefty price for one. Whose picture is on it?"

Mike squinted to read the bill, "Grover Cleveland."

"What picture is on the back?"

"There is no picture on the back, just the words The United States of America and One Thousand Dollars."

"Hmmm. What's above the portrait?"

"Right above Cleveland's picture? Federal Reserve Note. Is that important?"

"Since they have not printed those in decades and most people have never seen one, it really decreases the odds that it is counterfeit. I am about to close today. Can you bring it in tomorrow?"

"What time?"

"How about between nine and ten?"

"I will see you then, Mr. Addison, and thank you very much."

Mike hung up the phone and he gave the thumbs up and the three high-fived before they closed up the store and went home.

II

Mike awoke at six thirty the next day and showered and shaved. His wife had ironed his best pair of pants and a light blue shirt the night before, but he worried that his outer coat might appear too ragged, so he decided to leave it in the car. Randy called around eight to say that the car wash would open at ten thirty to give a snowplow time to clear his lot. In a few minutes, Jose and Quentin knocked on the door, excited as children at Christmas.

"Are we set, my man?" asked Quentin.

"Almost," Mike answered.

"What do you mean almost?" asked Jose.

"I need you two yahoos to dig my car out and clean the snow off of it. I'm a gentleman now and can't do such low menial labor," Mike teased.

"Yeah, right!" cried his colleagues as they began to horseplay in the kitchen. Quentin and Jose grabbed the snow shovel from the laundry room and soon cleared off the snow from around his car and made a path into the street. They had to push Mike's car out of the parking place into the street where several inches of new snow covered the road. They got into the car and Mike steered it onto the street.

He geared down to second as he crept along the nearly deserted highway. Addison's Shop was about five miles away from the car wash.

Addison was waiting for Mike in the shop.

"Good morning, Mr. Thompson, would you like a cup of coffee?"

"That would be great, but it will have to be a fast one since I have to get to work. Black is fine."

"Wonderful. I am anxious to see what you have. If it is real, it is a real rarity these days. Do you have it?"

"Sure thing. I put it in an envelope so it would not get crumpled. Here you go."

Tuttle took the envelope out of Mike's hand and gingerly slid the bill out of the envelope. He held it up to the light, turning it over and over to examine both sides.

"This is marvelous. I do have to check one thing."

He plopped a large book onto the counter and flipped through the page until he found the page he wanted. "I have to check the serial numbers to see that this bill has not been involved in a bank robbery."

After a few minutes he closed the book, smiling as he examined the bill with a magnifying glass. "Mr. Thompson, I will give you twelve hundred dollars for this bill even though you only asked face value. This bill is in mint condition. Where did your grandfather keep it?"

Mike stuttered, "I really don't know. I never knew he had it."

Addison knitted his brow before asking, "Can I give you a check?"

"Actually, I really need it in cash."

"Right, right. All I have I can spare until I go to the bank are hundreds and fifties. Is that alright?"

"That would be great. I really appreciate it."

"Oh, I want take your picture holding the bill. That is my insurance in case the bill winds up stolen recently or acquired by illegal means."

Mike started to object but agreed once he saw a shadow of doubt cross Addison's face. "All right, where do you want me to hold it?"

"About chest level facing the camera will be fine. Smile."

While Mike rubbed his eyes from the flash, Addison counted the money out and after chatting a bit, Mike left the store. He stopped by Kroger's on the way to get change for some of the hundreds so he could divide the money up evenly before hurrying back to work.

"Hey guys, we got it made!" he exclaimed to Quentin and Jose. "Got two hundred extra because it was in such good shape. We'll divide the money after work so we can shop on Christmas Eve."

The men danced for a few seconds before checking with Randy to see about closing time since only three people had come in to get the snow off their cars. Randy replied, "What the hell. Go do your Christmas shopping. See you the day after tomorrow. Have a Merry Christmas."

They thanked him and left. Though the roads had improved a little, the compacted slush made them treacherous, so Mike drove slowly, occasionally fishtailing as he turned a corner.

Quentin observed, "Randy sure is being picky about the books this year. I wonder why."

Jose frowned as he spoke, "Maybe he's about to sell the place. The books have to really honest for that."

Mike cried out, "God, I hope not. Where would we work?"

Quentin sighed, "They's other car washes, man, and always work if you want it."

Mike guided his car as best he could into a parking space. They bounded up the steps, excitedly stomping their feet before entering Mike's apartment. They hugged and kissed their families as Mike handed each of them $400.

Jose and Quentin gushed, "We're going to have the best damned Christmas ever!"

All three wanted to keep their secret so that all their families would have a genuine surprise on Christmas morning. They agreed to meet at Mike's Christmas Eve so they could go shopping.

On Christmas Eve morning, they joined the busy crowds of last minute shoppers in the malls and stores. They bought most of their gifts and decorations at Walmart and Target. Mike found three strings of lights he needed for his tree, Quentin found the star for his tree perfect and Jose bought a new angel and they bought new clothes and toys for the kids. Everyone bought food for a big holiday meal for their family.

Christmas morning was pandemonium at all three houses. The kids were in overjoyed with toys they never dreamed of getting for Christmas. Their wives quickly tried on new outfits and each household had enough food to invite some neighbors. Mike invited the caretaker of the community buildings, Joe Barber, to join them in celebration as they all knew he lived alone and would spend the day tending to his custodial duties and doing the daily crossword puzzle.

As dark approached, the neighbors and Joe left, leaving Mike and his family to clean up their apartment. The children, exhausted from playing all day, went to bed early so his wife Juana could wash dishes while he read the paper Joe had left behind. Mike enjoyed his favorite comics before settling down to read the newspaper. Suddenly, he sat bolt upright and cursed, "Son a bitch!" he exclaimed and dashed out of the house down the street toward Jose's and Quentin's.

III

"Jose, it's me, Mike! Open the damned door."

Jose shouted back, "Calm down and give me a minute. What's the problem?"

Mike pushed his way into the hallway. "This, this is the problem!" he shouted waving the paper in his face. "Call Quentin and get him over here now!"

Mike sat down at the kitchen table, waiting for Quentin to arrive. He dashed in out of breath and exclaimed, "Where's the fire man?"

Mike motioned for them to sit down and asked Brenda and the children to leave the room. Quentin and Jose looked at each other quizzically while Mike spread the paper out on the table and pointed to one obituary notice.

Mr. Johnnie Strickland, 825 Height Lane, eccentric
cofounder of Strickland Philanthropic Association,
died in a single car crash on December 22. A
preliminary autopsy indicated that Mr. Strickland
may have had a heart attack while driving. His black
Mercedes sedan crashed into a tree on US 48
some time late Tuesday. Authorities are
investigating further. No visitation is planned.
Interment will be in Rose Hill Cemetery
on December 28. The family has requested
that all expressions of sympathy take the
form of donations to Your Wish Come True
Foundation or one of the other charitable
organizations Mr. Strickland sponsored

(continued back page)

Jose and Quentin looked at Mike, and knitted their brows in puzzlement before they realized what he was getting at.

"Holy shit," said Jose. "Do you think it was the same guy?"

Mike snatched the paper out of their hands, folded the paper over itself and jabbed at a photograph as he snapped agitatedly, "What do you think? Same name, same car, same damned face. I think he probably realized he had just left us a thousand dollar tip and had a heart attack. Probably a rich old nut case with an unlisted number. How many old people in this town drive around in a black Mercedes sedan?"

"So what do you want to do, give back the money?" Quentin asked. "That is going to be hard to do since we don't have it anymore."

"Guys, remember that bill was in mint condition which means that the old man had squirreled it away somewhere for safe keeping. Some of his servants or family must know where it was. Believe me, the IRS goes through these rich estates with a fine tooth comb, and the existence of that bill will come to light."

"So what do we care? They can't trace it to us." Quentin said.

"Think, man. Didn't I tell you the coin man took my picture holding the bill? Didn't I tell you he checked a list of stolen bills? Doesn't this old man's estate have more money than God to track down where the money went? There must have been something special about that bill to hide that it away. Maybe you don't care about going to jail, but I don't want to go myself."

"Me neither," added Quentin. "I was there once for dope and I swore I wasn't going back. So what can we do?"

Mike shrugged, "I ain't got no thousand dollars. I might have some of it. Any ideas?"

Jose leaned forward to say, "What about this? What if we could scrape the money up somehow, write letter attached to it saying exactly what happened to it, and send it to that charity? We don't have to sign our name or say where we worked, but if anybody comes asking we have a good alibi. Plus, charities are tax free so the estate would be less a chunk of money."

Quentin and Mike pulled their chairs in closer. "How do we get this money so quick?" Mike asked.

Jose said, "We scrape together as much as we can and send it in. My kids had the best Christmas ever and I ain't going to change that."

Quentin exploded, "There ain't no way I am taking those toys from my children. There's got to be a better way."

The creaking chairs interrupted the silence of the room while they thought about what to do.

Jose crossed his arms, scowling, "I think we're overreacting. First place, maybe it's the same guy, maybe not. Second place, I doubt they'll come looking for a measly thou. Even if it is the same guy, who's to know?"

Quentin looked Jose in the eye and replied softly, "We will. Do you want to work with two guys who are dishonest?"

Mike mumbled, "You know what they say: 'No good deed goes unpunished'. Well, at least the kids won't hate us. Three days ago we said that all we wanted for Christmas was a star, lights or an angel. If we all agree to keep just them things we can always say that this is one Christmas we got everything we wanted."

IV

Over the next two days, they managed to scrounge up $325.19. Mike got a big manila envelope from Randy and carefully addressed it:

Your Wish Come True Foundation
857 Baltimore Avenue
Indianapolis, IN 46219
Then he scribbled out a note of explanation:

To Whom It May Concern:

Mr. Strickland left us a tip of $1000. We thought maybe he had left it by mistake so we called all the Stricklands in the book but could not find him. We spent most of the money for Christmas gifts for our families but we have managed to find enough to pay back a little. We are very sorry to hear of Mr. Strickland's passing and think it is only fair that we make this donation of $325.19 to your foundation in memory of his passing. We are only sorry that we could not return the full amount.

They sat staring at the package, bound together by a common regret, but separated by individual dreams. The next morning, Mike stuffed it into a mailbox as they drove to work and returned to their mundane lives.

V

After the first big snow the week after Christmas, the weather relented. A few shallow snowfalls threw city managers into a salt-spreading frenzy insured that many people stopped to get the whitish film off their cars. On a good day the men would split sixty dollars in tips. Fortunately, Randy did not hire any new workers.

Randy often sat in his office with his ear glued to a telephone receiver as his fingers busily punched calculator keys. He spent a lot of time policing the area around the car wash and putting up new signs. When Mike asked him about the new look, he replied, "Last minute capital expenditures, my boy. I can take this off my taxes for the year."

When Jose and Quentin heard the response they knew in their hearts that he was going to sell the business but they didn't say anything until they had a little more proof. They scanned newspapers during slow periods, looking for new jobs while hoping to stay at the car wash until spring when more jobs might be open.

In early March, Mike said to Randy, "Hey, quit bullshitting us, man! We know you're trying to sell the place, so don't give us that capital expenditures crap!"

Randy replied, "Actually, Mike, I really had started to clean the place up for a tax write off, but I now have a potential buyer. If all goes well, we'll close the deal by the last of this month. He said he wants a whole new crew that meets his image of how a business like this should be run, so now is as good a time as any to tell you all to start looking for other jobs and don't bullshit me because I know you've been looking. I explained to him that losing this job would put you guys in a tough spot, so he agreed to pay you two weeks pay on your last day as severance pay. Seems he can write that off. What can I say, guys? I guess we are all out of a job."

"Yeah, right," said Mike. "Difference is you don't have to work and we do."

Randy shrugged, "Nothing I can do. Sorry, Mike."

As Randy walked away, Mike said, "We might as well have a meeting tonight to tell our wives and decide what to do. Maybe they can arrange to take turns babysitting and do maid duty or something until we can find a job. Seven okay?"

When they told their wives, they agreed to help out by working part-time if needed. Frustrated by their bleak outlook, Brenda shouted, "All this started with that damned thousand dollars! Gave us the best Christmas ever—now we may lose our homes! Why did that old bastard pick you guys to curse?"

All at the table fell silent, considering Brenda's questions in a new light. Quentin sighed, "I feel just like Job. Living a righteous life. Good man with a happy family and then all hell breaks loose. Did he ever get an answer as to why all that crap happened to him?"

Everybody looked at each other and shrugged their ignorance. Mike suggested, "All of us need to start looking for jobs now, but I am going to work until the end of the month to get every dime of that severance pay!"

The month dragged interminably on. More cars came through the car wash as spring approached, so tips went up and the bright spring sun raised everybody's spirits.

A week before Randy finalized the sale; a city police officer parked his car in front of the office and strode around to where the men were working. He approached the men saying firmly, "Mike Thompson, Quentin Marksberry and Jose Garcia, you're wanted downtown for questioning."

Mike took a step back as if he was going to bolt away, but Quentin grabbed his arm. He asked, "Officer, what's this all about? Are we under arrest?"

"No sir, not at this time. You're only wanted for questioning. Please get into the back seat of the car."

The officer spent a few minutes chatting with Randy. Through the slightly ajar windows, Quentin could hear the officer say that the men were not under arrest, but may have witnessed a questionable transaction a few days before. Randy walked over, yelling into the small crack, "Don't worry boys, you're not in trouble. Just some sort of witness thing. Call me if you need anything like an alibi." He smiled broadly, and waved as the car drove away.

All three knew in their hearts that they had been found out, yet their heads told them not to discuss anything with each other that the officer could overhear. They began to sweat nervously so that by the time the cruiser reached the police station, dark damp circles stained their shirts. The officer led them past the booking desk where drug pushers and streetwalkers were getting fingerprinted to a gray room where a large table and eight chairs were already arranged.

The officer invited them, "Have a seat. The clerk will be here in a minute."

Shortly, a shapely blond in a tight skirt, blouse and high heels, entered the room, pulled a chair up to the table and began to ask questions.

"Good morning, gentlemen. My name is Susan Wilson. I am from the Make Your Wish Come True Foundation. I have a few questions to ask you.

"Which one of you is Michael Thompson?" she asked.

Mike raised his hand answering weakly, "I am, ma'am." as she wrote down a few notes. "Are you married, Mike? Any children?"

Mike nodded and held up two fingers.

"Quentin Marksberry?"

Quentin responded dryly, "Here."

"Married? Children?"

Quentin nodded, holding up one finger.

"So you must be Jose Garcia."

Jose nodded.

Married? Children?"

"Yes. One."

"Well, gentlemen, a few months ago we received a strange donation at the foundation and we have reason to believe that you know something about it. While I check on some information, the chief executive officer of the foundation needs to ask you a few legal questions. He'll be in shortly."

By now all three men were too terrified to speak. They began to shiver from fear of punishment and the cold evaporation of sweat from their bodies. Mike started to say something but Quentin and Jose stopped him, motioning the possibility that the room was bugged. Suddenly, the door opened, and an old man in and bespectacled man in a three-piece suit came in and sat down. Their jaws dropped as they recognized Ronnie Strickland.

"Well, gentlemen, do you take me for a fool?" Strickland thundered as he laid his briefcase on the table and took a seat and laid a large manila envelope on the table.

The three men blanched into a cold sweat as Mike stuttered, Mike stammered, "Bu...but... but it can't be you. You're dead!! We saw your picture in the paper!"

Strickland smiled mysteriously, "No, Mike, it wasn't me you saw. It was my twin brother Johnnie's picture in the paper. Sad affair it was too, but not totally unexpected as his health had been failing."

He saw the shadow of doubt clinging to their faces so he leaned over closer to Mike, "Mike, remember this scar? The one that hurts when it is turning bad weather?"

Mike nodded hesitantly.

"Well, then now that we are all convinced I am still alive, I believe you gentlemen should know that Johnnie and I were cofounders of many charities around the city. Before you ask, we preferred to stay under the radar to avoid the publicity and groveling that comes with celebrity and wealth and interferes with the mission of the charity. Your Wish Come True is such a charity and I believe you gentlemen owe me some something — at the least, satisfaction."

In near unison, Mike, Jose, and Quentin raised their upturned palms while a look of utter dismay crossed their faces.

"Hey, guys, I may be old, but I'm not senile. How many times do you think our foundation gets a donation more totaling over three hundred dollars and the whole thing is in cash and loose change? I believe, Mike, you know this gentle-man," Strickland asked as he pitched a business card from the coin shop toward Mike.

"Now, before you decide your next step, let me tell you a story about a man with two sons. The man was very wealthy, having worked hard but honestly, to make a fortune in manufacturing, raise a family and make a good reputation for himself. The father instilled a strong moral framework and keen business savvy into both his sons. First, but he demanded strict adherence to two tenets from the time the boys could understand: You will protect the integrity and honor of your family name with your last breath and second, you will never fight with family members. To do so flouts the first rule that the family name is worth more than mere money."

Strickland repositioned himself in his chair before continuing, "Now, of course, small boys had no idea of the value of money or honor, but they quickly acquired both. On their sixth birthday, the dad taped a one thousand dollar bill to the wall between their beds and quoted from the Lord's Prayer 'Lead us not into temptation.' He then sat us on his knee and warned us to never remove the money or the sign.

"Children reared in homes that provide them with a domestic servants have no idea of want and are really tempted by mischief, not need. But once the specter of adolescence rears it ugly head, new demons, driven by new needs, propel young boys down a dangerous path. One day, a servant cleaning the room noticed that the thousand-dollar bill had disappeared from the wall and promptly told the father. The man called his sons from their horseback riding and led them up to the room, forcing them to stare at wall where the money had been. The man sighed a long expiration of air and wept softly, "There is one less honest man in the world right now and, what's worse, he bears our family name."

Mike waved his hand slightly to interrupt. "Wait a minute. How did the dad not know it was a butler or something? Or a burglar?"

"Because the father hired servants whose integrity was as sterling as his own. Loose change from pants pockets or sofas was returned with a note of how much, when, and where the money was found. No, one of the sons took it and both of them knew which. But the father adhered to the principle that he taught his sons and nothing was ever said about it again."

"The sons grew up, earned Ivy League educations, and were empowered to expand the father's empire and his philanthropic endeavors. They married and raised families which produced grandchildren to insure the continuance of the family name. The family influence extended to major corporations, politics and even foreign countries, but both sons knew that the theft lying in their past prevented absolution of that sin. One son could not ask for forgiveness without admitting guilt and the other could not forgive without admitting knowledge of the crime. So as they grew old, the unimpeachable moral values the father bestowed upon them caused both to fear damnation for the same crime."

Strickland paused to catch his breath and surveyed his audience who sat in uneasy silence for nearly two minutes. He arose from his chair to stretch his legs, producing a crackling sound as his aged joints flexed and expanded. He straightened up, drew a long breath, and took up the story again. "As it turns out, some of the subsidiaries owned by each son used the same accounting firm, a firm dating back over a hundred years. A lot of the Fortune Five Hundred companies used the firm. An accountant embezzled from companies owned by each son and cost each son one million dollars and an audit by the IRS and the SEC. The money was less important than the dishonor and the aggravation. One son, exasperated, remarked, "I don't think there is an honest man alive anymore!" to which the other son replied, "I bet you there is! And I bet you, I can find him!"

Strickland massaged his chin. "The doubting son gave his brother a one thousand dollar bill and told him to go to the place where you least expect to find an honest man and you will find out that I am right! And once you find that honest man, you redeem your debt to him, not me."

Strickland's eyes teared up as he straightened himself in the chair. "By now, boys, you have no doubt surmised that the two brothers in question are Johnnie and I. We made that wager on Monday before Christmas, but I had to think where I might find men desperate enough to really test the issue. I gave you that thousand-dollar bill because you all looked so desperate three days before Christmas that surely you would not even think about returning it. Johnnie died before we could see the outcome of our wager, but I'll always be in debt to you men. Here."

Strickland pushed the envelope on the table toward them. "Open it!" he demanded.

Mike cautiously picked up the envelope and inverted it to catch the contents in his hand. The thick packet of paper was a deed to the car wash, applications to the local college for business and vouchers for expenses payable by the Strickland Corporation.

They looked up in astonishment to see Strickland's impassable face. He spoke, "When I saw the efforts you went through to return my money to me I knew I had found my man.er…men. Until you can find your footing in the business world, my staff of advertising and marketing, accountant will all be at your disposal. You are required to complete your education within five years. This arrangement must not be made public, but you can share it with your wives if you swear them to secrecy. Are we clear?"

The men nodded numbly before Quentin asked timidly, "Hey, man, I don't want to appear ungrateful, but ain't this a little over the top for a thousand dollars?"

"It is not for a thousand dollars, Quentin. This is the price of two souls."

Mike inquired, "Why two? Didn't you say that your brother handed you the thousand dollar bill so he must have taken it years ago?"

"No, I said that he gave me *a* thousand dollar bill?"

"So how can you tell the difference between two thousand dollar bills?" asked Mike.

Strickland rose from the chair, slipped on his coat, smiled at the three men and replied as he walked toward the door, "Because some thousand dollar bills are heavier than others."

A Thief in the Night

FOLKS IN TUGGLE Hollow knew that John Denny's destiny would be interwoven with coons and hounds from the time he was born. His mother, Meg Denny went into labor under a harvest moon while his father, Lige, was coon hunting across Slickford Creek, not knowing that the coon his hounds were chasing had doubled back down the creek to make a late night raid on the henhouse. Lige had left one of his older hounds home, and though the dog raised the alarm when the coon wreaked havoc in the henhouse, neither Meg, locked in the pangs of childbirth, nor Evadean Gregory, her midwife, could do much about the coon's raid. The ailing hound got his head stuck in a crack as he tried to force his way into the henhouse, and by the time he managed to free himself, the coon had stolen a fat pullet and disappeared into the deep woods behind the corncrib.

Realizing his hounds had lost the scent, Lige gathered his pack of blue tick and redbone hounds and returned home to utter confusion. A trail of bloody chicken feathers led into the woods, an exhausted dog lay moaning on the porch and Meg, recovering from the birth of an eight-pound son, was trying to nurse the baby before she fell asleep.

Lige sat on the porch in his rocking chair which creaked rhythmically in the pale moonlight. Deep in thought, he stood up and slipped quietly over to look at his new son. The people of the hills believed that Providence sent messages to those who were willing to listen and that unusual events were in some way revelations of those messages. Lige thought the raccoon's theft coincident with the birth of his son had a significance that would require the aid of a third party who could predict the future.

The next day, Lige caught a young rooster from his flock and walked over to Elmer Gregory's place to seek advice on the future of his son. Elmer was a kind of hillbilly shaman, a haruspex who could plumb the depths of the unknown by reading the entrails of a freshly killed animal. People consulted him for everything from marriage advice to crop planting to prophecies of a child's destiny.

The heavy dew had soaked through his pants by the time he reached Elmer's place. Elmer was sitting under a walnut tree whittling out a new hickory axe handle. Elmer laid the whittling aside and rose to greet his visitor.

"Mornin', Lige. I heard you had quite a bit of excitement over at your place last night. Got a new baby boy and a big one at that. What were you feeding that woman of yours anyway?" Elmer asked.

"Whatever I can catch, but after last night I may want to start eating more coon," Lige responded.

"Evadean said that one got in your henhouse and made off with a pullet. Was that the same one you was huntin?"

"Yeah, the dogs lost his scent in the creek and the son of a bitch doubled back. I figured that coon being there when the baby was born that's a sign of somethin'. Maybe the coon had marked the boy in some way. I brung a rooster to see if I was right," he said.

Elmer took the chicken. "Shore thing. Good thing you brung a rooster since it was a boy. Got a name yet?"

"Oh, we thought John was just fine."

"Yep. Well, let me get my axe and knife sharpened."

Lige waited for Elmer to get his divining knife and axe and sharpen them properly before he handed the rooster to him. Elmer took the rooster, and decapitated it in one fell swoop on a white oak chopping block. The headless chicken danced a horrific dance of death as Elmer got a white porcelain pan from the kitchen and set it on the stump. He waited for the chicken to fall lifeless to the ground, placed the body in the pan and retreated to the rear of the woodshed to perform his reading. Lige held the chicken by the legs while he split it lengthwise before laying it belly-up in the pan.

Lige took Elmer's seat and began whittling on a scrap of red cedar. He whistled "Amazing Grace" softly until Elmer returned.

"You was right, Lige. No doubt about it. A coon marked this boy. He'll have the best coonhounds in the country because he can think like a coon and teach the hounds a coon's wily ways. There was an odd sign in the rooster's heart, sorta a dark spot that I could not read good, but this boy will probably be the best coon hunter these parts have produced in years."

Lige bit his lower lip. "So he'll be healthy and all? " he asked.

Elmer nodded. "Best as I can tell."

"What do I owe you, Elmer?"

"Nuthin'. Give Meg my best and be sure that she don't eat no honey for at least six weeks. Honey'll kill a new mother, you know."

"Well, thank you. I'll owe you a favor. I've heard that about honey", Lige said as he headed back over the pasture to his home.

II

Lige told Meg what Elmer had said about their son's future. The excitement of having a son with such a promising future overshadowed the chaos of the night before. Perhaps their son would rise above the tedium of their lives. Most people in the community scraped a living out of the overworked soil. Almost everybody who had any money earned it through bootlegging or moonshining. But Lige found out that there was a market for raccoon furs that could make a good hunter a small fortune.

Unfortunately, he was not particularly good at it and sometimes the shotgun pellets ruined the fur. Carter Stinson had taught him how to make snares and dead fall traps, but his attempts were seldom successful. He thought that in some way the mark of the coon on his son would secure his future when he could not longer farm.

By the time John turned six months of age, he was sleeping with a small blue tick puppy at the foot of his crib. Lige and Meg figured, and Elmer agreed, that this was the best way to get little John to sense the rhythms of a true coon hunter because blue tick hounds were bred to hunt raccoons. When John took his first steps braced on the hindquarters of a year old blue tick hound, Lige thought about Elmer's prophecy.

John's first coon hunt was a shakeout accompanied by Lige, Elmer Gregory and Carter Stinson. Meg insisted that John not go on one of these late night jaunts until he was at least five years old. By then, he could keep up with the men as they clambered over split-rail fences and waded shallow brooks. After supper on his fifth birthday, Lige said to John, "Johnny, come here. I've got a surprise for you."

John ran over and jumped on Lige's knee. "What is it, Daddy?"

"Tonight, Carter and Elmer are coming over to take you coon hunting with us. It's important that you listen to everything they say. They know a lot about coons and coonhounds.

"Now, tonight is just a shakeout. There's lots of new coons that ain't learned all they need to know. Carter has two new pups that need to learn to hunt. All we'll do tonight is let the dogs tree the coons and then we'll shake them out. The new dogs will learn how to wrestle a coon. Coons can be mean, so you need to teach your dogs how to fight one."

John's eyes glittered with visions of battles between dogs and coons. Men used the dogs to subdue one small part of the wilderness in shifting balance of power between men and raccoons: the raccoons would raid henhouses and strip traps of their prey, but would suffer retribution wrought by dogs and guns. Tonight, John would take his first steps to manhood as he learned his role in the struggle.

Carter and Elmer arrived with their packs shortly after Meg had cleared the table. Amid the wild baying of the dogs eager for the chase, Lige took John by the hand, and the hunters disappeared into the warm night guided by the dim glow of kerosene lamps.

Carter whispered to Lige, "That boy has a good stride. Let's hope he can keep it up."

"Don't you worry about my John," Lige replied. "If he lags, I'll carry him."

Sudden sharp barks announced that the hounds had found a scent and the men picked up the pace. John had to run to keep up, but the rush of adrenaline thrilled and propelled him over shallow creeks and briar-infested clearings until they reached the ash tree where the dogs had treed a cantankerous raccoon. The dogs leaped wildly and clawed at the bark trying to reach their prey. The men held their lanterns aloft until Elmer said, "There he is!" pointing at the growling raccoon clinging to a low branch.

"I'll go shake him out," said Carter as he handed his lantern to Lige. "Now boy, you stand clear and watch these dogs work."

John felt Lige pull him back from underneath the tree where the coon would land. "Are they going to kill the coon, Daddy?" he asked.

"Not now. Carter just wants his dogs to practice tackling a coon before the hunting season starts. A big coon can kill a young dog because they can about turn over in their skins and they have a powerful bite." Lige answered.

He squinted to watch Carter climb the tree before he added, "And God help a dog fool enough to follow a coon into water. A coon drowns many a good dog. He'll grab hold of the dog's neck and set on his head until he drowns. It's a hard thing to break a good dog off the chase, but once they're in the water, they're playing the coon's game. You'd better hurry, Carter! He's about to move to another branch."

"Hold your taters! I'll get him. Watch out below. I'm goin' to start shaking now." Carter replied.

The branch began to sway violently until the branch broke and the coon fell to the ground with a heavy thud. Quickly, he quickly righted himself to face the swarm of dogs that lunged at him. John stood transfixed at the terror and determination of the raccoon to fend off its attackers, who matched his courage with their own resolve to win the battle. A dog would rush in only to have the coon grab him, bite him on whatever body part presented itself, release that victim, and grab another dog. The dogs began to circle, darting in from the coon's blind side to deliver a nip before retreating. They all had bites and scratches oozing blood mixed with saliva of both dog and raccoon, but the coon showed only a few drops of blood on his masked face and his left ear.

Carter stepped forward and yelled, "Here, Podge, Blue! Come here, boys! Elmer, you'd better get your dogs off him before he kills them!"

Elmer clicked his tongue, "Here, Duke, here Pooch! Come here!"

The older dogs broke off the attack, but Carter's two younger dogs ignored his command. They continued to circle the coon and looked confusedly at the older dogs.

Carter picked John up and said, "Now watch this, boy. Them pups don't got enough sense to quit when they're ahead. Now watch this old coon teach them two a lesson."

As the two pups got their second wind and took up the attack again. The coon backed up quickly then flung himself across Podge's neck and grabbed Blue by the ear. Blue yanked himself back, screaming in pain as the coon's teeth tore a gash in his ear.

"Now, maybe you'll listen to me, damn you! Come here!" Carter yelled. Blue slunk over to Carter. Podge turned to do the same. The coon hissed defiantly before scurrying off into the night.

Carter set John down, and knelt to examine his dogs' wounds. Terrified, yet wildly stimulated by all the commotion, John raced to Lige, who swung him up on his hip laughing, "I'll tell you boys, that was one tough old coon! Your dogs okay, Carter?"

"They's tore up a bit, but that'll learn 'em to listen to me, goddamn it! Well, boy, did you learn anythin' tonight, boy?"

With noticeable effort, John squeaked out, "Yes, sir! Not to feel sorry for no coons!"

The men erupted into loud laughter and took turns tousling the boy's hair.

"You're goin' to be a good one, Johnny boy, a good one!" Carter said, wiping the sweat from his face.

The dogs were rested now, and the men turned toward home, passing John from one to another. The men who were used to hunting would fall asleep quickly that night, but John would lie awake for most of the night reliving the hunt.

From that moment on, he, too, knew that a coon marked him.

III

The next year Carter brought John a blue tick pup and started to teach him how to train the dog to obey, follow a trail, do all the things a good coon dog would have to do. John instinctively grasped the nuances of voice and facial expression needed to communicate with his dog. Carter found himself standing aside, shaking his head at how gifted John was at training the dog. Sometimes the boy would act the role of an enraged raccoon and Carter would forget that he was only watching a boy wrestling playfully with his dog.

John accompanied the men on all their hunting trips. By age eight, he could skin and gut a raccoon, even stretch and nail a hide on the smokehouse wall to dry. The hunting trips became shorter simply because John's understanding of raccoons habits shortened the time needed to find and catch the raccoons. The older men began to acquiesce to his leadership, and let him keep all the hides to sell to the fur buyer.

The quantity and quality of furs brought John a great deal of money and a comfortable, but simple, life for himself and his parents. Lige and Meg were happy that their son could afford to buy them false teeth and new glasses, and they gloried in the recognition they received as the parents of the greatest coon hunter around. Lige watched his son grow into a giant of a man, six feet seven inches at age nineteen, but he realized that John someday would have to give up the wild carefree days of a young man for the tedium of adulthood and family life.

One day as they were chopping the weeds out of the tobacco patch, Lige said to John, "Son, come over here and sit a spell. We need to talk about something."

They walked over to the shade of a white oak at the edge of the tobacco patch. where they took drinks from the half-gallon jar of water Meg had placed there for them. After taking a long drink, Lige set the jug down to roll a cigarette, sprinkling loose-leaf tobacco from a pull-string bag into the paper trough before handing the bag to John who rolled his own cigarette.

"Son, you're nineteen now and you're purty well off for a young man. Everybody says you know more about coon dogs and coons than any ten men. But you can't keep hunting forever before you run out of coons. Besides, you won't always be a young man. You'll want to settle down and raise a family. I seen how you look at that Dovey Marcum at the revival at Piney Woods."

John's face flushed in the embarrassment of knowing that an older person recognized his yearnings. "Oh, Pop." he said, casting his glances self-consciously toward the ground.

"T'ain't nuthin to be shamed of. It's only natural. Just like it's natural that your Ma and me want grandchildren. But what I'm saying is that if you want to raise a family, you cain't keep hunting coons for a living. I was thinking that as good as you are at it, you could start training dogs for other people. Ma and I thought we'd give you two acres over there by the creek. You could build a house and some sheds to keep dogs while you're training them. People in four states know how good you are and they'd pay top dollar for you to train their dogs. You could still hunt when you want, but you'd have a lot better income and reputation."

Lige took one last drag on his cigarette before flicking it into the tobacco patch. John did the same, and mused over the idea before he said, "That ain't a bad idea, Pop. I got all kinds of trophies and ribbons from all over these parts to show I know what I'm doing. And I bet Dovey would be a lot quicker to say 'yes' looking at that kind of future instead of being married to coon hunter."

"Carter and Elmer think it is a good idea. Tell you what let's do. We'll start building a house and a couple of sheds. And you git to courting that Dovey," Lige said, laughing and slapping John on the back.

They finished the last few rows of tobacco and silently reflected on the future they had just built in their dreams.

IV

By the end of autumn, Lige, John and their neighbors had erected a simple house and two sheds by Potts Creek that ran through Lige's property. John gradually started to see more of Dovey, taking her to revivals and singings in the Baptist churches of the rural community. A proper courtship in this part of the world ran at least a year or longer but everyone knew that it was just a matter of time until they got married. Dovey spent a lot of time learning housewife skills from her mother, and John worked on getting his business off the ground.

He paid the local newspaper to run advertisements for him and to print up two hundred handbills that he could post in the small post offices and stores in the surrounding area. His sheds were soon full of packs of blue tick, red bone, and black-and-tan hounds the owners wanted trained. Sometimes his neighbors went with on nighttime training sessions, but usually he went alone. From time to time, people would kid him about being marked by a coon the night he was born because one had stolen a hen from Lige's henhouse that night. Clients from the bigger cities found the quaint idea of animals or events marking infants at birth amusing, but no one disputed that John did indeed have a special gift for training coonhounds. They would watch as John's dark eyes scanned their dogs, and let his nimble fingers ply the dog's fur to find the special spots that tapped into the very core of the dogs' nature. They gladly paid the hundred dollars for training that John assured them would make their dogs champion hunters.

By the end of a year, John had saved enough money to ask Dovey to marry him. They married in a local church and moved into their new home where they spent the time fixing it up to make it comfortable. One day a black Packard pulled up, and a man wearing a three-piece suit got out leading a blue tick hound got out. He climbed the steps to the porch and hailed John through the screen door, "Are you the John Denney who trains coon dogs?"

"Yes, I am," John said, stepping out onto the porch. "What can I do for you?"

"My name is Royce Getz. I run a furniture store in Glasgow. I heard you can work magic with coon dogs."

"People say I do a good job."

The man yanked on the leash and the hound stepped around to stand by his side. Getz continued, "I got a boy soon be old enough to go hunting, so I bought this dog. He's a registered offspring of the grand champion in the state fair two years ago. Do you think you can train him?"

John's eyes were transfixed on the dog. He was the finest blue tick hound he had ever seen: well fed and sleek with a light coat dappled with steely blue gray spots. His coal black eyes shone with the vigor and spirit of a true champion as he sat statue-like staring up at John with an intensity that pierced his very soul. Awkwardly, John replied, "That is one fine animal you have, Mr. Getz. What's his name?"

"Oh, he had some big long name on the papers, but we just renamed him Moses. How long will it take to train him?"

"It depends on the dog. Some dogs learn quick but others take longer. I can keep him here if you like or you can bring him back in a couple of months."

"I don't want to have to make a bunch of trips I don't have to make. You'll take good care of him I'm sure. Do I need to pay for his food now or later?"

"We'll settle up later. And don't you worry. I'll take extra special care of this dog. He is a beauty," John replied as the dog nuzzled an licked his hand.

"Well then, Mr. Denny, you'll give me a telephone call when he is ready."

"Actually, there ain't any phones around here yet. I'll send you a letter or postcard."

"That'll be fine. Here is my card with my address. Thank you, Mr. Denny and good day."

"Good day to you, sir. Have a safe trip home. You'll hear from me as soon as he is ready."

Getz drove his car back to the road and John knelt down, stroking the dog's handsome head and ruffling the short mane around his neck. The dog leaned into his caressing hands, whimpered a little bark of pleasure, and licked John's hand again.

At that moment, John knew he had to have this dog.

V

The bond between man and dog grew stronger each time John worked with Moses. John saw a dog of incredible beauty, the very essence of coon hound, a wild spirit filled with lust for the chase, a struggle whose roots grew from the deep recesses of the forgotten time when man gave the first dog a place to sleep by the warming glow of a fire. For the citified Gentry, the dog was chattel, a mere amusement for his son, but John and Moses were kindred souls, aching to range over forest and streams, their senses united in the wild joy of the hunt.

John had never seen a dog that responded so quickly. Moses came at the slightest click of his tongue and heeled at a low whistle. On his first shakeout, Moses knew precisely when to press the attack and when to retreat, emerging without the smallest trace of torn skin or blood. The other dogs quickly learned that if they followed Moses' lead, they would have far fewer wounds to lick.

Knowing that he would have to return the dog to Moses, John tried to put emotional distance between Moses and himself; but with each excursion, he knew that he must acquire this dog for his own. He knew that Getz would never agree to sell Moses since he had purchased the dog as a gift from father to son. Every day, he would pet and examine Moses from head to tail, memorizing the shape and location of every spot and the subtle curve of every leg.

Gradually, he devised a plan. Somewhere there must be a blue tick hound with markings so similar to Moses' that the untrained eye of Getz would never notice the difference. If he could find that dog and buy it from its owner, he could swap it for Moses and return the impostor to Getz. He could easily train the new dog to come to the call "Moses" and even train it to be more than an adequate hunting dog for Getz and his son.

Now twenty three, newly married, and anxious to start a family, John had his hands so full he had precious little time to scour the countryside looking for a suitable hound. His best bet was to go to the bigger coon club hunts and hope that he could find a dog there. He would load two or three hounds into his buckboard, head out midday Saturday and return late Sunday afternoon.

John hit the jackpot on his fourth trip. The Pickett County Coon Club in Tennessee hosted a big shakeout inviting hunters from four counties in Kentucky and three in Tennessee. As he walked among the cages of baying hounds, he found a horse drawn cart bearing a rickety old cage with a single occupant. John walked over and examined the dog closely. It was a male and at first glance the size and markings resembled Moses's. The twilight made seeing fine details difficult, but he could get a better look in the morning. The sudden approach of the owner startled him.

"Can I help you?" the owner asked.

"I'm just admiring this fine piece of dog flesh you got here. How old is he?" John replied.

"'Bout two. His name is Joe; mine's Bart Piercy."

John extended his hand, "John Denny. Pleased to meet you, Mr. Piercy."

"John Denny? I've heard of you! They say you are the best coonhound trainer in these parts. This is a pleasure."

"Thank you, but the real pleasure is in seeing this beautiful dog. Did you ever think about selling him? I'd pay a good price for him."

Piercy smiled and shook his head. "Sometimes I'd like to sell him, since I don't really coon hunt that much, but he is pretty good with kids."

John could barely contain his exuberance. "I understand. But it is such a waste to let a good coon dog like this just be a play pretty. Let me see how he works tonight and look him over tomorrow and maybe we can work a deal."

"A deal?"

"If he shows any hope at all, I'll pay you top dollar for him. What do you say?"

Piercy was flummoxed by the offer. "I wasn't thinking about selling him, but as you say, it is a shame to not use him as a hunter. I don't have any idea of what he would be worth, but I can ask around here and get some opinions."

"Well, let's see how it goes then."

Word spread quickly that John Denny was here and he was soon cornered for advice on training hounds. He answered a few questions before reminding them with a laugh that he could not give away too many secrets. Still, he sensed that his assessment of Piercy's dog would not be questioned, and he marked time until the hunt began.

He partnered up with Piercy for the hunt that night, and their dogs soon had treed a coon. Piercy climbed the tree and shook the coon out while John stayed on the ground to tend the dogs. Piercy's dog, Joe, was inept at harassing the coon, but John saw that the deficiency lay in the lack of training and not inherent ability.

He examined Joe the next morning and, satisfied that the dog could pass for Moses, he offered Piercy $200, which was quickly accepted. After loading Joe and his cage onto his buckboard, he began the trip home.

When he got home he compared the dogs while they sniffed around each other friskily; he could barely tell them apart himself. Getz had not even seen Moses now for two months so the chances that his amateur eye would detect any difference were small. Joe was missing one small spot on the right hindquarters. John thought about dyeing a spot there, but decided that the disappearance of a spot might cause more trouble than it was worth. He thought about trying to retrain Moses to come to a new name, a precaution he wished he had thought of earlier, but feared that might confuse the dog. His best option was to hide Moses in the deserted Cooge Bertram house the day Getz came to pick him up.

The house had been abandoned for several years since Cooge was killed in a logging accident and his wife remarried and moved out of state. Some people thought Cooge's ghost haunted the house and people told scary tales about disembodied spirits and will-o-the-wisps that floated in and out the broken windows. The locals steered clear of it, so the possibility of anyone discovering the hidden dog was remote. Since it would only be for a day, he could put food and water there for Moses until Getz left, and then Moses would be his alone.

He began to work on training Joe, making sure that the real Moses was tied up out of earshot. Within a week, Joe had forgotten his name, responding only to "Moses." John found it easy to teach him the mechanics of being a good coonhound. Joe-Moses would be a respectable coonhound in his own right, more than good enough for Getz and his son.

Shortly before he finished training Joe-Moses, Dovey told him she was pregnant. The baby was due in mid-July, which would give him time to care for the baby and Dovey. He would have free time for a little fall hunting with Moses and the men in the community.

The next day he gave Joe-Moses a run-through of his training; the dog passed with flying colors. Satisfied that Joe could pass for Moses, John addressed the postcard and carried it to the post office at Dumpy Ingram's General Store. He bought a stamp and the groceries Dovey had asked him to pick up as she was craving a few things and chatted a while with Dumpy before starting home.

He arose early the next day to prepare the Cooge house for Moses. The sun brightened the May morning and birds sang in the fencerows along the road. While he was secretly wanting a son, he pictured a pretty little girl growing into a beautiful woman. He and Dovey were young and they wanted a big family so he was content to bide time until she bore him a son. He began to whistle an old gospel tune, "Power in the Blood," one of the hymns that was a favorite among the primarily Baptist community.

As he rounded the last turn in the dirt road leading to his house, he glimpsed something moving in the bushes. A large, shaggy raccoon burst from the undergrowth and stood defiantly growling at him. Raccoons seldom left their dens and hollow trees during the daytime, but John knew that sometimes mothers with big litters would sneak out for water. He stood still, studying the animal as it wavered between standing its ground and running for cover. With one final hiss and gnashing of teeth, the raccoon slipped noiselessly into the low brush and continued its journey to the creek below the road. John shrugged his shoulders at the strange incident and made his way home.

IV

Getz replied to the card as requested, saying he would be there on June eighth in the late afternoon. The week before the appointed date John investigated the Cooge Bertram house, and prepared a place to keep Moses. Unwilling to tie the dog lest he start barking or howling, he prepared the largest room in the house so that Moses could move around freely to bask in the sun or cool off in the shade. He nailed some boards nailed over the windows and doors prevent the dog from escaping. Moses would need something to lie on so John figured he would bring a burlap bag filled with fine straw.

On June eighth, John fed all his dogs, paying particular attention to Moses. About mid-morning, he pumped a pail of fresh water, gathered up a huge plate of table scraps, Moses' bed and walked the dog to the old house. Moses whimpered slightly as John cradled him in his arms to set him over the barricade into the room where he had placed the food, water and the bed onto the floor. He sat down, caressing and cooing to the dog of his dreams. When John finally rose to leave, Moses licked his hands, as if he knew that his task for the day was to remain here quietly. John shook the barricade to assess its sturdiness left the room. "I'll be back for you tonight, Fella. You behave yourself."

He walked home and ate dinner with Dovey. In one more month, their daughter would be here and John would have his dog: he felt a glow of warm satisfaction knowing that his life was perfect. After dinner they sat in the swing on the porch, talking casually, but mostly just sitting, waiting for Getz to show up.

VII

Moses had to get up from time to time and move to a new warm spot. Summer temperatures had not yet become unbearable so he liked lolling in the warmth of the spring sun. He dozed lightly, but the scritching sound of claws on old wood awakened him. A large raccoon living in the chimney of the old house had smelled the food John had left for Moses and was greedily helping himself to the free meal. Quick as lightning, Moses ran at the raccoon and grabbed him by the back of the neck. The coon twisted himself around in his loose skin, snapping at empty air until his sharp teeth clamped down on Moses' front leg. Moses shook his head, contorting his body to remove his tormentor; the violent actions tore the coon loose and threw him toward the stone hearth. The enraged animal quickly scurried to safety in the chimney. Moses danced around, barking up the chimney until the coon climbed out the top of the chimney and sought refuge elsewhere. With the heavy scent of coon fading, Moses sat down to lick his wounds. The bite had startled the dog more than it harmed him. After a few minutes of licking the wounds, the blood had disappeared, and the pain abated enough for him to eat a few bites before returning to his nap.

VIII

Getz's car appeared on the eighth about one thirty. He and his son got out of car and walked up the porch.

"Hello, Mr. Getz. Who's that with you?" asked John.

"Mr. John Denny, meet my son William Royce Getz the third. You can call him Billy. Well, don't just stand there boy, shake the man's hand!" exclaimed Getz.

"Hello, Billy, I'm pleased to meet you. Is Moses your dog?"

"Yes, sir. Is he trained to hunt coons now?"

John knelt on both knees, placing his hands on the boy's shoulders. "Billy, that is the finest dog I've ever trained. And such a beautiful animal. Do you want to see him?"

Billy jumped up and down in excitement. "Yes, yes, yes!"

John led them to the barn where he had kept Joe-Moses waiting for this day. Nervously, he wondered if Getz would notice the switch, and rationalized his plan. *Everybody is going to come out ahead.*

Joe-Moses barked as he jumped and paced the enclosed pen. John opened the gate and the dog ran to sniff them, satisfied himself they did not pose a threat. Billy reached out his hand to pet the dog. The dog cautiously sniffed it and let the boy stroke his head. Getz stood and eyed the dog.

"I'd forgotten how pretty he is. Looks a little bigger. Heavier. Guess that comes from all the training." he said.

"Well, I do work them pretty hard. He has a good appetite and a lot of exercise will make some dogs bulk up. Ain't his coat shiny though?" John responded, annoyed that he had just invited a closer scrutiny of the very thing that could give the whole game away.

Getz grunted and bent over to examine the dog's fur. "Yes, it is. I think I got my money's worth. I understand there is quite a market for stud fees for top coon hounds."

"Oh, yeah. But there's people that will steal him from you. You might try to find a way to mark him so you can always tell he is your dog. He sure likes Billy."

The dog and the boy were romping over in the yard. Billy had discovered that the dog could heel and come when called.

"That's amazing, Mr. Denny. You certainly know what you are doing! Is he as good at hunting commands?"

"Like I said, the best I've ever trained. I wrote out a list for you of what to say to get him to do certain things. I keep an old stuffed coon hide out in the smokehouse to practice with. Do you want to try it?"

"Absolutely. I am anxious to see how he does."

John got the stuffed coon hide and threw it on the ground. Getz and Billy put the dog through his paces and were bowled over with how enthusiastically the dog obeyed. Getz took out his billfold. "What do I owe you, Mr. Denny? I don't mind paying extra for these results!"

Feeling relieved that the plan had worked so well, John replied magnanimously, "I had such a good time training that dog, how about a hundred dollars? I'm just so tickled to see him and the boy getting on so good. I'm going to be a father myself in about a month, you know."

"Well, congratulations! I don't think that is nearly enough. How about two hundred?"

John shifted his position, "Oh no, no, that's way too much. A hundred is fine."

"Not for me it isn't!" thundered Getz as he stuffed a wad of bills in John's pocket. "And not a word out of you!"

Finding himself filling with contrition and guilt, John started to speak "I..."

"Not a word!" repeated Getz. "Billy, let's go before I have to fight Mr. Denny."

Billy got into the back seat of the car and called the dog to join him as Getz got in behind the wheel. He started the car and hollered at John, "You're a good man, John Denny! I'll spread the word about your business. If you ever need my help, let me know!"

After Getz left, John counted the money, all two hundred dollars, and walked up the hollow to get Moses from his hiding place. He whistled as the dog gamboled in wide loops on the way back home.

"Yes, sir, everybody's happy," he said softly.

IX

For several days after Getz left, John seemed jittery to everyone. The entire crew at the store had heard of his good fortune with Getz and figured that he was just a nervous expecting father. He still spent a lot of time in the twilight hours roughhousing with Moses, and he soon let go of the fear of discovery of his scheme. Carter, Elmer, Lige and he often went coon hunting and he glorified at the envy of the others for his new hound.

Finally, Lige asked, "Which dog is this? I would sure use the same parents again to raise another litter."

John knew he had to lie since he had no pedigree for Moses. "I bought him over in Pickett County. Yep, he's the best dog I have ever seen. I hope to raise some litters by him next year."

John took one last short trip before the baby arrived in July, so one night he let his dogs loose. The pack ran off toward the old house and found the scent but Moses tore away to go in another direction.

The baying led John to the dogs that had treed a family of coons in a big hickory tree. A big female raccoon and three kits were clinging to the branches. The sight of the terror-filled eyes of the kits stopped him dead in his tracks. Perhaps it was his own impending parenthood that made him wonder how many young coon kits had starved to death because hunters had shot their mother. He tried to call the dogs off, but the smell of four coons inflamed their primal instincts into a frenzy. One of the kits lost its hold and fell to a lower branch, dangling just out of reach of the pack swarming like angry bees. The mother coon backed down the tree to help her offspring, but he managed to pull himself back onto the branch. Horrified at the plight of the little coon, John yelled and at the dogs and waded into the swirling mass of dogs, battering heads and rumps with sticks and feet. Finally, the exhausted dogs withdrew to rest and await further instructions. John sat down beside the pack, staring pensively up at the frightened coon family as they struggled to reach higher branches. In a few minutes, the mother coon had collected her kits onto a large horizontal branch about twenty feet from the ground, and they lay there terrified.

After the mother had collected her kits, John summoned the pack, and they began the trip home. In the confusion he had not noticed that Moses was not in the pack. But as they came to the house, Moses knew the terrain well so John was confident he would show up in the morning.

He arose a little before dawn to find the pack asleep in the yard. He stepped out onto the porch and whistled. The dogs raced to the porch and dancing in the yard, but Moses was still missing. John called, "Here, Moses! Here, boy. Come on."

John walked around the house and outbuildings, whistling and clucking as he went, desperately searching for his prize dog, but he found sign of Moses.

John walked up the hollow to the old house, only to find it empty. He cursed himself for not noticing that Moses was missing from the pack of dogs the previous night. On the way home, he found himself hoping that the dog had not fallen over a cliff or been stolen, but after two days the dog had not shown up and John was heartbroken that his well laid plan had gone awry.

X

Moses lay by the creek on the other side of the ridge. He was too weak to walk from exhaustion. His head lay at the creek's edge with his tongue trying to lap up a drink. Abruptly, he jerked himself upright in an agitated state only to collapse again, whining piteously as his tongue and throat began to spasm. Fever gripped his body but he could not drink the water needed to cool him off. He finally slipped into a deep sleep.

When Moses had not returned by Sunday, John organized a search party at his house. Men and women and dogs stood in the shade of the walnut tree, and decided who would search where. Dovey was making coffee when someone yelled, "There he is, John!"

Sure enough, Moses appeared coming from the direction of the old house. His behavior seemed erratic. He spied the people and ran toward them, passing all of them to go to John. Exhausted, he jumped at John and bit him through the wrist leaving globs of foamy drool dripping away. John collapsed in shock as he realized what had happened.

"Oh, my God, he's a mad dog! Mad dog! Get a gun!" yelled Lige as he ran to rescue John. "Hurry, Goddamn it!"

By now Moses had turned himself on the other dogs and a swirling mass of gnashing teeth and infected saliva. Maddened by the disease attacking his nervous system and starving for water, he tore into his old hunting partners with blind fury. Someone thrust Lige a twelve-gauge shotgun and he drew a bead as best as he could on Moses and pulled the trigger. Moses yelped and collapsed into a pool of blood; some of the other dogs fell as they were wounded by the spreading shot. Lige and Carter looked at each dog; every one had a wound either from the shot or Moses' teeth. They decided to take no chances. They collected the dogs into the pen and one by one shot them through the heart.

The news spread quickly. Doc Powers rode out as fast as he could. No one had been exposed but John who sat under the tree, and squeezed his wrist trying unsuccessfully to stop the pain and the flow of infected blood. He asked about Dovey weakly; she was okay, but had fainted from the shock. All that was left to do was to bury the dead.

Lige, Carter and Elmer dug several graves by the woods beyond the tobacco patch. One by one, they laid the dogs in separate graves and covered their torn bodies with the dusty reddish soil, marking each with a sandstone bearing its name; at John's request they made a real fancy one for Moses. When the dogs were buried, they built s split rail fence around the makeshift cemetery.

Dovey went into labor the next day and gave birth to a beautiful little girl. They let John name her and he named her Hope. No middle name, just Hope. Elmer had told him that he should never touch her or even breathe on her too much as she might get the rabies if he did have it. Only time would tell. He would have to wait for the signs to appear, and that could be a long time Elmer had said.

In the days after Hope's birth, John grew listless and distant. He seemed preoccupied, spending his time standing gazing at his daughter. Tears of longing to hold his daughter streamed down his cheeks, and his arms ached to cradle her against his chest, and let his fingers tickle her chin. He spent a lot of time sitting near the graves of his dogs, lost in thought.

The first spasms did not occur until about two months after the bite. John dropped his coffee cup at the breakfast table and felt his arm muscles tighten and lock up. Two days later, his legs throbbed with paralyzing pain. Within a week, the spasms had grown into full-body seizures that twisted his body into ungodly shapes and he began to avoid drinking. The seizures became so violent that Lige and Meg and Dovey had to hold him down until the convulsions passed. Late one Saturday afternoon, Carter and Elmer came by to visit for they knew his time was growing short.

They pulled up a chair in the living room beside John, now nearly too weak to talk. "You'll take care of Dovey and Hope and Mom and Dad, won't you boys?"

Choking back tears, they assured him they would.

Between moans and paroxysms of weeping, Elmer sobbed, "I spent my whole life figuring out how to read the signs the good Lord gives us all around us. I told your Daddy you was marked by a coon and your life would be devoted to coon hunting and coonhounds. And you grew into a fine young man with a good kind heart. I didn't understand that dark spot on the chicken liver but now it makes sense. A mad dog. Wonder where he got it?"

John had never revealed his duplicitous dealings with Piercy and Getz. Now as he faced dying seemed as good a time as any to confess his sin.

"Boys, I got to tell you something. I...."

The seizure gripped him so violently that he threw himself out of his chair. He thrashed wildly on the floor and knocked over tables and chairs. Lige raced into the room yelling, "Get the mattress to hold him down! The mattress!"

Lige, Elmer and Carter quickly slung the mattress over John's flailing body, and pressed as hard as they could. They maneuvered the mattress to cover John's body to keep him from cracking his head open on the floor. Their actions seemed only to invigorate the madness devouring his brain and spinal cord, and he surged up in a fury. They responded with adrenaline driven strength, and pressed harder until at last they felt his body go limp and the convulsions cease. They eased the mattress away to find John lying slack-jawed, his windpipe broken: they had accidentally suffocated him.

People from miles around came to the funeral: Getz and Billy, Mr. Piercy and dozens of fellow coon hunters said a mournful good-bye as John Denny was laid to rest beside the dogs he had loved so much. They recounted stories and said prayers before going home to their own lives and families.

That night Lige and Meg sat consoling Dovey as she nursed Hope by the glow of the oil lamp in the kitchen. There were no dogs now to alert them that a furry dish-faced intruder bearing a mask and a quivering moist black nose had emerged from the woods. He scraped under the bottom rail of the fence surrounding the makeshift cemetery, where he curiously snuffled the newly upturned dirt before turning his bright eyes and predatory intentions towards the henhouse.

Where Lies A Man's Treasure

Tim Collins steered his Jeep Cherokee with his left hand while his eyes darted back and forth from the road to the folded yellow-highlighted map clutched in his right hand. Just as Jimmy had said, there was the END OF STATE MAINTENANCE sign at the bottom of a graveled road that arced gradually along the sides of the wooded hill. On the right was the gray clapboard general store with its ridge row swaybacked like an old mare's spine. As he signaled and turned the Jeep into the dusty graveled parking lot, he thought to himself *Gosh! Look at that creek– clear as glass! and those dogwoods and redbud! This is right out of a picture book!* He parked in front of an antiquated gas pump — the kind with a big round glass top and a single hose swinging from its side — stepped out of the Jeep and strode through the yawning double wide wooden doors into the store. Two men sat engrossed in a checker game, barely acknowledging his entry.

Tim said, "Hi there. Can I get some gas and directions here?"

One man with kindly eyes peering from a fedora hat looked up and smiled to reveal a gold left incisor. "Well, sir, you can get one of them and it ain't gas."

Tim frowned before he replied, "You sold out?"

"Lord, yes! About ten years ago. Most everybody quit farming before then, so warn't much use in keeping gas in the pump inviting a leak and the gummit down on me, so after I pumped out the last bit, I just let it be. Now if you are needing gas, I can siphon some out of my truck, but it'll cost you as I don't care much for the taste of gas anymore."

"Oh, that won't be necessary. I have enough to get back into town. I am Tim Collins and I am looking for the Pat Kelsay farm."

The man extended his right hand, "I'm Cletus Wayne Stinson. This here is Homer Jay Hancock. Now, I know you ain't one of Pearl and Pat's kids or you would know where it was. Right up that holler yonder."

"No, I am a friend of Jimmy Kelsay in Louisville. Jimmy wanted me to come down and take pictures of his boyhood home for a book he is putting together, in case anyone tries to sell the place."

Cletus drew back in shock. "Sell it? Why, I didn't think the way it was deeded it could be sold. I was given to understand that it was deeded to all eight children and then to Jimmy's oldest son after they died. It has been abandoned since the day Pearl died eight years ago but I think the renter up the holler looks after it. Mows the yard, keeps the weeds fit back. Runs the kids out of the house when he catches them in there screwing."

Homer hissed, "Cletus! Such talk to a man you just met!" In a normal voice, he continued, "So, how do you know Jimmy?"

Tim replied, "He is the owner of Meridian Productions where I work. I am the main staff photographer. He plans to produce a coffee-table book of shots around his home place for all his brothers and sisters. Just being sure the grandkids have a point of reference. Yeah, he explained the inheritance to me, but he also knows wills can be broken."

Cletus sighed, "They sure can. 'Course, Jimmy's son Kevin must be in his forties. Time don't wait for nobody. Most of the people round here have either died or moved off. Used to be tobacco was a real moneymaker but with all the antismoking stuff nowadays small farmers can't afford to raise it."

Tim fetched a Coke from the cooler at the back of the store. The store's shelves were mostly vacant except for bread, soups, cereal and other foodstuffs that would keep well. He downed a swig of Coke before he asked, "So, what keeps you two here? Are you partners in the store? Don't look like you have much business traffic."

Cletus replied, "We are just too stubborn and too old to leave. We draw Social Security and so do our wives. School cafeteria workers. Our houses are paid for and we can grow a lot of our food. We are just simple folks who prefer to live out our days here."

Homer chuckled. "Yeah, and the fishing in the creek is good. Our old ladies ain't about to give up their gardens and chicken flocks for city living."

They all had a good laugh as Tim set the bottle on the counter. "Guess I had better head up that way. Is the road good?"

Homer replied, "Oh, yeah, now it is when nobody lives up there. I will just go with you if you like. I grew up with the Kelsay boys and know that place like the back of my hand."

They climbed into the Jeep, forded the shallow creek and Tim steered the jeep onto the narrow gravel that clung to the mountainside. Along the way, Homer provided commentary on the countryside and the lives of the people who once lived there.

"Damnedest thing. Forty years ago there was a lot of people living back in this here holler, but the state would never fix a decent road. That place right ahead had big boulders sticking up. Man get a tight asshole going over them, especially during winter. Old people died, young people didn't want to farm, then the tobacco buyout, and the next thing you know I think only one family lives up here 'cause Jimmy don't make them pay rent. Right there is where Jimmy's mother turned a tractor over on herself. All that timber there on the left was broke off when we had that big snow a few years ago. Now, right here is the old Cooge Bertram house that was built just after the Civil War. Been deserted a long time, kids say it's hainted. Used to be a little store right there. Fell in around fifty, but you can still see the roof. Now we go down this hill and cross the creek and there it is, the Pat Kelsay place."

Tim was enjoying all the local color as he guided the Jeep across the shallow creek and stopped in a wide-open expanse before a two-story white clapboard house capped by a rusty tin roof. "Let me just start here and take a picture of the house the way you first see it when you pull up. Now, Homer, you will have to be patient as I try a lot of different angles and views, so this may take a while."

Homer nodded and resumed the narration as they walked around the farm. "Take all the time you need. I was losing the checker game anyway. I will show you around. Stay out of the high weeds unless you want to get rattlesnake bit. When Jimmy was here, all these fields were in tobacco or corn. 'Course they picked up walnuts and hickory nuts. Pat always kept beehives over there for honey. That barn up there was used for horses and cows in the bottom and tobacco was hung in the top. Corncrib next to the hog pen. Apple and pear trees. That's a sugar cane patch up there where they gathered seed to use to grow cane for molasses. Pearl had ten mouths to feed so she always had a big garden. Sold eggs, milk and butter. Truth be told, Mr. Collins, most farms around here were pretty self-sufficient. Bet you didn't grow up like that."

"No, I am a city boy, though I guess all city folks dream of moving back to the simpler life with less stress."

"Yep, it was simpler, but harder too. Only went to town for coffee, white sugar, clothes, and banking or legal business. Some people never came out of these hollers more than once a year, some never went to town at all except to be embalmed."

"Really? Didn't they ever need to see a doctor? Go to a bank?"

"Nope, not as long as they could get to Elmore Hancock's place two hollers over. Most people here did a lot of swapping or trading, some never trusted banks. Kept their money in mattresses or buried somewhere."

"I just can't imagine a life like that."

"Well, you need to remember that the gummit raided a lot of stills in these parts and a lot of people lost sons to the wars. Kept interfering with tobacco production even before it was controlled by pounds, then there was the milk subsidies. Most people here cast a jaundiced eye even on census takers. Back then someone like you might have been shot for just being up here. There was some strange birds up here, but they was still good people. Give you the shirt off their back."

"Now, Jimmy said he had seven brothers and sisters?"

"Yep, Pat's first wife Nelly died of cancer and he married Pearl Lewis, whose husband had died. Came up here and took on eight kids two years to fourteen and made this a respectable farm. Worked them about to death, but they all made something of theirselves. Did Jimmy tell you she had to carry his brother around for almost a year when he burned his leg in an explosion? He was a great big kid, too, maybe twelve or fourteen. 'Course Pearl was a big raw-boned woman, strong as an ox. Probably the best farm in these parts. Hey, look! That porch swing looks like it can still hold us. Let's sit a spell."

They mounted the steps to the porch where they found a used condom and wrapper lying in front of the swing.

Homer snickered, "Looks like Cletus was right. Don't know what they was a-doing here in the swing, but I would have paid to see it."

They swung back and forth in silence for a few minutes before Tim said, "I guess this way of life is a thing of the past. Today's people are too soft to live this way. Still, sometimes I wonder if I could get married and start a life up here out of the rat race."

Homer chewed on a long straw he had picked in the yard. "Be mighty hard today 'cause you got no help. All these big farms that had families of eight or ten kids are gone. Land is so rough it wouldn't be profitable to invest in fancy machinery. You might make it a vacation home. I hear some people are looking into putting up vineyards or orchards. Still a lot of work and you got no neighbors to help. And you need that."

Tim stretched back to slow the swing. "Yes, I guess that is important. Unless you want to be a hermit."

Homer slapped his knee and laughed, "Ask Cletus about hermits! His father-in- law pretty much became a hermit after his wife left him and kids were grown. Elroy Marsh was his name, and he was one of them strange birds I told you about. See that knob yonder?"

He pointed to a high cliff topped by scraggly trees. "That's Pinnacle Cliff. You can see Monticello on one side and Albany on the other if you are on top of it. Elroy owned that and a lot of woods and some right good bottomland on the other side. Hard worker and honest as the day is long. Used to run a little store up here at Chestnut Grove. One night the register total was off by three cents and he stayed there till past midnight to square it. Another time, a customer overpaid by a dime. Elroy got in his car and ran the man down to give him the dime."

"That's pretty amazing today, when people just walk over loose change in the street."

"Back then a nickel was as big as a wagon wheel. Between the farm and the store, Elroy made quite a passel of money. Never trusted banks. Just kept his money hid up there. There are several caves in the Pinnacle Cliff. Anyway he caught wind that the gummit was going off the gold standard so quicker than spit he converts all his paper money and silver money to gold just ahead of the changeover. 'Course then he had to take paper money and silver at the store. The whole family lived on that hill until Lizzie said enough of this and left him. So he spent the rest of his life up there alone, scrounging to get by. People said he made a mighty fine possum and dumplings and squirrel pie. Never had any hankering to try them myself."

Tim shivered in disgust, "I think I would have to pass, too. You can eat squirrel, I know, but possum? Yuck!"

Homer grinned. "He got to be mighty peculiar. Sold the store. Cletus married Flora, the youngest girl. The rest of the kids moved up north like everybody else and pretty much disowned him. Elroy did keep a still going year 'round and got a little money that way until he died."

"What happened to him?"

Homer spat a long stream of spittle off the porch and wiped his mouth. "He was eat up with sugar. He had told Pat and Pearl if they never saw the lights in his house by eight o'clock at night he was probably dead or dying. Their boys used to check on him every other day...it's a long hike up there and it is steep. One day, a hen had pecked him and took a piece out of his arm. Jimmy told Pearl that Elroy was real bad and the wound didn't look good. Sure enough in a couple of days, there ain't no light so all four of Pearl's boys took off up that mountain in the middle of the night. August, hot as hell. They find him barely conscious. The peck had set up gangrene and he was about to die. Them boys had to carry his sorry ass off that mountain in a homemade stretcher in the middle of the night right in the thick of rattlesnake season. I told Pearl I would just let the mean old bastard die but she said that was not the Christian thing to do. That's the way she was — it was real hard to win an argument with her."

"So did he live?"

"In a manner of speaking. Lost the arm. I think he willed Flora and Cletus everything he had. Like they was going to go back up there to live. He hung on for about a month and then died."

"What happened to everything that was up there?"

"Foxes caught the chickens, and the hogs ran away. Cletus, Flora, and me went up there and collected a few items. Most of it not worth trying to bring down."

"Never found any of the gold?"

"Cletus poked around a little and never found any sign or mention of it in Elroy's papers. Figured it was just a story people made up. That's been what, sixty years since we lost the gold standard."

"I guess the house fell in by now."

"Maybe. It was built out of chestnut logs with clapboards. Termites don't eat chestnut, so it lasts a long time. Like I said, it is a damn long hard climb up there and I ain't that curious."

"Me either. I need to be getting back."

They got back in the jeep and Homer resumed his colloquial banter back to the store. Tim pulled up in front of the store and they got out to go back inside.

"Hey, Cletus! I have been telling Tim about your father-in-law!"

"Damn your eyes, Homer Hancock! I would have the meanest man God ever made as my father-in-law. He tell you all the stories people told on the poor old crazy man?"

"Yes, he did tell me about his idiosyncrasies." Tim replied.

"I don't know about them thangs, but he was crazy as hell. Homer tell you about the fortune in gold up there?"

Tim laughed, "Yes, but he said no one ever saw it."

Cletus gets up from the chair and walks over to the cash register which he opened as he motioned Tim to come over where he stood.

"I am going to show you the only gold coin anyone has ever seen of Elroy Marsh's vast wealth. One day he ran out of silver money and had to pay for supplies with a twenty dollar gold piece. This is that gold piece. I keep it here under a secret false bottom for good luck. Elroy tried every way he could think of to swap me out of that coin, but I flat refused. It has been here for over forty years and you are the first person I have shown it to in ten years. 'Course, you're leaving town so I ain't worried."

"Don't worry, Cletus. Your secret is safe with me."

"I know that. I know an honest man when I see one. Hey, wait a minute!"

Cletus trotted to the back of the store that was separated from the front by a burlap bag cut lengthwise. Shortly he returned, furiously blowing the dust off something in his hand. "Flora gave this to Elroy one year for Christmas. We found it still in the box when we went up there. Doubt he ever used it and it's probably no good now but if you a camry buff you can have it."

As he finished explaining, he handed the camera to Tim.

"This is one of the early Kodak Instamatics with flashcubes. Don't make these anymore, but it sure will be a novelty. Looks like some of the film has been shot."

Cletus asked, "Really? How can you tell?"

"This little window here. See that little orange stripe? That means the film has been used. Let me rewind it. I doubt the film is any good, but I will develop it and see what was on it. It might be interesting to see if he took pictures of his place before it was abandoned. You know, just to see how it's changed. I can send you the pictures if you give me the address."

"Don't know what that old cuss took pictures of, but now I am curious to know. My address is Cletus Wayne Stinson, Star Route 4, Sunnybrook, KY 42633. I'll pay you for the pictures."

"Forget it. You have been so helpful to me and I have really enjoyed the day. I am sure Jimmy will be happy. Say, I need to head back home. Maybe I will come back in the fall to get some nice color shots. Thank you very much. It has been a pleasure."

They all shook hands and Cletus and Homer waved good-bye before returning to the store.

When Tim was gone they looked at one another and broke out laughing so hard the tears rolled down their cheeks.

Homer caught his breath and said, "Guess we ought to call Jimmy and tell him the fish is on the line. You gotta admit, it was a clever plan sending that man down here supposedly to take pictures of his home place."

"And then just matter-of-fact tell him about this creepy old miser and his pot of gold up in the mountains. So, how many pictures did you leave on the roll?" Cletus asked.

"Oh, about half a roll. I figured I had to make it look like a tightwad wouldn't waste developing half a roll," Homer replied. "And I am sure showing him that twenty dollar gold piece your daddy left you whetted his appetite. All we have to do is wait. Soon as he sees them pictures, he'll be back."

They laughed loudly again and slapped each other on the back. Cletus gasped for breath as he said, "I have to call Flora and tell her. Now you took pictures of the old house and springhouse, didn't you?"

"Of course. You know, it looks real even up close."

They opened a door under the counter and pulled out a rusty old blue and white speckled cold-packer. The pot was filled with crumpled newspaper, but it was topped by enough fake gold pieces to give the illusion that the pot was brimming over with gold coins.

Still chortling, Cletus asked Homer, "So, where did you take the picture of the bait?"

Homer grinned. "Right in front of the biggest cave on Pinnacle Cliff. I set it sorta in the mouth of the cave so you can see it, but not too clear. Made it look a little out of focus like a shaky old man was holding the camry. What did Jimmy think we could get out of this dude?"

"I think he said we could convince him to buy the whole property for $150,000. Jimmy said that if he didn't buy it he was certain Tim would show it to someone who would. Maybe even pay more."

"Sure he will fall for it?"

"Cletus, I took a picture of it with my Nikon to see how real it looked and if I didn't know better, I'd swear it was real. Then I took a few pictures of the pot and some of the surrounding terrain with that old Kodak. If that picture I took with my Nikon could've fooled me, you know a picture with that old Kodak will fool people. Still, he seemed like a nice young man. Almost makes me feel guilty about taking him for a big chunk of money. Almost, until I think of that ten percent Jimmy promised us for setting him up."

Cletus laughed, "Yep, we'll get at least $10,000 or so between us. Easiest money I ever made. Ain't photography wonderful, Homer?"

Imago

A CEMENT BLOCK and a handful of red oak acorns mid-wifed the birth of my friendship with my closest boyhood pal Joe Thompson. The children of the communities of Wayne County attended the vacation Bible schools of the small churches peppered throughout the country where they found new friends, simple Bible lessons and folk handicrafts aimed at young people. It was in this rural milieu that I found a mentor who taught me the true meaning of friendship.

Most of us kids attended Bible school at Bethesda United Methodist Church. The redbrick church had replaced the white clapboarded church and the children enjoyed the shady refuges of two red oaks that graced the front lawn where the children played simple games. In those simpler and indeed happier times, when the boys and girls were flirting with the cusp of puberty, no one ever discussed sexual matters at all.

Young and middle aged men used pamphlets to teach well-known parables of Jesus to the boys. After a half-hour of discussions and prayers, the boys built small birdhouses for house wrens and bluebirds using simple hand tools because power tools were too dangerous. The girls made homespun jewelry and trinket boxes by gluing various pasta shapes onto cigar boxes with Elmer's Glue-all and spray-painting them with gold and silver spray paint.

After the time for projects passed, we snacked on lemonade and cookies before engaging in team games. On one fateful day, the boys lined up against the girls for a rousing game of Red Rover. One team dared a chosen member of the other team to try to run through their interlocked arms. If successful, the victor chose a member of the opposing team to join his team. If not, he was required to join the daring team. A few rounds had been played when I heard, "Red rover, red rover, we dare Alan over!"

Encouraged by the boys, I charged full speed toward the girls' waiting chain. Abruptly, the girls broke ranks, and I slipped on the acorns and fell face first into a cement block that marked the front line of the graveled parking area.

The bridge of my nose broke across the top edge of the block and my inertia knocked the block over and skinned my face. Angry rivulets of blood squirted down my face, blinding me as they flowed. Screaming in pain and feeling faint, I heard a voice say, "Oh, gosh, you're hurt bad. Here take my hand."

Through bloody tears, I saw a young blond boy two years my senior reach out his right to clasp mine and felt his left hand slip under my left arm to support me. "I'm Joe Thompson. You're Alan West, ain't you?" I nodded and leaned on him as he helped me stand up. By now the adults had run over to see what had happened and quickly took me to the restroom to clean the blood and dirt from my face. One of the men gave me a ride home and explained to my mother what had happened. My nose had suffered a small crack, but I returned to Bible school the next day wearing the abrasions of my accident. Joe sought me out and reassured me, "You got some bad scabs but I bet you won't have scars. Say, you want to hang out?"

A wave of a curious warmth swept over me as the comfort of a newfound friend bound us together. We began a journey of discovery and wonder that sustained me through the tumultuousness of surging and lonely adolescence. Some fifty years later, I reminisce about how two souls were knit into one on the sacred ground of a church auspiciously named Bethesda.

II

The seed of friendship planted that day germinated when school started in August. We rode the same bus to school driven by a sour little man, Ephraim Upchurch, with a crippled right hand twisted into a crablike paw by a childhood accident. He was generally unhappy but he never missed a day of work and always reminded the little kids when it was their stop.

Joe lived at Flat Springs in a gray house perched on a cliff that dropped precipitously to a narrow tributary on one side and to the road on another. A grassless path twisted between the tussocks of fescue where Joe slid down to catch the bus to school. On rainy days, Ephraim would bet Joe that he could not make it back up the hillside without falling and sometimes he would win that bet.

My house was about five miles from school so Joe and I had little time together to visit. I always took the same seat three rows back from the front and saved Joe a seat. We discovered we shared many interests: we loved science in all its forms and speculated that we once lived as Cheyenne Indians hunting buffalo on the Great Plains. Both of us had collections of arrowheads scrounged from the patchwork plots tended by farmers who grew tobacco to get a small windfall for their meager Christmases.

Sometimes we both attended a church social and used the time after Sunday potluck to explore the fields and woodlands near the church. One day, we were feeling braver than usual and we slipped away to investigate an old home place about a half a mile from the church. All that remained of the house was a tumbledown limestone block chimney jutting upright from a field haired over by amber stems of sage-grass. As we neared the chimney, we began to speculate about its origin.

Joe said, "So do you know much about this chimney?"

I replied, "No, do you?"

"I asked my dad about it and all he said was that it has been here as long as anyone can remember. He said it might go all the back to the Indian days. Hey, do you think maybe the Indians attacked the people here and burnt their house?"

As we inspected the lichen-encrusted blocks, we chattered possible stories of what that battle must have been like. We returned many times to relive our exciting former lives and we fascinated the kids at school with our fabrications about the chimney's origin.

Joe was a freshman, two years ahead of me, but we shared recess, a time we devoted to discussing the latest science news. We devoured the latest news of the Apollo lunar expeditions and swapped stories of our latest science experiments with our chemistry sets and microscopes. Our wanderings at church became fossil hunts for petrified brachiopods we found along a shallow stream in the field below the chimney. Soon we had assembled extensive collections that earned us A' s in our science classes.

One Sunday afternoon we had returned to the stream looking for fossils when we noticed several butterflies sipping water along the stream. We sat and watched them fluttering in fits and starts as soft breezes blew them aloft.

Joe said, "Hey, I'm tired of collecting fossils. I heard the other day that I will have to make an insect collection in biology next year. Let's start collecting butterflies."

"Will they keep until then?"

"Oh, sure. There's not much to them really. We can catch them and kill them with alcohol and pin them onto pieces of styrofoam. Museums have all kinds of collections from around the world. So what do you think?"

"So what do we need. A butterfly net?"

Joe laughed and replied, "We can always catch them with our hands but a net might make it easier for some of them. Why don't you start collecting them around where we live? I know you have alcohol and a Mason jar with a lid."

"Oh, yes, but I can't get the styrofoam until we go to town. Where do you get it?"

"You can get it at the dime store or the variety store. It ain't expensive. Tell your mom you need it for a school project, which is the truth, ain't it?"

"Well, yes it is. Do you think the butterflies will last long enough to use them next year?"

"Oh yeah, they just dry out. They are pretty fragile though so once you get them pinned down you have to be careful with them. Hey, if I see more than one of one kind, I will catch one for you and you do the same for me. Deal?"

"Deal. I had better get going home. Mom will be worried."

"Me too. Race back to the church?"

"Yep" and we dashed back to the church.

III

We live our lives without seeing the world around us. Until Joe and I started our butterfly collections, I had no idea of how many kinds there were. Mom's zinnia garden teemed with butterflies of every description, but I never knew their scientific names.

Joe fixed that. One day when he got on the bus he brought me a copy of The Golden Guide to Butterflies and Moths.

"Wow, thanks, Joe. Look at this. This is really neat."

"I bought two copies so you can have this one. Have you started catching any yet?"

"Yeah, I caught some black ones and yellow ones. Let's see that they are."

I flipped through the book until I found a black one like I caught."

"It's a spicebush swallowtail. **Papilla troilus**. This is great, it gives the scientific name."

Joe took the book from me and said, "Let me show you something." He quickly turned to the page with a large yellow striped butterfly.

"Tiger swallowtail, **Papilo glaucus**" Joe said, "But look. The females come in two forms. A black one and a yellow one. The black ones look a lot like the spicebush butterflies, but they're bigger and have different colors on the hind wings. If you look close you can see the darker vertical stripes."

Sure enough, there were faint darker stripes in the picture in the book. "Gosh, I had no idea there were so many kinds."

"And look, it even shows what their caterpillars look like and what they eat. I bet we can find some larvae and hatch them out."

"I bet so too. We're going to have the best project ever."

So using the pages of the guide as sails, we began our voyage into the world of butterflies and moths.

What a world it was. We began a friendly competition of collecting and learning about our subject. There were the orange and black monarchs, the greater fritillary with its beautiful silver spots under its hind wings, the zebra swallowtail, the monstrous giant swallowtail with its black wings spotted with yellow spots, the tiny blues and dozens of others.

Then there were moths. Our favorite moths were the giant silk moths. We had both the beautiful sea-green luna moth, the giant polyphemus moth with its huge blue eyespots, and the brilliant orange and yellow royal walnut moth. Invariably, when we were together we recounted our fantasies of finding the Holy Grail, the giant cecropia moth, to complete our collections.

"Can you come over Saturday? We can go hunting for new specimens and I want to try to make a rocket."

"Sure, I can ride my bike over."

"Your bike? Are you crazy? You have to ride up that hill from the creek. That hill is almost a mile long and then there's Dave's hill on my road. I can barely make it up that."

"That's because you're a sissy. See ya Saturday."

IV

When I got home, I told Mom that Joe was coming over Saturday before I went to the basement to mix up a crude batch of gunpowder for a rocket. I got up early Saturday morning and waited until I saw Joe coming out the road on his bike.

"Hey, buddy. I told you I would make it."

"I bet you're tired. Legs sore?"

"Nope, but it was hard going up that long hill. After that, Dave's hill was a piece of cake. Got anything to drink?"

"Yeah, Mom bought some Cokes. Come on up."

Joe rode up the drive, parked his bike outside the kitchen door and followed me into the kitchen.

"Mom, this is my friend, Joe Thompson."

"Hello, Mrs. West. Mom said to tell you hello too."

Mom replied, "Your Mom and I met at a Stanley party once. How's your brother?"

Joe had a brother, Ralph, who had muscular dystrophy. He seldom left the house as the disease had progressively weakened him mentally and physically. He had a small metal loom that he used to make potholders to sell.

She held up a potholder and said, "I bought this from Ralph. It's a real good potholder. You tell him that. I'm going to fry hamburger for dinner so you go on outside and play."

"Let's go, Joe. I got to get your help on something."

We ran outside and chatted about the trip over and school. I leaned over and whispered, "I need your help on something. Come up to the barn."

When we reached the barn we climbed into the loft where I showed Joe my gunpowder mixture.

"I mixed this up for rocket fuel. I used the recipe you gave me. Sulfur, charcoal and salt peter. Let's see if it works."

We jumped out of the loft and poured some of the powder onto a flat rock in front of the barn. I had sneaked some matches out of the kitchen and we lit the little pile. It spat sparks before shooting up a plume of stinky black smoke.

Joe knitted his brow. "Well, it ain't great, but it works. Do you have more of the stuff? We can make a new batch."

"Sure, I have it in the basement. I want to make a rocket."

"What're you using for the rocket?"

"I thought we would test it on a corncob. If it works, we can build a better body."

We picked up a corncob from the basket where we collected them. I hollowed out the pith center, placed a fuse from a string of firecrackers into the hole, and held it while Joe poured it full of the powder. Joe lit it and we ran back a few feet.

The fuse splattered sparks but died out when it reached the cob. Joe rolled it over to dislodge the fuse.

"Somehow your powder ain't right. Got any more?"

Before I could stop myself, I blurted out, "I can get some shotgun shells from the house. We can cut them apart and get the powder."

"I guess that'll work if we're careful. How are you going to get it?"

"Mom is doing the washing today and she will go outside to hang it out. I'll sneak into daddy's bedroom and get them."

We watched until Mom came out of the house carrying a big load of laundry to hang out on the clotheslines behind the garage. I ran into my dad's bedroom where he kept his twelve-gauge shotgun in a gun rack. Dad had warned all of us kids to never mess with the guns so I was more than a little nervous. Still, his warnings should not stand in the way of scientific progress, so I crammed three shotgun shells into my pants pocket and ran back to the barn.

I sat down and handed the shells to Joe. He said, "Good job. You gotta knife?"

"Yeah, here it is," I said as I gave him my pocketknife. We both began to sweat and shake as neither of us was sure what we were doing. He carefully pressed the knife down on the shell at the juncture of the brass cap and the plastic housing until it started to slice into the plastic. Using short saw-like strokes, he soon cut the shell away and poured the gunpowder into the hollowed out corncob we were using as a rocket body.

I inserted a long fuse from a package of Black Cat firecrackers into the powder and tamped in some modeling clay to seal the makeshift rocket. Joe held his breath as I lit the fuse and quickly backed away when the fuse ignited. Suddenly, the powder exploded and blew the cob into smithereens. We looked at each other in astonishment at how our well-laid plans had gone seriously awry.

Joe laughed and said, "Well, Al, I guess we're not rocket scientists!"

We decided to return the unused shells to the gun drawer and use the rest of the afternoon pursuing butterflies for my collection.

V

Joe and I had traversed the surrounding countryside for several weeks in search of new specimens, but at times our searches were excuses for tangential pursuits. Any excuse was sufficient to search the swamp next to Gossage's farm or the fields on the top of the mountain. Sometimes we found species that I did not have in my collection and sometimes we just had the time together doing what young boys did as they staggered into adolescence: trying to understand the mysteries of sex and girls.

By now, our collections had grown to include nearly all the native butterflies. People had heard that we were working on a collection, and many neighbors caught some for us. My father brought home a male tulip tree moth one day, followed by the female two days later. But one species had eluded us: the cecropia moth with its ornately colored patterned wings that reached over six inches.

The species was single brooded so we had only a narrow window in late July or early to mid-August to catch them. One Saturday in early August, Joe and I scoured Gossage's Swamp again. The summer heat had dried up the swamp so we did not have to wade water but the ground felt squishy. As we neared a stand of willow saplings, we felt our hearts racing with excitement as we saw a large cecropia moth clinging to a branch about seven feet off the ground. We crept silently toward the tree to stand under the moth, but it was just out of our reach.

Joe turned to me and suggested, "We might knock it down with a stick but that might damage it. Give me a boost and I can grab it."

I knelt down and cupped my hands to form a makeshift step. He put his right foot into my hands and steadied himself by laying his hand on the top of his head and waited for my signal.

"Are you ready? Here goes!"

As I rose, I lifted him off the ground. He tried to grab the moth but lost his balance and succeeded only in brushing the branch. The sudden movement of the branch frightened the moth and it fluttered further up the tree to perch on a branch ten feet above us.

I asked, "Do you want to try to knock it down?"

"No, let's not. We found him so I bet we can find others. If we don't we can get him later."

We searched the swamp for over an hour without success. Disappointed, we returned to the tree only to find the moth gone.

Joe turned to me and suggested, "Maybe we can find a cocoon and let it hatch out next spring."

We knew that the adults emerged in spring and the larvae spent the summer gorging themselves before spinning a large tough cocoon wrapped around a sturdy stem. In the fall, we managed to find one of these cocoons and kept it in a jar over the winter.

Boys our age are not particularly known for their patience. One day in February we decided to check on the development of the moth. Joe's mom dropped him off when school had been called off because of snow. We used a razor blade to carefully slit the stubborn silken pocket open and poured the pupa onto a table. The transformation has indeed begun as we could see the faint tracings of the outlines of antennae and wings wrapped around the pupa.

Joe said, "It looks like it has changed. Let's split it open and look at it." With the skill of a surgeon, he gingerly slid the tip of the razor blade into the pupa's skin and opened it up. To our disappointed surprise, there was no adult moth inside, just some amorphous brownish goop.

As I looked at the goop, I said, "It looks like this one had already died. It may have been too hot in the house."

Joe replied, "I bet you're right. Maybe we should have left it in the tree and got it later in the spring when it was older. Maybe we can find one this spring. Hey, I have to go. See ya tomorrow."

He got into his mother's waiting car and waved as she drove over the hill.

A major cold front dropped a foot of snow in the county that night. School was canceled and a secondary blast of arctic air kept the snow from melting. Many of the roads in the county remained covered in ice and snow for two weeks so schools stayed closed.

My brother and I spent the snow days playing Monopoly or Yahtzee. We were playing Yahtzee on the kitchen table while we listened to the radio to see if the school was open the next day. The announcer said that schools were still closed for the rest of the week before he finished the rest of the local news.

The radio crackled out the next announcement. "Joe Thompson, son of Ray and Bess Thompson, died suddenly this morning. Funeral arrangements are incomplete and will be announced when they become available."

My heart raced as the shock of the news sunk in. I cried loudly and rambled wildly while I tried to understand what I had heard. Only a few days ago, Joe and I had spent the afternoon in our usual pursuits and had tried to speed up the metamorphosis of the cecropia. He had been perfectly healthy with no sign of any illness, not even a cold. Mom called our neighbor Wilma Brown who served as the source of news for everyone because her kind heart and sympathetic ear made people trust her with any important news.

After a few minutes of conversation, Mom hung up and said, "Joe had leukemia. No one knew anything about it. Wilma said that he must have developed it a long time ago but he had not shown any symptoms until it was too late."

Still weeping, I asked, "What's leukemia?"

"Wilma said it is like you have too many white blood cells that fight disease and they eat up the red blood cells. At least that was her understanding of what Bess had told her."

By morning, the family had made funeral arrangements. The visitation would be the next day and funeral the day after that. The shock of losing my best friend had transformed me into a zombie-like existence and the time between Joe's death to the time of the funeral became just a blur.

I caught a ride with Wilma to go to the funeral. By the time we reached the funeral home, I had no more tears to shed, feeling only a dark hollow in my heart. The funeral director opened the casket and the crowd passed by to pay its final respects. I crept up to the side of the casket and saw the lifeless body of my best friend reposing in the white satiny lining of the casket. Other than a cold pallor in his face, I saw no difference between now and when I last saw him alive. The crowd pressed me to move along so I looked at him once more and wiped away a tear as I wondered if his insides were the same goop as we had seen when we tried in vain bring a new cecropia moth into the world.

VI

Time speeds by to heal the wounds of our youth and leaves us with memories as fragile as a dried butterfly's wings. Shortly after Joe's passing, I entered high school and later moved away to college. As new stresses and responsibilities assailed me, I left the memory of those long ago days buried in the past and pursued my career in entomology.

Unsurprisingly, my interests centered on the Lepidoptera: butterflies and moths. The misconceptions of naïve youth were replaced with the clinical reality of an excruciatingly detailed study of the life histories of these insects. My doctoral dissertation investigated how different species of butterflies reduced competition for resources by niche separation of the food plants eaten by the larvae. In a few years, I became an internationally recognized expert on these insects.

The puny collection of my youth has mushroomed into an enormous museum containing a menagerie of thousands of species. As the curator of the university insect collections, I revel in the gasps of admiration and awe when the breath-taking blue morphos of South America or the huge Atlas moths and bird wing butterflies of the Far East stunned visitors.

My classes in general biology and entomology are popular and challenge me to impart my love for the subject to my students. As in any science class, students have to learn basic facts and terminology to pass the tests: larva, pupae, thorax, spiracles and more complicated concepts. Some insects, like grasshoppers, are hemimetabolous meaning that the various stages of the nymphs differ only in size with no pupal stage. The Lepidoptera are holometablous, meaning they go through a complete metamorphosis from egg, larvae, pupae, and the adult stage, which is called the imago. My exams always asked students if humans are holometabolous or hemimetabolous and to justify their answers. Occasionally, a bright student saw the flaw in the question: our bodies are hemimetabolous because babies look like adults, but our lives are holometabolous as new experiences change who we are and how we view the world.

An advanced class in insect evolution and ecology encouraged students to ask more general and conceptual questions. The beautiful wings of insects have evolved designs that serve many purposes: they may camouflage the insects and some of the large eyespots may frighten away predators. Coevolution of flowers and their insect pollinators can explain why some butterflies and moths have long proboscises to reach the nectar and pollen in long tubular flowers. Students are surprised to learn that giant silk moths have no functional mouthparts at all and never eat anything: their only purpose is to mate, disperse to new habitats to lay eggs and then die, leaving the eggs to hatch into larvae that eat until the pupal stage.

Butterfly pupae are cased in a translucent chrysalis while those of moths are concealed in tough silken cocoons. During the metamorphosis, the innards of both are basically dissolved into goop with only a few cells called germinal cells left intact to direct the construction of the imago phase as if by some magical abracadabra.

Inquisitive students ask how butterflies and moths survive the winter and the answer to that question is multifaceted. Moths overwinter snug in their warm cocoons as do some butterflies; but some butterflies, (like the mourning cloak), hibernate in a tree hollow. For decades, scientists were confident that those were the only strategies available to survive the harsh winters.

All that changed in the seventies when a chance discovery by a German scientist, Frederick Urquhart, working in a secluded part of Mexico shook the scientific community. He found a small heavily forested region where monarch butterflies from North America gather in billions hanging in gargantuan masses from the trees. This was the first evidence that a butterfly species migrated to escape the winter chill.

In the following years, Urquhart studied the life cycles of these migrants. As the days ushered in the new spring, the masses shook off the slumbers and prepared to return to their northern homes. As the flood of butterflies moves north, they timed their odyssey with the warming temperatures so that three or four generations would be born along the way until the last generation would finally reach their ancestral homeland to reproduce that would return to the winter refuge to begin the cycle anew.

V

Fifty years ago, I began my journey into the intoxicatingly beautiful and mysterious world of Lepidoptera and followed my fortunes wherever the vagaries of fate took me. Now that I am nearing retirement, I find myself yearning to go back home, to those lost days of innocence, those times of treasures found and treasures lost. My children have started their own careers on the west coast and my wife has gone out of town to visit relatives in Boston, so there is no reason I can't go back home for a visit.

As I drive back home, I realize I am not the same man who left fifty years ago and it is not the home I left. When mom and dad died, the rest of the kids overruled me and sold the home place to a residential developer. The money from the sale did little to assuage the feelings of betrayal that eventually drove us apart and much like the adult silk moths we dispersed from our home.

The countryside along the road back home has changed drastically. What once were open fields, farms and woodlands now lay in fallow fields, small bedroom communities and shopping malls. Out of curiosity, I drive by my childhood home and see that it is unrecognizable. The Bethesda Methodist Church is still there but it clearly needs some routine maintenance. During one of my academic searches for some obscure bit of knowledge, I discovered that the word Bethesda derived from a Hebrew word meaning 'house of mercy' and I smiled at the memories of Bible school there. The old chimney still kept its lonely vigil over the sage grass-covered field, looking the same as it did when Joe and I had played around it and imagined wild tales of pioneers and Indians locked in mortal combat.

The church cemetery lies in a small area between the church and the field where the chimney stood its sentinel. I park my car in the graveled drive in front of the cemetery, tuck the small box I had brought with me under my arm and begin to stroll between the tombstones until I find Joe's grave. Small grass clippings spewed out by the weed-eaters are splattered over the dark gray granite and there is a splotch of bird droppings on the top of the stone. As I kneel down to clean the stone, I begin to weep as I trace over Joe's name etched deep into the stone. I recall that day of crashing headlong into that cement block and the friendship that sprang from that accident. Memories of corncob rocket ships, hunts for arrowheads, and searches for butterflies and moths flood over me and for a few fleeting moments I see both Joe and me gamboling over the fields and swamps.

I wipe my tears away with a handkerchief, pat the stone and whisper, "You know Joe, we never did ask what 'cecropia' meant. Well, I found out. Cecrops was the mythical Greek king who founded the city of Athens and taught people reading, writing, marriage, and ceremonial burial, among other things."

Carefully, I open the small box and gently place the beautiful cecropia male moth atop the tombstone and smile as it flutters across the stone before coming to rest. I realize that the moth would be an easy target for birds so I help him crawl onto my open hand and carry him over to the small patch of willows growing along the edge of the cemetery. After I place him onto the slender branches, he swings gently back and forth until a light breeze makes him lose his grip. He languidly flaps his huge beautiful wings before nestling into the uppermost branches, a little closer to heaven.

Pearls Before Swine

VIDA DENNEY HUMMED along with the nightly parade of gospel music presented by the local radio station as she prepared for her trip the next day. Someone always requested her favorite hymn, "Amazing Grace" and tonight was no exception. Instinctively, she began to sing along in a raspy voice tempered by years of hard work in dusty fields and rearing of six children.

"A-maazing grace, how sweeet the sound, that saaaved a wretch liiike mee…"

The lyrics alternated with low humming as she continued laying out her clothes to visit her son in Burnside the next two days. She ran through her packing list, "There's my blue dress, my shoes, my Bible, and my new necklace. The cat has enough food and water for two days, and I changed the litter box tonight. I think I'm all ready. I think I'll fly up."

She went to the bathroom and washed out her dentures before she placed them in their special cup with two Polident tablets. After she returned to the bedroom, she changed into a checkered fleece nightgown, clicked off the small table lamp, and called the cat to come to bed.

"Rastus, it's time for bed!"

A yellow Persian cat jumped onto the bed and crouched on her abdomen to gently knead her stomach while she scratched his ears.

"I've spoiled you so much, big fellow. You're just rotten. Ow! Not so hard. That's enough."

She gently pushed the big cat off her body and waited for him to settle beside her leg. Though she lived alone, she said her prayers quietly, her old-woman lips twitching as she thanked God for his mercy and her children and her dear husband Benton, dead now for fifteen years. Then she made more general prayers for the sick, the hungry, and the victims of the hand of man or heartless fate.

"In Jesus name, I pray these things, and if they be your will, Amen." She concluded her prayers and stared at the dresser and the crystal vase of flowers as she drifted off to restful dreams.

II

Harold Young was sitting on his porch mulling over the text for Sunday's sermon when he heard the harsh *braang* of the telephone. He walked quickly into the house and answered, "Hello," and heard Iris Brumley sobbing on the other end.

"Brother Young, this is Iris Brumley. It's Momma. I found her dead in the bed this morning. Can you come up here, please, before the ambulance people take her away? I want to show you something."

"Sure, Iris, I'll be right there as fast as I can." He hung up the phone, bolted out the back door and quickly drove to Vida's house. Iris was waiting for him on the porch outside the front door. He trotted across the yard and embraced her, "I am so sorry, Iris. This is a real shock. Vida seemed the picture of health in church Sunday, but when I dropped by Tuesday she did seem a little agitated. Had she said anything to you?"

She stammered, "I don't know, Brother Young. She was just fine when I took her to the doctor Wednesday. Said she was in great shape for an eighty-five-year-old woman. She never told me about anything that was upsetting her." She wiped her eyes again. "You'll have to excuse me; I'm still a little tore up. This is all so unexpected."

The ambulance drivers walked past them to radio in the information as Harold gently asked, "Can you tell me what happened? Take your time."

Iris nodded feebly and sat down on the couch. "Well, I told her that I would take her up to Jimmy's today for the weekend. This morning I got here around nine. Mom is usually piddling around her flowerbeds or sitting in a chair so it struck me as odd that she was not out here. I knocked and hollered, and when nobody answered I used my key to get in. She's still lying there just like I found her. I asked the ambulance men to wait so you could see this. Come on in."

Harold followed her into the house and into the bedroom where Vida reposed with a soft smile.

Iris took his hand and led him over to a small daybed under the window. "Look at all this and read that note," she said, indicating with a sweeping gesture a dress, some papers, a necklace of a lace kerchief woven around iridescent glass stones, and plain black shoes.

He picked up the letter written in plain pencil on notebook paper.

"Everything you need is on the bed. I'm going to see Benton about a new vase."

Iris's eyes welled up again and she gasped, "The medical examiners found no pills, no heart attack, no reason she should be dead. From the looks of it. I guess she had just lived long enough. She always said she wanted you to preach her funeral."

"I would be honored to preach her funeral. Do you know what she meant by this remark about a new vase?"

Iris wiped her eyes with a tissue and softly blew her nose. "Here, I'll show you. Daddy bought Mom this cut glass vase for their first Christmas together. Mom liked to grow flowers, so she always kept two roses in it for them and added a new flower when one of us was born. Lately she used silk flowers instead of real ones. That's me there, that white rose bud, that lavender bud one is Lily and that yellow one is Rose. They just used opened-up roses for the boys. Willie is the red one, Charlie the white one, and Tom is the yellow one."

"Who is that dark red one there?" Harold asked.

Iris wiped her eyes as she took the rose out of the vase. "I don't know. Momma's mind had slipped a bit, so she might have put it there by accident. Looks like a new one. Don't reckon she has had any more kids at her age," she said with a wry smile.

Iris stroked Vida's hand as the ambulance attendants entered to carry her body away to the hearse in front of the house. Harold hugged Iris again and whispered a short prayer. She straightened herself and patted his shoulder.

"Well, Reverend, I have a lot to do. I got to call the rest of the kids and try to pull myself together. I guess I'll leave everything like it is here until the rest of the kids can see it. By the way, Momma wanted 'Amazing Grace' and 'Will the Circle Be Unbroken' sung at her funeral."

Harold fumbled a card from his wallet to give her. "Iris, here is my card. If there is anything I can do to help, please call. If you need me to help make arrangements, let me know. I don't think 'Will the Circle Be Unbroken' is in our hymnal, so we may have to get copies made."

Iris smiled, "You know it never dawned on me that people might not know that song. Mom used to sing it a lot when we were young. Your mind remembers a lot of things at times like this, I guess."

"But that's exactly what you should remember now. You're just stressed out and confused. Would you mind if I took the scrapbooks with me to look through? I had grown very fond of your mother and want to preach a good funeral that recalls her whole life, since I bet a lot of people from Duncan Valley will attend. I'll be very careful with them."

She handed him the books and answered weakly, "No, that will be fine. You can return them after you're through with them."

III

Harold leafed through the scrapbooks, and thought about his visits with Vida since his arrival from Danville two years ago. He had worked hard to prepare a good sermon that first Sunday and was gratified to hear the compliments "Good sermon, Brother Young. Glad to have you here," as people filed past him to their cars, even if in his heart he knew they were just being polite.

But Vida was different. She took his hand, and offered, "You got a good speaking voice, Reverend. Now if you just had something to say, you'd be all right."

He remembered blushing as he stammered, "Thank you, I'll try to do better next week."

She invited, "You drop by this week, and I'll give you some tips."

"I would appreciate that and I'll try to drop by. Where do you live?"

"Good pastor ought to know where his sheep live, but you're new here. I live four houses up the street from the church. You see that row of rose bushes yonder? That's my place. Ain't no need to call. I never go anywhere during the week."

"I'll call, but is Wednesday around eleven okay with you?"

"That'll be fine. I'll try to have some gingersnaps made."

He greeted received the other parishioners, but he could not forget the image of those snapping hazel eyes set above the cheekbones made prominent by the sunken flesh by toothlessness. A short silver-haired woman said, "Hello? Reverend Young? I'm Lula Martin. I enjoyed your sermon today. Now don't let Vida throw you. She never was one for sugarcoating her opinion. I've known her for most of my life. She's a wonderful woman once you get to know her, but she's had a hard life."

"Really? Well, Ms. Martin, it sounds like I need to find out more about her before I meet her. I don't want to say anything else she doesn't agree with. I'm supposed to see her Wednesday. Is there any time we could meet so you could tell me more about her life?"

"Well, can you stop by Tuesday afternoon around two? I volunteer at the senior citizens home in the morning and that will give me time to fix us a late lunch."

"That would be great, if your husband doesn't mind."

She laughed a sad soft laugh, "Reverend, my Paul has been dead for ten years so I don't expect he'll mind. I live about three miles from here at 110 Chesney Street, a brown brick house with metal awnings. I'll see you then."

IV

The night of Vida's death, Harold sat at his kitchen table for two hours poring over the scrapbooks that told the story of her life. Wearied by the constant sitting, he decided to take a walk to clear his head. A light rain misted the air so he grabbed his umbrella to take a short walk.

As he walked along, his mind turned back to the lunch with Lula. She had prepared tuna fish sandwiches and chips with iced tea for lunch and he suddenly recalled her cackling, "I drink tea sometimes, but if you're going to Vida's you can expect coffee or maybe Kool-aid. She don't put on no airs with tea!"

"I've noticed that very few people here drink tea. Don't they like the taste?"

"No, it's mostly because their parents never drunk it. Traditions around here are hard to break."

"How did you come to break tradition?"

"I was one of the lucky ones. My daddy saw to it that I went to college, and I learned about lot more of the world. Picked up a lot of new habits, some good, some bad. I taught at the high school for thirty-five years."

"Now, you said your husband died ten years ago. Did you have children?"

"Paul died from diabetes, but we had three of the best children in the world. Margie, Becky, and Mark. Margie lives in Indianapolis, and the others in Kokomo. The sixties flight north, you know."

Young nodded his understanding before changing the topic, "How do you know Vida? Childhood friends?"

Lula sat her tea down as she repositioned herself in the chair. "Like I said, I was one of the lucky ones. Vida was one of the unlucky ones. Now, Brother Young, some things around here have changed some, but not as much as you think. Oh, you've got your conveniences, but people around here still look at life much the same way as when Vida was born. A woman born back then in the hollows around here lived her life with little expectation of fortune or fame. Vida's life was already mapped out for her the minute she was born: grow up, get married, have a bunch of kids and hope to God you could make that your idea of happiness and purpose."

"I take it that once you got away, you developed a different idea of happiness," Young said between sips of tea.

"Let's just say that I learned there was more to happiness than struggling to survive. My husband was a liberal from Michigan who taught me to appreciate life and all that different people bring to it. We lived in Michigan for the first eight years of our marriage, and it changed my view about black people, Catholics, Polish people, and nearly everything else."

"But surely, it was very hard to move back here. Why did you choose to move back?"

Lula smiled at his ignorance of the obvious. "Because this is home, Brother Young. And Paul said that he wanted our children to have that innocence he had found in me. He got into back-to-nature stuff. Still, we raised three good kids here, and I got to teach the children of my classmates. But enough about me. You came here to find out about Vida."

"Yes, ma'am, if you don't mind."

"Vida never made extravagant demands out of this life. She started out pretty rough up in the head of Dry Hollow. Her parents were Lester and Maybelle Denney. An outbreak of red measles had swept through the whole county, orphaning some and marking others for life with blindness or scars. Vida herself was laid out for dead when she was only six weeks old. Luckily, her father felt her faint breath as he was about to lay her in a coffin. Both her parents died from the measles a month later, leaving the people in that part of the county the task of divvying up the five orphans amongst themselves."

"So both parents died from measles, and neighbors had to raise the children?"

"There were several families like that. The Asberrys. The Watsons. The Fausts. No such thing as state aid then. People had no choice but to adopt them. Just the way it was."

"Did any of your family catch the measles?" Young asked, incredulous at the revelation of Vida's childhood.

"No, they didn't, because we lived way up in Sandy Valley and none of us ever had any contact with anyone who had it. Somehow Vida's family caught it."

"So who raised Vida?"

"Jay and Willadean Stinson over at Hidalgo adopted Vida to raise with their daughter Elaine. Only two years separated the two girls, so it was very easy to let Vida grow up as a member of the family. She was sixteen before she learned of her true parents, and had started courting Benton Denney. They had to say something, because they did not know if he was any kin or not. Turns out he was from a fourth cousin or something of her father, so it didn't matter."

"I imagine everyone knew who had adopted each of the children. Did she ever make any contact with her brothers and sisters after she found out where they were?"

Lula got up to refill the tea glasses. A studious look filled her face as she replied, "I think she tried after she was grown. A couple of them had moved to Tennessee and I think one had died from typhoid. The only one she found was Molly Keeton. They got to be real close, but I don't know if I would call them family, you know what I mean? You can't walk into a family; you sort of have to grow into it from the git-go."

"I hadn't thought about it that way, but I can see your point. I imagine living on a farm was a lot of work, especially back then."

"You can say that again. Most of us around here grew up on a farm and learned to work as soon as we could walk. Vida had no use for people who whined and prayed for the Lord to save them when they weren't doing anything to save themselves. She used to laugh that she prayed for an angel to come milk the cows at 4:30 in the morning, but none ever showed up. But she learned everything she needed to be a good wife and mother. Worked hard for everything she had. She had no use for laggards or thieves."

"I gather she learned a lot about the Bible from an early age. She seems pretty sure of her knowledge."

"Goodness, yes. The Stinsons were hard-shell Baptists. No music in church. Strict reading of the Bible. And, whatever you do when you meet with Vida, do not mention Catholics."

Young grimaced. "I know a lot of people who feel that way, but as I have grown a little older, I have a more ecumenical approach to religion. I take it Vida doesn't see it that way."

"No, she doesn't. Her mind is pretty made up when it comes to religious matters. I used to go home with her from the one room school. Early on, her mother discovered that Vida had a green thumb and helped her grow old-maids, marigolds, bachelor buttons, and hollyhocks."

"How old was she when she got married?"

"She told me once that she was a week shy of her seventeenth birthday when she married Benton Denney from Duncan Valley. He had bought a big farm and they raised six kids. Six good kids. Vida missed the farm after they moved into town."

"So why move into town? Just getting too old to handle all the work?"

"Partly, but the house burned down one night. Vida and Benton decided that it would make a lot more sense to sell the farm and move into town after Benton started having heart trouble. They bought that little house about twelve years ago and joined the church. Benton died of a heart attack eight years ago. Vida's been there by herself ever since, but the kids keep a check on her. And, of course, the church does too. She donates a lot of flowers to the church for Sundays."

"That brings me up to date. So, what about now?"

Lula laughed, "I'm not going to tell you everything. Vida is full of surprises. You've already seen she doesn't mince words. You can't help but love her. Now I have to go to get my hair fixed, so I'm going to kick you out. Good luck Wednesday."

<h1 style="text-align:center">V</h1>

As he prepared to see Vida Young he thought about the life Vida had lived and from this part of the world. He had never dreamed of people having such a tenuous hold on survival and he wondered how he could find any common ground to relate to the people. The world of seminaries, biblical commentaries, and liturgical funeral and wedding ceremonies seemed useless and alien, but he had taken the job and could only trust that his faith in God's guidance would prove sufficient for the tasks set before him.

He arose Wednesday morning, and busied himself around the church until 10:30 before he walked over to Vida's home. The house was a simple clapboard affair with a white picket fence around the yard. Flowerbeds and rose bushes lined the fence and surrounded the house in a wild profusion of colors and forms. Before he could ring the bell, Vida met him as she opened the screen door.

"Good morning, Brother Young. Well, it's good to see you're on time. I hate waiting on company that is late. You can come in if you like, but it's such a beautiful morning, I thought we might sit outside if that's all right with you."

"That would be fine, Ms. Denney. It is indeed one of God's beautiful mornings. Is that chair okay?"

"Yeah, that's good. I'll get the coffee and cookies. I hope you have a King James Bible. Don't put no stock in them other kinds. And you can call me Vida."

He laid his hat and Bible on a small wicker table and settled in for the visit. The air was thick with the sweet smell of the morning blossoms, and he smiled, and watched so he could open the door for her. She carried a tray with two china cups, a small percolator and two small dishes of homemade gingersnaps.

"Oh, set down, preacher. I ain't helpless. You might move that hat and Bible though, so I can use that table. Put them over there in that other chair. I always liked a man who wears a hat. Benton always wore a hat. I still have several of his old hats. Can't bring myself to give them away. "

"Absolutely. Everybody I know hangs onto keepsakes of loved ones who have gone on to the Church Triumphant."

"The Church Triumphant is sorta the whole point of our Lord's work, ain't it? To triumph over sin and death."

He could not help but notice a sly smile turn up the corners of her mouth, and he chuckled aloud, "Yes, I have the King James Bible. I have always liked its language and poetic style better than the others, but I do use some others for research and different points of view."

"Well, as long as you preach from King James, you'll be fine. Have a cookie. I made them last night. Benton and the kids always liked them. Kids, of course, liked their milk. Back in the country we got it straight from the cow. Nowadays, they say that ain't safe, but it never killed any of us. Lordy, I do miss them old days. Times was a lot simpler. Are they good?"

He paused to swallow before answering, "They're delicious. Much better than store-bought ones. I'm sure you got to be a good cook raising a large family of kids on the farm. Do you still do a lot of cooking?"

"Benton and me raised six kids, three boys and three girls, so I had to learn to cook a lot. I don't seem to have much of an appetite anymore and I hate to waste food. Iris stops by a few times a week and brings me McDonald's or Long John Silver's. It ain't as good as home cooking, but it is a lot easier. Here, have some more coffee."

He reached the cup to her. "Thank you. You make good coffee too. Whoa, that's enough. Don't want to spill it. I see you have a lot of flowers around here."

"I've always loved my flowers since I was a little girl. I've got so many I let the neighbors cut bouquets if they want. There has been several Mexican families move in around here and some of the kids pick a flower or two. They're always so nice and ask. They don't speak very good English, so I can't understand them much."

"We are all God's children, aren't we?"

"Well, that's one thing I wanted to talk to you about. I hear most of these people are Catholics. I don't know much about them, but I've heard they worship the pope or the Virgin Mary."

"Well, it's rather hard to explain. They still believe that Jesus Christ is the only way to get to heaven, but they believe that there is a chain of being that has degrees of holiness. They revere the Virgin Mary only as far as she gave birth to the Savior. They tend to emphasize Christ's suffering for us. Catholics have a crucifix with the body of Christ still on it. Protestants emphasize the risen Christ, so they use a cross without the body of Christ."

"I guess to each his own, but I'll just keep believing what has served me pretty well so far, and let them answer for what they believe. Now, about your sermon."

Young straightened himself up and leaned toward her. "I'm anxious to hear your review."

"Well, to start, you might want to not use so many big words. People here are pretty plain speaking."

He smiled, "I think that's probably a good point."

"I'm just saying how you need to talk to people on a level they understand. These people expect to see a lot more fire and passion in your sermons. Raise your voice, walk around, slap that pulpit! How can anyone believe that you have the fire of the Holy Spirit in you if you don't show it? Church is supposed to wake folks up about being saved and you can't talk them into it if they don't see it in you."

Young nodded slightly, and realized the differences between the preaching courses he had taken in school and this church's members. "I never thought about that."

"And there is one more thing. You need to get married. You're good-looking and personable enough, but people are suspicious if such a good catch ain't got a wife."

Young felt a wave of consternation wash over him at Vida's candid but non-judgmental comment. "Well, to be honest, I haven't found the right woman yet, and I was really waiting to find out where I might wind up first."

"Now, I ain't trying to fix you up. I'm just saying."

"I appreciate that, and I'm grateful for our talk today. I need to go visit some other folks, but if you don't mind I would like to stop by and check on you from time to time."

"I live in this world, not like some people. Some people are so heavenly-minded, they are no earthly good; that's what my daddy always said."

Young realized that in their conversation she had never mentioned her childhood, but he instinctively knew not to mention it. After the exchange of a few more pleasantries, he bade her good day and left.

VI

Young and Vida forged a deep affection and friendship over the next few weeks. Sometimes they just made small talk, but on occasion, they would get into some deep conversation about the Bible. He was astonished at her knowledge of scripture and her faith in Christ as her savior. She could recite long passages of scripture and was particularly fond of the need to supplement faith by works. One day, a little Mexican girl walked by the house, and asked politely if she could have a small bouquet of flowers for her mother and Vida would interrupt their visit to pick the girl a handful of flowers.

The wind blew Vida's birdbath over and broke it in a bad storm Young saw this as an opportunity to show his appreciation for Vida's friendship, so he bought her a new birdbath.

Humbled by his generosity, Vida said, "Well, preacher, that is awfully nice of you ain't it a purty color?"

"Well, actually, it was my pleasure to get you one. I got you these for decoration."

He reached into his pocket and pulled out a handful of iridescent glass globules that florists use in arrangements.

"Well, ain't them purty? They're almost too purty to put outside. So what am I supposed to do? Put them in the bird bath?"

"Yes, they'll add a touch of class to it, don't you think? You'll probably be the envy of your neighbors."

"Let me get some water. I think over there by the fence would be a good place?"

"I think that would be lovely."

After the birdbath was filled and the glass stones were scattered over the bottom, Vida stood admiring the new addition to her garden. "Now, that looks really nice. Thank you again for thinking of me."

Young said, "You're welcome. I will see you Friday."

He returned on Friday to find Vida in a mood he had never seen before. She was angry, agitated and talking aloud to herself.

"Preacher, come here. I want to show you something. You just can't be good to some people. I want you to look at this."

She led him over to the birdbath and pointed to it. "Somebody has done stole them little glass things."

Sure enough, the glass baubles were all gone. He knitted his brow and suggested, "You think maybe birds or squirrels got them?"

"Now what use would a varmint have for them? I think it was that little Mexican girl, — I think her name is Dulce— fooling with them the other day when she thought I wasn't looking. Pearls before swine, preacher. After all the flowers I gave her, this is the way she repays me. Stealing from me. Well, I'll put a stop to this."

"Have you asked her about the stones?"

"What's the use? She would just lie. You know how kids are. No sir, I will just tell her no more flowers. You can't be good to some people."

Young decided to stay a while to let her vent her anger and calm down. As they sat on the porch, Dulce walked by and waved to her. Vida's face hardened, and she ignored the gesture. She motioned for the girl to come over. Dulce hesitantly entered the yard and stood before her.

"Now, little girl, I don't want you to pick any more flowers. Somebody stole some stuff from my yard, and I don't want anybody poking around here. Do you understand me?"

Obviously embarrassed, the girl replied, "Si, Mrs. Denney. I'm sorry that someone stole something from you, but I will not pick any more flowers."

Young waited for her to leave before asking, "Mrs. Denney, don't you think you were a little harsh with her? You don't know she had anything to do with the theft. I still think it was squirrels. Some of them like shiny things."

"No, it ain't no squirrels except the two legged kind. Pearls before swine, preacher. I just don't want them bothering me anymore. Pearls before swine."

Her anger abated somewhat after a few minutes, so Young said goodbye and left. She was still fuming when he stopped by the next day. Two days later, he found her in a quiet, pensive mood.

"Good afternoon, Brother Young. I really appreciate you checking on me."

"Well, I've been worried about you. Have you heard anything about those glass stones?'

"You know, I'm getting over that, so let's don't bring up a sore subject. I'm ashamed at how angry I was over something like that, so let's just let it be. I have something to give you."

"Mrs. Denney, you've been too kind to me already. You don't need to give me anything."

"Now, I'm not going to argue with you. Wait here."

She entered the house and returned with a Bible whose covers had worn thin from years of use. He noticed an odd expression sweep across her face.

"This was Benton's Bible and I want you to have it."

Flustered by her generosity, he stuttered, "Mrs. Denney, I can't take this. You need to give this to one of your kids."

"I thought about it and figured it might cause bad feeling to let one of them have it. I told Iris I was giving it to you and she agreed that was the best thing. There are lots of notes in the pages, and we thought you could make better use of it."

Young felt a wave of embarrassment course through him. "Mrs. Denney, I really wish you would reconsider."

"Now, don't argue with me. My mind is made up. You take this and use it in good health. Would you please pray the Lord forgive me for the anger I have shown lately? I'm really ashamed of myself."

Seeing there was no need to protest anymore, he accepted the gift and replied, "Mrs. Denney, I'm sure the Lord has already forgiven you for that. Even he lost his temper in the temple with the money changers."

"But he had a good reason and I didn't. I shouldn't put so much stock in worldly things like them little glass things."

After a short chat Young left, not knowing that was the last time he would see her.

VII

Young scanned through the scrapbooks over the days before the service and presented a wonderful funeral for Vida. He extolled her faith in Jesus, her down-to-earth theology, consoled the family as much as he could, and assured them Vida was indeed in heaven with Benton. Sensing a deep sorrow in the crowded church, he felt himself choking up with the sense of loss. The procession to the small cemetery behind the church provided time to prepare the interment with the song of Simeon from the gospel of Luke.

"Lord, let your servant Vida go in peace according to your word. Her eyes have seen salvation's dawn so long your word has foretold."

Slowly, the crowd scattered, but Iris lagged behind and asked, "Mom said she wanted you to have Daddy's Bible. Did she give it to you?"

"Yes, she gave it to me the last time I was there. I'm truly sorry for your loss, Iris. If you need to talk or need help, let me know any time, day or night."

"Brother Young, you have done so much already. I hope you enjoy the Bible. There's a lot of life poured into its pages."

He hugged her and whispered, "The Lord give you peace, Iris," before saying good-bye.

After he returned home, he changed into casual clothes, made a pot of coffee, and went to his study to think about the day's events. Then, he noticed Benton's Bible lying near the upper right corner of his desk, and picked it up to examine it more closely. The book flipped open and a small leaflet of paper fell out.

He opened the note as he stood up. Inside was a note clearly inscribed by a child's hand.

'Mrs. Denney, I'm sorry that I took your little glass stones but I wanted to give you something special. I gave the flowers you gave me to my mother. She has been very sick. She helped me make you a lace necklace with the stones.

Then she died. I think it would look really good on you. You have been so nice to me. I'm sorry you're mad at me. Please forgive me and wear this necklace my Mom made you. Love, Dulce.'

Young's face blanched as he felt his body tremble with emotion. He fingered the note thoughtfully and glanced at the page the note had bookmarked: the book of Matthew 7: 1. 'Judge not that you be not judged...'

He continued to read through tear-filled eyes until verse six: 'Do not give what is holy to the dogs; nor cast your pearls before swine, lest they trample them under their feet, and turn and tear you to pieces.'

A Voice Heard in Ramah

THE HINGES OF the oak door to the County Judge Executive's office squeaked softly as Steve Hamlin entered the room where Joann Gehring sat typing at her secretary's desk. She swiveled around in her chair to peer over her glasses at him as she asked, "May I help you?"

Hamlin smiled and approached her desk. "Yes, you can. I would like to speak with Judge Steele, if I may. Is he in?"

"He's not in right now. I think he went to the poolroom for a hamburger. I can call over there and see if he can come back now. Whom should I say is asking for him?"

Hamlin extended his arm and replied, "Thank you, Steve Hamlin. I really appreciate your help."

Joann extended her hand and said, "Joann Gehring. Pleasure to meet you, Mr. Hamlin. And what is your business with Judge Steele?"

"I'm from the University of New York at Stony Brook where I'm working on my dissertation on the sociology and culture of people from the southern mountains. I thought Mr. Steele could introduce me to some people to interview. Doesn't the county judge executive know a lot of people personally?"

"Yes, Judge Steele is very popular and well liked. He really gets out in the county and tries to help people with their problems. Mostly road maintenance, bridge repair, things like that. Have a seat, Mr. Hamlin and I'll call over there."

Hamlin sat down in a naugahyde wing-backed chair where he could enjoy the cool breeze of the oscillating fan. He took a white handkerchief from his back pocket to wipe the beads of perspiration from his forehead and wondered how Joann could look so crisp in the summer heat.

Joann dialed the phone and answered when it rang in the poolroom. "Hello, George? Is Wendell there? He is? Please tell him there is someone here from New York to see him. He's on the way out? Good. Thanks, George, and tell Betty hello for me."

She returned to her typing as she reported to Hamlin, "He's on the way back now. He should be here in a few minutes unless someone who needs his help waylays him. He's so good about that. Would you like a cup of coffee?"

"As hot as it is, a cup of coffee would be nice. It's always easier to talk over coffee."

"Let me make a fresh pot. That's been there since this morning. It ruins on the burner. The judge always wants a fresh cup after lunch."

She pulled the glass carafe from the coffee machine and filled the pot from the drinking fountain. Humming softly, she threw out the old grounds, spooned four measures of coffee into the filter-lined basket, poured the water into the back of the pot, flipped the switch and returned to her work as the fresh coffee trickled into the carafe.

The door creaked as Steele entered. He placed a grease-stained brown bag on her desk. "Diet or no diet, I brought you a burger. You gotta eat something."

"Wendell, you know I can't resist these things. Judge Steele, this is Mr. Steve Hamlin from New York."

Steele walked over to greet Hamlin who rose from his seat to shake hands. "Glad to meet you, Judge Steele."

"Likewise, Mr. Hamlin. What can I do for you?"

"I'm doing some research on the sociological and cultural aspects of the people from the mountains."

"Well, we're not exactly Appalachia, but we do have mountains here in Wayne County. Help yourself to a cup of coffee and come into my office. You need cream or sugar?"

"No, thanks, I take it black."

"Well sir, you're off to a great start. Most people around here don't trust a man who adulterates his coffee with cream or sugar. Too citified. Come in and tell me what I can do for you."

Hamlin grasped the Styrofoam cup gingerly and slipped into the inner office lined with old-fashioned wooden filing cabinets and a large oak desk. Well-worn legal volumes filled rows of shelves and another oscillating fan droned along on the main desk. Steele rolled a squeaky wooden chair from under the desk and motioned for him to sit down.

"Now, what brings a New York Yankee down to these parts?"

"I'm working on a doctoral dissertation that will explore the roots of the strong feelings of attachment people have to their home place."

Steele stiffened in his chair. "So you're one of them fellers that wants to make fun of us hillbillies."

Hamlin realized that the conversation was taking a bad turn and hurried to interrupt. "Oh, no, sir! I am not making fun of anyone. I've noticed that the sense of belonging to their home places is especially strong among people from the southern mountains. I want to know why that emotional bond does not seem to lessen even after these folks have lived for most of their adult lives away from their place of birth."

"So how is that any different from anywhere else?"

"Well, I guess it is difficult to explain. It has been my experience that most people from away from here don't use the word 'home' for their birthplace, especially after their parents have died. They identify home with their spouses and children; but that is not true for people from here."

Steele leaned back in his chair. "Oh, I think I see what you are saying. In your mind, home is where you live, not where you are from. I think you'll find most people around here will see it the other way around. Still, I guess it would be interesting to see if that theory holds water. So how can I help you with your project?"

"I'm pretty sure that people around here would be more willing to talk about themselves if they knew you were willing to introduce me to people so they will feel more comfortable with me."

"So how are these folks going to know that you are not spying for the revenuers? There's a lot of drug traffic - like pot - and an occasional still to be found. Frankly, I think you should not venture off into these hills and hollers by yourself. Tell you what. Let me call a couple of people in some of the more remote places and see if they would meet with you. It would be a lot safer, I imagine."

"That does sound better than just letting me traipse off alone. Is there a hotel in town I can stay in?"

"There's the Tiffany Inn just off the bypass on ninety above town. They have a good buffet too. Here, wait a minute. I have a couple of books you might want to look at until I can arrange some trips."

He rose from his chair and pulled two thick spiral bound paperback volumes from the shelves. One was titled "Historic Wayne County" and the other "The Good Old Days in Wayne County."

"The local paper and the historical society put these together several years ago. Ran an ad in the paper asking for old photographs and got an unbelievable response. I think you will find them very useful."

"Thank you, Mr. Steele...I."

"Call me Wendell. Now to get to the hotel: take the main street here up to the bypass and turn right. You will pass by a KFC on the way. I think you'll find more variety of food at the buffet, but you can do as you please. Stop back in about ten tomorrow morning and I'll have something lined up."

Hamlin stood and shook hands as he said, "Thank you for your help. I'm looking forward to meeting the folks around here. I'll see you tomorrow around ten."

Hamlin drove to the hotel, registered, and left his bags in the room. Then he took the books with him to eat dinner at the buffet. After dinner, he flipped through the books to get a feel for the local community.

II

After breakfast the next morning, Hamlin drove back to the courthouse to meet the judge. Steele's office door was ajar, but Hamlin knocked gently even as he pushed the door open to find Steele hastily signing some paperwork.

"Good morning, Mr. Steele. I'm here to pick up that list of names."

"Come on in. I was just approving some roadwork up Catron Holler. I tried to think of people who still live on their original home-places that you could get to easily. So far, I think the first ones you need to see is the Hoover family up in Tuggle Holler. The road there is a bit rough in places, but you should still have no problem getting there. I didn't know how many people you expect to see in a day so I just have one name. Shelby Hoover."

Hamlin jotted the name down in a small memo book.

Steele continued, "As I recall he is the fourth generation to live on that plot of ground. Not much of a farm. Maybe ten acres."

"Will he be expecting me?"

"Yep, already called him. Let me draw you a map. It ain't hard to get there."

He took out a piece of paper and sketched out narrow lines that he labeled with highway numbers. He accompanied his map with verbal instructions. "Head south on Main Street until you get to a big fork in the road, then veer left onto Kentucky 200. There's a county road called Tuggle Hollow Road coming off on the right side of the road. Take that road all the way up to the Hoover place is where the road ends. Park in front of a big gate. Shelby told me to tell you to be sure to lock the gate back when you come through so his cattle don't get out."

"Cattle? Is there a bull in the field?"

"Nah, just a few Hereford cattle. They won't bother you. Now, Shelby will talk your ear off. He can tell you all about his family and everyone else in the holler."

Steele laughed before continuing, "Hell, he can tell you about all the people in any holler thereabouts. Now the weather says there are storms heading this way. Don't get caught up there and let that creek get high."

Hamlin thanked him, "Thank you for all your help. Probably one person on the first day is enough."

Steele pursed his lips. "Well, there are other people up in the holler you might run into. Maybe not with that storm coming. Just be careful on the road."

Hamlin nodded and said, "Will do. If I get back before your office closes I'll stop by. Otherwise, I'll stop in tomorrow morning."

III

Hamlin had no trouble following the directions. As Steele had warned, in places the road narrowed to a thin ribbon clinging precipitously to the wooded mountainside. A creek ran parallel to the road for long stretches and it crossed the road twice but was shallow enough to ford.

After much trepidation, he emerged into an open space just outside Hoover's place. He parked the SUV on one side of the road and stepped out to view the five red and white Herefords apprehensively as he stepped inside the pasture. The cattle ignored him and he walked toward the weathered house where he could see a man standing on the porch motioning him to come up.

The man shouted, "Come on up, young man. Them cows won't bother you. Just don't step in cow shit."

Hamlin nodded and picked up his pace until he reached the wooden steps leading up to the porch.

"Good morning, Mr. Hoover. I'm Steve Hamlin. I think Judge Steele called you about me coming to visit."

Hoover nodded, "Yep. Call me Shelby. Have a seat."

He pushed an old homemade rocking chair toward him.

"I just made a pot of coffee. Would you like a cup? Black?"

Hamlin grinned, "Is there any other way?"

Hoover laughed before he entered the house and returned with a white ceramic mug filled with strong coffee.

"The old lady went to town so we won't have any interruptions. Coffee okay?"

Hamlin sipped the coffee and nodded. "It's fine. Thank you."

"Now, what can I do for you, Mr. Hamlin?"

Hamlin shifted himself in the chair. "Call me Steve. I'm doing research on the reasons why people in the south, particularly the mountains, maintain such strong ties to their birthplace. Do you mind if I take notes?"

"That's fine. Well, that certainly is true for a lot of people. Some people leave to find work somewhere, but a lot of them come back after they retire. My brothers and sister are doing that. I have lived my whole life here. My dad did the same. So did my grandpa and his dad."

Hamlin listened intently, scribbling notes as Hoover talked.

"So your family has lived here for four generations? Your great grandpa settled here? When?"

Hoover laughed, "You might say settled. Grandpa Jacob got drunk with some of his pals one night and won this place in a poker game. All ten acres of it."

"Really? That must have been quite a poker game."

"The man he won it from, Wheeler Bertram, didn't have much use for it. Too hilly and rocky to grow much. Too little pasture for livestock. I guess he figured he wouldn't have to pay taxes on it."

"I hadn't thought about that."

"Grandpa Wheeler and his brothers built a little log cabin here in 1888, I think. He and Granny Ather moved in and raised a family of four."

"Log cabin?"

"Well, after a few years, they added a room at the back and cased the house in poplar clapboard. Gave it a more modern look. Still pretty damned drafty."

"Really? I bet that made it hard to heat."

"Originally, they had a fireplace. Then they got a pot-bellied stove."

"So you still heat with wood?"

"Mostly. We have some space heaters we use in the winter. Mallie, that's my wife, took the wood cook stove out so she could have an electric one. A lot less work. No ashes and not as much wood to split and tote in."

Hamlin wrote furiously. "So how big is the house?"

"There's four rooms down stairs and three upstairs. We had a bathroom put in about forty years ago. The trip to the outhouse got cold when there was snow up to your ass."

Hamlin chuckled. "I bet. So some family members have lived here since it was built?"

"Yep. Some of the kids had to buy their own places when they got married. Mostly whoever took care of the old folks got the place."

"So you looked after your folks?"

"Yep. Dad and Mom died thirty-four years ago. We got the place when they died."

"Do you have any children who will get the place?"

"We only have two kids, William and Pat. Pat lives in Louisville, but William still lives up at Chestnut Grove. He checks on us every day and takes us places. He'll get the place when we die."

"So why do you think this hold on people is so strong?"

Hoover smiled. "Take a look out there at those mountains. Ain't they beautiful? Like big arms hugging you. You don't get that in the flatlands. Let me get my stick so we can go for a walk."

He shuffled into the house and returned with a gnarly walking stick and gestured to the right of the house. "Let's head up this way."

They left the porch and walked across the pasture until they got to the edge of the woods.

Hoover motioned in a wide swinging arc, "We own to the top of the mountain. They cut the timber for the logs for the original cabin from this part. Now it's mostly grown back. A man who owns a sawmill asked me about buying the rest of the timber, but I turned him down. I like gallivanting over them woods looking for ginseng or dry land fish. It gets me out of the house and a little exercise."

"Ginseng and dry land fish?"

"Well, ginseng is a plant used in medicine. Hard to find, but it brings a good price. Dry land fish is a mushroom you can find only in April. The cap is like a sponge. They're really good and taste like fish. I hear they are very expensive."

"Oh, I think you mean morels. Yes, they're very expensive because they can't be cultivated. So you don't sell them?"

"They're too good to sell. Roll them in flour and fry them up. Here, let me show you something."

Hoover bent over, raked the leaf litter away and scooped up a handful of the rich moist dirt. He presented it to Hamlin who held in his cupped hand.

"Now squeeze it real hard." Hoover said.

Hamlin squeezed the dirt into a small blackish mass.

"You can't do that with sand. The harder you squeeze sand the faster it squirts out of your hand. People today are like sand. They got nothing to hold onto. Always moving around. A lot of them have no kids because they don't want to be bothered or had rather spend the money on themselves. And when they get old they got no roots. Look here."

Hoover folded his fingers back over his palm so the nails were visible. Thin black traces of dirt lay under the edges of the nails.

"Living here is different. See how the dirt gets under your nails? That's what it is like here. That dirt that was here for thousands of years and supported your folks for a long time sorta collects in your soul too. You can't get it out too easy."

Hamlin eyed the dirt before tossing it to the ground. "That's an interesting way of describing it. I guess it means something that I don't have dirt under my nails."

"You didn't dig it out of the ground. You just let me hand it to you. Ain't the same. When your life depends on that dirt it means something."

Hamlin replied, "I think I see what you mean. So can you tell me more about this place?"

Hoover nodded and they spent the next couple of hours walking around while he told stories to Hamlin who was trying to take notes while they were walking. Hoover recounted tales of the other people who lived in the hollow and what life was like for people living in such a remote place.

Dark clouds had started to roll in from the west and a breeze began to sway the trees. Hoover advised, "You had better get going. There's a storm heading this way. The creek might rise."

Even as he talked a few large raindrops splattered onto the ground around them. They walked quickly back to the house, but by the time they got there, the rain had become a steady drizzle.

Hamlin said, "Mr. Hoover, I mean Shelby, you've been very helpful. This is exactly what I'm looking for. I really can't thank you enough. But you're right. I need to head out before the storm gets too bad."

"No problem, glad to help. Now be careful going out. There's a place or two that can get slick in a rain. Come back any time."

Hamlin shook his hand before getting into his SUV and heading back the way he came.

IV

Hamlin had scarcely got out of sight of the house when the storm erupted with full fury and jagged lightning streaked across the dark sky. He turned on the headlights and crept along the muddy road. Suddenly, a lightning bolt struck a tree by the road and the flash startled him so much that he yanked the steering wheel to the right violently. The SUV slid off the road over a slight embankment before hitting a tree beside another narrow road. He had neglected to put on his seat belt, so the sudden stop slammed his head into the windshield hard enough to knock him out.

By the time he came to, the rain had stopped and the sun was trickling in between the trees. He was still groggy and so disoriented that he started down the narrow lane he had landed in instead of returning to the main road.

After a few yards, he emerged into a clearing where a house stood reflecting the sunlight off its wet roof. He had not seen the house coming up so he thought he should make sure he was not lost. He pulled the SUV into the grassy yard and got out.

He walked up to the door and knocked. A short middle-aged woman answered. "Can I help you?"

Still woozy, Hamlin explained, "I am doing some research. I was talking to Mr. Hoover and was heading home. I'm a little fuzzy. I crashed my car and bumped my head. I think I'm lost. Is this the main road?"

"No, this is the road to Denney Hollow. Why don't you come in and clear your head? Maybe a drink of water."

"That would be great. I'm Hamlin Stevens."

The woman extended her hand and replied, "I'm Hattie Denney. Glad to meet you. Here have a seat and I'll get you a drink."

She returned from the kitchen with a glass of water. "What brings you to these parts?"

"I'm working on a project exploring why people have such a strong attachment to their home places."

He looked around the neat room. "Mrs. Denney, do you live here by yourself?"

"Oh no, my husband Ernest is at work and the boys are out playing in the woods. We have three boys, Willie, Ollie and Allan."

The water helped Hamlin settle his nerves. He looked at his watch and asked, "Say, I have some time. Would you mind talking to me about your life here?"

"Why, no. There ain't much to tell. We're just plain folks."

"How long have you lived here?"

"Well, me and Ernest moved here when we got married. He bought the place from Arlene Hatfield. Her husband Herbie got killed in a logwoods and they never had no kids. As she got older she figured she wasn't able to tend to the place so she moved closer to town. Poor thing died a few months after she moved. She never did get over Herbie dying."

"So what happened to Herbie?"

"They was cutting some trees to sell for lumber. They was cutting a big red oak tree and as it fell, it kicked back and ran a big splinter right through his heart. It was awful."

Hamlin shuddered. "Sounds pretty gruesome."

"Oh, it was bad. People talked about it for years. Logging is dangerous work. Lots of people killed or crippled doing it."

"So tell me about your boys. How old are your sons?"

"Willie is twelve, Ollie is eleven and Allan is ten. We had them close to-gether. All boys. I wanted at least one girl but that didn't happen. Still, I'm happy with the boys."

"Do you farm much here?"

"Not much. Too steep and rocky. We grow a little garden and some tobacco. We have a few chickens and a pig and a cow."

"I didn't see them when I came up."

"Oh, we just let them run free so they wander around the woods and fields. Every once in a while, a fox'll catch a hen, so Ernest will have to hunt him down and kill him. Mostly though, not much exciting happens around here."

"Well, that's all interesting. Can you tell me more about your family and life here?"

Hattie nodded and scooted her chair closer so he could hear her better. Over the next hour, she told Hamlin dozens of stories about their lives. Before he knew it, the sun had started to slip behind the treetops and he realized that he needed to get back to town.

"Oh my, I need to get back. I really appreciate your talking with me. I bet you have to get supper ready, so I'll leave you to your work. How do I get back to the main road?"

"Just go back out this road and turn right and it'll take you to the highway. It was nice to meet you, but I do have to get supper going."

Hamlin returned to his SUV and followed her directions until he got to the highway. Back in town, he stopped at the KFC before he went back to his room and fell into bed without even taking off his clothes.

V

The next morning he felt refreshed and anxious to get back to work. He stopped at KFC for coffee and went back to Steele's office. Steele was already there working.

Hamlin rapped lightly on the door. "Are you busy?"

Steele looked up, "Not too. How was your visit with Hoover? Did he talk your ears off?"

Hamlin smiled, "He is a talker, but that's what I like. He had a lot to tell me. I sort of had a little crash on the way out and took a wrong road. But it worked out fine. I got to meet Mrs. Denney and interview her."

Steele leaned over his desk. "Did you? How was that?"

"She gave me a drink of water and told me about her family."

Steele smiled and repeated, "Did she?"

"Told me her husband's name was Ernest and her boys' names were Willie, Ollie and Allan. They were all out playing in the woods."

"So you never met them, huh? They're an interesting family. You really should meet them. Tell you what. Why don't we go back up there and see if we can catch them at home?"

Hamlin really wanted to go elsewhere, but he agreed. They left the building, got into the SUV, and started back up the road. Along the way Steele told him about some of the people living by the road and occasionally described some landmarks as they rode. Hamlin turned onto the road up Tuggle Hollow and wound along the road until they got to the Denney Hollow road.

Steele motioned, "Turn here up this little road."

Hamlin veered left onto the road and crept along until he reached the opening. The house was nowhere to be found.

Steele asked, "So this is where you were yesterday? You sure?"

"I'm positive, but I don't understand where the house is."

Steele said, "Let's get out and walk around."

They got out of the car and meandered around the open field until they came upon some large limestone foundation stones among clumps of orange daylilies scattered across the field.

Steele turned to Hamlin. "This is where you were, ain't it?"

"I think so, but I don't see the house."

"Well, this is the old house place. You can always tell by them daylilies. Anytime you are out in the woods here and find daylilies you are at an old home place. They'll grow for years after the house is gone."

"But what happened to the house?"

"This house burned down a long time ago. Here, let me show you something."

Steele led Hamlin around the scattered stones to a small cemetery at the edge of the woods. He pointed to four small weatherworn tombstones inscribed with names and dates:

Willie Denney Born March 2, 1902 Died March 2, 1902

Ollie Denney Born April 22, 1903, Died April 23, 1903

Allan Denney Born April 4, 1904 Died April 6, 1904.

Ernest Denney Born June 7, 1875, Died April 10, 1904

Hamlin felt the hair on the back of his neck quiver. "She told me they were out playing in the woods."

"But you never saw them, did you? You never even heard them. Now did you meet her husband, Ernest?"

"Well, no, she told me he was at work."

"Let me guess. She told you about Herbie Hatfield getting killed in a logging accident?"

"Yes, but..."

"It wasn't Herbie, it was Ernest. He was killed by that tree four days after they buried their third child."

"So ..."

"So what happened to Hattie? Nobody knows. There was a big storm that night. People came to check on her the day after Ernest was buried but she was nowhere to be found. The door was open but there was nobody home. The fire had gone out in the stove, but there was no sign of Hattie."

"Hamlin shivered. "Did they look for her?"

"They searched everywhere for her. Somebody found what looked like her footprints heading up to the woods, but then they lost them in the leaves."

"So I guess you're telling me I saw a ghost or I was still hallucinating from bumping my head."

"No, I'm not telling you anything. You ain't the first person to see Hattie and the house. I doubt you'll be the last."

"Well, Mr. Steele, I don't believe in ghosts. I must have hit my head harder than I thought."

"Maybe yes, maybe no. Like I said, a lot of other people have seen her. Most usually around a storm. Nobody can explain it so we quit trying to."

Steele pointed to the tombstones. "You see, Hamlin, there's something outsiders don't get. You can come down here with your questionnaires and so on, but you'll never understand life here. Hattie and Ernest had three boys a year apart and they all died the same day or a day or so later. Now you think about that. They were on a first name basis with death and yet they didn't give up. I'm pretty sure that if Ernest had not got killed they would have kept trying until they got one to live."

Hamlin felt himself quaking. "That is really tragic."

Steele bent over and dug out a large handful of dirt that he squeezed into a moist longish lump.

"Hamlin, I'm sure Shelby showed you this. Here when you squeeze a handful of dirt it just gets into a tighter clump. The dirt gets under your fingernails and it's hard to get out. Well, that's the way it is with death around here. Sure, you folks from away from here have people die. You have a funeral, you have a wake, bury them, and go on. Oh, you probably visit their graves for the first few years, but as time goes by you stop doing even that. Oh, you might tell a story in some reminiscence, but you move on."

Hamlin pursed his lips. "Maybe you're right."

"Well, it's different here. Like Hattie, the spirits of the dead get lost in these woods, but you can't find them. Nobody comes to visit these graves or a lot of others like them scattered around these hills and hollers, and nobody puts flowers on them. But in the spring, them little pink flowers pop up and cover these plots. I think they're called spring beauties."

"Yes, that's right. Spring beauties."

"Well, like I said, outsiders will never really understand us. You have no connection to this place. Ashes to ashes, dust to dust. But this ain't your ashes and it ain't your dust. People around here never lose sight of the fact that they are made of this dirt, and they know they will return to it. A pine box rots in time, and the bones and flesh go back to the dirt. But some small bit of that person's soul lingers here I guess until Judgment Day, when all the souls are called up in the resurrection. No matter how hard you try, you can never get your head around living that close to death. For you folks, death is a single event in time. Here it is a constant stream that never stops. You just can't understand it."

Hamlin stood reflecting on Steele's words. He spoke softly, "You're right. I really don't get it."

"Oh, from time to time, people have seen Hattie and even spoken to her like you did. Around here, we don't give it no mind. We don't even talk about it much and just accept it."

As they stood looking at the stones, a tiger swallowtail butterfly floated over the field before settling on one of the daylily flowers to sip nectar. She flitted among the flowers before drifting on a languid breeze to disappear into the nearby woods.

Steele smiled and turned to face Hamlin. "So what do you think? You think that was Hattie?"

A Still Small Voice

THE BRIGHT MOONLIGHT glinted off the hand-hewn sandstone of the old Wayne County High School as Darrell Ramsey drove his black Monte Carlo speckled now by the dust of the dry October winds blowing off the surrounding streets and antiquated baseball field. He eased his car into the space closest to the building that had been constructed by WPA to give the workers money and the next generation hopes for a better life through education. He thrust his arm through the straps of a bulging book bag and anxiously checked his watch when the light came on as he opened the door.

"Oh damn! It's 9:02! I'm two minutes late and she'll never let me live it down! Not after all the trouble she went to," he whispered under his breath. "I hope the key I bought off Elmer opens the door."

After racing to the far side of the building, he could see a bright light pouring out the windows of a first floor room. Breathing deeply from the running, he fumbled the key into the lock that yielded with a click, admitting him into the foyer where he ran up the small flight of stairs. At the top of the stairs, he turned left and entered a large room cluttered with educational posters and paraphernalia. A lone, silver-gray haired woman turned up her bespectacled, tanned face from grading papers to greet him.

"So, it's you! I'd about given up and gone home. Maybe I should send you to the principal's office for tardiness. I'm a busy woman," she teased through a toothy grin.

"Now, Helen, you know there is no principal here this time of night."

"Excuse me, my name is Mrs. Bertram and I may even let you call me Honeybee, but not Helen. I don't know you that well."

"Don't know me…! I had you for five classes here thirty years ago. Don't you remember that?"

"Yes, yes, I remember: Algebra two, geometry, physics, trigonometry, and calculus. So what? You still can't take such liberties with me as I'm a lady," she said as she reached out her hands. "Come here and let me see you. It's been a long time."

Darrell walked toward her, and plopped the book bag onto a large square wooden table near her desk. He bent low, feeling her cool kiss on his forehead, and spontaneously started to hug her.

"No hugging, now, Darrell. You know, I'm old and I break easily," she clucked.

He laughed aloud and stood up, "Old? Honeybee, you'll never get old. Decrepit maybe, but never old."

"Very funny! Thirty years go by, and you still crack the same jokes. Didn't I teach you anything?"

His mouth curled into a soft, wry smile. "More than you know, Mrs. Bertram, more than you know. I'm a teacher now and I teach a lot like you taught me."

"Don't you have any original thoughts? You can't teach like me because I'm so much cuter than you are. And smarter. Quit boring me with your life story and show me how much math you remember. Did you bring your books like I told you to?"

"Of course, I was always your slave."

"Spare me the melodrama and turn to the section on solving quadratic equations by factoring. Impress me with your math ability instead of your conversation skills. Turn to page forty-five in the Algebra Two book … the big yellow one."

"Har, de, har, har," Darrell replied as he fished the book from the book bag. "Still the perpetual charmer, aren't you?"

"But of course! It is in my blood, you know. Now do these twenty problems in about a minute or I'll come back there and hurt you!"

"Now, Mrs. Bertram, you can't talk to me like that these days or you'll get sued. Wanna race?"

Helen sighed as she replied, "Yes, I know. That is why I quit teaching years ago. Nobody had any sense of humor. Everybody became so serious. Sure, I'll race and I bet I'll win, because I have the teacher's edition with answers."

"Yeah, yeah. For number two I get x is four or x is five. What did you get?"

"Why, the right answer, naturally. X is four or x is negative five. I can see why you missed it; you had to work with big numbers like four."

Darrell slapped his thigh and roared loudly, "See there, the trouble you got me in? I used that same line my first year at my new school and the parents had the principal call me and chew me out, because I had hurt their daughter's feelings. Do you believe that?"

Helen raised her eyebrows. "These days, I'll believe anything. I'll give you an E for effort on that one. What's next, geometry?"

Darrell pulled the worn book from the bag. "What do you want me to do, prove the Pythagorean Theorem again? I was the only student in your teaching career you ever made prove that thing by Euclid's method and for what?"

"Well, it kept you out of my hair, so I could help other students who needed it. Didn't kill you, did it? Made you what you are today."

"Give me a break!"

"Right arm or left? You got a break. You got me for a teacher."

"You can joke all you want, Honeybee. I know you loved me."

"Who told you that?"

"Well, Betty Lou West, for one. And she was your best friend, so she should know."

"Betty Lou West? Are you so naive you would believe a driver's education teacher? And a Democrat at that! Tsk, tsk. Have you hit your head lately?"

"Now, come on. Everybody knew she was your best friend."

"Maybe yes, maybe no, but you can't hold that against her."

"By the by, I have always wondered if you had anything to do with her daughter marrying the son of the top Republican in the state. 'Fess up!"

"Why, l'il ole me? Of course not, but you have to admit that was funny."

"Actually, ironic."

"Now there you go using big words. Ten-dollar words out of a five cent head. Can you get that head to state the theorem about two tangents to a circle from a common exterior point?"

"No problem: Two tangents drawn to a circle from a common external point are congruent. Impressed?"

"Well, like I always say, even a blind pig finds an acorn once in a while."

"You know what?"

"Of course, I do. He is a cousin of mine."

"I went out to your old farm last week."

"Without my permission? I think I'll call the sheriff and have you arrested for trespassing. Sheriff! Sheriff!"

"You are just a barrel of laughs. Anyway, I found this."

He stood up, reached into his right pocket, and pulled out a perfect flint arrowhead. "Here," he said, sliding it across the desk toward her.

"Ooh, that's a good one! Have I told you how we used to see how far we could throw them when were kids?"

"Only about a million times, but tell me again."

"Well, we used to throw them when were kids to see how far they would go."

"Another knee slapper. Wanna know where I found it?"

"Probably in the lower tobacco patch near the peacock house. Did you see any of my peacocks?"

"No, but I heard them. You know, it sorta sounds like a rusty nail being yanked out of an oak board."

"'You know' is not a correct way to start a sentence. Now please use good grammar or you'll sound like an ignorant hick."

"Do you want this one for your collection?"

"Are you trying to bribe me? No, thank you very much, but I had to quit collecting them after Dennis and I moved to a smaller house. We had to give up so much: arrowheads, peacocks, and antiques. My knife collection."

"How is Dennis? Still bothered by arthritis?"

"Oh, no, he's all well. We do reminisce a lot about the farm out at Cooper. Do you still collect knives?"

"A few. Boker Tree brands, Case double x's, Kissing Crane, Hen and Rooster."

"What? No Russell Barlows? And you call that a knife collection?"

"I only had one Russell Barlow and I gave it to you when we were named Kentucky Star Student and Teacher. I always thought it would be sacrilegious to cheapen that moment of achievement for both of us."

"I suppose, but let's not get maudlin just yet. Hey, let me tell you something funny. Remember how I told you about the rooster that got drunk on pumpkin brandy from rotting pumpkins behind the barn? He was so drunk he couldn't even roost."

"Yes, you told us that in trig class. All three of us."

"Peggy is principal of Wayne County High now and Grady is president at a bank?"

"Yes, I see them from time to time, but I don't get home much from Lexington. Me, I sort of wasted my life. I became a teacher."

"Ain't it the truth?"

"Hey, but your life was exciting. How many different colleges and universities did you attend?"

"Who knows? Eight, I think. Did I tell you that I was the first woman admitted to Case Western Reserve?"

"About how you and three other women earned the right to attend a summer session and had to stay in a men's dorm?"

"Yes, and I how I saw the sign that said 'Women Only Past This Point' and I ran the other way because I thought it didn't mean me?"

"Where you saw all kind of men in various states of dress and undress? Yes, I do remember that yarn."

"Well, aren't you the clever one? Are you clever at trigonometry? Solve this right triangle."

"Oh, Honeybee, I can do this stuff in my sleep. Here."

"Well, I can see your study methods have not changed any for thirty years. Do you still paint those wonderful bird pictures? I bought two of the owls, you know. And by the way, did you ever finish that saw-whet owl you promised me?"

"'Well, I have it with me, but it is not finished. I stay pretty busy. Every time I start to work on it, something comes up. Sometimes I imagine that I can make it look like you, if I painted horn-rimmed glasses like yours on it."

"Humpfh! I'll thank you that these glasses make me look smart!"

"Don't you mean visually challenged?"

"Well, I attended Harvard which is more that I can say for my present company. In fact, I took classes in the medical school."

"Good thing you spoke up or they would have mistaken you for a cadaver!"

"Pure corn. Have you been watching "Hee Haw" again? I think I told you about having to study a rat skeleton."

"Yeah, and you dumped a rat on a chain in a vat of maggots to digest the flesh. Then you had to come home suddenly for an emergency only to get the rat skeleton in the mail in a few weeks. Yes, Honeybee, that's a good one."

"Did you ever understand continuity in Calculus? I recall that it drove you nuts your freshman year in college. Not that that was hard to do…"

"I got my degree in math, so I guess I got it. Say, wasn't the senior citizen home renamed in your honor?"

"Honor, schmonor. When I retired, I was so bored I had to do something. Then I figured a lot of other 'old' people would like to have some place to go. We turned out some beautiful quilts. By the way, do you still have all those awards you won at honors day? You did set a school record, didn't you? You must have had superior teachers like me."

"Yes, they were good teachers, but none of them were like you, thank God for small mercies."

"Yuck, yuck, yuck. How do you get all that hair on such a little head?"

"I use glue. Nearly all of the teachers I had are gone now, retired or … so why did you leave me? I thought you loved life too much."

"Well, I have had my close calls. Remember when I was in the hospital and you came to visit from Michigan?"

"How can I ever forget that moment? There you sat upright in a hospital bed reading a book and the hollow look in your eyes tore my heart apart. Talking to you was like grabbing a fistful of sand. The harder I squeezed to keep you here, the faster you ran away. So I just stopped squeezing and you ran away anyway."

"Just call me quicksilver. But I never abandoned you, did I? Did you hear me calling you when you needed it?"

"And sometimes when I didn't. Jesus Christ, now *you're* getting maudlin. Let's change the subject. I would suggest physics, but I guess we are beyond that. Look what I brought you. Remember the picture Kenny Crabtree took of us at that special luncheon when we won that honor? Here is my copy all framed and nicely matted."

"I guess mine has disappeared over the years. Say, there is that Russell Barlow you gave me and the new slide rule I gave you. I guess they are both useless now, huh?"

"Helen, nothing you ever gave me will be useless."

"Well, if it was, I'd never have given it to you. We were quite a team when we were younger. But as the poet says, nothing gold can stay. Here, grab hold of this frame. Okay, take the back off of it and hand me the photograph. That is all I need. Now watch this magic trick."

"Magic trick, schmagic trick. Wait, how did you do that?"

"Well, if I told you I would have to kill you. Still want to know?"

"Why not? You always were just full of surprises."

II

The phone call jarred Sheriff Kenny Crabtree out of bed a little before six o'clock. His wife mumbled her annoyance as he turned over to answer the call.

"Hello, Sheriff Crabtree."

He listened to the agitated voice of the janitor at the local middle school enough to recognize the need for immediate action before school started.

"There in five, Arnold. Keep everyone out until I get there. Everyone!"

Kenny hurriedly dressed himself and rushed to the door of his modest home. Still shoeless, he bolted into the cruiser and tore away to the middle school where the janitor and ambulance workers paced around awaiting his arrival. He had managed to pull his sockless shoes on while driving so that he could run to the middle school building.

"Arnold, for God's sake, what's going on?"

Arnold's still blanched face twisted in horror and pain as he spoke, "It's a mess, Kenny, it's a mess. Blood everywhere. I think we'd better get the superintendent on the horn and have him cancel school today."

"Let's see what is going on. Get me a doctor or a coroner or some such damned thing. Get them lights on in the back!"

The men hurried around the building to enter through the still open door and face a scene of nightmarish horror. Darrell's body slumped over a student desk so small that the hands of his long arms brushed the tiled floor. Piles of papers and books were scattered among large pools of dark blood that had drained from the long thin slits in his wrists, and had traced irregular rivulets among the shards of glass of the picture frame.

Gagging and heaving in disbelief and nausea, Kenny excused himself to go back outside to vomit. Pale and wiping his mouth with a handkerchief, he returned to the room still shaking with pain.

"What a damned mess! Who was this guy anyway? Why did he do this here? How did he get in here? Anybody got any answers?"

"No, sir, we didn't touch anything until you got here."

Arnold interrupted, "My helper, Elmer, told me he lost his key two days ago. I thought maybe this guy found it, but we can't find it anywhere."

Kenny walked around carefully, and took a few pictures for the coroner's files. He rolled the body over and gasped, "That's Darrell Ramsey! We graduated together thirty-two years ago. I think his brother, Bobby, lives out in Slat. Somebody call him and get him here now."

Arnold ran to his office and flipped through the thin phone book to find Bobby's number. When he returned, Kenny continued where he left off.

"Darrell was the valedictorian in our class. Damned genius. Moved away to teach in Louisville... no, Lexington. I hadn't seen him in years. He never came to any of our reunions. Wait a minute. What room is this?"

Arnold replied, "Room two. Art room."

Kenny shook his head, "No, it's an art room now in the middle school. But when this was the high school, this was a math room. In fact, this was Helen Bertram's room. Darrell and I had geometry together in this room. Man, they were a pair."

He looked at the other men who stood speechless and ignorant of his reference, before continuing, "Helen Bertram was probably the best teacher ever to teach here. Had a really weird, but gentle, sense of humor. She got the funding for the senior citizen's home. Great lady and a genius, too. Everybody knew that she and Darrell were closer than mother and son."

Kenny pulled up a chair, sighing as he sat down. "My senior year they were named State Student and Teacher of the Year or something. It was a big deal around here. First and only time that had happened in this school. I was the photographer on the school newspaper and I took a picture of them together for the paper. Seems like they were handing each other something."

The whine of an ambulance interrupted him. The driver and his helpers rushed into the room. The driver asked, "Any evidence of what happened here?"

Kenneth replied, "Just the books and papers there on the floor. There might be something in that book bag over there."

He hoisted Darrell's book bag over a table in the corner of the room and dumped its remaining contents onto the tabletop. "My God, I ain't seen a slide rule in years, but it's the same books we used in school here. I guess he kept them all this time."

The driver asked, "Who? Mrs. Bertram?"

Kenny looked at him and sighed softly. "No, Darrell. Mrs. Bertram died twenty something years ago. I think Darrell was in school in Michigan, but he didn't make it to the funeral. Seems like she died of cancer. Not pretty. Big funeral and visitation. Lot of people loved her. I was a first year policeman who had to escort the procession to the cemetery. Wasn't easy, knowing all the people she had helped over the years."

He wiped his eyes and nose. "So what did he use to slash his wrists? Piece of glass?"

"Haven't found it yet. It's hard to get around all this bloody mess without disturbing the crime scene."

Kenny looked around the room. Most of the desks stood in neat rows, but three near the bloody pools were overturned. He saw the broken, empty picture frame lying under a desk near Darrell's body. He bent over to examine the frame's pieces to examine for traces of blood. "Wonder what was in here? Why would he bring a picture…." his voice trailed off as he saw the slide rule lying on the table.

"It was a damned knife and slide rule they were holding! A Russell Barlow knife and a slide rule. That's what was in the picture. Anybody find a picture?" he asked as he dropped to his knees to look under the desks. There it is!"

He retrieved the picture from under one of the desks. As he stood up, Arnold returned and said, "I told the brother what happened. He said he would be right up, but in a way he was glad it was over. Said that Ramsey was dying of colon cancer anyway, and was really suffering from the treatment. Said at least now he wasn't in pain."

Kenny knitted his brow as he asked, "But why do this here? Why not blow your brains out in the woods? Why not just eat pills at home or whatever? This makes no sense."

He fell silent as he examined the picture to verify it was the picture he had taken in high school. "See, I told you guys," he gloated as he held the picture up for all to see. Only then did he notice the small irregular point of light showing through the picture as if a shard of glass had jabbed out a hole as the frame fell. He flipped the picture over, pressing the jagged tears back together to form a complete picture that revealed a small white imperfection in the portion of the picture showing the gifts they were exchanging.

"Jesus Christ! What in the hell?" he cried as he pulled the photo closer to his face. "What in the damned hell is that?"

He studied the picture closely before exclaiming, "I can see the slide rule, but I know he gave her a goddamned Russell Barlow knife! I took the picture and I know."

The ambulance driver asked, "Is it okay to load this guy up? I mean you got all the pictures you need?"

Kenny nodded, "Yeah, let's get this mess cleaned up. Probably a good idea to call the superintendent and have him cancel school today. There's no way we can get this mess cleaned up before school opens."

He righted one of the desks and said, "Somebody get a broom and trash pan. We're going to need some plastic trash bags."

Arnold handed him a broom, and he began to carefully sweep the broken glass and scattered papers into a wide blood-soaked pile. "Probably just as easy to pick up this trash before we try to sweep," he said.

He knelt down and began to pick up the gory trash. He used both hands to grab a large pile, but suddenly froze as he lifted it off the floor.

Arnold asked, "Something wrong, boss?"

The color drained out of Kenny's face and he pointed at the floor. There, partially covered by the trash and debris, lay a Russell Barlow knife and an unfinished painting of a saw-whet owl.

Believe In The Light

THE MORNING SUN off the shiny tower of Jordan Osmund Incorporated temporarily blinded Woodrow Barnett as he turned his green Ford farm truck into the parking lot just off Fourth Street in Louisville. He straightened his tie and breathed a soft sigh before he got out of the truck and walked to the building.

With his right hand, he shaded his eyes against the bright light as he looked up at the penthouse of the modern high-rise building. It was topped by the strange emblem of the Jordan Osmund Inc. Corporation: a simple capital O superimposed on a taller capital I. Woodrow felt his heart race as he wondered if the symbol really represented the power he so desperately hoped lay within the inner offices.

"My God, it must be true!" he muttered under his breath.

He had never met Osmund, but they were both from Pine Knot and shared a mutual friend, Chester Criswell, who had passed on the rumors of Jordan Osmund's meteoric rise to wealth, power and philanthropy. Chester had called Osmund and he had agreed to meet Woodrow to discuss his situation. As Woodrow limped into the revolving door, he questioned his sanity for believing in a miracle in a story from a comic book.

A smartly dressed receptionist greeted him with a warm smile, "Can I help you, sir?"

He quickly read her nameplate: **Margaret Thornton.** "Good morning, ma'am," he replied. "I have an appointment with Mr. Osmund at ten o'clock this morning."

She scanned the ledger before answering, "Certainly, Mr. Barnett. Please have a seat while I let Mr.Osmund know you are here. There's fresh coffee over there if you would like some."

Woodrow nodded in response and poured a cup of coffee before easing himself into a comfortable chair. The receptionist smiled sweetly as she made conversation, "I see you are from Pine Know too. Did you know each other?"

Woodrow sipped his coffee as he shook his head. "I never knew him directly but everybody in Pine Knot knows who he is. He's the biggest success story in the history of the town. Chester Criswell went to school with him and he called Jordan for me."

"If you don't mind me asking, are you here for your leg? I noticed you had a limp when you came in."

"No," Woodrow replied laconically.

The elevator door opened and a tall well-built man in a neatly tailored suit emerged from the car. He strode over to Woodrow, smiled and extended his hand, "Jordan Osmund, Mr. Barnett. I'm glad to meet someone from my old stomping ground. Any friend of Chester's is a friend of mine. Bring your coffee with you and let's see if we can be of any help to you."

"Nice to meet you, Mr.Osmund," Woodrow replied, at ease with Osmund's genial manner. "Chester is a fine feller. I guess you graduated from Pine Knot together."

"Yes, before they consolidated the schools. Big mistake as far I'm concerned. But that's progress for you."

"Do you still see Chester much?"

"Not much. This keeps me pretty busy. We exchange Christmas cards and maybe a phone call from time to time. Say, is Blevin's Grocery Store still there outside of town?"

"It's still there, but it's been sitting empty for several years. I hear it's up for sale."

"Really? I wonder what they want for it. Who owns it, if I was interested in buying it?"

"I guess Jim Duncan, but I can find out for you for sure. Why would man as rich as you want to buy a rundown store in a place like Pine Knot?"

Osmund smiled, "It never hurts to diversify, Mr. Barnett."

"You can call me Woodrow," Woodrow replied as the elevator doors opened into the penthouse suite.

"Only if you call me Jordan. Do you need a warm-up before we get started?"

"No, thank you," Woodrow answered as he sat down in the overstuffed chair in front of Osmund's desk.

Osmund pulled his leather swivel chair closer to the fancy cherry desk as he asked, "So what can we do for you?"

Woodrow took his wallet from his pants pocket and took out a picture of frail young boy. He handed it to Osmund. "It's my boy, Andy. He was born with a bunch of things wrong with his heart, and the doctors say if he don't get it fixed soon he's going to die."

Osmund looked at the picture before he leaned back in his chair. "Wouldn't a heart transplant fix the problem?"

Woodrow shook his head. "He's so small they can't find a heart to fit and they say he's too frail to fight the 'mune response. So fixing his heart is the only hope he has."

Osmund smiled at the mispronunciation of immune, but graciously nodded acknowledgement of the child's predicament.

Woodrow fidgeted in his seat, hand-wrestling with himself to pass the suddenly uncomfortable silence. As he felt his last hope slipping away, tears welled up in his eyes he blurted out, "I was hoping for a miracle, and you're the only man who can make it happen!"

Osmund sat up straight. "Mr. Barnett, I am truly flattered that you think I can actually work miracles, but you've been grossly misinformed. All I do is run a business which makes enough profit margin to help those in need. But I don't work miracles. I'm sure I can convince the governing board to cover any and all expenses for your son's surgery and recuperation, but that's all I can do."

Barnett sighed deeply as he struggled to contain his emotions. "That's just the thing. We have had a slew of doctors look at Andy and they all say he can't survive the surgery because he is too weak." He stopped and muster the strength to ask, "Can't you use that special ring of yours to make him well?"

Osmund sunk back into his chair as he asked, "And what ring would that be, Woodrow? All I have is a wedding band, which performed a miracle in its own right by marrying me to my wonderful wife, but I don't think it can help Andy. Is that the ring you had in mind?"

"No, sir. But everybody in Pine Knot knows that you have a Green Lantern ring, just like in the comic books. Nobody knows where you got it, but everybody knows you got it! If you didn't have it, how else could you have done all this?"

Visibly agitated, Osmund slumped forward, sighing heavily as he replied, "Okay, let's see if I can tell you the story you heard. They say I got this mysterious ring when I was a teenager. I wore it everywhere, and people made fun of me: a man going off to college on a full scholarship wearing a ring from a comic book character. Then one night I had a bad wreck when my car plummeted one hundred feet at Pump Station Hill, but I was not hurt at all other than a few bruises. So it must be the ring saved my lucky ass. How am I doing so far?"

Barnett sat stupefied at the accuracy of the story Osmund had just told him. "That's what I heard. Everybody I know tells that story and believes it is so. That's how I got the idea of coming up here for your help. I even told Andy where I was going." His voice quavered and he began to cry again.

Osmund slid the box of Kleenex across the desk and waited while Barnett collected himself. "Regrettably, Woodrow, that story has become so widespread that people from other states come in here reciting that tale, hoping I will use the ring to solve their problems. Wait a minute."

He rose from his chair, walked over to a file cabinet where he pulled out a tray full of bright green translucent rings bearing the Green Lantern emblem. Returning to his desk, he offered the tray to Barnett, "Woodrow, I will do all in my power to help Andy. Take one of these rings and give it to him to reassure him that all will be well, and if it gives him the hope he needs to survive, so be it. But you need to be man enough now to face the fact that happy endings are only in comic books and fairy tales, and we don't live in either. If I may keep Andy's medical records, I'll have my staff begin an exhaustive search for surgeons skilled in cases like this. I will contact you as soon as I can find out what can be done."

Barnett rose from the chair and took a green ring from the tray. "Thank you, Mr. Osmund. I'm sorry if I seem foolish to believe all those things, but he's my only son and I love him."

Osmund shook his hand, "Woodrow, it's never foolish to love one's children and to try to do as much as you can for them. Now you be careful on the way home."

Barnett face twisted into a weak smile and he choked back one last sob before he left to begin the long trip home.

Osmund picked up the medical file, flipping through the charts and graphs as he walked out to his secretary's desk. Handing her the file, he said, "Carol, get the medical resource team in here and have them locate the best pediatric coronary surgeons in the world. Once you find at least five or so, fax them the relevant information on Andy's situation on a piece of my letterhead. If they think the surgery can be performed successfully, get them to tell you what support staff facilities they will need and work out the time frame to get them here. I want this list by end of business today."

Carol smiled, "I think we had a similar list from two years ago. I can give that to the team. I'm sure that those doctors would all be willing to come back."

Osmund smiled back as he closed his office door, "Then that would be an excellent place to start."

II

"Jordan Osmund, have you been wasting your money on comic books again? Didn't I tell you to stop buying them things?"

Ten-year-old Jordan answered, "But Mom, it's only some of the money I made from mowing yards. I get them second hand from the guys at school."

"They're the tools of the devil and just a bunch of nonsense. Next thing you know, you won't have any money left for school."

"But Mom, I get straight A's in school, and I always do my chores. Most of the time I even do a lot of Tommy's chores."

Realizing she had little chance of winning this battle, Lena Osmond handed him the comic book, saying, "Well, at least don't let your daddy find out about them."

Jordan bartered for comic books with his school buddies, but guarded his enjoyment of the adventures of Superman, Batman, and Green Lantern just as well as the fictional heroes guarded their own alter egos. In the small rural town of Pine Knot where men slaved away in low paying jobs and women were house wives and mothers, most of the town's children never finished school. However, the state testing program had identified Jordan as an exceptionally intelligent young man, and his father vowed that this son would escape the tedious existence that had kept the family in poverty for generations.

Jordan's dad encouraged him to read, a skill he himself lacked, and somehow he finagled the driver of the public library book mobile to risk the bumpy ride up their hollow. Jordan had figured out that his dad's objection to comic books had less to do with the local Baptist preachers' damning of the magazines than it did with the more pragmatic problem of scratching together every penny possible to pay his way into college.

Although his pragmatic parents did not understand that the boy's boundless imagination needed heroes and villains no more substantial than those in the pulpy pages of a comic book, Jordan's friends did. They, too, reveled in reading and discussing the adventures of their favorite superheroes. Inevitably, each of them began to identify with a particular hero, and strove to justify their preferences to their peers.

Each of the boys in Jordan's group of closest friends had a favorite superhero. Bobby Criswell liked Superman, Billy Roberts was a Batman fan but Jordan loved the stories of the Green Lantern whose magic ring powered by his will power that could do almost anything. They spent many hours discussing the merits and weaknesses of their heroes in scenarios they conjured up in their imaginations.

At first, Bobby and Billy teased Jordan when he pretended to charge his power ring by reciting the sacred oath of the Green Lanterns. "In brightest day, in darkest night, No evil shall escape my sight. Beware my power, Green Lantern's Light!" Eventually, they relented in their mockery, preferring to enjoy their flights of fancy that diverted them from their mundane lives.

One day, their conversation took a more serious turn. They pondered their futures when they would have to abandon their fantasy lives. For a few fleeting moments, the boys felt a bit guilty that they did not concern themselves with more serious matters to prepare for adulthood. Billy spoke up, "My Dad says that we had better get some out of our childhood, cause there sure as hell ain't none when you grow up."

III

As the boys grew into men, they had less and less time for comic book reveries. They took on part-time jobs and school became more demanding. Bobby dropped out in his junior year, and took a job with a local sawmill to make enough money to buy a used car. Billy used his diploma to get into a car mechanics program at the vocational school in Somerset.

Jordan graduated valedictorian of his class and was offered several thousand dollars worth of scholarships. Bobby and Billy volunteered to help Jordan's parents move him to the University of Kentucky dormitory. They tried with mixed success to hold back the tears as they hugged each other good-bye, languishing one more time in the unspoken fantasies of three boys joined by strands of childhood memories now separated by the realities of adulthood.

Jordan earned perfect marks his first year, and settled into an electrical engineering major as his career. A falling tree splintered as it fell, crushing Bobby's leg, and left him with a gimpy leg. Billy got his girlfriend pregnant and a forced marriage hamstrung his financial situation as he scraped by as a mechanic at a local service station.

Jordan's visits home became less frequent as his studies and research into new approaches to integrated circuit design consumed more of his time in Lexington. He always took the time to visit his childhood buddies, but the visits increasingly left him agitated and fraught with a sense of impotence at his inability to help his friends.

Jordan did stay home during the summer months. After the second year in college, he took a job as a stock boy at Willard Blevin's Grocery Store for the exorbitant pay of ten dollars per day. Long regarded as a bookworm and educated fool by many people in the community, Jordan went to the first day of work with more than a little apprehension.

The store was built of plain stone with black four-inch steel poles supporting a long roof over a smooth concrete porch with cinder block steps at the sides and the front. Jordan remembered coming here as a child when Jack McCutcheon had owned the store, but it had changed hands several times after Jack had retired. Jordan did not know Willard and Fannie Blevins, but his dad knew them from attending the church where Willard's dad, John Blevins, had preached for several years. Jordan took a deep breath and pushed the door to go in the store. There he discovered Willard and Fannie struggling to replace the cash register tape.

"Come in, young man," Willard said without looking up from the task at hand. "So you are Jordan Osmond. Caleb's boy. Your daddy and me used to go coon hunting when we was growing up. You ever go coon hunting, boy?"

Caught a little off guard by the brusque greeting, Jordan responded hesitantly, "Yes sir, I've gone with my dad a few times."

Willard stopped working on his cash register work and turned his thin, furrowed face toward Jordan. Deep-set gray eyes complemented the light gray combed hair on his head, and the loose work clothes hanging on his scrawny frame reminded Jordan of a scarecrow flapping in the autumn winds.

"Well, I'm glad that Caleb is taking you. Coon hunters are dying breed. Dammit, woman, I just about had that that danged thing in there! Show Jordan around the store, and tell him what we want him to do while I will fix this damned thing."

Fannie was a tall woman with a husky frame and large doleful eyes. Her aquiline nose had been broken in a car wreck. She took one last draw on her Winston before extinguishing it in a green ashtray she kept by the register. "Willard, I wish you would watch your mouth around these young people. Don't look good. I knew what I was doing until you came along and messed it up. Jordan, I'm glad to meet you. Let me show you around."

The store had a tongue and groove oak floor that covered about two thousand square feet. Soda pop bottles and empty cases were stored temporarily under the large window to the left of the door awaiting the trucks to return them to the bottling plants. Milk coolers and small freezers lined the back wall by the butcher counter where Willard cut and weighed the meat products he sold: chickens, sausage, pork chops, hamburger, hot dogs and, during the holidays, a few turkeys.

Simple wooden store shelves lined the aisles. They held dry goods and canned goods. Detergents or other products that exuded a strong smell were never displayed near cereals, flour, or breads that might pick up the odor. A produce cooler and stacks of soda pop cartons lined the back wall, while the western wall was reserved for household items and detergents. Jordan noted that the items on the shelves were the old standbys of several generations because many of store's patrons relied on food stamps, pensions and the minimum wage paychecks of unskilled workers. This was the environment he knew best, and he took comfort in that.

Over the next few weeks, he figured out that Willard's grouchy nature was only a facade and, in idle moments, he listened to Willard's coon-hunting stories. Fannie busied herself with paper work or word searches during the lulls between customers.

Business was brisk at the first of the month when welfare checks and food stamps came through the mail. Among the regulars, Jordan noticed some particularly intriguing and even appalling characters, and he became more acutely aware of to the tragedy of the human condition.

One man who worked at the quarry would stop nearly every day to buy a few items to take home, attempting to shake the rock dust from his clothes and white crew-cut before entering the store. On most days he would commandeer one of Willard's two grocery carts, which he would steer back and forth until he had traversed every aisle only to check out with a single can of pork and beans or chili. After two weeks of this odd ritual, Jordan asked Fannie, "Fannie, who is that older man who works at the quarry? He always gets a cart but usually only buys one or two items."

Fannie blew a puff of smoke as she extinguished her cigarette. "That's Harley Burkhart. Wife's name is Wilma. She's diabetic and she had a heart attack two years ago. Pretty bad situation."

"Don't they have any children to help?"

"They have children, but they ain't no help. Most of the kids live away from here. Billy lives in Knoxville, Annie lives in Georgia, I think. Anita used to live here. Wild child, into drugs and drinking. She got pregnant and had a boy, Rocky. When she found out that Rocky was Mongoloid, she left him on Harley's doorstep one night before she took off for California. Harley and Wilma raised him. He's ten now. Sweet kid, but he's got no life ahead of him."

"Does Rocky ever come in here?"

"Oh yeah, they bring him in every few weeks. Keeps him happy to meet people. He knows Willard and me. A few other people. Sort of puts you in mind of one of them chipmunks on the Bugs Bunny cartoons."

Jordan whispered, "So why does Harley take so long to buy a can of chili?'

Fannie lit another Winston, "Probably avoiding going home to all that. But Harley don't ask for nobody's pity. I think he's trying to make some money to take care of Rocky when him and Wilma dies. 'Course Rocky will be put in a home somewhere, but Harley hopes he can delay that some."

One Wednesday afternoon as he was lugging the noisy cases of glass bottles to the end of the porch, Jordan saw a blue-green station wagon pull into the graveled parking area. A dirty unkempt woman, beaten down by living, got out of the car and went into the store. Jordan pretended to be busy, but out of the corner of his eye he could see a paralyzed man lying naked in the fold-down back of the station wagon. The sight of flies buzzing around his motionless body made Jordan feel like vomiting.

By the time he had re-entered the store, the woman had bought a loaf of bread and a gallon of milk, which Fannie was adding to her monthly bill.

The woman spoke, "I think that is all he wants, milk and bread. I think he wants to go to Keith's Market for something but I don't know what he wants to go there for. I'll pay you when I get my check, if that is okay."

Fannie nodded, "That'll be fine. Now, you be careful."

After she had driven away in the station wagon Jordan asked, "Fannie, Who is that? I have never seen such a sight in my life!"

"She's bad off. Name's Norma Jean Matthews. She's Delmar Tucker's girl."

"Delmar Tucker, that everyone talks about being so poor and dirty?"

Fannie replied, "Yep, but you have Willard tell you about Delmar sometime. Norma Jean married this man William Matthews several years ago, and they was doing pretty good. I think he worked for Richardson Lumber Company in the logging woods. They had two beautiful little girls. Hair like little lambs. Then one day a tree fell the wrong way and hit William. Paralyzed him from the neck down. That's who she's hauling around in her car. She leaves him naked so she can clean him up better. Summer or winter, he lays there buck naked in that car. She throws a sheet over him the summer and a quilt over him in the winter.

'Course he has bed sores all the time. Don't weigh nothing. I hear she throws him across her shoulder and takes him in the house at night. The state took her children a long time ago because she could not take care of them. They visit once in a while; beautiful little girls."

"So she lives on welfare?"

"Can't do much else. She can't get a job, cause she can't afford to get care for William. Can't leave him home alone so she has to take him with her. Not much of an education."

Fannie wiggled her finger to entice Jordan to lean over the counter so she could whisper in his ear, "I hear she sells it to earn extra money and that some times they even do it in the car beside her husband. You know some men ain't too particular when it comes to getting laid."

Jordan felt a general queasiness creeping over him, and he shivered in disgust, "Damn! I ain't never going to be that desperate, Fannie!"

By now Fannie was bending over and slapping her thighs laughing. "She's not your type, huh? I hear she's cheap. Want an advance on your pay this week?"

Willard came up to see what the commotion was all about.

"Willard, tell him about Delmar Tucker while I go fix my makeup. I ain't laughed this hard in years."

"Now I know you've heard of Delmar Tucker, Jordan. You've probably seen him in here, a tall, tanned man with a grizzled beard and dirty old khaki clothes."

"Yeah, I've seen him, but I try to stay up wind. He's got weird eyes. Light gray and the clearest eyes I have sever seen. Looks like he's always looking at something a million miles away."

"That's Delmar. Lives down at Cabel. So damned much junk in front of the house, the state highway department had to go down there with a bulldozer and push it off the highway. Twice."

"I know Mom always told us to clean up the house or people will think we are as bad as Delmar Baker. I don't understand how people can live like that."

Willard shook a Winston out of Fannie's pack on the cash register and lit it before continuing; "Now let me tell you some things about Delmar you don't know. We used to live down at Cabel and Marvin Davis used to cut hair for us neighborhood men. One day Delmar was there with a bunch of us and we started talking about our years in the service. Directly, Delmar pipes up and claims he was in the service, the Army. Well, people was falling down laughing and making jokes. Delmar got up and drove off in that old beat up truck of his. 'Course everybody felt bad about hurting his feelings. But, directly, he comes back with a cigar box full of war medals and papers to prove they are his. We didn't know what to say."

"Guess he got the last laugh. So what happened to him to make him go to the dogs so bad?"

Willard shook his head, "Nobody knows. I heard he used to work for the electric company and was doing very good for himself. But whatever it was must have been pretty bad. You can't judge a book by its cover, huh?"

Fannie returned to her post as light rain began to patter on the tin roof. Jordan knew that business dropped off in the rain and was hoping to get a rest but Willard said, "Come back here, young'un. I got a job for you."

Jordan followed him to the back corner piled full of odds and ends that had collected over the years. Willard pointed to the corner, "I want you to clean that corner out and throw that junk away. Anything that might be useful put in that box. Most of it is junk like that big box of concrete paint. You find something you want, you keep it." He paused before adding, "Assuming it ain't money or gold. You might as well pull that big trash can back here now."

Jordan placed a few horseshoes and harness rings into a box and a few other items that might have antique value. Most of the stuff had rusted or mildewed, or had a purpose that modern society no longer needed. As he picked up one large mass of moldy reins and bridles, a black box about six inches on a side and a foot tall fell to the floor. He threw the tangled leather into the trash can and picked up the box. After he had wiped the grime away, he saw that it contained a replica of the Green Lantern Power Battery and the Power Ring.

"Hey, Willard, I think I found something I want. Here take a gander at this."

He raced over to the meat counter where Willard stood grinding hamburger. Without looking up from his job, Willard growled with a low whisper and twinkling eye, "What is it, one of them blow-up dolls?"

"No, it's much better than that. Look. It's a Green Lantern Battery and Ring. I used to play Green Lantern with my friends when I was a kid. I never knew they even made these things. I wonder how long this has been back there in the corner. You remember Green Lantern, the old one, don't you, Willard?"

"Vaguely, but I never read comic books much. Is there a date on the box? Go outside and clean that thing so you don't get dust in my hamburger."

Once outside, Jordan used his handkerchief to wipe years of accumulated dust from the box. The label had disintegrated in large spots so no date could be found and only the INC portion of the manufacturer's name remained. Jordan opened the top of the box and gasped at the exact replica of the power battery he had dreamed of in his adventures with Billy and Bobby. He carefully lifted it out by the handle. There was an emerald green ring taped to one side and the back of the box bore the Green Lantern oath with only the line, "No evil shall escape my sight." He came back in to show Fannie his find.

"We used to play superheroes and I was always Green Lantern. Do you know how long this has been sitting back there?"

"If Willard don't know, I don't know. So what does it do? Act like a little lamp?"

Jordan picked the lantern up, turning it over as he searched for a battery compartment. "No, Fannie, I think it is just a collector's item. I don't see any place for batteries. It seems pretty solid based on its weight what do you think, Willard?"

"I think you need to get back to cleaning that corner out. Maybe that ring will do it for you now."

They all laughed as Jordan pointed the ring toward the back corner, "I am commanding you to clean up the corner, magic ring!" When nothing happened, he shrugged and returned to the task. As he was carrying the last load of junk out the door, Alene Catron and her two young daughters, Sherry and Susie, held the door open for him before they entered the store to do their bi-weekly shopping.

Alene was a slight, thin woman who seldom said much of anything above a whisper. Since she could not drive, she always brought at least one daughters with her to carry the groceries home. One day Jordan had seen them walking the three miles from town back home in the rain. He had offered them a ride, but Alene refused, saying it was not that much further.

Jordan had often watched her shopping, checking prices with a grim determination to make the meager food stamps and welfare check go as far as possible. The children seldom enjoyed the luxury of candy or even gum, yet they seemed genuinely happy, never whining for things that Alene had told them in privacy they would have to sacrifice for the good of the family.

After they left the store, Jordan said to Fannie, "I have never seen her husband. Is he dead?"

Fannie stopped organizing the bills to answer, "Worse. Jerry ran a bulldozer for Wayne Construction. Made good money when they married. Then something happened to his bowels so that he can't control them. He has to stay around a toilet all the time. Somebody told me that he only weighs about a hundred pounds. They have a little boy named William that stays with Jerry to help clean him up when she comes up here. You noticed Alene buys the cheapest food she can get. They have it pretty rough, but the kids never complain. Amazes me."

"I offered to give them a ride home a few weeks ago when it was raining, but she wouldn't take it even though one of the little girls already had the door open. I guess she doesn't want charity."

Fannie blew a long stream of smoke from her pursed lips. "Jordan, one thing I have learned in years of running a store is that most people don't mind charity, but they had rather have dignity and self respect. There's some people come in here who are willing to take a handout and you know who they are. They think the world owes them a living and complain when they don't get it. We all hate to see them come through the door."

Jordan said, "The Bells, the Brummett's, the Rigneys…"

"Yep, you know them. But people as bad off as Norma Jean bother us because she never whines about her life. One time she asked to borrow ten dollars for a week. When I cashed her welfare check the next week, she handed me back ten dollars and thanked me. I think we make remarks about people like her so we don't have to admit we're not willing to help her more, and we don't believe in miracles to do it for us. What are you going to do?"

Deep in thought, Jordan walked away biting his lower lip and shocked that a hill woman in a country store had such insight into the human condition. He looked at the green ring in his palm and remembered thinking as a child how easy it would be to fix people's problems if he only had the Green Lantern ring. Now, in the face of the desperation and frustrating poverty in this little corner of the world, that seemed shamefully childish.

A few days later, Harley and Wilma brought Rocky to the store. Harley walked with a spring in his step as he led his grandson into the store where Rocky cried out, "Hi, Fannie. Where's Willard?"

"I'm back here, Rocky," Willard replied.

Jordan watched Rocky maneuver his stubby-limbed body down the aisles while Harley and Wilma glowed with pride at how far their only grandson had come.

After he had shook Willard's hand, Rocky looked at Jordan and boldly asked, "I'm Rocky. Who are you?"

Jordan extended his hand, "My name is Jordan. I've heard a lot about you, Rocky."

"That's a pretty ring. Can I see it?"

"Sure," Jordan replied as he slipped the ring past the first knuckle on his finger. "I found it in the corner over there."

"It's pretty. Can I wear it for a while? Do you think you could find me one?"

Jordan thought for a few seconds, " Sure, you can wear it while your grandparents shop. If I find another one, I'll give it to you. Now don't lose it, Rocky."

Jordan did his work while keeping an eye on Rocky, not for fear he might lose the ring, it but to see what he would do with it. Rocky walked in his stiff-legged way around the store, showing the bright ring to people he knew and a few he didn't, until Wilma told him to give it back to Jordan.

"Here's your ring back, Jordan. That's a pretty name, Jordan. We have to go home now, but I'll see you again soon. Can I play with the ring then, too?" Rocky said.

Jordan smiled as he remembered Fannie's comment about his looking like a chipmunk. "Sure, Rocky, as long as I work here you can play with it," Jordan said as he pushed the ring back onto his finger.

As they watched the Burkhart's leave the store, Fannie patted Jordan on the arm and said, "That was mighty nice of you to let him play with that ring.

Don't it look shinier now? He might have gotten something, probably potato chip grease on it. Here's a paper towel to clean it up."

"Thanks. He's a nice kid," replied Jordan as he wiped the ring until a new luster appeared.

The following week Jordan was stocking canned goods when Norma Jean Matthews came in leading two beautiful little fleecy-headed girls. They were neatly dressed in frilly dresses, and Norma Jean herself was cleaner than Jordan had ever seen her. A bright smile and dancing eyes replaced her usual hangdog look.

"Girls, you remember Ms. Denney, don't you? Ms. Denney, do you remember Katy and Elizabeth?"

Fannie smiled broadly as she bent over the counter, "I sure do remember them and their beautiful heads of hair. And such pretty dresses. Are you helping Mommy shop today?"

Katy replied, "Just a little for us and Daddy. He wants a sandwich and Mommy promised us some candy and a Coke."

The three of them danced back to Willard's meat counter where Norma ordered ham and sandwiches for all of them. Watching them take Cokes from the cooler, Jordan could scarcely believe this was the same woman he tried to avoid. Willard cleared his throat loudly to get Fannie's attention so she could see his slight headshake telling her not to charge Norma Jean for the food. She and the children laid the food on the counter so Fannie could get a total cost to add to the monthly tab.

Jordan asked, "Would you like a bag for that?"

Norma Jean replied, "Yes, that would be a good idea. I forgot to get a big box of Tide. Would you get one and bring it out to the car for me?"

This was the day that Jordan had feared above all others. In the past Norma Jean's purchases had been small enough for her to carry. Now he had no choice but to comply. He fetched the box of Tide, dreading the sight of the naked man who was probably lying in his own filth in the back of the station wagon. The girls were already in the front seat of the car with Norma Jean.

"Just set it there in the floorboard behind my seat," she said.

When Jordan opened the door, a few flies flew out and an odor of stale urine smacked him in the face. He had planned to deposit the box quickly, without looking at the naked man lying in the back, but he found his gaze fixed on the thin pale man who resembled a stick figure with a shroud of skin stretched over him. His genitals were half covered by a dirty washcloth that would certainly blow off when Norma Jean drove off. His limbs lay horribly twisted, like straws in a windstorm, and his eyes looked like the blots of a fountain pen were the ink had leaked out. The man gave him a weak smile punctuated by yellowed and missing teeth, and even said, "Thank you," in a raspy voice.

As the station wagon pulled off, Jordan stood frozen in confused disgust and compassion. Glancing down, he saw the translucent green ring glistening in the sunlight, and suddenly realized the fatal flaw of youthful imagination. Only children could believe in superheroes. They live in a world of possibility where they do not face the harsh realities of the everyday human condition. He returned to the store and bought a Coke to drink.

Shortly he said to Fannie, "Like you said, she is in a real bind. I ain't never seen anything like that. How can people live like that?"

"I don't know, but ain't them two pretty little girls? And did you see how happy Norma Jean was?"

"Yeah, but for how long? She gets to keep her own kids for what a day or so every couple of months. Then what? Back to the hell of her life."

Fannie sighed as she smudged out her Winston, "Still, if I lived my life in hell, just one day in heaven would be all right with me...all right with me."

Fannie wadded up the scrap of paper with the total of the lunches and tossed it into the trashcan. She said, "By the way, you know it meant a lot to her to have her children see you carrying that Tide out to her car."

Jordan felt his face flush, "Why? So they could think I am her flunky?"

Fannie replied softly, " No, so they could see that you treat her like everyone else who shops here."

Embarrassed at his egocentrism, Jordan looked at his watch. "It's after five. I'm going home. See you tomorrow."

All night, Jordan tossed and turned as the events of the day haunted him. His own face replaced the face of William Matthews lying naked and twisted in his own filth, and rasping a weak 'Thank you' to a cold, indifferent stranger doing a trivial service. He overslept and was two hours late for work the next day.

Willard met at the door. "Are you all right? We was getting worried. Thought maybe you was sick or had a wreck. Why didn't you call or something? You look like hell, boy! Go comb your hair!"

Jordan dropped his head, "I am sorry, Willard. I did not sleep much last night and I just overslept. I would have called but I figured I might as well drive up here. I'll work late to make up the difference. If you want to fire me, that's okay too. I messed up, and I am sorry."

Willard put his hand on his shoulder. "Fire you for this? How could I ever look your daddy in the eye? We all oversleep some time. We're just glad you're okay. Fannie, fix him a cup of coffee."

Jordan borrowed Willard's comb and quickly raked the tangles out of his wavy brown hair. The coffee smelled good and tasted better. The three of them stood around the counter sipping the strong black brew.

"Been a short summer, college boy. Back to the books! You never have told me what you are working on."

Fannie snorted, "Willard, if he told you, you wouldn't know any more than you do right now. Face it: we're just dumb hillbillies in the sticks. We don't even know what all them lines on the boxes are for." She pointed to the barcode on a box of cereal.

Jordan said, "Well, Fannie I am working on something that is related to those little lines. Someday every product sold in a grocery store will have those little lines on it. A special light called a laser will read the lines and send it into a computer that will decode it. The lines contain all the information about the box: price, size, manufacturer, and so on. So then you won't have to price everything by hand, or take inventory by hand. I'm working on ways to improve the computer that scans the code."

Willard and Fannie stared blankly at the UPC on the cornflake box Jordan handed them. "Like Fannie said, 'we are just a bunch of dumb hillbillies.' Put this back and get to work, Mr. Computer Genius."

The day passed uneventfully until Alene Catron and her daughter Sherry stopped in to buy a few groceries. Sherry seemed especially joyful, so Fannie asked, "Why are you so happy today, Sherry?"

"Because it's my birthday. I'm eight years old today and Mommy's going to bake me a cake with eight candles on it!"

"Eight years old. Boy, you sure are growing up fast! Won't be long until you will have your own little girls," Fannie said in a teasing voice.

While Alene gathered the groceries and mixes for the cake, Sherry made a bee-line to the section of the store where Willard kept a small supply of general-purpose toys: cap pistols, balls, stuffed animals and so forth. The supplier from Tennessee had just stocked new toys last week and no one had paid much attention to what he had left. As Alene was checking out, Sherry excitedly grabbed a fluorescent pink teddy bear with emerald green eyes and dashed to the counter. She gently touched touch the bear to Alene's arm while Fannie was adding up the groceries. Alene quietly took the bear, and inverted it to see the price. Though she thought that only Sherry would see her imperceptible rejection of her daughter's request, Fannie saw Sherry's eyes lose the twinkle they had when she came in the store a few minutes ago.

"So, Alene, is that pretty bear Sherry's birthday present? I need to check the price on that."

Before Alene could object, Fannie had taken the bear out of her hands and looked at the price.

"That price is wrong. Willard said these stuffed animals are half price. So it's only two dollars," she said as she handed it back to Sherry.

The child's eyes searched her mother's face for any hint of hope before a soft smile acknowledged that her dream had come true. Sherry grabbed a sack of groceries and raced out the door. Alene and Fannie stood staring deeply into each other eyes for what seemed an eternity before Alene whispered "Thank you." in a strained tremulous voice, "Thank you." Then she, too, grabbed a sack of groceries and headed home.

Willard came to the counter where he slapped Jordan on the back. "I think you should thank Fannie for getting rid of that damned bear. I believe it was the ugliest thing I have ever seen. Damned green eyed monster."

Jordan laughed. "I have to agree with you, Willard. But it made one little girl very happy," he replied as he realized that he had fidgeted with the green ring on his finger.

"Made me happy to get rid of it, boy," Willard laughed. "What about you, woman? You happy?"

She blew out a languid stream of smoke, "I sure am. Bought a lot of happiness for two dollars. I say we got a bargain."

The delivery truck did not run until seven thirty that night, so Jordan's staying late was fortuitous. No one in the small rural community shopped after seven o'clock so Willard and Jordan concentrated on storing the goods in the stockroom and restocking shelves while Fannie checked the accuracy of the order. Around ten o'clock, Willard said, "Let's go home. I'm tired and you look worse than you did this morning. Missing sleep will do that too you. See you in the morning."

Jordan dragged himself to his car where he sat resting for a few minutes. As he pulled the car onto the main highway, he found himself thinking of Sherry and her ugly green-eyed bear. He placed his hand on the top of the steering wheel so he could better maneuver the car around the first turn atop Pump Station Hill where the narrow road clung to the steep mountain that plunged over a hundred feet to the creek bed below. When he rounded the second turn, the lights from an oncoming car blinded him; he lost control of the car and crash through the guardrail over the cliff into a pale green glow at the creek bottom below.

IV

"Mr. Osmund, Mr. Barnett and his son, Andy, are here to see you. Should I see them in?" Margaret announced over the intercom in Osmund's office.

"No, I'll come and get them in a minute. Offer Mr. Barnett some coffee and Andy a juice, please." Jordan replied.

Hurriedly, he shuffled the papers on his desk into a manila folder and exchanged that folder for the one containing the Barnett file in his desk drawer. He quickly strode over to the filing cabinet where he retrieved the power battery he had found in Denney's store and placed it in the lower drawer in his desk before taking the elevator to the first floor to meet the Barnetts.

"Good morning, Woodrow. And this must be Andy. How are you Andy?"

The small boy, frail and insubstantial as a puff of cigarette smoke answered, "I am okay, Mr. Barnett, but I am a little scared."

Osmund squatted down to face the boy eye to eye, placed his hand on Andy's shoulder and reassured him, "There's no need to be afraid, Andy. You're going to be fine and when you get well you can play ball, and go fishing, and horseback riding, and do all the things your friends do. Now come with me to see a surprise."

Osmund stood up, winked at Woodrow and led the boy past Margaret's desk. "Margaret, please see that we are not disturbed for any reason," he requested as the three of them went into his office.

"Please pull up a chair in front of my desk. Here, Andy, let me help you. Would either of you want something to drink?"

"No, thank you, Mr. Osmund." Woodrow replied, "To tell the truth, I'm as scared as Andy is."

Jordan smiled as he spread the folder out in front of the Barnetts, exposing a photograph of a handsome young man in a suit.

"The Osmund Foundation conducted a worldwide search and found a surgeon, Dmitri Armitrov, in Moscow who seems to be especially gifted in repairing the kinds of damage to young hearts that Andy has. We flew him into town last week to check out the hospital facilities and assemble his support staff for the operation that we scheduled for later this week. The foundation has arranged for him to stay in this country until Andy leaves the hospital and will pay for any return trips for checkups or emergencies should they arise. We do need you to sign this waiver that in the event of something going wrong, which is very unlikely, you will not pursue legal action against the foundation. Do you understand, Woodrow, that you have no financial obligation for any of this?"

Woodrow looked at Jordan through tear-filled eyes and replied in a quavering voice, "Yes, but I wish there was some way I could repay your kindness."

"There is. You must see that Andy leads a healthy lifestyle. No smoking, no drinking, no drugs; cut down unhealthful foods. Now, Andy is a child and he will best do these things if you do them too. There is one more thing you must agree to, Woodrow."

Woodrow snapped to attention, eager to satisfy the request of the man who was going to save his son's life. "What is it, Mr. Osmund? What do I have to do?"

Jordan leaned back in his overstuffed leather swivel rocker and quietly replied, "Let Andy have his flights of fancy. You'll know what I mean in a few minutes."

Woodrow's face wrinkled in the puzzlement and frustration of a man who desperately wants to do the next right thing but has no idea what that is, and no guide to judge if his choice of action is the right one.

"I don't understand. How can I...."

Jordan held up his hand to cut off Barnett's objection. "Like I said, the answer will come to you. Now Andy, did you bring the ring I sent you?"

Andy flashed the cheap green plastic ring and smiled, "Yes, Mr. Osmund. Here it is. Daddy even bought me some Green Lantern comic books to read. I've even learned his oath. 'In brightest day, In darkest night, No evil shall escape my sight, Beware my power, Green Lantern's Light!'

"That is wonderful Andy. Have you been able to make the ring do anything for you?"

"No, not yet. I don't think I'm strong enough yet because I'm too weak."

Jordan motioned for Andy to come sit on his knee. He hugged the boy close and said, "Now, Andy, I know you have seen a mule pulling a loaded wagon or a plow. That mule is pretty strong to work all day, isn't he?"

"Yes, sir, he is. Real strong."

"Well, how does that mule work all day? Which is stronger, the mule's body or his will that drives his body?"

"Gee, Mr. Osmund, I don't know."

"Knowing the answer to that question is one key to getting the ring to work. The other is making sure that your ring is charged up. Now you almost got the oath right. Here, let's take the power battery and charge up our rings together."

Jordan opened the drawer and placed the power battery on his desktop, winking at Woodrow from the eye that Andy could not see.

"Wow!" Andy cried "A real power battery! Where did you get that? Can I get one too?"

"Boy, I don't know. I found this one a long time ago in the most unlikely place, but I've never seen another one. I guess you'll have to just use mine. Here we go. Now listen carefully."

They pointed the rings toward the battery, and repeated the oath in unison. Jordan felt Andy's body tense up with excitement and expectation.

"You do know that the ring will protect its wearer from harm, don't you? I have checked with Dr. Armitrov and he sees no reason why you can't wear the ring during your operation. So you know everything's going to be okay."

Andy replied with a new confidence, "You bet I do! Thanks, Mr. Osmund!"

Jordan tousled the boy's hair, "You're welcome. Now I believe that you have an appointment with the doctor this afternoon and I have work to do. I'll sneak the battery in for a booster shot before your surgery and every day or so until you're well. I'll see you soon."

The Barnetts left the office, Jordan returned to his work. As promised, he smuggled the power battery into Andy's room just before he was wheeled away for pre-op. The surgery lasted over four hours, a little longer than expected, but Armitrov assured Woodrow and Jordan that Andy's condition was better than he had hoped for. In a few days, Andy was walking by himself, and ten days after surgery an astonished Dr. Armitrov released him from the hospital, and returned to Moscow.

Six months later, the Barnett's reappeared at Jordan's office before their appointment with Dr. Armitrov. Neither Margaret not Jordan could believe this was the same boy they had met a few months before. He had gained twenty pounds; his once vacuous eyes danced with a new life and a rosy blush shone from his face. He had earned A's and B's in school and was playing Little League Baseball.

Jordan asked, "Baseball, huh? What position do you play?"

Andy bubbled, "I play left field, but I want to be a pitcher next year. I'm a good hitter too. So far I hit two home runs!"

Jordan could see Woodrow's proud countenance and posture out of the corner of his eye. "Two home runs? You must have strong arms."

Andy leaned over the desk and whispered, "Actually, I cheated. I used this." He thrust the green ring toward Jordan's face.

Jordan's face darkened as he puckered his lips and turn towards Barnett. "Woodrow, I think Andy and I have a few things to talk about. Would you please wait in the outer office for a few minutes?"

Somewhat surprised by the sudden change in Jordan's demeanor, Barnett had little choice but to comply. Jordan placed a chair beside Andy's chair and held his hand bearing the green ring in his own.

"So you cheated using the power ring. Could you demonstrate how it works for me? You see, your dad did not pull the door quite closed. Do you think that you can push the door closed from here by using your ring?"

"Well, I'll try," replied Andy. But no manner of facial grimacing or verbal commands could summon the power of the ring to do his bidding. After a few minutes, Jordan took his hand, "Andy, this ring doesn't work anymore. Never did."

"But it does work! It got me through my operation! I would have died without it!" Andy cried.

Jordan released his hand and stroked his hair, " No, Andy, it didn't. You were so young and scared that I knew you needed something to believe in, a source of strength, to harden your will to survive. You believed in a light you thought you saw in that ring, and that became your good luck charm. The light that truly saved you was your father's love. He would not give up on you, and his determination gave you strength to get well. Do you want to know where I got this ring?"

Andy sat sobbing quietly at the deception played on him. "Ye...es."

"Well, let me give you a little background. When I was a young man just a little older than you, I took a job in Blevin's Grocery just outside of town. And you wouldn't believe some of the people who used to come in there to shop..."

As Jordan told him about Harley and Norma Jean and Alene and the green-eyed bear, Andy, enraptured by the tales of these and other poor desperate souls, forgot why he was crying as he envisioned what it must have been like to see this first hand.

".... and after a while I realized that I really wished there was some way to help these people. Then I remembered pretending I was the Green Lantern as a boy and I began to hope I could find a power ring to heal the evil and pain in these people's lives. And, lo and behold, I found this power battery and ring in a pile of junk in the back of the store! And do you know what, Andy?"

"You helped them people?"

Jordan dolefully shook his head, "I wish I could say I did, but believing in a superhero to come save us is a game for children. Each of us has our own battery inside us," he said gently tapping Andy's scarred chest. "Good and evil both live in the same house, the human heart, and they live there side by side. Look at this room, Andy, how bright it is. But look under my desk or in that far corner. Do you see the shadow that lurks there?"

By now Andy was alive with the story, "Yes, yes, I see it."

"Those shadows are the choices we make that hurt others. Even if my ring could wipe out evil, it still could not have helped those people."

"Why not?" Andy asked.

"Because there are a lot of bad things that happen that are not caused by evil. There was no evil in the tree that crushed Norma Jean's husband. There was no evil that gave you a deformed heart. The only thing that can help people who need help is the light of human compassion of others and they will help those in need. I realized this too late. I never did anything to help those poor people I met and now they are either dead or scattered so I can't find them. And that is the shadow that dwells in my heart."

"But Daddy says you help a lot of people like you helped me."

"I used my money to start this foundation to help those in need, but it is not nearly enough. We need more people out there who believe in the light. Remember I asked you a question about a mule or its heart?"

"Yes, I think it is his heart because it gives the mule strength to go on."

"That's right, it does. Keep this ring to remind you to believe that the light of good shines in the hearts of all people. Some day, you might run into someone else who has a ring like yours. When you do, touch the rings together, look each other square in the eye and say the Green Lantern Oath."

By now Andy's was sitting slack-jawed and mesmerized at Jordan's speech. "Now remember, this is our little secret, Andy, and come see us around here once in a while!" laughed Jordan.

He buzzed for Margaret to send Woodrow back into his office.

"Woodrow, it looks like things are going extremely well. I'm asking you to check in with us now and then for the next two years. Of course, feel free to refer others to us as you see fit. And, Woodrow?"

"Yes, Mr. Osmund?"

"Please see what you can do about those power ring rumors."

Woodrow turned red and laughed, "Okay, I'll try, but people are sort of set on that idea! But I ain't figured out what was that other thing was that I have to do."

Jordan winked at Andy and patted him on the back. "I believe Andy can help you with that. Have a safe trip home."

As they shook hands and said good byes, Jordan resumed his seat behind his mahogany desk and turned his attention to a new plant construction. A few minutes later, he heard the door open slightly, although no one came in. Realizing that the Barnetts had not latched the door behind them, he pointed his hand with the green ring at the door and an enormous translucent green hand emerged from the ring and gently closed the door.

The Road to Damascus

THE FAMILY TREE Restaurant lying five miles from the foot of the steep incline of Jellico Mountain, Tennessee, was a last chance for the semi trailer truckers to fuel up themselves and their rigs before tackling the ascent up the long tortuous highway. The interstate from the base of the mountain provided a long straight shot to gain speed to start the climb preceding many gear changes needed to negotiate the only north- south corridor in this section of the state. The road clung like a four lane ribbon winding up the mountain before reaching a straight stretch along the top of the ridge where the steep sandstone cliffs plunged into the abyss on either side. A panoramic vista lying on either side invoked a real sense of vertigo for those unfamiliar with the route. Wintry weather often closed the road for short periods thereby aborting futile attempts for traffic especially long-distance truckers from attempting the life-threatening conditions.

During these times, travelers and truckers alike took refuge in the Family Tree while they waited out the delay. The restaurant served typical southern comfort food, but it was noteworthy for its homemade meatloaf, chicken and dumplings and delicious pies. A retinue of truckers traversing the north-south road formed the nucleus of a sort of fraternity of habitués whose lives depended on making the trip several times a week. George Bates, Harold Shearer and Junior Rigney stopped in to eat and shoot the breeze on both the trip up and down the mountain and each delighted in picking at the waitresses Lois Riddle and Imogene Cooper. A lot of good-natured teasing with a heavy undercurrent of sexual innuendo flowed constantly, but everyone knew that such indelicacies were just talk, as acting on such fantasies would destroy the camaraderie and platonic affection binding them together.

A typical day in the restaurant started around five in the morning when George, a large bearded man habitually dressed in flannel shirts and greasy khaki pants, would bluster in with the subtlety of a north wind. Three or four days a week his compatriots, Harold and Junior, would join him as they made their trek either up or down the mountain.

On a warm July morning George burst in with his usual bluster, "Morning, Lois, Imogene. How are my two best girls?"

Imogene nodded and replied, "We're fine. Yourself?"

"Great. Heading down to Atlanta. Hey, Doll, how about the breakfast special eggs over easy and a cup of your world famous coffee?"

"Coming right up," said Lois as she motioned ever so slightly with a head motion to tell George to look to his left. A gaunt, unshaven man sat hunched over his plate, eating his breakfast.

George turned toward him, "Howdy, partner. You're up early. You a trucker?"

"Yep."

"Where you heading?"

"North."

George began to feel uncomfortable with the stranger's laconic replies. "You know, I passed a wreck in the north bound lane about half an hour ago. You might get held up."

The stranger nodded without making eye contact. "Thanks for the heads up."

George knitted his brow as he walked over to greet the man. "I'm George Bates," he said, extending his hand.

The man turned for a quick handshake. "Paul Koger."

"Who do you drive for?"

"Latham."

"I have not seen you in here before. Every trucker on seventy five stops here. How long have you been driving?"

"About six months."

Sensing the man was not interested in conversation, George said, "It's nice to meet you, Paul. Have a safe trip north. I guess you know about Jellico Mountain."

"Yeah, I have been over it a few times."

George returned to his seat to eat his breakfast as Paul quietly finished his meal, paid, and left for his truck. All three of the people at the counter watched as he pulled out.

George said, "Not much of a talker, is he?"

Lois shook her head in agreement. "Something about him kind of creeps me out. Ordered his breakfast and never said a word. Just held up his cup when he wanted more coffee. Creepy."

Imogene added, "Maybe he was just tired. He ain't been trucking long. It takes some getting used to. I'm not going to worry about it. Probably never see him again."

George shrugged, "I ought to have got his CB handle, but I doubt he'd have given it to me. You're right. Probably never see him again."

They were wrong. In a couple of days, the man walked in while George, Harold and Junior were noisily eating lunch and flirting with the waitresses. The man slipped in the door and took his seat against the wall.

George welcomed him. "Well, howdy, partner. Fellers, this here is a new trucker. Name's Paul ain't it? This here is Harold and Junior."

The man shot them a quick glance and muttered, "Nice to meet you."

"Didn't you tell me you were out of Lexington?"

"Yeah."

"You get caught in that wreck Tuesday?"

"No," Paul replied as he pointed out his lunch selection to Lois, "This here and coffee to drink."

"I meant to get your handle but forgot. You got a CB handle? Mine is Loudmouth, Harold is Big Daddy and Junior is Papaw."

"You can call me Nashville."

"Well, it is always good to know your name in case you need help along the road."

"Appreciate that."

"You heading north or south?"

"North."

"Well, have a good trip. We're all heading to Tampa. Always nice to have running buddies on long hauls."

"I guess so."

Feeling an uncomfortable pall settle in, George turned to rejoin his friends to finish his lunch. Paul ate his lunch hurriedly, paid, and left without saying a word.

Harold watched out the window as Paul got into his truck and pulled out of the parking lot. "Not much of a talker is he?"

"Nope. I think you're right Lois. He's kinda creepy. Well, we tried to be friendly so I ain't going to worry about it. Let's hit the road. Lois, give me a cup of coffee to go."

"I didn't hear the magic word."

"Please? Damn, woman you're such a hardass."

A wave of laughter washed over the diner. The men paid and drove off.

II

Paul became a regular at the diner, but never revealed any more details about his life. Soon trying to decipher him became a cottage industry. Occasionally, one of the men would say they had heard him on the radio, but even there he refrained from idle chitchat.

After he left one night on a northbound trip, Imogene said to Harold as he finished his dinner. "I don't care what you say. There is something not right about that man. Never seen a trucker so quiet."

Harold responded, "Quieter than a church mouse. Lois is right ... sorta creepy."

"Sorta? Damned creepy, if you ask me."

"I heard a Smokey pull him over the other night for being in the left lane up the mountain. I think it was Larry Powell. I'll try to raise him on the radio and see if he found out anything about him."

"You know, he comes off as being real empty inside. Never talks about family or women or drinking or nothing."

"You sure he is a trucker?" Harold asked.

"Good point. See what you can find out."

The usual gang happened to meet three days later. Imogene brought a coffee pot and three mugs over to their table. "Morning guys. Harold, you learn anything about Mr. Blabbermouth?"

"Not one damned thing. Larry checked his license and registration. Paul Koger like he said. Clean driving record. Told Larry he had a headache and was a little slow in changing lanes."

"He give him a ticket?"

"Nope, just told him to pay more attention and have a safe trip. I mean, what can he say to the man, tell me your life story?"

"You know if any of you fellers had any sense you might try to get the ball rolling by telling him more about yourself. He might open up a little. I don't mind telling you that I'm getting to be very curious. Ain't right for a trucker to be that quiet."

George and Junior nodded. "You know, you might have something there. Next time I see him I'll try that," George said.

The opportunity presented itself three days later. George and Junior had stopped by for dinner on their way to Detroit and found Paul sitting at the counter instead of his usual table because a young couple eating quietly took it. They sidled up to the counter to take a seat beside him. "Mind if we join you, Paul?" Junior asked.

"Free country."

"George was trying to tell me that his daughter looks like him. George, show him that picture."

George pulled his wallet out of his back pocket, flipped open the picture sleeves and slid the wallet to Junior. "That's her on the right. What do you think?"

Paul looked at the picture quickly. "Yeah, she looks like you."

George asked, "You got any family?"

"No."

"I have to tell you, Paul, you're the quietest trucker I have ever met. After all these months we still don't know much about you."

"Not much to know."

George said, "Hey man, that's cool. We're just trying to be friendly. You ain't been trucking too long or you would know how important it is to have friends on the road. You never know when you might need them."

Paul pursed his lips, lowered his head and took a deep breath. "Okay, here is the story. I used to have a family but I don't now. I used to be an accountant, but decided that long distance trucking might help me think some things through and maybe forget some things. Sometimes I don't talk because I get migraine headaches. Sometimes, I just don't have anything to say. Sometimes I have things on my mind. Look, it is not like I don't appreciate your interest and I don't mean no disrespect, but I just need to work through some things, okay?"

Shocked by his candor, George and Junior got up to leave. "Okay man, but if you need to talk to somebody let us know. Us truckers are just one big family. Be glad to do what we can."

"Thanks. Like I said, I appreciate your concern, but some things you have to work out alone."

"Hey, Buddy, we'll put a good word for you with the man upstairs."

"Do me a favor. Don't." Paul snapped back as he threw a ten-dollar bill on the counter. "Keep the change."

He walked swiftly across the diner and disappeared into the night.

Lois came over and said to the men, "Like I said, he is one creepy son of a bitch. Have you ever known anyone turning down a prayer for him?"

Junior replied as he scratched his head, "Can't say as I have. He seemed real pissed off by it too. Now he's got me wondering what his story really is. Why would anyone turn down an offer of prayer for him?"

Imogene sniffed, "Must be one of them atheists. They don't believe in God. Never thought I'd see the day I had to serve one of their kind. I wonder if I have to serve him?"

George made a clicking noise. "Now, let's not jump to conclusions. He never said he didn't believe in God, just not to pray for him. Some people are just naturally afraid of such talk. I say we go ahead and pray for him and just go on treating him the same way. Maybe he'll tell us what he is thinking."

Harold added, "I told you that he seemed empty inside. Now I know why."

George replied, "Now hold on, everybody. Maybe he is just going through a rough time and has lost any faith he had. Don't tell me that all of you have not done the same thing in rough times. Lord knows I have."

Junior nodded in agreement. "You all know the story of Job. Even he lost faith in God. Just because he asked us not pray for him doesn't mean we can't.

I have always felt that as strange as he is he is basically a good guy. What do we have to lose anyway?"

Everyone agreed and pledged to pray for Paul to be able to confront whatever demons possessed him. George whispered, "And nobody tells him anything about this. No point in risking making him mad at us."

III

Paul appeared only sporadically over the next few weeks, and many of the group feared that their nosiness had driven him away. When he did show up, they all tried to treat him the way they always had without betraying any hint of their plan. Paul obliged them by remaining as quiet and stoic as he always had been. He continued to respond to questions with terse, even abrupt, answers and deflected any attempts to delve deeper into his personal life. Weeks became months with no perceptible change. One by one, each of the group began to doubt that their efforts were worthwhile.

One day after Paul had stopped by and left, Lois said, "You know some people can't be saved. The Bible says so. I have prayed and prayed that he'll tell us what's wrong. I ain't afraid to tell you that I'm wondering if we're wasting our time here. He ain't changed any."

Harold agreed. "You know, this would be a lot easier if we just got some kind of sign that he was trusting us or something was happening."

Imogene added, "I find it real easy to forget to say a prayer for him. You'd think he would be a little more appreciative. I mean why is he so down on God? Everybody has trials, so why does he think his are so bad?"

Junior echoed her doubts. "They say faith is believing in things unseen and I gotta tell you I have faith that he ain't going to change because I sure have not seen any."

George listened intently. "I thought we were doing the right thing when we started this but now I'm not so sure. Maybe he is an atheist and God wants nothing to do with him. Maybe some of us are not praying hard enough. I gotta tell you I find myself praying for a sign that something is going to happen and I don't see any such sign. It's real tempting to just give up and wash my hands of the whole thing. I guess we can still be civil and courteous toward him, but if he is unwilling to confide his troubles with us there is no point in keeping up this waste of time."

They all nodded their silent assent. As the weather turned wintrier, Paul stopped by more frequently, but more and more Lois and Imogene noticed him taking painkillers. When asked if he was okay, he replied with "Just another damned migraine. Sometimes they blind me. Is there some place I can sit that is not too lit up? The light makes the pain worse."

Little by little, the people who were so concerned about Paul's health and spiritual came to regard him with the same indifference they showed a chair in the restaurant. Conversation deteriorated to a series of grunts, a specious "How ya doing?" or sometimes just a silent nod of acknowledgement. As the Christmas season approached, a last ditch effort to spread good cheer toward Paul fizzled out when they saw him sitting in his dark corner crying to himself.

Lois took some coffee over and asked, "You okay, sugar? I hate to see you so down. Anything I can do?"

Paul wiped his eyes and nose with a handkerchief. "No, thank you very much, Lois. I appreciate your concern but the holidays are tough on me sometimes. Could you put that coffee in a go cup? I gotta hit the road."

"Sure thing. I'll get you an extra large cup. Looks like you could use it. Sure there is nothing I can do?"

He shook his head as he wrestled some bills from his wallet. He poured a little cream and sugar in his coffee, placed the lid on tightly and left the diner.

Lois sauntered over to the counter where Imogene and Junior were chatting. "I really hate to see a man so down in the holidays. But it ain't like we haven't tried to help. Shame, real shame. Maybe we should say some more prayers for him," she said.

Junior replied, "Hey, we tried that and nothing changed. Some people just want to be miserable and I think he is one of them. Pour me another cup of coffee to go. I gotta head out too."

By the end of the week, all the regular customers knew about the crying episode. Some began to speculate on how Paul would spend the holidays.

George threw up his hands. "Hell, I would invite him to Christmas dinner, but we don't even know where he lives. Guess we could ask. Day after tomorrow is Christmas Eve. Wonder if he'll be back in."

Lois said, "If he is, I'll ask him to come to Christmas dinner at my house. I felt so sorry for him that night, but I don't know what we can do. I'm pretty sure he would not accept any gifts from us."

Junior shrugged. "Guess we'll play it by ear. I should see you all before Christmas, but if I don't, Merry Christmas. G' night."

IV

Paul did not return until Christmas Eve. He sought out his usual seat in the low light section and popped a pain pill. He motioned Lois to bring him coffee and a menu.

"Evening, sugar. You still feeling bad?"

"Just the damned headache. I think I'll have the roast beef dinner with mashed potatoes, green beans and a piece of pecan pie. And a glass of water and a cup of coffee."

"You know, if you're going north you might want to hurry, honey. It is supposed to snow tonight and they might close the road. You got big plans for Christmas?"

Paul exploded into a standing position. "Do I have big plans for Christmas? Let me tell you about my damned Christmas. I used to be an accountant with a beautiful wife. We were expecting our first child. Something went wrong during the delivery and our son was born with severe brain damage from hypoxia… oxygen shortage to the brain. But he was our son and we loved him. For ten years, we raised Stephen and helped him learn to function at a minimal level. Then, last year we were going to Nashville for Christmas with a friend. I hit a patch of black ice and turned the car over three times. Stephen was thrown out of the car and broke his neck. Ginny sustained burns over half of her body and died. I wound up in a coma for three months. I never got to see my son's or my wife's funeral. When I woke up, my whole world had vanished. I became a trucker hoping to get way from all the pain and endless questions. Seems like I can't escape those."

He pointed over to where the regular crew was sitting. "So now you know why I don't want your goddamned prayers. What kind of God would do such a horrible thing to anybody? I'll have to relive that nightmare every Christmas Day for the rest of my life, so please don't tell me of how Jesus came to save us from sin and death. He ain't done too good a job by me. If I wasn't such a coward, I would kill myself but I'd probably screw that up too and wind up in worse shape. So if you want to believe all this Christmas story crap, whatever gets you through the night, but please spare me and let me grieve in private."

He stormed out the door, walked swiftly to his rig and began the drive to ascend the mountain road that snow was rapidly obscuring. Lois gathered the dishes from his table and carried them to the kitchen sink. She poured herself a cup of coffee before joining the others at the counter. A cold blast blew into the diner when George and Harold entered, stomping their feet to remove the snow.

"You people look like your best friend just died. Why is everyone so down?"

Junior motioned for them to take a seat. "We know Paul's story now and it is a real bummer."

They listened intently as Junior and the waitress's recounted Paul's story. Harold and George sat silently before Harold said, "Well, we kept bothering him to find out his story. Now I wish we had let well enough alone."

Lois said, "I don't know about you guys, but I'm going to be thinking about that all day tomorrow so Christmas is really going to suck. No wonder the poor guy is so down on religion. I would be too. I'm not sure I could even go on living."

They all nodded. George said, "Yeah, I think tomorrow is going to be pretty hard for me too. Like Harold said, though, we brought this on ourselves. We kept sticking our nose in somebody else's business."

Imogene interrupted, "We were just trying to help the guy as he seemed so miserable. It seemed like the Christian thing to do."

Junior added, "Maybe so, or maybe like George said we were just being nosy. Well, like the old curse says: 'May you get what you think you want.'"

After a few minutes, the men went out to sleep in their trucks and the women put things away before they too left to go home. The snow was falling heavily as they looked up the mountain and wondered how Paul was making out on his drive.

V

After he left the diner and started up the mountain, Paul spent a few minutes regaining his composure after his outburst. He regretted snapping at Lois and the others.

"I'll apologize next time I stop by. Damn, this snow is really coming down."

He maneuvered his truck slowly up the sloping road, finally reaching the level stretch running across the top of the mountain. He geared down as he entered the downhill side.

Suddenly, a sharp pang ran through his head and a bright light flashed from the rear view mirror. He eased off the gas so the truck slowed down. He rubbed his eyes with one hand, but the light had blinded him, so all he saw was the bright light.

"Holy shit, what am I going to do now? I can't stop here."

The CB radio crackled and a voice asked, "You got problems, man?"

Panicked by his predicament, he picked up the CB phone and screamed back, "I can't see where I'm going. I think I had a migraine that has left me blind. I'm trying to hug the right side of the road until I can feel the guardrail but…."

The voice answered, "Yeah, I saw that. Just stay calm and listen to me. There is a pull-off for people to see the view not far from here. I'll guide you the best I can. You with me?"

Paul felt his heart pounding violently, "Dammit, I'm a dead man…"

"No, you're not. Just listen to me. Now your trailer is drifting too close to the rail. Ease it back to the left a bit. That's better. Now don't go too far. Straighten her up. Not too fast or you'll slide. You can straddle both lanes. There's no one behind you. You're doing fine. Whoa, back to the center again… There, that's better."

Paul felt his panic subside a little as he struggled to hear and obey the instructions.

"Okay, the pull-off is just up ahead, so start gearing down. Now this is going to be tricky, so don't rush it. Start steering to the right a little. That's good. Okay, you can probably put her in neutral and let her coast to a stop. Slow, slow… you got it, Nashville."

The truck coasted to a stop and Paul collapsed over the steering wheel. Still unable to see clearly, he listened for the other trucker to either come up to check on him or drive by in his truck, but he heard nothing. He fumbled around until he found the CB radio. "You there? Hey, man you saved my life. I owe you big time. How did you know my name?"

He heard no answer, so he repeated, "Hey, man, thanks for saving my life. Can you hear me?"

He heard no answer, so he reached over to the radio to turn up the volume. His body went limp as he heard the radio switch click from "off" to the "on" position with a static crackle.

The Better Angels
of Our Nature

CLINK. CLINK. AVERY Pittman slid the last two shells into the empty chambers of his Smith and Wesson .38 and gave the cylinder a quick turn. He pushed the pistol across the small table where he ate his meals and walked over to the bug-fouled window, raised it on its creaky pulleys and leaned over the paint-peeling casement to view the dingy Chicago streets four floors below. The air was humid, smelling of an approaching thunderstorm, but it pulsed with the drone and sharp cries of the pimps, prostitutes, and drug addicts wandering the streets in front of the dirty flophouse. The rickety chair creaked as he pulled it over to the window, sat down and began to practice aiming at their blurry, anonymous shadows.

"Bang, Bang, Bang, you're all dead!" he said menacingly. Smiling a deviant grin, he repeated the ritual over and over like a kid shooting ducks in an arcade. Tiring of his imaginary target practice, he scooted a table and lamp over to the window, laid the pistol and his wallet on the table as he began to whisper the words to Steely Dan's *Deacon Blues*.

As he watched the sea of losers below, wondering if they knew they had an anthem. When the moonlight supplemented that of the yellowish streetlights, he often sat watching the johns propositioning the hookers. Desperate women and men hustled their flesh for a living, and when a price and method were agreed upon, the parties would often come into this sleazy hotel Avery had called home for his first three months out of prison. If they went to a room adjacent to his, he would often masturbate and groan in response to the fornications he could hear being transacted through the thin walls of the hotel. He dropped his head, chewed his lip in deep thought about the times he had resorted to whoring his own body to make enough money to survive and shuddered as he relived those horrible moments of shame, degradation and desperation so far removed from his former life as a successful bank manager.

"Thank God that Dad can't see me now," he muttered. "How the mighty have fallen, that is what he would probably say and as usual he would be right. And Mom would…. I guess Mom would try to…" His voice trailed off as he considered the uncertainty of her response.

Still whistling the tune running through his head, he set a large cardboard egg carton on the bed, began to fold his clothes, and laid them in the box in neatly arranged layers. After the clothes were packed, he laid the picture of his family, the eight-by- ten photo of his former fiancée, and the few remaining articles into the box. After he wrapped two strips of duct tape across the lid and the bottom and wrote his parents' address on the box, he set the box on the table, and sorted through the papers and cards in his wallet After recounting the four hundred dollars, he crammed the wallet into his back pocket.

"Well, let's get this show on the road," he said, as he looked over his room once again. He put on a rain-jacket, picked up the box, left the room, and locked the door to the hallway that reeked of urine and sweat. A bare bulb shone dimly in the hallway, but it was enough for him to find his way down the stairs and into the noisy Chicago night where a light drizzle had begun to fall.

The box was cumbersome, but he managed to carry and drag it to the convenience store on the corner of the block where he shopped there for his meager needs, and knew the manager, Harun, well. Once there, he wrestled the door open and forced the box into the dingy store.

"Hey, Harun, I have a favor to ask. Can you help me out?"

Harun replied, "Only because you are my best customer. What do you need?"

"I'm moving, but I need to send this box to my folks. I won't have time to send it tomorrow, because I'm working a double shift. It's just personal stuff that I need them to store until I get a better place. I need you to drop it off at UPS tomorrow. Here."

He reached into his wallet and handed Harun a fifty-dollar bill. "That should be more than enough to send it. Just keep the change."

Harun recoiled, "Now why should I help you if you are taking your business elsewhere?"

"Oh, don't be so melodramatic. I'll still come by every few days to check on my best friend, but I can't take this dump anymore. So what do you say? Deal?"

"I guess I can do that. Hey, wait a minute, you don't have a return address on it. I don't think UPS will take it without one. Here write your address on it."

He handed Avery a Sharpie pen. "You know, I think you're right," Avery said as he scribbled his address in the upper left corner. "Hey, man, I really appreciate your help. I got to be somewhere. Let me see … here, add this candy bar and chewing gum to my bill. Thanks again, man. See ya later."

Harun said, "Hey, hold on there a minute. Take it and put it in the back of my car. I think it'll fit." He threw him the keys.

"Okay," Avery replied as he pushed the box toward the door, picked up one end, and duck-walked it across the damp sidewalk toward Harun's SUV. He opened the back door, wrestled the box into the back, locked the door. Satisfied the box was secure, he re-entered the store and returned the keys.

"Thanks again. You're a real lifesaver. See ya around."

The rain started to pepper down more heavily. Avery pulled his coat closer and made his way to the buildings that afforded him a little shelter from the rain. He recognized familiar faces of hookers on their home corners along the way. They braved the elements to make enough money to support their drug habits or pay the rent they could not afford from their day jobs. Occasionally, one would nod or say "Hi" or "Evening", but most recognized him only as the competition for their squalid business.

As he turned the corner, a scruffy black teenager stepped in front of him. "Hey, Mister, you feeling lonely tonight?"

Avery felt his blood rush to his head as he exploded back, "No, goddamn you!" He snatched the kid up by the lapels and threw him against the wall.

"Hey, man, I don't do that rough stuff. Just the best blow job you ever had."

"Why, you little punk. What the hell are you doing out here?"

"Trying to make a quick buck like everybody else."

Avery relaxed his grip on the boy's jacket and pushed his face closer to the boy's face.

"Hey, kid, that wasn't what I meant. I want to know what you're doing here at all. Don't you realize how dangerous and degrading this is? I know. I used to work here, too."

"Hey, look around, you see any other way for a brother my age to earn a living? I just want to earn enough to buy an iPod. I swear."

Avery grabbed the kid again. "So, let me get this straight. You're going to whore yourself and lose all respect for a fricking iPod? How stupid can you get? Here. Wait a minute."

He pulled his wallet out, fished two hundred dollars out, and waved it in front of the kid's face.

"If I give you this money, will you take it and never come back here or anywhere else like it? You gotta give this life up, period."

"Damn straight, but I don't want to be beholden to anybody. How about a quick handjob?"

Avery slapped the kid across the face and screamed, "You're not listening! I want you to quit this life altogether. Now, not later, now!"

The kid rubbed his hand across his cheek, "All right, all right, you don't have to get violent. But if I take your money, how you going to know that I kept my word? I may never see you again."

"Because you're going to swear to me on your honor as a man that you'll keep your part of the bargain. If you lie about it, there is not much I can do, but I'll rest easy knowing I had tried to help you. I'll have no trouble standing in judgment, but you will. Son, I don't even know you, but you had better learn this now. You can't afford to throw your life away like this. You can't. Look, here's the money. Swear you'll go home and never do this again. Swear."

The kid took the money suspiciously, half expecting another slap but Avery simply folded the money into his hands. "I swear! Man, you're one crazy son of a bitch."

"Don't worry about me. Now get out of here. Go."

He watched the kid turn and disappear into the night.

"Stupid little bastard."

He continued along the storefronts for three blocks until he saw the all-night liquor store's neon sign flashing 'OPEN'. The gun bulged in his waistband as he took a deep breath and started toward the store.

II

For as long as he could remember, Avery Pittman could recall his father's constant admonition to respect himself and his name, and to be a man. He distinctly recalled falling out of a small tree when he was three, lying on the ground crying in pain, only to have his father, Raymond, hoist him up by the arm, and dust him off as he said, "You ain't hurt none. Now quit crying like a baby. A man don't cry just because he fell down. Now stop it! You're a big boy now, so act like it."

He would be taught that lesson again and again during his youth. The only son in his family of three kids, he came to understand the weight of obligation resting on his shoulders. Neither a skinned knee nor a knot on his head was reason enough to show pain, and his stoic father would tolerate only a few minutes of whimpering from a broken forearm.

The family lived on twenty acres of land that supported a small tobacco crop, two fields of tomatoes and peppers, a cow, and a small herd of Yorkshire hogs. Scraping a living from the rocky dirt was not easy, and the family struggled to make ends meet between crops and litters of pigs. Raymond scoffed at the idea of applying for welfare, food stamps, or any other kind of assistance. He constantly reminded his wife, Alene, and his kids, "We got no use for charity. Ain't no Pittman ever took it, and we ain't going to be the first. Ain't going to dishonor our family name now or ever."

Raymond and Alene were barely literate, but they worked hard to make sure all their children got a good education. Avery's sisters, Peggy and Annie, earned associates degrees at the local community college, but Avery's academic record qualified him to attend the University of Kentucky. Seeing how gifted his son was at academics, Raymond doubled the size of the hog herd to help fund his son's education. Fortunately, Avery earned enough scholarship money to concentrate on his studies without having to work a part-time job.

When he graduated from college, Raymond's chest swelled with pride as he told him, "Son, you're the first Pittman to earn a four year degree. Now you can write your own ticket to a good future."

Avery took a job with Ohio Casualty and rose quickly through the ranks of its accounting department. Soon he was engaged to a coworker, Cheryl Evans. They planned an elaborate wedding for the following summer.

But as swift as his meteoric rise was, his fall was even more sudden. One night after an evening of carousing with some of his friends, he had a wreck, killing a young girl in the other car. He was charged with driving under the influence and vehicular homicide, convicted and sentenced to five years in prison. So Avery Pittman, the pride of his father's dreams, became prisoner 576432.

His incarceration was a nightmare. Cheryl tried to maintain their relationship, but ultimately broke off their engagement. A month into his term, he was attacked and brutally gang-raped by other prisoners. He spent the duration of his term constantly fending off similar attacks with only intermittent success.

After his release, he found out how hard it was for an ex-con to find a job. In desperation, he began to work as a male prostitute. Wishing to spare his family the shame of his life, he had little contact with his family. To his horror, the further he withdrew from his family, the more deeply he fell into the street life, until the embrace of an anonymous john offered him the only comfort he could find. But self-loathing for having lost not only his family name, but also his identity as a man, plagued him with sleepless nights and days filled with despair. His life had lost all meaning, and he struggled to find a way to regain it.

III

The rain had slowed to a constant drizzle when he entered the liquor store. He meandered along the aisles, and examined bottles and carafes, while two late night customers finished their shopping. After rechecking the position of the gun under his jacket, he walked toward the counter. As he pretended to survey the array of cigarette brands the clerk asked, "May I help you?"

Feeling his heart pounding so violently that he was sure that the man could see his chest vibrate. "Yes, a box of Marlboro lights," he replied.

The clerk got the box from the display and turned around to face him. Avery stuck his gun in his face and said in a quavering voice, "All right, mister, I don't want to hurt you, but give me your money."

Obviously shaken, the man replied in a meek voice, "There ain't much here, but just don't shoot. You can have it."

Avery's glance shifted to the small safe behind the counter, and he didn't see the man press the silent alarm button under the counter.

"What about the safe? What's in there?"

"I don't know the combination."

He aimed the gun at the man. "You're a liar. I've seen you open it before when I was in here. Now open the safe or lose your face. Your choice."

The clerk's face blanched, but he nodded and slowly made his way over to the safe and started to turn the dial.

"Hurry up. I ain't got all day."

"It's hard to think with that gun pointed at me. Let me see. Four right, five left, six left, two right." The door opened, revealing several stacks of bills.

Avery pulled a large paper bag from under the counter "Put it all in this sack. Hurry up, damn you!"

The man did as he was told, neatly stacking the bands of bills in the sack.

"I said hurry up."

"If I just throw them in there, they won't all fit."

"Dammit, give me what you got!"

The man handed him the sack. "Please don't hurt me."

"I ain't going to hurt you. Lay down on the floor there. If you get up before I get out of here, I'll blow your head off."

The clerk lay down, and Avery watched him as he backed away. He pushed the door open with his body, and turned to run, but a loud voice yelled, "Drop your gun, and put your hands on your head!"

Avery saw a number of cruisers with four policemen leaning across them as they aimed their guns at him. He fired blindly in their direction and ran away from the store. One officer yelled, "Stop or I'll shoot!"

Avery continued to fire rapidly and tried to escape. The officers returned fire, and he felt sharp hot pains tear through his back. His legs collapsed, and he crumpled onto the wet blacktop where he lay breathing in labored gasps and feeling his warm blood oozing from his body. He fired the gun once more before his eyes closed and everything went black.

Two of the policemen went into the store, while two others approached him. One officer gave him a soft kick, but getting no response, he knelt and turned Avery's body over.

"He's dead as a door nail. Dammit, I guess we got a lot of paper work to do tonight."

The other police officer said, "I'll go call it in and get the forensics unit here. See if he has any ID."

The officer slipped his hand under the bloody jacket and pulled out Avery's wallet. He shuffled through the contents, while the other officer wrestled Avery's gun from his hand.

"So, what do you got?"

"Old license says he's Avery Pittman. About a hundred fifty dollars. Hey, look at this. Organ donor card, a newspaper clipping seeking a liver donor. Some kid on the east side. Pretty damned weird that a perp thinks he could be an organ donor. Never seen that before."

The other officer motioned with his head to the spent shells lying in his outstretched hands. "You think that's weird, look at this! Blanks! Every damned one of them was blanks!"

Prophesy To These Bones

THE CROWD AT Redd's Tavern had dwindled to a handful by the time Keith Crocker shuffled in to take his usual seat at the usual time. His tired and disheveled look made Greg, the bartender, sigh in resignation to his fate of having to listen once again to Crocker moaning about his job. He walked over with a Pabst he had already drawn as a part of a near-nightly ritual he danced with Crocker.

"How ya doing tonight, Crocker, or should I ask? Rough day at work?"

Keith inhaled deeply and he lifted the beer to his mouth for a quick drink before he set the mug down and responded in an exhausted voice, "Oh, same old, same old. Ya know, that boss of mine is just like a diaper."

Greg raised his eyebrows as he busied himself with the chores of closing the bar at midnight. "How's that?"

"Like my Daddy back in the mountains used to say: Always on my ass and full of shit."

Greg twittered a soft laugh before inquiring, "Okay. So what has he done this time? Fired you?"

"I wish. Then I could sue his ass. No, it's just the same old stuff. No matter what I do, I can't please him. Crotchety old bastard."

"So what has McGill done now?"

"You know, he's been the curator of the University's antiquities collection so long he probably was around when some of these antiques were made. They let him get by with a lot of shit that would get another man fired."

"Seems like I have heard this before."

"Sorry, but I have to vent to someone or I'll go nuts. I bust my ass in that place for almost a year and he won't even recommend me for a raise. Says the university is on a tight budget and there's no point in wasting the time and paperwork asking. If I was unhappy with my pay there, I could always go somewhere else."

"So why don't you? You're still young and got a good education."

Crocker took another sip, shaking his head slightly. "It's not that easy, and he knows it. Most universities are under the gun and have closed a lot of their collections and museums to save money. McGill has such a great reputation and the collection is so extensive that he had the clout to keep it on the budget. Don't get me wrong. The man knows New World archaeology probably better than anyone in the field, and God knows I have learned a lot from being his assistant curator. I just don't understand why he has to treat everyone else like dirt."

"Guess it is a perk of the job."

"I guess. He demeans everybody and hits on the young undergraduates helping there. Dirty old man. Looks like freaking Ebenezer Scrooge: tiny round spectacles, sourpuss drawn-up mouth and squinty little eyes. Reeks of Aqua Velva aftershave. Thinks he's a player. Girl would have to be crazy to sleep with that."

Greg's eyes twinkled as he offered, "Maybe he ain't after girls. Maybe he's got the hots for you. Ever think of that?"

"Hey, watch it! I'm trying to drink here. Damn, that's too gross to even think about."

"Oh, can't you take a joke? I guess some people are just naturally mean. I know he's been there a long time. What, thirty years or more? As I recall, he and his wife were on a team that discovered some Aztec burial tomb."

"Actually, it was an Inca city. Ingapirca. Oh, I've heard that story a lot. He reminds me of it whenever he thinks he can use it to belittle me. It's not like he led the team. Sure, that was a great find. Some wonderful gold jewelry and interesting pottery pieces."

"Ain't that where they got that big urn or whatever it was that contained the mummified body?"

"Oh, yes, that thing. Well, it came from that site, but it was found on a much earlier expedition. It's the reason later trips to the site were funded. That damned thing sits on a huge pedestal right beside his office door. The mummy is in a separate air-tight case to preserve it."

"I've seen it. Took my family from out of town to see the stuff there. After they read the writing on the urn that said there is a curse on anyone who disturbs the tomb, they were so freaked out they didn't finish the tour. They lit out of there like a bat out of hell."

"For Pete's sake, how many times do I have to hear that bullshit? Every visitor of the museum wants to hear that story. Someone will die as retribution for disturbing the grave."

Greg's face froze and darkened with resentment. "Don't be so sure about that being bullshit. I've heard that the leader of that team, Dr. Willis, was killed in a car accident just days after making that find. Several members of the original team have met strange ends. Some have just disappeared without a trace. Some people say that the ghost of that Indian guy comes and steals them away. McGill's wife was one of them. She disappeared without a trace. No body, no weapon, no clues of any kind. It was the talk of the town. A lot of people come to town to see the relics because they were cursed. I'm sure he's told you about that."

"Yeah, yeah. She disappeared without a trace. No clues of any kind. No body, no weapon, no nothing. The old man reminds me of his personal tragedy to manipulate me to do things I don't want to do. How many people on the team have not died under strange circumstances? It's just human nature to single out the few cases that match our perception of reality and forget those that don't. Greg, you're a smart man. Why do you believe that bullshit?"

"All I'm saying is that there's a lot of weird things we don't understand. You have to admit it's strange that there has been such a high turnover rate in that job. Six new directors in the last twenty years. I think McGill's held it longer than anyone."

"Coincidences." A wry smile crossed Crocker's face. "You think we are overdue for a new director? Maybe that old curse will get him."

"You can always hope. Want another beer?"

Crocker did not answer because he was watching the man at the end of the bar put out a cigarette in the ashtray before he got up to leave.

"Hey, Keith. You awake? Another beer? Last call."

"Nah, I gotta go. I have an early day tomorrow. We're cleaning out some old pieces that we don't need any more. Thanks for listening to me bellyache. Good night. See ya tomorrow."

"And try to have a better attitude, okay? See ya then."

II

Crocker rose early the next day and grabbed a to-go breakfast from McDonald's on the way to work. McGill's car was already in the parking lot. Crocker steeled himself as he entered the museum, expecting to catch hell for whatever malfeasance of duty his boss perceived as today's shortcoming. McGill's office door was open, but he was not there. Crocker heard some noises in the basement and took the elevator to the basement to see if he was needed.

McGill was by the furnace, throwing stacks of old paper inside. "Crocker, you're just in time. I've cleaned out a lot of old papers and damaged pieces we don't need. I have to make room for that traveling exhibition of Pre-Columbian art. You can take over for me here. Just throw these old papers in the furnace."

"Where did all this stuff come from?"

"Here, yonder, and about. A lot of newspapers that are already on microfiche or transferred to computer files. That stuff takes up a lot of space we'll need if we want to put up a good display. Hop to it. I'm going back upstairs to see if there's any more."

Crocker nodded and started to stack the papers on a small wheeled cart, rolled the cart to the furnace, and threw the papers in before he went back up stairs and headed to the main office. He paused and patted the huge urn as he walked into the office.

"Say, Dr. McGill, have you ever thought about moving this urn? It's really a magnificent piece and could probably be shown more effectively in the center of the room."

"No, it's just fine where it is. There are a couple of cracks in it and I'm afraid if we move it, the whole thing may crack. It's been sitting there since it was given to the museum. Besides, if we put it in the center of the room, it would not be long before some little bastard running around it would push it over. That urn is far too valuable to risk damaging it. Here, get busy and take this trash down to the incinerator. And see if there are any pedestals or display cases down there we can use in the new exhibit."

Crocker shrugged and pushed an empty cart down the hall into the elevator. When he got to the basement, he carefully steered the cart through a maze of boxes and crates to the old furnace. Ansel Graham, the founder of the museum, had a vindictive streak and had written into the policies of the museum that any materials scheduled for disposal had to be incinerated to keep people from rummaging through the garbage and finding pieces to sell to other museums or collectors. His dream was to make his museum the premier showplace for the archaeological discoveries from Central Mexico. He would have done anything to hold on to that distinction, even if over half of the museum's holdings were warehoused in the cluttered basement.

Crocker eased the cart to rest in front of the furnace, opened the door and tossed the papers into the fire flaring up through a large rectangular grate. The flames shot up more brightly, and forced a blast of hot air into his face. He shut the door, and lit a cigarette while he waited for the fire to die down enough to toss in the rest of the trash. He meandered through the maze of crates. Some were opened, exposing the shredded packing; others were still nailed tightly shut, and a few had the lids removed and lying crossways on the top. He dropped the cigarette, stepped on it to extinguish it, and began to explore some of the open boxes.

Some crates had manifests glued to their sides that listed their original contents of the crate: mostly pots and shards, a few weapons, and assorted odds and ends typically discovered in digs. A few made reference to gold and jewels that he knew were on display in the museum, but many of the unopened crates were not labeled.

"Damn! You got to wonder what is in these crates! And better yet, why has the old bastard never put these items on display? Just being contrary, I guess."

The alarm bell to the upstairs rang, and he knew he had better hurry back up or face the scolding he had grown used to. He hurriedly unloaded the cart, pushed it into the elevator and went up to the main office for the next load. McGill was waiting for him.

"What the hell were you doing down there for all this time? We need to get this stuff out of here ASAP, and you are down there diddling yourself or something. Now here, load this stuff up, and this time don't take all day about it!"

Crocker bit his lip before answering, "Actually, Mr. McGill, I didn't think that throwing all that trash in there at once was a good idea with that old furnace. I was waiting for the first half of it to burn before I tossed in the rest. You know, just to be safe."

"Safe? My boy, that old furnace will outlive both of us. Been there since the place was built and never had a bit of trouble with it. Burns like the flames of hell itself. You don't need to worry about it being safe. That heat keeps the steam-powered generator going. Damned cast iron walls must be a foot thick. Now, help me move this filing cabinet over there to the corner. That table needs to go under the window."

The two men wrestled the furniture around to the new locations. "Now sweep the floor, so we can put that display case there. You do know how to use a broom, don't you?" McGill sneered sarcastically.

Crocker paused before replying, "Gee, I don't know. I was hoping you would give me lessons."

"Okay, smartass. Hurry up. I want to close early today so I can go to Memphis to make sure everything is ready to ship the exhibit here next month. I want everything in order before I leave. By the way, you'll need to move some of those crates in the basement to make room near the loading dock for the exhibit. I'll be gone until the first of next week. I was going to close the museum for a few days, but I think you can keep it open. If there are any problems, you can call my cell or just have people come back when I'm here. Since you're getting the afternoon off, you can make up the time Saturday to move those boxes. I want you up here when the museum is open."

"Well, Dr. McGill, I'd planned to be out of town this weekend to visit some friends in Cincinnati."

"Well, I guess you have to decide which is more important, your friends or your job. I want this done before Monday."

Crocker swallowed hard. "What would you do if I just quit now and let you do it yourself?"

"Go ahead. You won't get unemployment, and if you apply for another job anywhere, I'll be sure to make them aware of your lazy work ethic. It's your choice."

"Okay, okay. You don't have to be nasty. I'll call my friends and tell them next weekend is better. The place will be ready Monday. I'll get paid overtime, won't I?"

"Oh, I guess I can manage that. Now take that next load of trash down to the basement. I'm closing up in a few minutes so you can start moving some of those boxes. I'll see you sometime Monday."

As Crocker turned to leave, McGill added, "One more thing. We will need some things from some of those crates. I'll leave you a list taped to my door."

"Okay. See you next week."

Crocker went back to loading old papers onto the cart. He took the cart downstairs, and busied himself trying to move some of the crates around. He looked at his watch.

"The old bastard won't know if I take a break. I need a drink," he said.

He took the elevator to the main floor, locked the door, and walked over to the bar.

Greg greeted him, "Little early today, Keith. You quit or get fired?"

"Neither. The old son of a bitch had to go to Memphis and left early. I have to work tomorrow, so I figured I can take off today."

"Working on Saturday? Well, I guess the cat's away, the mice will play. You want your usual?"

"Yeah, that would be fine," Crocker said as he took a seat on the stool in the center of the bar."

He slapped a pack of cigarettes against the bar a few times before he tore the plastic off and lit a cigarette. He nodded to Greg as he set his drink down before him. "Thanks. Run me a tab."

"No problem. So, why did your boss go to Memphis?"

"I thought I'd told you. We're getting a big exhibit next month after it leaves Memphis. He wanted to go check on the shipping arrangements and find out if there were any special things we needed to do to get ready."

"Oh. What do you have to do tomorrow?"

"Make room in the basement for the crates when they get here, and fish some things out of some of those crates down there."

He took one last draw on his cigarette and blew out a long swirl of smoke. "You know, Greg, there is one thing that bothers me sometimes. I think that old coot is living beyond his means. I don't care if he is the director. He lives in a mansion and owns a bunch of cars, even a Rolls."

"Maybe he made good investments, or maybe he had a life insurance policy on his wife. Who knows? I wouldn't worry too much about it. I figure the less you think about him, the better off you'll be. Need another?"

"Yeah, I was going to go back in tonight, but what the hell. I'll go in tomorrow."

"By the way, that blonde was in last night asking about you. I think she's got the hots for you. I told her you'd be in today sometime. She said she'll come back tonight about seven. You might get lucky."

"About damned time I had luck on something. Got the crossword I can work on till she shows up?"

"Sure," Greg replied, as he slid the newspaper down the bar.

The young blonde woman came in a few minutes later and they left the bar together.

III

Crocker left the young woman's apartment about nine the following morning, and grabbed a breakfast on his way to work. He opened the door to the museum, set it to lock after him, and walked over to the main office door. McGill had taped a note listing some items he wanted from the basement. He had added "I think this is in the crate labeled 8."

Crocker made a pot of coffee, checked the door to see if it was secure, poured a cup of coffee, and rode the elevator downstairs, thinking to himself, *I might as well try to get those things out now.*

The stenciled numbers on the boxes were easy to read and he found one with an 8 on it labeled nearly hidden in an unlighted corner. The smudges in the dust on top of the box were smeared, so he figured had been recently opened. It was labeled MISCELLANEOUS POTTERY. "I guess this is the one he wants," he muttered quietly.

Rummaging through the packing materials, he felt a metallic object that he pulled out to examine. A heavy solid gold figurine depicting an ancient Inca god made him gasp.

"What the hell is this?" he cried aloud. After pulling the box out to check the numbers and verifying that this was really box 18. The crates beside it had hidden the 1. He frowned, and started to pull out more gold and silver treasures. The crate was nearly half empty, though the amount of packing material clearly was meant for a full crate. Some of the shredded material still had a figure-shaped cavity molded into its twisted strands. By the time he was finished, he had pulled several hundred thousand dollars worth of artifacts from the crate.

Why in the hell are these finds not on display? I've never even seen any reference to them in the files. I wonder... Wait a minute! I think I'm beginning to get the picture.

As he pondered his discovery, he sat down on a nearby box and stroked his chin. *So that's where the old bastard's getting his money. He must have gotten rid of all references to these artifacts and just sells some of them when he needs the money. Crap! He'll know I found his stash when he looks in here. I've got to put this back as good as I can and think about what to do. I wonder if the board of directors knows about this."*

Crocker tried to remember the order in which he retrieved the treasures, returned them to their original places, replaced the top, and searched until he found crate 8. After loading the items McGill had listed onto the cart he took it back up to the main floor and rolled it to rest beside the office door before going back down to the basement to resume his work.

His mind ran through options of what to do as he worked. *If I say anything to him, God knows what he'll do. If I report him to the board, he'll find a way to wriggle out of it, maybe even blame me for the theft. Still, if he's doing what I think he's doing, he should not get away with it. I need proof he's stealing the stuff. I've got to think.*

By four o'clock, he had rearranged the crates to make space for the new display, careful to leave number 18 as undisturbed as possible. He closed up the museum and walked over to the bar.

Keith could tell that something was wrong when he came in. "Why the long face, Crocker? I figured you'd be happy having the old man gone."

Crocker winced and shrugged. "Just taking a break from re-organizing the basement. I guess I didn't get much sleep last night, if you know what I mean." He winked at Greg, who rolled his eyes as he replied, "Too much information, man, TMI! Beer?"

"Yeah, just need to wet my whistle. Dry and dusty in that basement. I bet some of those crates have not been moved in years."

"Probably not. My daddy used to tell me what a big deal that museum was when it was built. Old man Graham played it up big to the press. Cagey old bird. Never put everything on display at once. He would display a few new items every couple of years just to keep the museum in the news. He must have put it all out because after he died there ain't been any more pieces brought out. So, is there a lot of stuff still down there? Anything valuable?"

Crocker felt himself freeze momentarily, "Naw, just a load of old wooden crates and assorted junk. The old man just wanted to make room for the new crates so we can manage the exhibit safely. Just another of his bullshit jobs."

"That's what he's been training you for, ain't it?"

"Funneeeee. Say, what can you tell me about McGill when he came here?"

"Not much you don't know. He and his wife were hired to assist Anselm Graham's son, Andy, run the place. Andy was a big drunk and in constant trouble with the wrong kind of people. Left town sudden-like and left a note that he wanted to go back to the site and make a name for himself. Never came back."

"So, then McGill gets the job."

"Well, technically, the board gave the job to his wife with him as an assistant. They worked hard to revitalize the place. Even played up the old mummy's curse rumors. Had a few haunted Halloween nights there for the kids. Got a few of the old glory days back."

"So when did she disappear? How?"

"Let me see, that would have been about fifteen years ago. You know, my dad was a police officer here, and he told me he got a call to answer an alarm at the museum. He found the door wide open and the main window to the gallery busted out. He found McGill knocked out on the floor, but couldn't find any trace of his wife."

"Maybe she just wanted to rob the place and disappear. Ever think of that?"

"That was what the FBI and my dad said, but they never found any proof of it. The old man never changed his story. They were walking by the place, saw a light on, and went in to look around. Says he tried to stop the burglar, but tripped and knocked himself out on a display case. Nasty cut. Had to have stitches. Police found his blood and hair on the case and what looked like a few scuffmarks on the floor. Never found any trace of his wife."

"So what happened to her?"

"Nobody knows. The police thought maybe he'd killed her, but they searched the place over, and found no evidence to support that theory. Some people think she may have had a boyfriend, but I kinda doubt it. She wasn't much to look at."

"Maybe she was kidnapped."

"Nope. No ransom note or calls."

"So what did the robber get?"

"That's the funny part. McGill closed up the museum for two weeks for a complete inventory and found nothing missing. Some people speculated that McGill had stolen some stuff for the insurance money, but he never filed any claims. He did take an extended leave of absence to recover from the loss of his wife. You know, he still has a standing offer of fifty thousand dollars for anyone who can help him find his wife. Swears he'll make that offer till he dies, or until she is found."

"So, no one ever collected. No clues or nothing."

"Guess the old Indian curse got her. All the excitement did revive the museum, and the local color ghost story pulls in tourists, I guess. Another beer?"

"No, I have to get back to work. I'll probably be back later."

"What do you want me to do if your lady friend comes back?"

"Here, call me on my cell, and I'll come over to meet her. Thanks. Back to the salt mines."

IV

The woman did not come back that night so Crocker spent the time in his office thinking about what to do next.

Maybe that's the reason the old fart is such an asshole. I can't imagine losing my wife and not knowing what happened to her. That would sure screw with your mind. Still it doesn't make sense that a burglar would take the time to break into a place with lots of gold and stuff and not take anything after he has taken care of the old man and his wife. Even if he ran because of the police coming, he should have taken something. Then again, it might be hard to get rid of anything stolen from the museum. But people steal art all the time and manage to sell it on the black market. Maybe I need to look at that crate again.

He took the stairs to the basement, scooted the crate out and studied its markings. The crate had arrived at the museum in a shipment after the first big shipment from the Incan expedition. There was no list of its contents other than the words 'miscellaneous pottery' and 'DO NOT INVENTORY' which had been scrawled in rough handwriting, unlike the neatly stenciled labels on the other crates. The edges of the sides had gouges left when the top was pried off, and the accumulated dust on the top was lighter than the tops of the other boxes. There were tracings in the dust indicating something had been laid on the top of the crate.

The plot thickens. These artifacts would enhance the museum's collections a lot. Unless…unless McGill has been stealing this stuff all along. That could account for his high living. I wonder if there is any other record of this crate even being here. Wait a min-ute…maybe that is why he burning a lot of papers. I bet that any record of this stuff was in those stacks of papers I burned. All those papers are coming out of his office so no one else would have had access to them.

Come on man, get a grip here! McGill has an outstanding reputation, and no one has ever questioned his integrity. Maybe someone else stole the stuff without his knowledge. Or maybe nothing was stolen at all. Maybe the crate was never filled up. It was shipped later. They could have just put a lot of extra packing in the crate to keep it from rattling around. Maybe that thief did take things. Hey, wait a minute! Maybe there was no thief. McGill could have faked the whole thing. All the police had to go on was his story.

"Dammit! What should I do? You know, as little as he gets down here, he may not even know of the crate is here or that someone has taken anything. I really need to ask him about it."

He lit a cigarette and looked at the crate trying to decide what to do.

I can't think here. I need to get out of here and try to work this out. I'm going back over to the bar.

He walked over to the furnace and took one last draw before opening the door to toss in the butt. There was no trace of anything he had burned the day before, but the fire inside lay smoldering as a bed of glowing embers. His eyes widened as he eased the door shut.

Maybe I'm missing an opportunity here. What if I off the old guy and burn his body in here so there is no trace left. Then I could get his job and still have access to the treasure no one else seems to know about. A lot of people seem to believe that old curse story... Hmmmm

"Are you out of your mind?" he said aloud.

The police always catch murderers... except those that they don't. They never solved his wife's disappearance. So maybe if I'm careful and plan this well. How can I cover up his disappearance so I'm not a suspect?

Still in thought, he went upstairs, locked the outside doors and strolled over to the bar.

"Back again? Finish up your work?" Greg asked.

"Yeah, now I can enjoy the rest of the weekend. Give me some Wild Turkey on the rocks."

Crocker sat nursing his drink, stirring it idly with the swizzle stick while he ran through possible scenarios of how to kill McGill. He dared not risk anything that might cause a struggle because it might leave evidence for the police.

Greg came over as he was polishing up the bar. He flipped through the channels on the television, and stopped when he came to a station showing a crowd of people protesting. "You know, they're going to execute that son of a bitch who killed that little girl three years ago tonight, and these dumb bastards are out there hollering about his rights. I hope he burns in hell."

Crocker turned his gaze to the television. "Can you imagine what that man must be thinking about now? I mean, all you can do is to sit there and wait for them to come and get you to kill you. Wonder what goes through a man's mind then."

"Well, I bet it is not the same thing as what you used to think about. The old electric chair struck fear in people's heart, I bet worrying if you're going to feel anything or catch fire. If you ask me, this lethal injection business is for the birds. Make him suffer like that little girl suffered. All he does now is just go to sleep and not wake up."

Crocker replied, "Actually, they do it in stages. There're several plungers involved. The first one has a sedative in it, the second one has a muscle relaxer and the last one has potassium chloride to stop the heart. You're right, though: he doesn't feel much more than the needle stick. Always struck me as ironic how we keep coming up with humane ways to kill somebody."

"Hey, after tonight he won't kill anyone else."

"No, he won't. But I wonder if it really..."

His voice trailed off as his mind replayed his last words. *Potassium chloride stops the heart. That's it! I bet there is some of that in the chemicals in the museum somewhere. Hell, we had it in high school chemistry class. I can inject him with a massive dose to kill him and then dispose of the body. It won't even matter if he knows I have stuck him because he is going to be dead meat soon enough. And I know just how to get rid of the body!*

He sat up straight and smiled, bringing a quizzical look on Greg's face. "Hey! What's so funny? I mean, I'm glad that the bastard is checking out, but it ain't that kind of funny!"

Crocker lifted his glass to his lips to finish his drink before smirking, "I wonder if they read him a bedtime story."

Greg winced a light chuckle. "Ya know, I never thought about that. Now that is kind of funny."

"Well, I need to go back over and double check the locks. The old man is due back on Monday, so I'd better be sure everything is just perfect for him. I'll see ya later. Good night."

"Night, Crocker. Don't forget to celebrate that the world will be short one deserving bastard at five after midnight."

Crocker made a gun with his right hand and clicked it at Greg, "Yep! One bastard short." He closed the door as he left to return to the museum.

He scurried across the street, let himself in the front door and strode excitedly down the hall toward the lab they used for cleaning and restoring display items. McGill had insisted on putting locks on the storage cabinets in case some kid got into them so he had to wrestle his key out of his pocket to open the cabinet. The lock and chain slipped easily out of the handles so he could swing the doors open wide. His eyes raced along the top shelves, hoping that the jars were in alphabetical order. They had been at one time, but now there was a hodgepodge of various-colored glass jars. He moved a few around until he found a deep brown wide-mouthed jar bearing a skull and crossbones and the words Potassium Chloride (KCl) printed on the peeling label.

I wonder how much I need. It shouldn't be too hard to find out a lethal dose on the Internet.

After closing and locking the cabinet door, he took a seat before his computer screen. He started to Google 'potassium chloride' but froze in mid-motion. *Crap, I can't search here in case the cops search the hard drive. I can look it up in the library tomorrow afternoon and mix it up tomorrow night so I will be ready when he comes back. I might as well go home and think about how I can do this.*

V

The library opened at noon on Sunday, but Crocker waited till two to go do his search. He sauntered around the computer room until he saw a teenager leave the computer without logging off. Quickly, he typed in "potassium chloride lethal dose" and shielded the screen with his hunched-over body. The first reference gave the lethal dose — 100 milliequivalents — that he memorized before quietly slipping away from the computer. He drove back to the lab, mixed the proper solution in a small bottle that he hid with a syringe in a drawer in a cabinet.

On the way home he stopped by three hardware stores to buy some timers for the lights. He found a new message on his answering machine from McGill announcing his plans for the return trip.

"Crocker, my plane is supposed to arrive around five so maybe I'll be there by seven. I'll come to the lab directly because we need to go over some paperwork and check a few things. We should be finished by nine or so. Meet me at the lab around seven."

This is perfect. I can sit at the bar for a while before I go to the museum. I have this tape to verify his plans for the evening and with these light timers, it will look like someone is there working late.

VI

He could not sleep much that night as he spent the night going over his plans, trying to think of anything he might have forgotten. He arose after a fitful sleep and drove to a diner for coffee before going to the museum.

There he set the light timers on the room lamps for different times before installing them in various rooms that had a window facing the street. A few things needed his attention, but after he had completed those tasks, he went for lunch and then dropped by the empty bar where Greg sat working a crossword puzzle.

Keith said, "Afternoon, Greg. How about a beer?"

"Sure thing. You seem awfully happy today."

"Just enjoying my last few hours of freedom before the old man returns. He is due back sometime around seven and wants us to work some tonight. Might as well spend some time goofing off."

"So the museum is closed today?"

"No, but I just put a sign on the door explaining that due to circumstances beyond our control the museum would be closed today. I have to get back in a few minutes. I figure what the old man don't know won't hurt him. Damn, I need to go."

He gulped down the last of his beer before hurrying out the door. "I'll probably be back after I get off if you're still open. See ya."

After some thought, he doubled-checked the timers before settling down to read while he waited for McGill to return. Still tired from not sleeping well, he dozed off for a few minutes.

When he awoke he anxiously went to the chemical room to check the solution and syringe. From there, he went to the basement to check that the furnace was still burning. Returning upstairs, he went online and researched some articles about Pre-Columbian archaeology.

About six-thirty, he heard the back door open and close. McGill's footfalls echoed in the hallway as he climbed the stairs to the main floor. He paused in Greg's doorway to flex his umbrella, covered in a fine film of the misty rain that had started to fall outside.

"Welcome back, Dr. McGill. How was your trip?"

"Fine, fine. I found out a few details we need to check. Our constant temperature and humidity chambers need to have their filters cleaned, and we need to empty some of the larger display cases temporarily. Follow me to the office so I can show you pictures of some of the pieces."

"Sure thing, but I need to go to the bathroom before we begin. I put the artifacts you asked for on a cart by the door to your office. Be back in a bit."

"Hurry up. I don't want to be here all night."

Crocker walked toward the restroom until he saw that McGill had entered his office. Then he walked swiftly to the chemical room, and palmed the syringe so it would be unnoticeable. His heart was racing and his breathing became more rapid as he entered the main office. As he settled into a position beside McGill, he managed a weak smile and asked, "Did I get everything you needed?"

"It looks like it. Was I right? Were they in crate eight?"

"Oh, they were there, but I opened crate eighteen by mistake. Guess what I found?"

McGill blanched momentarily before his face turned bright red with rage. "Can't you read? I said crate eight!"

"It was an honest mistake. So, guess what I found? A whole bunch of gold and silver artifacts that are not catalogued anywhere. It looks like some of them may be missing, based on the packing. Did you know they were down there?"

McGill pushed him away, snapped open his briefcase to grab a pistol that the pointed in Crocker's face.

"You're damned right! I know all about that. But you are about to forget everything — even to breathe. Step back."

Crocker lunged at him, knocked the gun loose, and jabbed the syringe deep into McGill's thigh. McGill tried to get past him to retrieve the gun from under the desk, but he staggered and gasped for air. He clutched his chest, and fell to the floor, wheezing badly. His breathing became more labored and then stopped. Still shaking, Crocker sat down in the chair, trying to catch his breath and calm down. His body was trembling so badly he could not light a cigarette. Finally, after he managed to light up and smoke a few puffs, he rolled a cart into the office, loaded McGill's body onto it and pushed it into the elevator. In the basement, he pushed the cart out of the elevator over to the furnace where he struggled to place the body over the main burners. He tossed in the syringe, closed the door, and flicked the switch to turn on the forced-air blower and the exhaust fan. When he heard the whoosh of the fire,

Roger L. Guffey

he took a deep breath and turned to take the cart back upstairs. He collapsed into his office chair to calm down.

I wonder how long this will take. I'll wait here for a spell, and then go over to the bar for a few drinks. Ya know, I can leave this all night, come in early tomorrow and get rid of any remains. I just need to be sure that Greg sees the lights upstairs.

He went to the main floor, checked the timers, locked the door and went over to the bar.

Greg hailed him, "So, is the old man back?"

"Yeah, he's back. Mean as ever. I told him I needed a break and would come back if he's still there. Gimme a beer and slide those pretzels down here."

"You got it, buddy. So, what's the big news from the museum set?"

"He brought back some more detailed information on special needs for some of the display items. When I left him, he was checking out the constant temperature display cases. He wanted to get them all done tonight. I told him I'd come back over if I saw the lights on. Hey, make me a club sandwich on whole wheat. I might as well eat now in case I have to stay late."

They chatted idly as Crocker ate his sandwich. He glanced at his watch after he finished eating. "How about getting a breath of fresh air while I grab a smoke?"

"It's slow, so I can step out for a minute."

They stepped out onto the sidewalk to see that two rooms of the museum were lit up.

"Dammit! I guess I need to go back over there. Maybe it won't be an all-nighter."

"Oh, suck it up, you big baby. It won't kill...hey, look, he turned off one of the lights."

Right on time. Now we wait a couple of minutes.

"Looks like you might luck out."

"I hope so. I'm really tired. Well, son of a bitch! He must be calling it a night. He just turned out the other lights. I'm out of here."

"Lucky bastard, I'm stuck here for another hour to close up. See ya tomorrow, I guess."

Crocker's mind was racing as he turned to walk away.

This is going perfectly. The deed is done, I have a great alibi witness and nobody is the wiser. I'll get up early and come in to take care of business in the basement.

A rush of excitement at committing the perfect crime and now being the sole owner of all that loot made him too antsy to sleep well. About two he managed to drop off, giving him four hours of sleep before he got up at six,   showered, drove to the museum. A faint sickening odor met him as he raced down the stairs to the basement. He opened the furnace door, and found that most of the body had been reduced to ashes, but a few ends of the larger bones and the burnt shell of McGill's watch lay on the grate. After fetching a metal bucket and small long-handled shovel from a janitor's closet, he carefully removed the pieces of bone and watch. Then, he ran the shovel over the grate to sift all the remaining ashes onto the pile of ashes accumulated during the trash burning, using the shovel to mix the ashes up some and closed the door.

After he return the shovel to the closet, he grabbed a small stepladder and the bucket of bone fragments, and made his way awkwardly over to the elevator. The bucket was not heavy, and he easily loaded it into the elevator, rode to the main floor, and worked his way over to the pedestal holding the large urn. He paused to look at the door's title, and imagined what it would say if he were named the curator. **"Keith Crocker, Ph.D., Head Curator"** Barely able to contain his glee, he opened the stepladder up, set it up beside the pedestal, grabbed the bucket of bones, and climbed the steps.

The ladder wobbled a little so he steadied himself on the lip of the urn, and hoisted the bucket up to dump its contents into the urn and thought to himself.

This is too perfect. Just another mysterious disappearance with no clues or body. I'll be the new curator and I'll make sure this urn will never be moved as long as I'm the boss.

He stepped up to the next rung and swung the bucket to throw the ashes into the urn, but froze in mid-motion as the color leached out of his face.

The urn was already filled nearly to the brim with ashes, bone fragments and fire-charred jewelry.

Through A Glass Darkly, Then Face to Face

EVERYONE KNEW THAT Hattie Glass was a witch, so when she died, feelings of grief in the Alex Valley were tinged with a general sigh of relief, especially from the children whose parents had told them that Hattie stole little babies and baked them into pies. An elderly black-shrouded spinster whom many thought to be over a hundred years old, Hattie saw little of the people in the valley unless someone ran into her rummaging through the woods for herbs and roots to make the potions she used for God knows what.

No one could recall the last time she went to town. She preferred to survive on the vegetables she grew and an occasional rabbit or squirrel she charmed to its doom in one of her snares. No one knew about any source of income she may have had, but the mailman sporadically delivered mysterious packages from faraway places. Even he did not dare to confront her face to face. So he would leave the packages near the front door, ring the bell, and hotfoot it back off the dilapidated porch. Sometimes a scraggly, withered hand would emerge from the door to retrieve the package, but usually the package would lie there until Hattie could fetch it inside under cover of darkness.

Her house lay in a shallow swale that people had dubbed "The Hainted Bottom." Even before Hattie's arrival strange apparitions and creepy goings-on had been reported there for years: a pig that had escaped the butcher's cleaver was seen to run along the top of a rail fence during the full moon and a young black man who had been lynched for some peccadillo would hitch a ride in the back of a pickup truck. The nearest neighbors claimed they heard piteous wails at night. Some folks claimed to have seen Hattie conjuring up spirits to join in the satanic revelry. One old man known for his drinking habits swore he saw Hattie bewitch a table and make it walk across the room, though most people discounted this story as the hallucinations of a drunk.

Such a character was bound to generate controversy, gossip, and feelings of distrust among the community. A few of the older residents in the valley recalled that when she moved there as a young lady, Hattie was quite attractive with long dark tresses, beautiful pale skin. Then she always wore a dark dress with a high bustle that had gone out of style in the last century. Elmore Hancock remembered seeing Hattie's parents move her into the house, but no one had seen them return for a visit after the last load of furniture — including a large steamer trunk — was carried inside. Neighbors who visited her recounted that her cool, but polite, behavior seemed nervous and suspicious, as though she was concealing something. There were no second visits.

To a community of folks on a first name basis with poverty and need, it seemed obvious that this well-to-do woman was hiding some kind of treasure in her house. Stories of money, gold, and jewels began to percolate through the community, with each teller adding something of even greater worth than the last. For all intents and purposes, Hattie secreted the Holy Grail itself on her premises. But the only thing anyone ever saw her bring out of the house besides herself was what appeared to be a long handled silver mirror. She would sit on the porch and look in the mirror as she combed her hair.

One determined young gold-digger, Otis Hurt, decided to relieve Hattie of her treasure by courting her until he could gain entrance to her house. He began to leave bouquets on her porch and send her candy through the mail until; finally, he received an invitation to join her for tea one afternoon. The tea was indeed a short affair; it had hardly started when an ashen-faced Otis stumbled out the door and fell off the porch. When Hattie's neighbors came to his rescue, they inquired about her house and habits.

Clearly shaken, he replied, "She told me that I had liver cancer and would die within a week." And sure enough, he died five days later.

Outraged by what was clearly the work of the devil, the community began to rally for expelling this she-devil from their midst. But with the disposition of a doctor performing an autopsy, Hattie informed them that she had no intention of leaving her home on account of the unfortunate death of a local resident, particularly since she had thought she was doing him a favor by giving him warning to get his affairs in order. When pressed for details on how she knew about Otis's cancer, she replied matter-of-factly, "I know the signs." Though unsatisfied with her answers, people lost their resolve to force her out when she stared them down, her black eyes burning through the wispy fingers of her breath in the cold November air.

But after mysterious letters written in elegant penmanship predicting severe illness and even death began to appear in the community the locals redoubled their efforts to ostracize Hattie. The letters appeared in the mailboxes of those people who had walked by Hattie's place when she was sitting on her porch fixing her hair. Invariably, trips to the doctor confirmed the warnings of severe illness; those unlucky enough to receive a death notice learned to make their funeral arrangements. The uncanny accuracy of these predictions convinced even the most skeptical that Hattie was a witch who had cast spells on these poor unfortunates. Fearing some supernatural reprisal, folks chose to leave her alone and the letters eventually ceased.

At last her isolation became so complete that the locals deduced her demise only from a pile of packages that accumulated outside her door. After a week, the foul stench of decaying flesh oozed from the crevices of the house and I, as the medical examiner, was called to verify what everyone already had guessed: the witch was dead. The sheriff and I found her shriveled body, clutching a worn Bible in her left hand and her notorious mirror in her right, lying on an overstuffed couch. Vials of strange potions and ancient books with magical-sounding titles cluttered the tables and shelves. As a forensic scientist, I later determined that the "eyes of newts" vials contained nothing but dolls' eyes, and the leathery "wing of bat" jar held only pieces of an old shoe. In fact, although the witches' "ingredients" of her containers bore a passing resemblance to the names on their labels, they were actually fake.

The house was furnished with antiques and the fine accoutrements one might expect to find in a European. The mantelpiece featured an ornate coat of arms bearing a griffin and a unicorn atop a carved gilt-framed oval mirror with the phrase **Homo Unus Facies Verus**, (one true face) inscribed below it. In the bedroom we found a baroque canopy bed and a matching vanity lined with bottles of perfumes and cosmetics. At the foot of the bed was an old-fashioned trunk with a domed lid and rusty iron straps holding it together, partially covered by a velvety maroon spread.

When the sheriff went to his car to call for an ambulance, I gently removed the mirror and Bible from her dead hands. The quicksilvered mirror was a trifle dark, but it still presented a clear image of my face. The Latin phrase from the large mirror over the mantel was also embossed in the tracery on the handle. The mirror intrigued me, and I made a mental note to ask the sheriff if I might keep it for my daughter. The Bible contained a picture of what appeared to be her family when she was a little girl. They were posed before what might have been a Scottish castle. As I thumbed through the ragged volume, a folded scrap of ratty parchment fell onto the floor. I laid the Bible on the sofa arm, retrieved the paper, and carefully unfolded it to reveal an odd poem written in Old English script:

The inky mirror you now hold in your hand
Has a power no mortal soul can understand.
I can foresee what will surely come by and by
To warn the sick and tell them when they will die.
I serve all good souls, but have only one master;
Death comes to some soon, but for others faster.
As soon as you take up this prophetic glass
You will know others' ills, but your own it will pass.
You must never sell me, for love or purse
For You are now trapped in my ancient curse.
On the day your eyes lose their lively gleam
I will snare a new master to damn with his dreams.

I read the poem again and tried to decipher its garbled verses. I looked at the mirror again. None of it made sense, so I continued to ponder the odd imagery until the sheriff returned to the room.

To my surprise, he said, "Doc, I bet your little girl would love that mirror. Hattie had no heirs, and I won't tell anybody if you take it to her."

Relieved that I would not have to make an awkward case for taking the mirror, I mumbled "Thank you," and placed the mirror along with the parchment scrap into my medical bag.

II

The local folks were glad to see out-of-town collectors buy most of the estate as they considered it good riddance to a blight on their community. My wife and I fell in love with the old steamer trunk and were determined to have it as a hope chest for our young daughter. The opposing bidder drove the price higher than I thought reasonable, but my stubbornness and two hundred dollars finally claimed my prize.

The auctioneer had not opened the trunk prior to its sale. We finally picked the lock and raised the lid. Inside we found pieces of paper bearing incantations and weird recipes. We put these inscriptions into a smaller box. I wanted to add to the romance of the mirror and also to cover the questionable way I had come by it, so I had carefully cleaned the mirror and hid it in the trunk. When my daughter, Janice, entered the room and opened the chest, I handed her the mirror and said, "Well, look here! A mirror fit for a princess! How do you look in a princess's mirror?"

Janice looked at her reflection and replied, "Why, I look perfectly natural in it. Where are all the Prince Charmings when you need one?"

We all laughed and took turns gazing at ourselves in the dark surface of the mirror. Janice put the mirror back in the trunk, and my wife, Gloria, and I carried it to the garage until we had time to refinish it. I returned to my schedule as a family doctor, delivering babies, binding wounds, treating fevers and, of course, occasionally serving as the official medical examiner.

In early April, Gloria was on vacation from teaching, and a warm breeze was blowing through the countryside, so she decided it was time to restore the trunk. We carried it out of the garage and opened the lid to find the mirror still there. I picked it up and laid it on a shelf above the garage door. We used noxious chemicals to strip away the peeling paint and varnish accumulated over generations. In two days, we managed to reveal light oak panels and dark metallic bands decorated with fine tracery of flowers and vines. We discussed how we could refurbish the trunk.

Gloria exclaimed, "I think I have it! We'll stain the wood a burnished mahogany and paint the metal a flat black. Then I'll paint the designs with metallic gold. It will still retain an antique look, but fit in with any décor Janice has when she is on her own."

"Yes, dear, that sounds quite nice. Make out a list of what you'll need and I'll bring it home tomorrow so you can start."

"Actually, I have enough stain from my last project to do the wood. I'll need a pint of flat black and a pint of the gold. Oh, I'll need some artist's brushes and some turpentine to clean up with, too."

With a lot of elbow grease and help from Janice, over the next two weeks Gloria and Janice transformed the trunk into a collector's item. When they were done, they had placed the trunk in front of the garage so I could not drive the car inside when I came home and ran out of the house to pose proudly by their work. Gloria handed me the camera and I shot several pictures of them with the trunk from different angles. A few gold flowers were still sticky, so I said, "We should leave it in the garage until it dries completely. Let me clear a little space."

As I pushed the lawn mower to one side and reshuffled garden tools, I happened to see the mirror I had laid on the shelf a few weeks before. Smiling, I turned the mirror toward them on the driveway beside the trunk, shouting, "Let's see how it looks in our enchanted mirror!"

I looked over the mirror as they primped and preened themselves and oohed and aahed over their work. Then I shifted my gaze to look directly the back of the mirror and nearly dropped it at what I saw. Viewed through the mirror, the trunk showed all its flaws and imperfections. I rubbed my eyes and checked again to see the same thing. When I looked over the top of the mirror, the trunk appeared in its new finery.

"Hey, Honey, would you come here for a sec?" I called to Gloria.

"Sure. What's up?" she asked as she walked to where I stood.

"Hold the mirror like this and look at it." I reversed the mirror and asked, "What do you see?"

"Well, silly, I am going out on a limb here, but it looks like me!"

I leaned in and looked with her, and sure enough, both of our reflections stared back at us. "I guess I'm working too hard. Here, help me put this trunk inside for the night."

I ate dinner so distractedly quiet that Gloria asked, "Honey, do you feel all right? You're awfully quiet. Bad day?"

"No, not really," I muttered. I wanted to say something about the weird hallucination I had seen in the mirror but I couldn't mouth the words. After dinner, I went back to the garage and held the mirror up to the trunk: same result as before. I looked through the mirror at the right front fender of the car where I had hit a tree in a snowstorm two years ago. The repaired fender looked as good as new, but when I turned the mirror around, it clearly showed the crumpled metal. I whistled for the dog. "Here Rex, come here, boy!"

The family Labrador bounced into view. As a pup, he had broken his right front leg. The vet had set the bone so well that the healed leg showed no sign of injury. But when I looked at the dog through the mirror, I saw the broken bone as clear as an x-ray. I began to ponder the true potential of this mirror and wonder why no one else could see its effects. Suddenly, Gloria ran out of the house crying, "Honey, come quick! Janice is very sick! She's throwing up and hurting in her side!"

I raced into the house, absentmindedly still carrying the mirror. Janice had collapsed into a pool of vomit on the bathroom floor and was barely conscious. I knelt beside her and felt her forehead to find her burning up with fever. As if in a dream, I stared at her right side through the mirror and saw her inflamed appendix on the verge of rupture. I laid the mirror on the vanity, loaded Janice into the car, and rushed her to the hospital for an emergency appendectomy.

Of course, I could check on her progress every day, but after a long day of seeing patients, I came home to rest while Gloria was staying with Janice. Gloria had laid the mirror on the dresser and I picked it up. I sat on the side of the bed, contemplating the meaning of the poem I had never shared with anyone. I wondered if the episode with Janice had been a fluke, so I decided to take the mirror to the office to see if I could diagnose patients' medical problems.

The results astonished me. I would joke with patients that this was a poor man's x-ray as I looked at them through the mirror. Then I would let them see their own reflections in the mirror to see it was just a mirror. I could see ulcers, infections, cancer, heart problems, blood clots, or any ache or pain. I soon learned that the mirror proved invaluable in discovering congenital defects in children. I was able to save many children who were too young to describe their pains because I could diagnose their illnesses so quickly. Then I had an epiphany. Hattie was not hexing people; she was actually diagnosing them! That was why only people who walked in front of her house where she could see them had received her letters. When people avoided walking by the house, the letters had stopped.

With my secret new diagnostic tool, I was able to see a lot more patients now and my income ballooned beyond my wildest dreams. Before long, our family moved into a custom-built mansion on a large farm outside the town. My reputation grew, and the next year several large city hospitals approached me about joining their staff. I really liked the quiet simplicity of the country life, especially for rearing Janice. Deep down, I feared that my secret might come to light, so I declined the big-city offers. I did agree to offer my services as a consultant for really difficult cases.

III

The power of the mirror had engendered me with an unforgiving and arrogant attitude. I had become sort of a medical celebrity over several states and that served to create in me a belief of my own omnipotence. I appeared on television talk shows where my following increased dramatically. When other doctors consulted me, I began to see signs of suspicion and envy. At the same time, a gnawing paranoia came over me, and I retreated into my own little world so I could jealously and constantly guard the mirror. Janice had gone away to college, but I spent as little time as possible with Gloria, for I did not even trust her. By now, I had interpreted some of the verse on the old paper and came to understand that I alone could use the mirror's power because I was the first one to touch it after Hattie had died. It was my secret and only I could make it work its magical spell.

They say that a doctor who treats himself has a fool for a patient. I had enjoyed good health my entire life and followed guidelines for diet and exercise and I avoided harmful habits. The demands and stresses of my busy schedule began to take is toll, but I was oblivious to the early signs of problems. A random pain here, a bit of weight loss there and a few episodes of neurological symptoms were dismissed as too much stress. But the problems escalated and their cumulative effect made me look emaciated and sick.

I made appointments with several doctors and specialists, but none could diagnose my illness. I had become the fool of the proverb, trying to use the mirror to diagnose myself. The veil lifted from the last un-deciphered verses on the paper. I could look at my limbs through the mirror, but no matter how I tried I could not position to examine my torso, back or head. Trying to look through the mirror into another mirror failed to work and because of the curse, I could not let anyone else use the mirror to diagnose me. Now I understood: I was the one the mirror could not diagnose.

Taunted by the mocking mirror, I tried to smash it with a hammer, but no blow could dent its shiny dark surface. I threw it into a roaring fire, but even that failed to have an effect. Apparently, the mirror was indestructible. All I could do was to tape over the surface with black tape so I did not have to see my withering self in it.

The first sign of insanity is the loss of a sense of time. That is true, for after I realized what was going on, I was not sure of the sequence of events that landed me here in a sanitarium, or how long I had been here. My condition continues to worsen and, although I spend hours poring over obscure medical texts, I am no closer to finding the problem. Gloria visits infrequently because it pains her too much to see me in this condition. The past and present meld into some disjointed jigsaw puzzle whose picture shifts continuously around a faint memory of my life before I found the mirror.

I sit rocking back and forth, muttering the last lines of the curse:

On the day your eyes lose their lively gleam
I will snare a new master to damn with his dreams.

All That Glitters

MOST OF CHASE Hunter's friends thought that he was a little neurotic because he built castles in the air, but no one thought he was psychotic enough to live in them. From his earliest childhood days, he had a very active imagination coupled with a very inquisitive mind that was not afraid to take flights of fancy some might consider imprudent.

Indeed, he showed enormous creativity and vision as both a visual artist and a writer of fantasy literature, skills that made him a recruiting prize for rival fantasy video game manufacturers. After taking a job with Imagineworld Productions he declined any offers of advancement to administrative positions to pursue his dream of becoming the apotheosis of game designers. He dated infrequently as no real woman could possibly measure up to his cerebral ideal of the perfect Sleeping Beauty. Eventually, his coworkers quietly accepted him as an affable real life Walter Mitty who earned an enormous market share that guaranteed them healthy bonuses at Christmas.

One day, the receptionist buzzed him that he had a phone call. When he picked up the phone, a jolly voice bubbled, "Mr. Hunter? Hi, my name is Carlton Trask. First, let me say what an honor it is to speak to the best game designer in the whole damned video game business! You are truly a legend."

"Thank you and I'm flattered by your comments, Mr. Trask, but I'm just living my dream life doing my dream job. Now, how can I help you?"

"I would like to meet you to discuss an idea for a new video game. I would be delighted to treat you to dinner so we can discuss my proposal."

"I'm sure that would be wonderful, but management frowns on us pursuing independent projects."

"Oh, don't misunderstand. I'm not asking you to violate any of your company's proprietary interests or procedures. Everyone knows that **Imagineworld** has the best games on the market and I'm willing to negotiate the exclusive rights to the game to your company. Why don't you see if your bosses are interested in hearing my idea? I promise it is a killer idea that will have very wide appeal."

"Well, I guess there is no harm in asking. Give me your number or email address so I can get back to you. 4-3-5-6-8-9-1. Is that a local number? Fine, I'll get back to you. Thanks for calling."

He hung up the phone and sauntered over to the office of Joe Durham, the head of project development. Joe looked up from his desk.

"Chase, what's up? Come in, come in."

"Thanks, Adam. I just had a phone call that I need to discuss with you. I got a cold call from a man who wants to see if we are interested in developing his idea for a video game. Name's Carlton Trask. Know anything about him?"

"Trask, Trask. Wait a minute. I think I got an email from him last week, but I told him that I would get back to him. He didn't give any specifics, so I sorta forgot about it. Did he tell you anything about it?"

"All he said was the game would have wide appeal. He invited me to dinner to present his idea. I told him I would have to check with you. Any objections?"

Durham shrugged, "I guess there's no harm in seeing what he's got. Just don't sign anything."

Chase smiled, nodded agreement and returned to his desk to phone Trask.

"Mr. Trask? Chase Hunter returning your call. Mr. Durham says it is okay to meet informally."

Trask replied, "Great. How do you feel about dinner tomorrow night at The Savoy, say 7?"

Chase replied, "Fantastic! I look forward to actually meeting you. I will get there early so you can just have the hostess direct you to my table. See ya then."

II

Chase parked his Volkswagen in the restaurant's lot and walked over to the door. Inside the lobby, he surveyed the crowd before a well-dressed handsome man waved him over to a table near the rear window. He hurried over to meet the man.

"Hello, Mr. Hunter. I'm Carlton Trask. It's an honor to finally meet you. Have a seat. Would you like a drink?"

"Nice to meet you, Mr. Trask. Yes, a strawberry margarita would be nice, thank you."

Trask motioned the waiter over. "Strawberry margarita, for my guest."

The waiter nodded and left to get the drink.

Chase settled into a comfortable position as he placed his napkin on his lap.

"This is very gracious of you to spring for a dinner in such a fancy restaurant. My curiosity is certainly piqued. You do understand that this meeting is just an informal discovery meeting. Of course, any ideas you give me will be protected so you won't lose any rights to the game won't be endangered."

"Oh, I'm not worried about that. Your company has a very honorable reputation. Ah, here's your drink."

The waiter set his drink in front of Chase. He eased the drink to his lips and took a small sip. He raised his eyebrows in approval and addressed his host. "That is good. What do you suggest for dinner?"

"Oh, this place only serves the best food in town. Steaks, chicken, fish….it's all fantastic. I am partial to the sea bass, myself, but order what you like."

The waiter returned to take their orders. Durham ordered his sea bass and Chase asked for Porterhouse steak, medium rare.

"I guess I'm not being very imaginative here," he chortled.

Durham smiled. "I bet it gets tedious, always being expected to be creative. Anyway, let's get down to business. I'm sure you have heard of the Philosopher's Stone."

Chase felt a letdown surging in his gut. "Of course. That is a staple of a lot of games. I hope that is not the gist of your idea."

Durham leaned forward. "Well, yes and no. I have done extensive research into the subject and think I have a different angle that will make it more intriguing."

Chase gestured politely. "So what's your idea?"

Durham stretched back into this chair. "I think that you will agree that the best video games are those that offer the players the possibility of actually representing events."

"As a rule, I would agree, but frankly, the philosopher's stone is a bit puerile. Third grade stuff."

"That's because most people never did any real research into it. Alchemists are thought of as buffoons, but they don't get the credit they deserve. I'm sure you know that alchemy was the forerunner of modern chemistry."

"Yes, but I don't see…"

"You know that the apothecary system of weights, symbols and measurements used in medicine is rooted in the alchemists' desire for secrecy. And therein lies the problem."

"What do you mean?"

"Alchemists practiced their art in deep secret for many reasons. At times, it was considered black magic, punishable by death. Most people believe the reason for the secrecy was the desire to keep their methods shielded from rivals or others who might steal their ideas. You probably know that alchemists made up cryptic symbols for the elements they knew."

"Yes, I have seen those. Their symbol for iron is the same as our symbol for man or male. I can't recall any others."

Durham leaned forward. "As I said, the problem here is the secrecy. Most alchemists developed their own language and obscure symbols only they could decipher. In fact, we have many alchemists' records that still have not been deciphered."

"And I care because…"

Trask bit his lower lip before continuing, "Okay, most people assume that alchemists sought the philosophers' stone as a way of making gold from lead or whatever. Actually, they were often pursuing other goals. Chinese alchemists cared little about transmutation, but eagerly sought to understand how the stone could grant healing or eternal life. Others saw I as a window to ultimate wisdom, while others were convinced that it could help them find a universal solvent…"

"Yeah, I have often wondered what they would store that stuff in."

"Okay, make your jokes. But here is where my idea of a game differs from others. The stone can mean different things to different people or even at different levels in the game."

"I am not convinced."

"As far as we can tell, every culture has stories about the magical properties of alchemy and the stone. We know that Egyptians and other Middle Eastern civilizations were heavily involved in alchemy, as were the Greeks and many others. The chain of belief spans millennia..."

"Yeah, so?"

"Did you know that some rulers like Henry IV engaged alchemists to make gold for them to fund wars. Others saw is as a real threat to the economic structure of their society. Thomas Aquinas actually wrote a treatise trying to resolve the question of whether gold made by alchemy was the same as gold found in nature. In fact, we know that he was heavily involved in alchemical studies. Which brings us to another point."

"Which is...."

Trask motioned with his hands. "Do you have any idea how many famous people dabbled in alchemy? Isaac Newton wrote extensively on the subject. So did Francis Bacon, Roger Bacon, Albertus Magnus, Paracelsus, Robert Boyle... the list goes on."

"And your point is..."

"Isn't it a little presumptuous to assume that so many of the greatest thinkers in our history were all taken in by a bunch of charlatans?"

Although he found himself increasingly intrigued, Chase decided to play his trump card. "Look, Mr. Trask, this is all very fascinating, but we know today that the only way to transmute one metal into another is through nuclear reactions of fission and fusion, and I really don't think that these folks had those tools available to them."

Trask took a deep breath. "Point taken, but as they say absence of proof is not proof of absence."

"I don't understand where you are going."

"Did you know that the ancient Greeks for all their mathematical knowledge could not fathom irrational numbers? The fact that the Greeks did not understand or recognize their existence did not preclude the very real fact of their existence."

"Well, mathematics is always evolving...."

"And which fields of human knowledge are not?"

"But it's a horse of a different color..."

"Okay, are you familiar with Fermat's Last Theorem?"

"Refresh my memory."

"Pierre Fermat was a French lawyer who did math as a hobby. He contributed a great deal of high-powered mathematics. He often made little notes in his books' margins. In 1637, in one of these books, he posed the following problem. Let a, b, and c be integer values. Consider the equation $a^n + b^n = c^n$. Are there any values of a, b and c that can satisfy this equation for n an integer greater than or equal to three? I have found the most marvelous proof that there are not, but the margin of this book are too small to contain it."

"So?"

"So mathematicians have been able to verify every other conjecture he put forth but this one. Hence, Fermat's Last Theorem."

"Again, what does this have to do with the price of tea in China?"

"The search for a proof took on a life of its own. Mathematicians around the world tried to duplicate his proof, but none succeeded. The good news was that a lot of very good advances were made in math trying to solve this problem. Eventually, a prize of one million dollars was offered for its solution."

"Go on."

"The situation took a strange turn in1937. Kurt Godel proved that in any axiomatic system, there are some statements that can't be decided to be either true or false. Based on this new theorem, a lot of mathematicians began to think that Fermat's Last Theorem was one of these. I mean for Pete's sake, after 350 years the proof eluded the greatest mathematicians of all time. Until..."

Trask's faced beamed as he continued, "Andrew Wiles, a British mathematician working at Princeton presented a valid proof in 1994. Three and a half centuries later and at last we have a proof."

Chase shrugged as if to say 'So what?' but before he could comment, Trask had settled back and continued, "Or do we? Wiles used some very new math techniques that did not exist in Fermat's time. Clearly, if he had a proof, it must have been very different."

Chase replied, "That's a single case in math…"

Trask interrupted, "Oh, but there are examples. David Hilbert put forth twenty-three questions he challenged anyone to solve. And lo and behold, several of them have now been proven. I repeat, "Absence of proof is not proof of absence.""

"Like I said, this is math. I agree that new discoveries are made in science all the time. So how does any of these concern the philosopher's stone?"

Trask leaned forward again.

"Have you ever heard of a man named Nicholai Flamel?"

"No, but should I have heard of him?"

"Nicholai Flamel lived from 1330-1418. Apparently. I'll come back to that. He was a poor scribe and book merchant in Paris. Nothing extraordinary about him until he had The Dream."

"The dream?"

"One night he had a dream in which an angel carrying a large ancient book appeared to him. The book was titled "**The Book of Abraham the Jew.**" The angel told him to look well at the book for it would reveal secrets only he could discern. The angel and book disappeared in a flash when Nicholai awoke."

Trask took a deep breath. "He thought nothing of this until a few weeks later a haggard looking man appeared at this shop to sell him a book called "**The Book of Abraham the Jew.**" Needless to say, he pounced on it and eagerly dived into reading it."

Chase had leaned forward expectantly as Trask continued, "But there was a problem. The book was written in Hebrew, which he could not read. And as usual the Jews were being persecuted so he was forced to leave France for Spain. Flamel took the book and headed to Granada, where he found a rabbi willing to decode the book. The book was a treasure trove of arcane esoterica. As best we can tell, the rabbi deciphered enough of the text to allow Flamel to concoct a red elixir to turn lead into silver and a white elixir to turn mercury into gold."

By now Chase was thoroughly caught up in the narrative.

Trask went on, "Remember I told you that Flamel was a poor scribe? After his return to Paris, he seemed to be wallowing in wealth, but according to the legend he only made gold three times and never used it to enrich himself. He donated huge sums of money for hospitals, poorhouse, churches and even the National Library of Paris. So where did he get the money?"

"Maybe he inherited it or was a better business man than people thought."

"No evidence of either exists. But it gets much, much better. According to the story, these elixirs granted the user immortality. Flamel's wife, Pernelle, died first and he soon followed. They were buried in a cemetery in Paris. When he had funded a church, he requested that a small image of himself be carved into the stones. According to the stories, when the grave was opened, the coffins were empty!"

"So what happened to the book?"

"Flamel willed the book, but not the translated pages to his nephew who could not make heads or tails of it. Then the book disappears for three hundred years."

He paused for dramatic effect. "Do you have any idea of where the book turns up? In the hands of one Cardinal Richelieu. I'm sure you have heard of him!"

Chase nodded.

"Richelieu had an interest in cryptography and tried in vain to decode the text. He ordered Flamel's house ransacked for his notes. By the way, the house still stands in Paris. Richelieu ordered the graves opened, but as I said, they were empty. Oh yeah, I forgot this little gem. From time to time, witnesses around the world report seeing someone who looks like Flamel. The textbook was never found, but there are copies of some of the diagrams, which so far have yielded nothing. When the cardinal died, the book vanished. But for all we know, it may still be out there lying in some dust-covered attic or pawnshop."

Chase leaned back and raised an eyebrow. "Interesting."

"But the quest for the stone did not die out. Isaac Newton spent a good deal of his life exploring alchemy, as did Robert Boyle and many others."

"But isn't it true that only radioactive procedures can cause transmutation?"

"And Fermat's Last Theorem was deemed unsolvable for over three hundred fifty years. Suspend disbelief for one moment. What if? Now whether you believe Flamel or anyone else was successful is beside the point. With your imagination and some more research, you could develop one hell of a video strategy or quest video game that involves a lot of the more illustrious people in history. So what do you think?"

Chase straightened in his chair. "It does have possibilities. Let me think about it, discuss with product development and get back to you. Thank you for the dinner."

The two arose, shook hands and parted ways.

II

Chase thought about the possibilities all night. The next day, he met with the product development department and after some back and forth conversation, the managers gave him the go ahead to begin the project.

He contacted Trask and they signed a letter on intent after Trask gave him copies of his research. The more he read and thought about their conversations, the more he was inexorably drawn into the slippery world of "What if?"

He took vacation time and booked a trip to Paris where he visited Flamel's house just where Trask had said it would be. As he toured the house, he tried to imagine what life would have been like when Flamel lived there. Where did he read the book and conduct experiments? Did anyone know what he was doing? Did he keep notes written in some secret code? How did he keep the faith for twenty-one years until he concocted the elixirs? Had he uncovered some rare catalyst that could do the impossible?

Still mulling these questions over, he visited some of the churches and other buildings Flamel had funded. Sure enough, in the churches he found a small likeness of Flamel carved into their pillars. And then there was Richelieu. Indeed an important figure in history, but not one of such acclaim that unscrupulous charlatans could count on their victims to have known him.

He recalled that Trask had said that the text of the book had disappeared, but some of Flamel's diagrams still existed. He ate lunch at a sidewalk café and sat, sipping tea, musing about the next thing to do. With some trepidation, he took a cab to the main branch of the Bibliotheque Nationale de France. Luckily, he found a librarian who spoke English who helped him find the archive section. Together, they rummaged through stacks of dusty tomes and age-marred parchments until the librarian happened onto a thin folder labeled Flamel in faded ink.

They took the folder to a table and carefully opened it to find pages of obscure alchemical symbols. Some of the pages were signed NF. Chase excitedly copied the symbols as exactly as he could and pored over the pages searching for any clues to deciphering the code. He recognized only a few symbols for the more common elements, but no hint of how to interpret the mysterious faded scribbling. Simultaneously exhilarated and frustrated, he thanked the steward and returned to his room. He spent the rest of the week exploring other possible leads before flying back home Saturday evening.

On Monday he met with the production supervisor to tell him that he thought this idea could be very profitable. The manager Joe Durham listened intently.

"Chase, I have to admit that this is intriguing. Do you have any ideas of the basic layout for a game?"

Chase replied, "I see several possibilities. The obvious one is a quest for the Philosopher's Stone, but the player must also search for the book or even the immortal Flamel himself. Then there is the enormous potential involving all the famous historical figures and locations, possibly a line of action figures with accompanying historical bios. Hell, we could even design a conspiracy scenario like *The da Vinci Code*. We can probably develop science and chemistry modules. The strength of this idea is rooted in all the research that suggests that the whole idea is not out of the world of possibilities. Pardon the pun, but we could be sitting on a gold mine here!"

"It sounds like you have really bought into this. I guess the trip to Paris will pay dividends. By the way, shouldn't we reimburse you for your expenses since it was clearly related to your job?"

"That would be great and I appreciate the support. I have tinkered with some basic outlines. I think I will need an expense account to buy odds and ends for research."

"That should be no problem. You can either submit requisition purchase orders or buy things yourself and get reimbursed. I'll alert purchasing to expect some bills. Oh, we need to get contractual issues with Trask squared away as soon as possible. I don't want any legal battles distracting you. You can submit progress reports as you work, but don't spoil the surprise. If you can keep me in suspense, it'll be a good sign for the product viability and marketability. Thanks for the update and go get'em!"

Chase threw himself into the project, consulting coworkers and game designers and doing more research. The creative teams developed a series of games that could standalone or could be nested levels within a grand overall scheme to make the stone reality.

As Chase was reviewing and editing the work, he realized that providing the names of actual chemicals that Flamel may have used would increase the product authenticity and plausibility. He researched on the net and interviewed chemistry professors from the nearby university about which chemical elements would have been known during Flamel's lifetime. Several professors suggested that Flamel could have actually used elements for which they had no names or perhaps the names were lost in the obscure symbology of the alchemists.

Chase next turned his attention to deciphering Flamel's diagrams. He met with cryptologists but all they could do was to suggest educated guesses with no real proof of their interpretation. He realized that the empirical approach might be the best one after all.

He began to investigate the market for pure chemical elements and how to purchase them. Scientific equipment warehouses that supplied schools and independent laboratories would supply most of the chemicals he needed as long as they were in appropriate quantities and were delivered to real addresses instead of P.O. boxes. A few elements were not available to the general public, but he figured that there might be a back door to getting these if he needed them.

As he began to make lists of the elements he needed, a feeling of uneasiness troubled him. If he ordered all the material to be sent to his home, federal authorities might suspect him of being a terrorist and start asking questions about what he was up to. The solution was obvious. He would have the materials to addresses of friends and coworkers with occasional shipments of glassware and lab equipment sent to the office.

His friends and coworkers who were happy to help him out. This latest project was just another exercise in fantasy that could bring the company a lot of money and they found his enthusiasm amusing. After disguising his orders, he submitted purchase vouchers for test tubes, retorts, flasks, burners, distillation tubes and storage bottles. He ordered small quantities of various salts and halides of elements that he deemed tom be possible candidates for the processes he would use: chromium, cadmium, lead, mercury, cobalt, thallium, palladium, copper, manganese, osmium, platinum, silver, gold and mineral acids.

As the materials arrived, he reorganized his basement into a chemistry laboratory. He opened the jars to inspect the contents and stored them on a shelf over his desk. Realizing how expensive some of the ingredients were, he decided that he needed more books that might help him build basic competencies with simple chemicals. Gradually, he worked up the courage to try some of the elementary experiments that the alchemy literature described. When these simple procedures produced the desired results, he dived even more enthusiastically into his research.

III

The work on the first components of the fantasy game progressed on schedule. Every morning he bounced joyfully into work and seemed to be emerging from his shell. Several times during the day he flipped through alchemical books he kept locked in a desk drawer. He and his teams produced a test version of the first fantasy game and received very favorable reviews. The office and everyday coworkers inquired as to how the games' developments were going. For the first time in a long time, Chase felt a new level of happiness that grew with each new successful experiment in his basement lab.

As his confidence blossomed, he began to tinker with his precious, expensive chemicals. Still, he was unsure that he was ready to attempt even the simplest tests. As he struggled over the arcane texts and diagrams, he became proficient in the language of alchemy. He found a listing of the steps for the synthesis of the Philosopher's Stone in an obscure text called the *Tabula Smaragdina*. When he produced liquid mercury from cinnabar ore, he felt the rush that he imagined that the ancient alchemists felt.

As his successes continued, his spirits at work continued to soar, but the late hours he was keeping in his lab left him drowsy by lunch. Occasionally, he would lock himself in his office for a power nap. Work on the next stages of the game's evolution continued, and he felt more comfortable delegating more of the duties to his colleagues. He told them that he was exploring the possibilities for a chemistry module, and that satisfied their questions about his experiments.

One Friday afternoon, Joe called him into is office to get a status report.

"So, Chase, I hear things are coming together. I gave the first module a trial run and I have to admit, I found it intriguing. If we can maintain that quality throughout the rest of the project, we could have the game of the year."

"Oh, I have every confidence that our guys will develop a great product. I guess we need to start thinking of titles."

"Meet with your people and see what you come up with. Oh, one more thing. I am a little concerned about you, Chase. You look tired. Are you getting enough sleep?"

"Not to worry. Some nights I get involved with the project and stay up too late. I appreciate your concern."

"Well, okay. Can I expect weekly updates?"

"Sure. Let's say Friday afternoons at 2?"

"Sounds good. Have a good weekend. And get some rest."

Chase left the office and went to the bathroom to see if he looked as tired as Joe had said. Examining himself in the mirror, he realized that he did look exhausted and a little pale. He left work early and after a quick dinner, went to bed.

He awoke about three in the morning and could not get back to sleep. After tossing and turning for a while, he got up and went to the basement to read and piddle around in the lab. At six, he showered, ate a hasty breakfast and drove to work. He had to squint in the bright lights of the lobby as he wound his way to his desk. After working at his computer for a couple of hours, he felt a headache coming on so he went to the bathroom to wash his face with cold water. That seemed to help and he went back to work.

His experiments at home had now outgrown the beginner phase and he had progressed to more elaborate tests. Every night he pored over Flamel's diagrams, occasionally being rewarded with a moment of inspiration. By coupling his interpretations with information from standard chemistry book he could produce a wide variety of colors and forms that resembled the stages of transmutation described in his obscure texts.

As his skills developed, he found himself needing less and less sleep. When he was late to work for the second time in a week, Joe called him in and expressed his concern.

"Chase, I appreciate your dedication, but you need to have yourself checked out. You' re losing weight."

Chase snapped back, "Why do you care? Truth is, I'm on a diet. Don't worry about me. I'm fine."

Joe was taken aback at the angry response from a man who had always been mild mannered. "Hey, man, don't have a cow."

Chase felt his anger seething. "Look, I'm working as hard as I can on this project. Why are you hounding me so much?"

"I'm not hounding you. Just forget I said anything. I met with your team and we have set a deadline for next month for completion of the project. Is that doable?"

Chase stood up quickly. "Now you are going behind my back. Look, if you just get off my case, I will make our damned deadline."

Joe shrugged, "Fine. I want a prospectus for completion on my desk by next Friday. Now get out of here."

Chase stormed out, glowering at the people staring at him after the loud altercation in Joe's office.

"So what are you looking at? I just wish everybody would leave me alone! Damn, it's hot in here!"

A wave of nausea came over him and he raced to the bathroom and threw up for several minutes. After splashing water on his face, he returned to his desk. As his nerves calmed down, he apologized to his coworkers and to Joe.

Joe said, "Look, I know you're under a lot of pressure. I don't want to lose my best designer. We can push back the deadline until you can get back to yourself. Take a few days if you need to."

"I'll be fine, but maybe I will take a couple of days. Thanks. I'll see you next Wednesday."

He stopped at a cafe for dinner on the way home. Once home, he tried to relax by watching television. Then he had a sudden insight; he turned the set off and went to the basement. After leafing through some notes, he said aloud,

"That's it! It's like growing rock candy crystals. Flamel must have realized that he needed to prime the pump."

He assembled his jars and vials, lit the burner and began carefully mixing the ingredients until he got a heavy viscous reddish coagulant that turned to shimmering gold as he heated it. But when he tested a sample with acids the shiny metallic substance dissolved with a fizzling sound.

"That's okay. I have the color, the luster and the density. Now let's see if I can use a gold nugget to congeal it into pure gold."

He took a small golden nugget from his jar, tied a thin copper wire around it and began to dip it into the liquid. Unhappy with the slow progress, he placed the beaker over a low flame as he continued to dip the sample. As the solution gurgled and spat out streamlets that ran down the sides of the beakers, he felt the weight of the sample gradually increasing. Before his astonished eyes, the nugget was growing in size. He continued to amalgamate the gold nugget until most of the liquid had evaporated. He tested it with acid and sure enough there was no reaction.

"Eureka! I've done it! Flamel was right. It can be done! Say hello to the latest millionaire, world!"

He called Joe's office and left a voice mail that he had great news for Wednesday.

V

Joe could by tell the excitement in the voice mail that Chase must have some wonderful breakthroughs. He considered dropping by his house to see what had happened, but realized that he should let Chase alone and mind his own schedule. He could wait for two more days.

He came into work early to see what Chase had found. When Chase did not show at nine, he called the house only to get the answering machine. He tried again several times throughout the afternoon. After work, he decided to check on Chase for himself.

As he turned into Chase's subdivision, he saw the flashing lights of several police cars, fire trucks and ambulances. Police tape cordoned off an area about one block from Chase's house. He pulled his car over to the curb and started to walk to the house. A concerned policeman stopped him.

"I'm sorry this sir, but this area has been quarantined."

"Quarantined? Why? I am just here to check on a friend who didn't show up to work today. Is he okay?"

"What is your friend's name?"

"Hunter, Chase Hunter."

"You need to wait here, sir. I'll be right back."

In a few minutes, the policeman returned with the medical examiner. Joe asked, "Is Chase alright?"

The examiner replied, "You know the victim?"

"Victim? What the hell happened to Chase? Was he murdered?"

"Not exactly. His neighbors called the police when they found the dead rats in the yard. I don't know what kind of witches' brew your friend was working on, but this whole area is so contaminated with heavy metals that we will have to evacuate the area until we can get a HAZMAT team to clean it up."

"So where is Chase?"

The examiner fished a photograph out of his pocket. It showed Chase slumped over at his lab table with multicolored spills scattered over the table and floor.

"Your friend is so laced with heavy metals that I'm not sure how we should dispose of the body. Had you noticed any changes in him the last few days?"

"Like what?"

"Insomnia, mood swings, weight loss, paranoia, digestive problems, hallucinations."

"I had spoken to him about his appearance, but he didn't seem too concerned. He had been on edge a lot at work, but I had no idea it was this serious. Why didn't he go to the doctor?"

"As near as we can tell, he was so out of it, he didn't even know he was sick. And on top of that, he was apparently suffering from hallucinations. We found a lot of extremely toxic chemicals and a lot of old books on alchemy down there. What was he doing? Looking for a way to turn lead into gold?"

Joe stuttered, "He was developing a game about alchemy and the philosopher's stone for my company, Imagineworld. I knew he was working on chemistry modules, I had no idea that he was playing with these toxins or I would have stopped him. Jesus Christ, this is awful. Do you think that the paranoia he developed made him distrust me? I wonder why none of us ever picked up on it?"

The examiner thought for a minute. "That is not surprising if your friend had deluded himself into thinking he was an alchemist. Does the name Flamel mean anything to you? He had it scribbled all over the table."

"I think that was the man who supposedly found a magical way to turn lead into gold. Chase has said he was trying to decipher some of Flamel's diagrams that had defied translation. I wonder what he thought they meant?"

"From my own little knowledge of alchemy, the practitioners were very secretive so no one could steal their secrets and to avoid charges of black magic. We may never know what those drawings mean or what delusions your friend was having."

A wry smile crossed Joe's lips, "Well, you know what they say. 'Silence is golden.'"

Song of the Clover Dancers

THE SUN APPROACHES the horizon so I know I do not have much time to return to the Hive, but I can fly by the patch of jewelweed on the way home. Jewelweeds have so many flowers so rich in nectar I am sure I can top off my load from flowers others have missed. I have to be careful not lose track of time and wind up stuck away from the Hive overnight. I hate being away from the Hive at night, and my sisters might worry that something has happened to me. We all worry about getting killed on the road. There it is now.

I hate this black road, but jewelweeds always grow in the ditches alongside it. The stalks are tall and strong and the flowers are huge and filled to the brim with delicious nectar, but you risk your life just to fly near them. The nursery bees used to tell horror stories they heard from the workers when we were still just grubs in the Hive, and I have had enough close calls along the road to know the stories are true. Once, several of us were flying back to the Hive but I lagged behind a bit with a heavy load of pollen. Good thing I was behind, because one of those big things on round feet roared by and splattered my Hive-mates everywhere. The wind somersaulted me backwards into the tall grass, and made me lose most of the load of pollen I was carrying. I crawled back up to the edge and saw wings and legs and dismembered bodies everywhere. There was nothing I could do but start gathering a new load of nectar and pollen. My allegiance is to the Queen and the Hive, not a few dead workers. While we Hive-mates may feel a sympathetic connection, the Hive has a single soul.

This jewelweed patch has always one of my favorite places to visit but I stay toward the back edge. I will land there if it is safe. No sign of birds, spiders or mantises. Looks good. I need to rest first. Ah, the leaf feels good under my feet.

My life in the nursery seems so far away. In my earliest memories, I dreamed of my future as a, for the nurses told me that the whole bottom row of cells was designated for Queendom. The workers and nurses constantly force-fed us royal jelly and tended to our every need day and night. I just ate, slept and dreamt of having my own Hive. But something went horribly, horribly wrong. One day the nurses fed me just honey and I never again tasted royal jelly. My dreams of being a Queen were over.

There is no shame in being a worker, but there is no glory in it either. I became only the worker from the bottom row next to the last cell. But just before I entered the Sleep I saw what the nurses forgot to tell me. Two new Queens were battling to the death, for a Hive can have only one Queen. I saw the body of the loser being dragged away as I began the Sleep.

I don't remember much about the Sleep at all. I recollect bits and pieces of a worker walling me into a cell. It was like being buried alive, but then everything went dark and fuzzy. I heard the soft murmur of the Hive and imagined dismembered parts of the Queen and the nurses and workers floating wistfully in my head, until a strange Voice gently wove them into the new bee that became me.

Maybe I will start to gather nectar. I will go slowly as I can't seem to move as fast as I used to. I haven't moved this slowly since I dragged myself out of the cell from the Sleep. I met the bee from the cell next to me and we watched the Queen pull her fat body along to start laying eggs in the empty cells. My sister said that everything comes at a price. We ourselves could never have children like the Queen. On the other hand the Queen was never allowed to leave the Hive. She will never see the wonderful world where we gather the good nectar that keeps the Hive alive.

I was fascinated that my sister and I had the same dream. I asked her if she too had heard the Voice in the Sleep. She said a nurse told her that every bee hears it. She said it was the Voice of the Hive that directed all the activities of all the bees in a wonderful dance that kept the bees alive, working together to keep the Hive happy and prosperous. I admitted that I did not hear the Voice right then, but she said not to worry. Every bee will hear the Voice when she needs to change her part in the dance.

We had to rest from the struggle of awakening from the Sleep and dry our wings until they were strong enough to fly. All the new bees were told to clean the Hive of debris and stray pollen that had fallen off the workers returning from gathering nectars. Oh! I guess I had better get back to that. Let's see: I land on the lip of the flower, head down and push in past that fuzzy thing hanging down and there it is! Liquid gold, the lifeblood of our Hive. Delicious — enough to fill my stomach now and my pollen sacs until they are full. It is getting late. I must head back to the Hive.

The sun is low. I can make it if I can rest along the way. At least I won't run into butterflies on the way home. I hate those big yellow and black striped ones. They are so pushy on the flowers and they only half gather the nectar. Some bees won't gather nectar after them because they foul it up so much. A bee can't do her job if those butterflies are around. Flit here, flit there, and fly so slowly! The little blue ones are the worst for flitting around while you are trying to work. One of them knocked me so hard that my head went all the way under the nectar pool. I nearly drowned. But what do butterflies care? They don't have a home to go to and there are no hungry grubs waiting to be fed. I used to chase them away from the flowers I was visiting, but I gave that up. I was wasting time and energy. I don't have time to be bothered by ne'er-do-wells.

Maybe I need a short rest. There's a nice patch of milkweed. Looks safe to land. Harder to see than I thought, but I am almost home. One worker told me while I was on cleaning chores that if I could find one when I took my first flight, I should go for the milkweed. Thousands of flowers! All designed with bees in mind. I was so excited about visiting that I dreamed of those great big heads of tiny flowers just waiting for me. If it was not for that dream, I could not have gotten through my mortuary days. I hated that time in my life! We had to find the dead and dying bees throughout the Hive, drag their bodies outside and drop them over the side of the Hive. Once, a few bees stung the drones to death and we threw their bodies out because they did not contribute to the welfare of the Hive. After they mate with the Queen, they only consume honey that is better spent on workers and grubs.

One day I found the same bee that had told me about the milkweed dying from a spider bite. She warned me to watch out for spiders. Spiders make my legs tremble. Some of them spin webs that you can't see until it is too late. Others jump on you while you are busy working. That was the kind that bit this bee. She managed to lurch away but the poison was already in her and she was doomed. She was almost unconscious when I tossed her body out, and her abdomen had grown mushy from the poison.

I once saw a spider attack a bee in a web. The bee was flying close to me, but I went between the web strands that she hit. Like lightning, the spider ran down the web and bit her. She died instantly and the spider started sucking her soupy insides out. Sometimes a bee gets lucky and stings the spider to death but most of the time there is nothing other bees can do but go back to work. My right hind leg got caught in a web once, but I managed to break free just as the spider got there. It cost me a leg that the spider threw away as I left.

I am getting my second wind again. Still enough light to make it home. This is a very heavy load, but my sisters will be there to help me with it. I used to really like that job. I could hear all the stories of the workers and sample all the varieties of nectars and pollens. I got to watch the dance bees do to tell other bees where the good flowers were and how far it is to them. I did not understand it at first, but I soon learned it. It was exciting to know that I would be doing that dance once I was strong enough.

One day the Voice told me to start hovering outside the Hive as a sentry. Dozens of bees patrolled the entrance to the Hive, and chased away any intruders. Sometimes we hovered near the entrance to cool the inside of the Hive. One day a dog ran too close to the Hive and we attacked him. Bees stung him wherever they could and they died to do it. Their throbbing hindquarters ripped away from their bodies but still pulsing venom into their target. I stung him on the nose, but he yanked away before my barbs could go deep enough to pull me apart. After order was restored, we could see dozens of bees torn apart, guts streaming out of them as they died. It is a gory death, but it is an honor for a bee to die defending the Hive.

One more rest stop will do me. That evening primrose will make a good resting place. These things are the bane of every bee. They only open when the light is dying, so we get little time to feed on them. There is a lot of nectar, but a bee can't get to it very well because her tongue is not long enough. I have tried on many of these flowers with nothing to show for it. I could smell the nectar and sometimes, on really full flowers, I could get a drop or two, but never enough to make up for the effort I put into it.

Despite the dangers and the frustration, I really like my job. The Queen misses so much, locked away in the Hive all of her life. I remember my first flight outside. New delights waited me everywhere I looked and smelled. Star-shaped and pocket shaped, single flowers and clusters of flowers. Blue and yellow and purple and orange and white. Then there is what we bees call the ghost color: you can smell the nectar but can't see the flowers. I thought I had found them once when I saw hummingbirds flitting in and out of some big vine that seemed to have a rich nectar smell. I watched as the hummingbirds would stick their necks out and their beaks and face would just disappear, completely erased from their bodies. Other bees had seen the same thing and we all agree that it is really creepy. But sometimes I wonder if we are missing something wonderful just because we can't see it.

There is a lot to see in my world. Honeybees from other Hives buzz among the flowers along with big fat bumblebees. Little butterflies and skippers are darting here and there. Slow-moving swallowtails ride the breezes over mud puddles where bees drink. Mud daubers gather mud for their homes. Most birds leave us bees alone because we sting them, but a few will risk it from time to time. A few bees sacrifice themselves to teach birds the lesson so the rest of us can live in peace. Frogs are not as smart as birds, and more of us must die to teach them that lesson.

Bees that die by the mouth of a bird or frog meet a quick death. The real monster is a praying mantis. I once saw a praying mantis grab a worker from a flower I had just left. The mantis ate her alive while I watched from a safe distance. She tried to sting him, but her sting could not pierce his shell. So bit-by-bit he ate her, leaving only legs and wings to flutter away in the wind. At least a spider knocks you out, birds and frogs crush you. Those big animals on round feet hit you so fast you never know what happened. But mantises keep bees awake at night!

The smell of this primrose is really intoxicating. I guess I can sit here for a bit until the first hawk moths arrive. I smell bees from the Hive flying by. It can't be far away. I don't see how any bee could survive for long outside the Hive. The

Voice told me some things, but mostly I learn from the other bees in the Hive. I used to watch the scouts returning to do their little dance, gyrating wildly on the Hive wall, but none of their dances made any sense to me until one day the Voice said, "**Watch!**" and the veil of confusion was lifted. I learned to count the times she wagged her abdomen, the number of circles she made and the angle of the dance. I followed an older bee who seen the dance before and, to my sheer delight, I found myself in this very patch of jewelweeds with their flowers bulging with delicious nectar. I gathered so much nectar I had to fly low to the ground going home, where a younger bee met me to help with the unloading task that I had done the day before. The Hive is everything, and each bee has a part to play to make the Hive survive.

Our Hive is struggling to survive now. We have always had a few beeswax moths in the upper part of the Hive. They eat the old honeycombs, but we could keep them under control by throwing their grubs out of the Hive before they hatch. Now I hear their numbers are growing. A strange new disease is spreading through the Hive and thinning our ranks. I have seen its victims. Some of the dying bees complain they can't breathe and they suffocate. The first signs of the disease are fatigue and erratic flights and staggering when they walk. We watch each other's walks, dances, and flights and try to avoid anyone who acts out of the ordinary. Many of us think the disease is spread by touch. And our society communicates by touch and smell. It is hard to avoid touching others. The Queen seems to be safe for now, since she is insulated from touching any bees that fall victim to the disease. They are usually the workers, unloaders, and mortuary workers. One day I thought I had the disease. I was bouncing around as I flew from the Hive, but it was just a tear in my right hind wing that threw me off.

One day I watched a bee in the final throes of the disease and I wondered why the Voice did not tell us what to do. Then I heard the Voice whisper to me: 'Bees live, bees die. Whether you die from spider, mantis, or disease doesn't matter in the end. I guide the lives of bees, not the Hive. The welfare of the Hive is the bees' responsibility. A storm may topple the bee tree or a bear may raid the Hive, but as long as there are bees who listen to their inner voice, the Hive will recover and thrive. Each bee who does her part, however small, insures the Hive will survive.'

Ah, I have just enough time to reach the Hive before dark. Sometimes I wonder if I would have made a better Queen than worker, or if she would have made a better worker than Queen. Then I think of the day I set out from the Hive with several other bees to the clover field west of the Hive. Heavy dew glistened on the grass and clover flowers. The entire field was quiet except for our buzzing. The butterflies and skippers don't like heavy dews on their fancy wings, so we had the whole clover patch to ourselves. We dived head first into the nectar flowers, dancing the dance the Voice called out while our wings sang a melody of life over the blossoms. That is bee happiness, doing what we do best.

I can barely see the Hive in the dim twilight. I guess missing a leg and part of a wing takes its toll on a bee, especially one with such a big load! I really can't see the road too well. I wish there was more light. Maybe I need to fly a little higher, but I can't. If there were more light, I would know what to do. I guess if I just creep up to the road a little at a time it will be okay. A little closer...yes, a little closer...so far so good.... a little closer ...so far.....

Even the Memory
of Them Is Lost

WILLA, THE WOOLY bear, never knew her mother or why she chose the particular leaf of plantain on which to lay her eggs during the late summer. Willa's first memory was an overwhelming urge to wriggle free of the creamy egg her mother had deposited a few weeks earlier, and to start eating as soon as possible. Her thin, black bristle-covered body struggled to emerge from the egg. She lay quiescent on the leaf to recover from her struggles, and then ate the eggshell.

The plantain leaf was covered with her brothers and sisters. Some were beginning to eat little holes in the leaf, but others had crawled off the leaf and ventured into the nearby weeds where they began to eat. Willa nibbled small holes in the leaf, but she abandoned the leaf, now crowded with new arrivals.

Slowly, she made her way through the maze of weeds and grass peppered with tiny wriggling bodies. Willa ignored them as she sought a new food source. A small spider had already eaten one of her siblings, and birds were eating others. Instinctively, she crawled under leaves to hide, and she soon found a clump of new plantain.

Still hungry, she ate voraciously and moved to a new part of the plant and pursued her drive to eat, eat, and eat. After a few days she cramped in her skin. Her eyes glazed over, and she felt her skin tear along her back. With much effort, she struggled and freed herself of her old skin, and dreamed ever so briefly she could fly.

She was exhausted and rested while her new covering of chestnut brown and black bristles dried in the morning sun. Once again, she began to eat until she had eaten most of the leaf she was on. She left the leaf and sought a new food source.

Occasionally she would meet other wooly bears along the way. Some were surely her siblings, but she did not remember them. She had no time to waste in her search for food.

Willa found a new plantain, and gorged herself on the tender blades. Soon she had that strange feeling again, and again fell into a semi-stupor. Her eyes clouded over, and her old skin split along her back. Her dream of flight was stronger now. Her new coat was larger, and it had a reddish-brown band between the black ends. The hairs were longer and more densely spread along her soft body and they took longer to dry. The eating urge returned, so she sought a new plantain.

A spider attacked her along the way, but she instinctively to curled herself into a tight coil. That frustrated his attempt to penetrate her thick coat. When the spider had gone, she uncoiled herself and returned to her dinner.

She shed her old skin several more times. Each new coat had a larger reddish brown stripe between the black ends. Each time, the dream of flying became stronger. Her appetite redoubled and she shed her skin for the last time; she was two inches long.

Her appetite subsided, and a new restlessness gnawed at her. She rested on the last leaf, but the warmth of the autumn sun drove her to seek the shade. One morning, she crawled off the plantain leaf and searched for a place to be alone It had to be a special place that she had not sought before. She wriggled her way into a tussock of fescue, but abandoned it to search for a new resting place. The urge to find just the right place drove her across the hot pavement of a road littered with other wooly bears crushed by passing cars. She ignored everything but her instinct to find her special place. She tried and rejected a new tussock of grass, the cavity under a small limestone rock and even an old chipmunk hole. Finally, she found just what she was looking for: a secluded, snug depression under a piece of bark from an oak tree.

After inspecting her resting place, she settled down. Another strange new feeling seized her, and she extruded a sticky thread of silk from her body. She writhed and rolled, and spun her silken threads until she was completely encased in a beige cocoon.

Willa rested from her labors, and drowsed into a deep sleep. Slowly, she her body dissolved into an amorphous soup. Her old bristly coat sloughed off, and her chewing mandibles and tiny soft feet disappeared into the gooey morass. Eventually, only a clump of isolated cells remained, and she lay, safe and snug in her pupal cocoon throughout the cold, snowy winter.

She had chosen her resting place well. Snug in her haven, she was safe from deer mice and shrews who would eat her. When spring arrived the quiescent group of cells stirred with a new energy that marshaled resources to construct her new body. A long hollow proboscis replaced her mandibles. Spindly new legs replaced her stubby thick feet. She forgot her life as a larva and grew beautiful wings.

On a warm spring morning, she felt the urge to free herself of the silken cocoon that had protected her through the cold. It was harder to break free, because the cocoon fibers had toughened over time. A small tear appeared in the silken shroud, and she wriggled vigorously to enlarge the hole so she could pull herself out.

Once outside the cocoon she rested while her new heart pumped fluids through her wings. They stiffened into ochre-colored membranes. After the wings had hardened, she dragged her new furry body from under the bark and onto a fern frond. A new urge to find a mate and reproduce possessed her. In her new body, she forgot the trials of her old life as a larva. She found a firm footing on the topmost frond, and beat her wings slowly.

Then Willa launched herself into the air with a gentle push, and the dream she could fly came true.

Made in the USA
Lexington, KY
13 July 2017